Blake's Hope

By Kelly Miles

Cover Design by Marianne Nowicki

ACKNOWLEDGEMENTS

To everyone who has supported me…. there aren't enough 'Thank You's' to express what it means to me. My family and friends have shown me unrelenting, unconditional love and have stood behind me throughout writing this series. It means more than I could ever express.

To my illustrator…. Marianne Nowicki. When I started this journey, I had no clue what I was doing. None, but you made it so easy and gave me beautiful covers for all of my novels. Thank you for working with me and bringing to life the characters exactly as I pictured them. I will forever be grateful and look forward to working together in the future.

To my readers…. I wouldn't be able to do what I do without you. The whole reason I write, besides the fact that I love it, is because of you. To hopefully bring you joy and happiness and give you a little break from reality. I appreciate each and every one of you who have given me a chance and invited my characters into your life. Thank you! Thank you! Thank you!

To Phil Price… who helped write the fight scenes in this book and has helped in so many other ways, I owe you. Blake's Hope would not be what is it without you. You have opened my eyes to a whole new world of possibilities when it comes to writing and friendship. You'll never know what it means to have you in my corner. Thank you for everything.

When I started this series, almost three years ago, I was a completely different person. Shy and unsure, scared and inferior. A lot has changed since then, and several have helped mold and shape me into the woman I am today. I won't name individual names, but you know who you are.

Those that took a chance on me, gave me hope, and helped me to believe in myself; those gifts are way above and beyond anything I have ever received. Feeling safe in your own skin is immeasurable, and I will never forget those who have traveled this road with me; pushing and encouraging me every step of the way. True friends are hard to find. If you're lucky enough, the right ones will stick with you. For those of you that stuck, know you forever have a place in my heart.

1

Moonlight danced off the waves as the foamy billows crashed into one another; a reminder of lover's past, intertwined in a passionate tango. The flames of the fire twisted around the now charred logs, skewing them into unrecognizable embers of fiery-orange ash. The music was loud, the roar of the partygoers even louder. Brown liquid sloshed over the rim of red solo cups as they were passed from person to person, most of them laced with GHB, or some other drug of choice for the unsuspecting girls that had been invited; though perhaps *lured* was a better word. The years I'd spent undercover had taught me lots of things, one of them being that there was always a method to Raul's madness. His debauchery knew no bounds. I would be so thankful when all this was over, barely able to stomach much more.

I'd been watching her all night and unbeknownst to me, so had Raul. She was different, always had been from the first moment I laid eyes on her. As usual, she wasn't dressed scantily like the others, instead she was trying desperately to fade into the background. Keeping to the shadows, her eyes wandered to those same waves I'd been watching just moments ago. Momentarily dazed, I stared in awe as she stole the show from the ocean's love affair with the moon. Suddenly, the faint glow had decided to cast its shadow upon her, and rightfully so. In that moment, it struck me how the waves now seemed violent; too violent for her delicate curves. Innocence wrapped around her like a cloak, as she tried in vain to shield herself from the damp night air. There was no denying she'd captured the moon's attention… and mine.

I could feel the sand shift beneath my weight as the waves lapped over my feet, leaving a cool sensation against my scorching skin. Unable to move, thoughts of laying this gorgeous creature across my bed and having my way with her ran rampant through my mind's eye. God, she was incredible to look at. Her long, blond hair blew around her bare shoulders, eventually tangling in the crook of her neck. She reached around and gathered it in her hands and as she did, her ridiculously outdated blouse rose high, revealing a flat, firm stomach and a small tattoo. From a distance I couldn't make it out. Just swirls of color and intricate detail etched on silky smooth skin. I wanted to run my tongue along the outline, leaving drops of moisture on her pebbled skin. Then….

"See something you like?" Raul slapped me hard on the back, breaking the spell the goddess-like creature in front of me had managed to cast. When did I get so googly-eyed over a girl? *Never.*

"Just thinking." I shrugged my shoulders and feigned indifference. I knew Raul for the bastard he was and there was no way he was going to let this go.

He smiled a devilish grin as he pulled a long toke from the end of a joint. "Get her." His black eyes bore into mine, waiting to see what I would do, but he already knew. If you valued your life you didn't say no to Raul, and since I didn't feel like being shark food on the bottom of the ocean floor, it left me with no choice.

I gritted my teeth, calming my temper. What I wouldn't give to put a bullet right through his miserable brain. "Yes, boss."

He moved away slowly. "Smart move, son." He disappeared into the shadows, or even more likely, the fiery pits of hell. I wasn't sure.

I returned my attention to the woman. She was in the same spot, this time her eyes on me instead of the crashing water beating along the shore line. *Showtime.*

I smiled, revealing my perfectly white teeth. My dimples had always been a chick magnet and I had no doubt they would affect her, as well. I slowly advanced, maintaining eye contact the whole way. A slight grin pulled at the corners of her beautiful lips and I knew I had her, hook, line and sinker.

As soon as we were within touching distance, her friend came bounding down the hilly terrain, slipping on the soft sand. I'm sure the drugs and alcohol were a factor, too, and I grimaced at her unfortunate fate.

"Hope, c'mon!" She pulled on the blonde's arm. *So, Hope was her name*. I let the word roll around in my brain a few good seconds before I realized she was being drug away. My feet moved quickly.

"Wait!" I shouted from behind. "Where are you going?"

Hope turned and glared at me, her friendly demeanor just seconds ago now replaced with fear. She looked scared to death and it caused a pang of regret to course through me. She scampered even faster over the sand, eventually breaking loose from the hold of her friend. I was going to have to change tactics.

"Hey!" I shouted again, but her feet only moved quicker.

Her friend stopped and waited for me to catch up. She eyed my six feet plus frame, shamelessly. "Like what ya see, sweetheart?" I held my arms open wide, giving her an eyeful of my rock-hard abs and tanned physique. I felt like an ass, but he was watching. I could feel him. I had to keep up my asshole appearance for the sake of the case.

The girl licked her gloss-smeared lips. "What can I do for you?" She leaned in closer, the alcohol wafting from every pore of her body. I wanted to gag.

"What's your name, sweetheart?"

She looked deep in thought as if she didn't know the answer. As drugged as she was, she probably didn't, but after a long pause she surprised me. "Simone."

"Well, Simone. It's nice to meet you."

She swayed unsteadily on her feet. I held my arm out to catch her just as she was about to fall once again. Her arms wrapped around my neck and clamped tightly, moments before her lips sealed over mine. I pushed against her waist, careful not to hurt her. Our mouths broke apart with a popping noise. I wiped the pink lipstick from my lips as she looked on with lust. Not what I was hoping to accomplish. I knew I could drop her down in the sand right then and there if I wanted, but she's not the one that had my attention. She didn't have delicate curves, or the colorful and intricate tattoo that I wanted to run my tongue along.

"I'm sorry, I was looking for your friend. Hope, is it?"

Simone let out a chuckle. "Boring Hope? Trust me sailor, you'll have more fun with me. Hope doesn't put out, but I do." She edged closer once again, like a piranha dying to sink her teeth into my flesh.

"I like boring." I stepped back and went around her in the opposite direction. I didn't want Hope out of my sight for too long, or Raul would take matters into his own hands. I began walking away.

"Wait! C'mon, I'll help you find her." Simone walked by my side, holding the crook of my arm for support. "See that bungalow?" she pointed. "I'll have her there in five."

She gave me a push in that direction and I complied. I turned and spotted Raul, watching me cautiously. A man in his position couldn't be too careful and he is as untrusting as they come. Ironic, I know. I gave him thumbs-up and continued along the flagstone path. I needed to get Hope alone and explain the danger she was in. Something deep inside me ached to keep the beautiful stranger safe, and it was a bit unsettling. I pushed it away, focusing on the job at hand. I was about to break a rule and blow my cover, knowing it could go one of two ways, neither of which was satisfactory to me. I was headed for trouble.

The bungalow was plush, nicely decorated in teakwood and earthy tones. White linen curtains blew in the breeze, free from their prison of glass. The octagon structure was slightly elevated to protect it from the onslaught of the ocean waves. Wispy ferns and giant potted palms took up every available space of the entrance and surrounding deck, offering privacy. It was tucked away in the crook of the dimly lit pathway, and the perfect place to get Hope alone.

I entered, listening for any sounds of possible occupants. It was empty. I switched on the lights, lowering the dimmer to a soft glow. Being too anxious to sit, I paced the wooden floor, running my bare feet over the plush rug that sat just inside the French glass doors. Within minutes I heard the scuffling of high heels and drunken laughter that hung in the balmy air. Simone had managed to get Hope away from the party, though I suspected she had no idea what awaited her. As the women reached the porch, I opened the door wide for them to enter.

Hope had to help steady Simone when her heel caught in the doorway, causing them both to topple and land in the floor. I sighed in frustration. I really didn't have time for her drunken antics. I placed my hand around Hope's arm, taken aback by the jolt of electricity that sparked between us. She looked at me with wide eyes, apparently feeling the same. She was frightened, if not a bit cautious.

"I won't hurt you, Hope. Promise." I bent down and got a firmer grip on her, pulling her up with me until our torsos were touching. In that moment everything else fell away. I had forgotten all about Simone still on the floor, struggling to get to her feet. Her flailing limbs broke the spell I was under. Huffing in frustration, I held my hand out to her.

"Here, let me help." I reached for her, all the while keeping one arm firmly planted around Hope's waist. I didn't want her to take off, a good possibility given the look on her face.

Once Simone had regained her footing, she smiled and straightened her skin-tight dress. She winked my direction. "I'm going to head back to the party. You guys have fun!" She waggled her brows before bounding unceremoniously back down the walkway.

I watched until she was out of view and then faced Hope. She looked like a deer in headlights as she shivered beneath my touch. "I need to get back, too. I'll see you around." As confident as she pretended to be, her voice warbled, immediately giving her away.

"Hope, I'm not going to hurt you. I'm trying to help you." She backed away quicker than I liked.

"Help me what? Are you going to rape me?"

I scoffed. "Rape you? What the hell?" My temper flared briefly, the same one I'd always had trouble controlling when accusations started flying. "No, Hope. I'm not going to rape you. I won't even touch you, but you have to listen to me."

She had backed up even further, positioning herself directly in front of the door. I watched as her eyes darted between me and the open escape, waiting for her to make her move. She looked fit and no doubt would be quick about it. What she didn't figure was that I was even quicker.

In a split second, she darted towards the exit, running smack dab into a brick wall of me. She struggled, each thrust and brush of her body causing a reaction that I was trying my best to keep under control. My arousal would definitely send her over the edge, and more than likely screaming at the top of her lungs. I couldn't have that.

I turned her so that my front was to her back. One arm was locked firmly around her waist, holding her in place. The other was against her breast, my hand over her mouth. The rise and fall of her chest pulsated under my touch as she struggled to catch her breath. I leaned down and put my lips against her ear, watching my skin as it pebbled over with chill bumps and a tingling sensation trailed its way up my spine.

"Don't fight me, Hope. Relax." I felt her give in, momentarily allowing the fight to leave her. She melted into me and nothing had ever felt so good. I cleared my throat and forced myself to focus. The hardest damn thing I'd ever done.

"I need you to look at me. Can you do that?"

Hope nodded her head against my chest. "I'm going to uncover your mouth. Whatever you do, don't scream. You'll only make things worse." Again, she nodded her head in understanding.

I turned her slowly and moved us away from the door. "Come with me." I thought she was going to protest, but instead she dropped her head and allowed me to lead her to the bedroom without a fight. She sat on the edge of the king-sized bed, after much prodding, and I kneeled on the floor in front of her. I was afraid if I sat beside her she'd try to bolt again, and I was too tired to give chase.

"Hope, I need you to listen to me, okay? Hear me out. Can you do that for me, babe?"

"Yes." Her voice was small and timid. She looked so frail. I knew what was coming, and I didn't think she was strong enough to handle it. I don't know anyone who would be.

"What I'm about to tell you, you can't tell anyone. Understood?" She nodded in compliance. "Good. Hope, I'm an agent with the FBI. I'm undercover so no one can know. *Ever.* There's a man out there. His name's Raul and he's one bad son of a bitch."

"I met him earlier. He invited me and my friends." Her voice was detached and void of any emotion.

I hung my head. I didn't want to be a part of this in any shape or form, but it was my job. I didn't have a choice. "Look, all your friends out there are drugged into oblivion at the moment. This whole party was a set up. Have you had anything to drink?"

"No. Someone offered me a cup, but I didn't take it."

"Good girl. Anyone back home gonna be looking for you? An overprotective dad or asshole boyfriend?" I smiled, trying to lighten the mood, but it was to no avail. Hope was trembling as tears rolled over her perfectly sculptured cheekbones.

"No. No one to care that I'm gone. But why? Aren't I going home?"

I hated to break the bad news, but she needed to know. "I'm afraid not, babe."

She stood abruptly, nearly knocking me in the chest with her knees. "What do you mean exactly? Of course, I can go home! I *am* going home."

I stayed rooted to the floor on my knees. From this angle I was able to get a better view of the intriguing tattoo. It was a butterfly breaking free from its cocoon; brown and blues mixing together in a vibrant twist as the butterfly took flight. My mouth watered until finally I had to mentally slap myself back to reality.

"I mean just what I said. Sit down, Hope." My voice was commanding, but soft. You catch more flies with honey, after all.

Her foot stomping caused a chuckle to escape me. Perhaps I was wrong about her. A little bit of spark was a good thing, as long as she didn't use it with me. Or Raul.

"Hope, Raul is a drug lord. A murderer. A pedophile. A sex-trafficker. A demon. Want me to go on?" She stared blankly at the wall as I continued. "You were all lured here tonight, and I'm very sorry about that. I'm sorry you got mixed up in all this and I promise I'll do everything I can to get you out, but you have to listen to me."

"I wasn't even supposed to be here. I told them I didn't want to come!" Her sobs were getting louder and more uncontrollable by the minute. With no choice but to quieten her down, I sat beside her on the bed and put my arm around her shoulder. She leaned into me without much coaxing, causing a swell of pride to bubble in my chest.

"What do you mean?"

"My mom died last year. Since then I've been taking care of my father. I told my friends I just wanted to stay home. If I hadn't let them talk me into coming..."

"It's gonna be alright, babe. Somehow, I'll get you outta here, but you gotta trust me."

"What about them?" She was referring to Simone and the others she'd arrived with. I didn't want to give her false hope. The truth is I didn't know. I wasn't even sure how to get *her* out. Raul had seen her. What's more, he'd seen me watching her and he ate that shit up. Anything he could do to make another human being miserable seemed to be his number one goal in life. I knew he, too, had his sights on her. She was a target. A plaything. A prize to be won. Looks like I was going to have to beat Raul at his own game because hell would freeze over before I let him harm one hair on her head.

"I'll do my best, Hope, but right now my concern is you. Let's focus on that."

She sat up straight, breaking the contact between us and leaving me with an immediate feeling of loneliness. I didn't like it.

"I'm nothing special. It doesn't matter."

"Why would you say such a thing? Of course, you matter!"

She shrugged her shoulders and played with her hair in a nervous manner. "My father barely even notices I'm there. He's so grief-stricken over my mother's death that it's like he doesn't even see me. I work a waitressing job. Waitresses are a dime a dozen. It's not like I can't be easily replaced. My friends aren't really my friends. They're just people I talk to on occasion to remind myself I'm not dead."

It bothered me greatly that she felt the way she did. I knew there was more to Hope than she was willing to share, or possibly stuff she couldn't even see.

"Well, you matter to me, Hope." I reached down and took her hand in mine.

"Here's what's going to happen. We're gonna walk outta here looking all lovey-dovey. Raul doesn't need to know any different. I'm gonna tell him I'm taking you home with me for the night and then I'll think of something to make sure he never gets his hands on you."

Hope looked embarrassed as she quickly tore her gaze away from me. I placed my finger under her chin and guided her to face me. "What is it?"

"Nothing." Her hands wrung nervously in her lap as she chewed her bottom lip. Both classic signs of sexual tension.

"It is something and you need to tell me. I need you to be honest with me about everything. It's the only way I can help you."

Hope thought for a moment. "I've never… you know. Been with anyone. What will Raul think if I can't convince him?"

My heart raced. It's possible I even saw stars before regaining my composure and picking my jaw up off the floor. A pulsating sensation began building between my legs, but I ran through a mirage of images in my mind to keep it at bay. A bulging erection is not what she needed right now. *Nuns. Puppies. Football. My ninety-year-old grandmother.*

"So, you're a virgin?" My voice was squeaky, something akin to that of a pubescent boy.

Hope jumped from the bed. "It's not… You don't have to laugh at me!" She had mistaken my reaction as poking fun at her, but God, that's the last thing I was thinking.

"No, Hope. I'm not making fun of you." I walked to the corner of the room where she stood, looking out over the water. I was close enough that she could feel my presence, but I didn't touch her.

"I'm just surprised that's all. You're beautiful. You have an incredible body…." Going against everything I knew to be right; everything we were taught in training, including but not limited to getting involved, I sighed and moved closer, gently placing my hands on her shoulders and kneading the tight muscles underneath. “I’m just in awe that no one has swept you off your feet and made love to you the way you deserve.”

She was silent for several minutes, no doubt contemplating my words. I continued my ministrations on her muscles, loosening her up for what was coming. If she freaked out in front of Raul, he’d know we were lying. I couldn’t chance that.

“Thank you.” Hope whispered so softly that I barely heard over the clap of waves crashing together.

“It’s the truth. Now, do you feel better? We need to maintain a front in front of Raul. I just need to get you back to my place and hopefully this will all be over soon.”

“I’ll give it my best shot.” Hope gave a slight grin and waited for me to explain the plan. I prayed it would work. She nodded her head vehemently, seeming relieved I would do most of the talking.

2

Hope and I made our way back to the party, laughing and giggling. She'd since lost her shorts and that ridiculous out-of-date top. A white bikini barely covered her slender frame, making both my mouth water and my brain short-circuit. It also caused a jealousness within me. I didn't want her parading around like that at the party. I knew she'd be eaten alive, so I did the noble thing and offered her my button up to cover herself.

Hope's arm was slung low around my waist, mine around her shoulder. I held onto her tightly as she was clumsy on her feet. Colored lip stains were plastered on my face and chest, and hell if I didn't enjoy every single one of them. We continued laughing loudly, stumbling into bushes and trees, and incidentally each other.

"There you are!" Raul met us before we'd even stepped our toes into the cool sand.

"Well hello, púta." Raul licked his lips, soliciting a low growl from the back of my throat. Hope felt the vibration as she clinched her fingers tighter around my belt loops. It'd be nothing to put the little prick down, but his men were nearby as usual. I wouldn't stand a chance.

"Hello." Hope hung her head and spoke softly.

Raul wouldn't tolerate disrespect. He grabbed her roughly by the arm and shook her while I stood by and did nothing. To say it was difficult was an understatement. I wanted to rip his head clean off his shoulders!

“Look at me when I’m talking to you, púta, else I’ll have to teach you a lesson.” Hope’s head immediately snapped up, looking him square in the eyes. My arm was still around her shoulder which I squeezed gently for reassurance.

“Sorry,” she hiccupped. “I’m just a wee bit drunk.” Hope giggled and held up her thumb and pointer finger, leaving a bit of space between.

“That’s better, púta.” Raul gave me a funny look, questioning why I’d yet to let her go. I thought quickly.

Thinking fast on my feet, I leaned over and whispered in his ear. “She’s just a piece of ass, boss. Gonna take her home with me. Get better acquainted, if you know what I mean.”

Normally Raul didn’t like his merchandise to be touched, but the evil glint in his eyes told me he was enjoying this. He pawed at her breasts roughly. “Have fun. Bring her to me tomorrow when you’re done. Seems like she’s got more than enough to share.” He puffed his fat Cuban cigar, blowing the smoke out in ringlets, which hung in the thick night air.

Hope shivered. I knew she was freezing as she might as well have been naked, but I think the fear was chilling her to the bone. I didn’t know how, but I’d get her out of this. She was too good to be thrown to the wolves.

I grinned coyly. “Will do, boss. See ya tomorrow.” When we were fifty feet or so away, Hope fell into me, weary and dangerously close to falling apart. “I got you, Hope. It’s alright, babe. Almost there.”

We walked through the sand and rocky earth until we reached the parking lot. There, beneath the glow of street lights sat my prized possession; my 1979 Harley Shovelhead. My mother had a fit the first time she heard me pulling in the driveway, all 783 pounds rumbling beneath me. I was home from college and had paid for it by working odd jobs around campus. It was a piece of junk when I bought her, but I'd brought old Daisy back to life. I smiled proudly.

"You expect me to get on this?" Hope stood ramrod straight, glaring in disbelief.

I chuckled at her expression, which I quickly surmised wasn't winning me any points. "S'all good, babe. I've never laid Daisy down once." I chuckled again, but she obviously didn't find it funny.

"In case you haven't noticed, I'm half naked!"

I stopped and perused her womanly figure. "Oh, I noticed." I reached in the saddle bag and brought out another helmet and a pair of sweatpants. "Here, put these on."

She didn't argue. She took them willingly and slid them over her hips. They were baggy, but they'd do no further than we were going. "Ever been on a bike?"

"Um, no." She didn't look too thrilled about it either.

I had to reassure her. "Babe, trust me. I won't let anything happen to you. I got you out of here tonight, didn't I?" I pointed to the crowd. It was just a matter of time before the cops showed and I was more than ready to bolt.

She nodded her head. I straddled the seat and held out my hand to steady her as she climbed on. When she was situated, I put my helmet on, buckling the strap tight. Normally I didn't wear one, but I knew it would only freak her out even more. I grabbed her hands and pulled them around my waist snuggly, giving them a gentle squeeze.

"Hold on tight, babe." Daisy roared to life and I smiled proudly. Kicking into gear, we shot off into the darkness. I heard her giggle behind me and I knew she was enjoying herself. I'd give her a ride she'd never forget if it meant I could hear that just one more time.

We were almost to my apartment, but I wasn't quite ready to go back. I liked the feel of her on my bike; her legs squeezing my hips. The way she melted herself to me and the way she would occasionally rub her hands up and down my stomach left me feeling giddy. *Me*. A big badass was gushing like a school girl and I liked it. At the red light, I let my now booted foot fall to the pavement and settled my hand on her thigh. It felt natural and I was thrilled when she made no attempt to remove it.

The light turned green way too soon. I was perfectly content to sit there for hours but honking horns and angry motorists didn't exactly set the mood. I felt Hope shiver behind me, realizing she must be cold from the night air. It was fine if you were sitting still but zooming the streets at 50 mph was a different story. "Cold, babe?"

"Freezing!" she shouted over the noise of the engine.

"We'll be there in five."

I helped her from the bike then helped her remove the helmet. Her teeth were chattering, and I felt bad that I'd prolonged the ride unnecessarily. “C’mon. Let’s get you inside and warmed up.” Surprisingly, Hope laced her fingers with mine and followed me through the doors and to the elevator. It was as if we were a couple just returning from a romantic date. It was easy to forget the danger we’d both be in come morning, but I’d worry about it then.

I opened the door to my modest apartment, praying to all that was holy that I’d remembered to pick up my underwear from the bathroom floor. “Are you hungry?”

Hope looked embarrassed and I felt for her. She was in a stranger’s apartment, her bottom half covered only in baggy sweats. She must be wondering what the hell was gonna happen next.

“I’m starving.” As soon as the words left her mouth, her stomach grumbled loudly. We both laughed at the timing.

“I’ll make us some dinner. You wanna grab a hot shower? I’ll give you a shirt to sleep in for the night and you can have my bed. I’ll take the couch.”

“I don’t want to put you out. I’ll take the couch.” She fidgeted nervously.

“I won’t hear of it.” I spun her around and walked her to the bathroom. “Make yourself at home. What’s mine is yours.” I pointed to the fresh towels and showed her how to work the shower. It was a little cantankerous.

“Thank you.”

“I’ll be right back with some clothes you can borrow.” I left her alone and sprinted to my bedroom. I striped the bed sheets, picked up a pile of clothes from the floor, throwing them in the laundry, and made sure there were no empty condom wrappers laying around. Not a saint, remember? I remade the bed with fresh linens, happy with my progress. I checked my watch. All done in fifteen minutes!

As I made my way to the kitchen, I stopped in the hallway. Knocking on the bathroom door, I announced myself. "Hope? I'm going to leave you some clothes on the sink. C'mon out when you're done." I entered and exited quickly, resisting the urge to peek behind the clear shower curtain. I wasn't a total dick.

Rummaging through the cabinets I realized I desperately needed to make a run to the store. Being a bachelor, I didn't think about it much. It was usually takeout or eating at the club with the guys. Shit! I'd almost forgotten about our little predicament. I pulled my cell phone from my pocket, dialing the local Chinese place down the block. After placing a quick order for delivery, I hung up and dialed George.

"George? Blake." My fingers drummed the counter top as I bit my lip. He was gonna be pissed at me for bringing her here, but I didn't have much choice. "We've got a situation, man. I've got a girl here."

He chuckled on the other end of the line. "Well, son. If you don't know what to do with a woman by now, I don't see how I can help."

"Very funny. Look, she's one of Raul's girls, or at least she will be if I don't get her outta here by morning. Can you come get her, or send one of the other guys?"

George's heavy sigh didn't go unnoticed. "No, Blake. I can't. I'm tied up at headquarters and the others are making runs. Get her out first thing in the morning."

Did he think I was stupid? That was the whole damn point. "How? I can't leave her here by herself."

"Put her in a cab and send her on her way. Simple."

That might work but knowing Raul he had people watching the place. I should've settled us in a motel for the night, but it didn't cross my mind until now. "I'll see what I can do." I hung up without another word and rubbed the back of my neck to ease the tension.

"I hope I'm not being a problem." Hope had entered the room, unbeknownst to me.

"No, you're not a problem, babe." I uncrossed my ankles and stood up tall, turning to face her. My mouth went dry at the very sight. There she stood, hair dripping onto my black V-neck tee that had never looked better. I liked her in my clothes, oddly enough. What was happening to me? I didn't get all mushy about these kinds of things. I didn't do feelings and touchy-feely shit. I had no room for that in my life, and she didn't need it anyways. My line of work was dangerous enough for me, much less dragging an unwilling participant into the mix. I cleared my throat and regained my focus. I couldn't let her see me falter, and I definitely couldn't afford attachment, for either of our sakes.

Indifference was the way to play this. "I ordered us takeout. Should be here in a few minutes." I shoved the Chinese menu back in the drawer, focusing my attention anywhere but at her.

The room grew eerily quiet. I was uncomfortable, and I could tell she was, too. The whole night had gone smooth considering, but it was time for asshole Blake to make an appearance. She didn't need to get too comfortable.

"So, I know you don't have a lot to take with you when you leave here tomorrow. I'll see you off early, give you a bit of money to get wherever you need to go. That's it. It'll be done."

Her eyes glassed over with unshed tears. "Oh, okay. Sure. Um, that's great. Thanks for…"

I cut her off. I didn't want her appreciation. I didn't want gratitude. I wanted her to put on a damn coat and wrap up in a blanket. It was impossible to concentrate with her staring at me like that. "Don't mention it." My voice was curt and detached. There. That should get the point across.

"Why are you being like this? Cause I can just go now if you'd like." She moved to walk back down the hallway, but my long legs caught up to her in a few short strides. Grabbing her elbow, I spun her around and pinned her against the wall.

"What do you want me to do, huh? You want me to take you to bed? Is that it? You want me to promise you shit just so I can get in your panties?"

Before I could register what was happening, Hope brought her hand up and slapped me hard across the face. Can't say I didn't deserve it. I stepped back, releasing her from the weight of my body. I rubbed my face, already feeling the heat settling under the skin.

"I don't want anything from you! I didn't ask for this!" She ran full force towards the bedroom and slammed the door. Shit! Smooth move, dumbass. I threw my head back in frustration. This was the trouble with girls. Hell, with getting involved period. I had no clue what she wanted. She's a freaking virgin for God's sake! Pure and innocent.

Someone that deserves the best, and that sure as hell ain't me. Never will be. As torn as I was, I couldn't stand the sound of her crying.

I trudged down the hall, dragging my feet with reluctance. I had no clue what to say and in truth, she was right. She didn't ask for this.

"I'm coming in, Hope." I didn't wait for her to respond as I knew what the answer would be.

Hope; the beautiful woman I'd watched with fevered desire hours ago; the woman that felt incredible nestled behind me on my bike was now lying in the fetal position, protecting what little she had left of her broken heart. I stomped on the pieces as if they didn't matter, and for the first time in my life I cared.

"Hope, look at me please." I scooted closer, resting on one knee and waiting. I squeezed my eyes shut and silently cursed myself when she did just that, showing me her tear-streaked face.

"Don't cry, babe. I didn't mean it, okay? I'm an ass, it's really the only excuse I have." I shrugged my shoulders, playing it cool. Deep down though it wasn't cool. I'd hurt her, unintentional as it was.

"What's going to happen to me?" Her voice was barely a whisper.

"What do you mean?"

She scooted up the mattress, leaning back against the rod-iron headboard. I didn't miss the way my shirt rode high on her hips, nor the fact her bikini bottoms had shifted ever so slightly, but now was not the time.

"When I get out of here? What am I going to go back to? A father that hates me because I remind him too much of my mother? A job that I was going to lose anyway because I couldn't remember the stupid menu? What am I gonna do?" Hope dropped her head in her hands and began to sob louder.

Against my better judgment, I moved to sit next to her. "Hope, please don't cry. C'mere. It's gonna be alright, babe." I placed my arm around her and pulled her close. Without thinking, I placed a kiss on her head and she stiffened immediately.

"I'm not… This isn't." I was trying to explain, but had difficulty finding the words.

Hope placed a finger over my mouth to silence me. "I know."

I blushed. *I actually freaking blushed.*

"Good." I leaned forward to put some distance between us. "I don't know what's gonna happen, babe. I know that you deserve better than where you came from, so promise me you won't let them treat you like that. You gotta stand up for yourself sometime. Might as well start now."

She sniffled and wiped her eyes. "I know. I just don't know how. I don't like confrontation."

I laughed heartily. "Could've fooled me! You were standing up to me at the party earlier."

Hope playfully slapped me on the shoulder. "That's different. We were around people." When she wouldn't look at me I knew there was more to the story.

"Talk to me."

Her head snapped in my direction. I could see it written all over her face. Yeah, this girl was full of secrets, but then again so was I. "Out with it, babe. I'm just gonna keep asking 'til you do. Who hit you?"

"No one." Her stuttering said otherwise.

"Hope, I do this for a living. I interrogate people. I read their body language. Who did this and where can I find the asshole?" I knew I should stay out of it. I'd lectured myself on getting involved already, but I didn't like to see any woman hurt, especially her.

"It was a long time ago," she admitted. "It doesn't matter now."

"It does matter. You gonna have to worry about this when you get home?"

She paused. "I… I don't think so. He's probably quit looking for me by now."

"What does that mean. How long have you been missing?" The party tonight was the first time I'd seen her. She'd never been at Tommy's, the strip club where Raul conducted most of his business, and Simone hadn't made it sound like they'd been kidnapped.

"A couple of days." She shrugged, while picking at her nails. "Jason. He's my ex. I haven't seen him for several weeks. He hasn't called or anything so I'm sure he's given up by now."

"Jason, what?" I gritted his name through my teeth, complete with spittle. I was fuming, though trying hard to control it.

"Jason Owensby. Don't waste your time. He's not worth it." Hope let out a chuckle of despair.

"I'll handle it, Hope. Don't worry about it." The asshole was mine. I stood and paced a few laps the length of the room before coming back to stand in front of her.

"Look, I am sorry about what happened in the hallway. I let my anger get the best of me and I didn't mean to take it out on you. It's just… it's just you're beautiful, and you're here, in my apartment and…."

"You think I'm beautiful?" The longing in her voice for it to be true was unmistakable.

"Yes, Hope. I think you're stunning. In every way. But, this can't happen." I motioned my hands back and forth between us, and then watched as her expression fell. Classic sign of abuse.

"It's not you." *Great, Blake.* The it's-not-you-it's-me speech. But it was true. It had nothing to do with Hope. It had everything to do with my job and the uncertainty that came with it.

"This job, Hope. It's demanding. It's dangerous. My partner was shot years ago and almost lost his life. And I don't have to tell you how dangerous Raul is." I sighed, frustrated that I wasn't explaining myself very well. The last thing I wanted was to give her a reason to doubt herself. "If things were different…"

She cut me off. "You don't have to explain, Blake. I know." Hope forced a smile. I realized changing the subject now would be a good idea.

“Food should be here any minute. Why don’t you come back out? We’ll eat and then get a good night’s sleep. Things will look better in the morning.”

“Okay.” She stood and dried her tears.

“Good.” I got to the door then turned. “We’re okay, Hope. You’re safe here for the night.” I didn’t give her a chance to respond. Instead I shut the door, giving her time to compose herself.

3

I was hot. My leg was thrown over something warm and soft, and I was too comfortable to move. Thoughts of the night before came to mind, hitting me like a brick wall. Hope. Half-naked. Dinner. Talking. Laughing. Falling asleep. Somehow, we'd both ended up on the small couch, tangling ourselves around one another. I'm choosing to believe it was strictly for self-preservation, to keep one or both of us from falling on the floor, but I knew better. She was as drawn to me as I was to her.

I raised my head, getting a better view of her beautiful face that was tucked into the crook of my neck. She looked peaceful and content. I didn't have the heart to wake her, even though my morning routine was calling. I plopped my head back down on the couch and covered my eyes with my arm.

Just as I was about to drift back into a peaceful sleep myself, a loud pounding rang through the air. Someone was beating on the door so hard I worried the hinges would give way.

"Wake up, babe. Someone's here." I rousted Hope as best I could. "C'mon sleepy head. Rise and shine." She stirred and stretched as I looked on in awe. She was truly a beautiful woman.

"What time is it?" Hope murmured incoherently before rolling over and pressing her backside into my morning erection. I would have scooted back, but there was nowhere for me to go. My large frame didn't even fit the length of the sofa.

"Hope!" I whispered, loudly. "Get up."

She sat up quickly, a look of confusion on her face. "What was that?"

"Someone's here, babe. Get moving. Go to my bedroom and stay until I come get you." She was on her feet within seconds, high-tailing it to safety.

I stood and stretched, giving her extra time. I'm sure my neighbors didn't appreciate the noise, nor did I. Whoever was on the other side of the door was about to get an earful and then some.

I grabbed the handle, yanking the door open with anger. Just as I was about to tell whoever to go to hell, I realized it was Raul. Shit!

"Hello. I was expecting you much earlier, but of course you were a no show. I attribute that to oversleeping after a fun night because I know you wouldn't disobey me." Raul pushed past me, Sergio in tow. I didn't protest.

"Where's the girl?"

"Uh, she's not here. She took off on me during the night." I lied.

Raul turned and looked around the stark room as if she would magically appear. "Really. You don't say?"

He walked further into the living room, almost reaching the long hallway. "Must not have been too happy with your…. performance, shall we say, or she wouldn't have snuck out in the middle of the night. I'm surprised, a strapping young man like yourself." He spoke with an air of superiority and I chuckled within myself. He was my age and he was calling me a 'strapping young man'.

The condescending undertone didn't go unnoticed, but I let it go for the sake of not wanting my head bashed in.

"You got plenty of girls last night, boss. What's so special about this one?"

Raul's dark eyes bore into mine. I shrunk back, horrified by the evil that lurked within them. I seriously didn't think the man had a soul. "I got twenty, to be exact, but I'd be willing to let them all go for her." His devilish sneer told me that was a lie.

"For her friend's sake, Diego, just turn the girl over." *Diego*. I loathed the name. I hated everything it stood for and everything I'd done while having it attached to me.

"She's not here, Raul." I ran my fingers through my hair, nervous. If he caught me lying, I was in deep shit.

Raul's eyes cut to Sergio. "Find the girl."

Sergio nodded and proceeded to go through the apartment, tearing up furniture and anything else that stood in his way. My modest flat screen was busted into tiny fragments, the couch and its cushion were voided of their fluff, mirrors were broken into small glass shards, and my guitar was smashed over the kitchen counter. The place looked like an intruder had ransacked it, but I'd seen the whole thing. I watched in horror as what little I had was obliterated.

He was just about to step into the hallway when the bedroom door creaked open. Hope reluctantly stuck her head through the slit, surveying the damage.

"Ah! Púta!" Raul exclaimed. "Well, well, well… aren't we a sight for sore eyes. Diego must've really worked you over good!" He clapped his hands together in amusement. It was weird. Very weird. He was getting his jollies thinking of the two of us together, and it was then that I saw the true depths of his depravity.

"Raul…" I tried to interject, but he held his hand to quieten me.

"Come here, Hope, is it?"

Hope's eyes flickered to me and then back to Raul. She was scared to death as evident by her shaky hands. "Come on, my dear. I won't bite." Raul's voice lowered a few octaves.

Hope moved slowly towards him. As she grew closer, I stepped forward, trying to place myself between them. I have no idea what overcame me other than the thought of Raul touching her sent a rage of fire through my veins. My well-being wasn't a consideration.

Before I could react, Raul gave the signal to Sergio who grabbed me from behind and placed me in a chokehold.

"Watch this, lover boy!" Raul laughed just before grabbing Hope and ripping my t-shirt from her body. She stood, a look of shock and horror etched on her face. She was naked, all except for the tiny bikini bottoms, but I wasn't paying any attention to her breasts. My eyes were focused on hers and the fear that was reflected in them. I hadn't done my job. I hadn't gotten her out and Raul would make her pay for my mistake. For my lie.

Raul circled her like a vulture, making sure to rub his hands over her flesh. She shivered in terror. She knew as well as I did what he was capable of. "Please," she whimpered. "Don't hurt me. Don't do this."

"Oh, trust me, my dear. You will love every second. Perhaps I should even make old Diego here watch."

I could see the confusion on Hope's face. She didn't know me as Diego. She knew me as Blake. "I thought…."

She was silenced immediately by the stinging slap of Raul's hand to her backside. "You speak only when I say, púta. Is. That. Clear?"

Hope nodded her head as the tears welled up in her eyes. I couldn't do a damn thing but stand by and watch. This was all my fault.

"Enjoying the show?" Sergio's voice was menacing and low, and I was sure he was no better than Raul. All of them were low-life scumbags who deserved nothing less than a bullet through the head. Unfortunately, my gun was nowhere in sight.

I struggled against him, but as big as I was he was bigger. He towered over me, at least 6'4. The seams of his t-shirt strained against the bulging muscle in his arms and I knew I was outmatched.

Raul continued circling Hope as if she were a piece of meat on display. It was disgusting. "I think we'll have a little fun before we leave. How does that sound, my dear?" He stood in front of her, his back to me, but I could still see what he was doing. A low growl erupted from my throat and past my lips as he manhandled her; touching her delicate skin in the most intimate of places.

"Keep your hands off her!" I shouted at him, realizing my mistake too late. Sergio clamped down tighter on my neck until everything went black. I vaguely remember my knees hitting the carpet before I was out cold.

4

~Present Day~

I stand at the window, looking out over the city; the flashing lights and casinos draped in gold obscured by the drizzling rain. The streets glisten, shining with neon colors that bounce from the pavement like a Ferris wheel at a carnival. Fog is beginning to set in, hinting that debauchery is on the horizon. I'm nursing a warm bottle of beer and the TV is on, strictly for background noise. I don't feel like going out. The glitz and glamour of sin city holds nothing for me. Most single men are having a field day; placing bets and flashing wads of money, but this shithole offers nothing I haven't already experienced. I spent years as Raul's right hand man and lavishness was an everyday bonus, at least when I wasn't hanging out with dirt bags and drug lords.

I'm oddly fascinated by the people mulling around outside. They don't seem to mind the rain. They bustle about, shielded with over-sized coats and umbrellas, undeterred by the nasty weather. I guess greed will do that. Nothing matters except money, and who has the most money holds the most power. I come from money, so I should know. Some might even say I had a privileged upbringing and they'd be right. Except thankfully, my parents taught me the value of a dollar and instilled that hard work made the man, not the size of his bank account.

I'm not broke by any stretch of the imagination, but my hiatus from work has kyboshed cash flow. I have enough set aside to get me through this jaunt, but before all of this is said and done, my funds will most likely be bone dry.

Still, none of that is enough to convince me that sitting at the blackjack table is a good idea. I'm in a foul mood and not good company to anyone.

A break was good I suppose. In fact, it's just what the doctor ordered. After years of chasing Raul and collecting evidence against my boss, I am burned out. The end wasn't what I'd signed up for when I joined the agency. Sure, I expected to take out the bad guys. That was the whole point. The thrill of the chase. That thrill quickly died however, when working a case for six years resulted in my target escaping and my superior dead. It had been all for nothing after the FBI decided to abort the mission, and hadn't that just sucked the wind out of my sails? It hadn't made any of us look good, so the agency hoped that by laying low, pressure from higher ups would die down. Truthfully, I didn't know if it had or not. I hadn't kept in contact with George, my superior, or Billy, my ex-partner. Not since I'd been here anyway. They needed time and space to absorb all that had happened, and I vowed to give them that. Johnny, on the other hand, was in it up to his neck. Last I heard he was in Texas, handling some border patrol issues.

He called a month ago with a tip that Raul and his men had brought Hope and the other girls here. I questioned how he would know, but I tried not to pass judgment. I knew it was a long shot at best, but I had nothing to lose; if it meant finding Hope, I had everything to gain. So anyway, here I am in Vegas, handling things on my own.

My grip tightens on the less-than-satisfactory beer; the tension and flexing of my fingers causing the glass to shatter in my clutch. I'm angry. Actually, I'm down right pissed and there's nothing I can do about it. Not yet anyways. For the moment I'm biding my time, waiting for the perfect chance to make my move. I don't know how all of this will play out and right now I don't care. I just know I have to do something. Something to shake this fog from my brain.

I pace; the burgundy carpet with gold swirls sewn throughout rub against my bare feet. The walls are closing in with every lap and my stomach is in knots. Yeah, going out is definitely a bad idea, but I need fresh air. I'll mingle with the others and wander aimlessly about in the rain, but I won't shield myself. No coat and no umbrella. I need to feel. And I need to forget her.

The wind howled between the buildings and through the overcrowded streets. The sidewalks were bustling with people dodging in and out of the rain while street performers were undeterred by the damp weather, carrying on with life as normal. It wasn't. It was anything but normal. Hope's face haunted me, whether I was wide awake or fighting to stay asleep; yet no one, not one damn person cared.

The blood pumping through my veins fueled my feet forward and warmed me under the pelting rain. Before I realized, I was running. My sneakers were pounding the pavement, sending droplets of water flying and soaking the bottoms of my jeans. I didn't care. I kept running until my lungs hurt, but just like always, it wasn't enough. I couldn't outrun my last damn memory of Hope; standing there and silently begging me to help her. It was still fresh in my mind, even almost a year later.

I was about to fall from sheer exhaustion, so I stopped and paced, cooling my body and trying to catch my breath.

When I took the time to look at my surroundings, I noticed the absence of bright lights and drive thru wedding chapels. The streets were void of people and the area looked like an abandoned war zone. I had run way beyond the limits of sin city and now I was surrounded by a host of what appeared to be abandoned buildings; a dense fog rising among them. Where the hell was I? It was like stepping into another world.

My training kicked in as I took stock of everything, making mental notes of every detail. A chain link fence with barbed wire wound around most of the structures, all except one. There was something about that building, something peculiar, but I couldn't quite put my finger on it. I proceeded towards the one less guarded; my sneakers scraping along the broken asphalt and every lose pebble echoing in the silence. As I neared I could hear garbled voices. The faint glow of lights in the background illuminated a secret entrance hidden beside a loading dock. An unexplainable pull kept me trudging forward as my heart rate accelerated. I couldn't pinpoint what it was, but a force greater than me insisted I get up close and personal with whatever the hell was going on.

Two burley men stood at the entrance, blocking the crude metal door. The larger of the two stepped forward, exhibiting authority behind his dark shades. He didn't utter a word but proceeded to pat me down, checking for weapons, microphones and wires. He gave a slight nod for me to walk further when the second man, slightly smaller in build stepped in my path. "Twenty dollars."

"Excuse me?" Twenty dollars for what? What the hell was I expected to pay for.

“Twenty dollars or you can turn around and go back where you came from. Tell anyone about this place and we’ll hunt you down and gut you. What’s it gonna be?”

I swallowed the lump in my throat and reached for my wallet, thankful I hadn’t forgotten to shove it in my back pocket. I had no idea what the hell I was walking into, but that same force that dragged me this far was getting stronger and stronger.

I handed the money to the man and only then did he step aside for me to pass. I paused at the door before pushing it open. The thick, commercial steel screeched against the concrete floor and banged shut with a loud clap.

The cement floor was damp, and my rain-soaked sneakers squeaked loudly, reverberating off the unwelcoming walls. There were no doors or windows, just single bulbs hanging from exposed wiring. Stairs descended into a basement, reminding me of a horror flick with a gruesome discovery lying in wait. I briefly contemplated turning around, but that damn pull kept nagging at me, boding me forward. I’d been so lost in thought I hadn’t even heard the stampede of people rushing past me until it was too late, and I was knocked into the unforgiving cinder block.

A strong smell of astringent and cigar smoke assaulted me when I reached the bottom of the stairs. The smell was distinct and unmistakable. Expensive Cuban cigars. *Raul.* Now I understood everything. What were the odds? I’d not had a single lead, and now here I was in the devil’s lair. My blood boiled as the heat rose through my body, finally making its way to my ears. The cool basement suddenly grew hot. Too hot.

My eyes darted around the room in search of the man that had eluded me for so long. I couldn't find him amongst the crowd, but I knew he was hiding there somewhere, as usual. Money was being waved around in the air and exchanging hands faster than I could see, obstructing my view.

I moved through the sea of bodies, all pushing and shoving against one another, hoping for a better view of the fight that was about to start. Loud shouts of excitement bounced through the air. It was draft and damp and sent chills up my spine. The place was crawling with an infestation of scum; less than desirable characters, each one looking shadier than the next. In reality, the crowd wasn't unlike what I had dealt with in the past, but this time I had no backup. I was technically off duty and had no jurisdiction here. Besides, this didn't strike me as the type of establishment where law mattered anyhow.

Fights like the one about to take place were illegal, and out of the limelight of Vegas and the usual UFC circuit. Underground fighting was taboo, with next-to-no rules or regulations, but that wasn't all that made it dangerous. The men who participated in these bouts were usually hot heads; men who had been banned from the UFC and other fighting regimes, or who had never been allowed in at all for failing psych evaluations. Their rage knew no bounds and unfortunately people like me fed off that anger, making for a mosh pit of instability.

However, in my line of work, I'd had to maintain self-control. I couldn't afford to lose my shit and blow my cover. It had taken great restraint on a daily basis to control the urge of putting a bullet through Raul's brain, and my psyche had suffered for it. I needed to get back in the ring myself, but for now I had to be extremely careful.

My eyes attempted to focus through the cloud of smoke, watching as spectators moved from one side of the narrow room to the other, leaving a small path for the contenders to move through. Catcalls and whistles seemed particularly loud, and I covered my ears to protect them from the assault. It didn't take long to realize who was the cause of the ruckus.

Hope sashayed around the ring, which was nothing more than chain-link fencing attached to a makeshift octagon. Her white shorts rode high on her thighs and her tank barely covered the bottom of her breasts as she held a sign overhead.

The room spun around me as I struggled to take air into my lungs. Overhead lights swung from lanterns like pendulums, each sway echoing loudly in my ears as seconds ticked by. Those brief seconds felt like hours as my mind recalled the last time I'd seen her.

Rage festered inside me. My eyes narrowed into thin slits as I watched her move seductively. I thought briefly of throwing her over my shoulder and running, and as appealing as that was, there were a couple of reasons why it was a terrible idea. One, there wasn't an exit in sight. The stairs were no longer visible through the crowd packed into what could quite possibly be described as nothing more than a shoebox. Two, Raul was nearby. If he wasn't his men were, as the girls were never outta his sight. I was on uneven ground, away from my turf, and I certainly didn't have the upper hand. The best I could do was wait it out, all while trying to maintain anonymity.

"Watch out, man!" I shoved the asshole roughly, making no apologies. He was practically salivating as he watched Hope strut her stuff. I'm fairly certain he had a screw or two lose, if you know what I mean. Truth be told, I suspected none of these people were all that sane, myself included, but I would never cause her harm like these jackasses.

I glared at him with wild, menacing eyes; as threatening as I could muster. For all he knew, I was one of the fighters and everyone knew not to mess with them. The degenerate backed down without a comeback and quickly disappeared into the crowd.

"Ladies and gentlemeeeennnnnn!" The announcer's voice boomed loudly through the bullhorn. "Give it up for the lovely Hoooooope!"

The crowd went wild as she once again looped the circle, receiving pats on the ass and money shoved into the waistband of her skimpy shorts. The humiliation on her face was evident only to me, but her fake smile seemed to appease her fans. They ate it up.

I fought my way through to the front of the crowd, making sure to stay in the corner where I'd be less visible. As she made one more round, I grabbed her around the waist and turned her suddenly. The swift motion caught her off guard and she fell into me, knocking us both backwards.

"I want in on this!"

Apparently, the douche bag next to me had ideas of his own and it wasn't long before others jumped in, offering to join in on the fun. I pulled Hope around behind me and shielded her small body with mine, the same protectiveness

I'd always felt for her kicking in. Staring the hecklers down with malice, each one slowly raised their hands and backed away in surrender.

"You alright, babe?" I scanned her body, looking for any sign of harm. My fingertips lightly brushed her waist and she fell apart like putty in my hands, or so I thought. I smirked with satisfaction, earning me a slap to the face.

"You jerk! How dare you!?"

I looked at Hope in disbelief. Did she not recognize me? I'd just saved her from a pack of piranhas, and she hit me?

"What the hell was that for?"

"Stay. Away. From. Me!" The sweet voice I remembered was not what I just heard. She wasn't the same woman I knew a year ago, but what did I expect?

Before I could say another word, a big, burly man towered over me. "There a problem?" He stood with his shoulders squared as he peered down at me over a pair of sunglasses. Hope shrunk back in what looked to be submission and hung her head.

"There's no trouble, Jax. I'm fine." Hope continued to hang her head, almost as if it was against the rules to look him in the eye.

"You don't touch the girl. Got it?" He glared at me some more, but I wasn't one to back down.

"That's what she's here for, right? I mean, you can't expect to parade something so delicious and men not want a little taste. How much?" I jutted out my jaw and smirked in her direction. She never looked up, but I could see her facial expression change.

"No. She's here to get the fight going. To get everyone riled up. Hands to yourself, boy." The man named Jax dared me through his dark lenses. A pissing contest had ensued.

"We'll see about that!" I reached out suddenly and grabbed Hope by the arm, pulling her towards me.

"You know me, babe. Let me help you!" I pleaded with her, but her face remained stoic and blank.

After a few long seconds, Hope stared at me with eyes wide and shook her head vehemently. "I said I'm fine!" She enunciated each word carefully, never giving me any indication that she was lying. Maybe I'd been wrong about her. Maybe she liked being a play toy. Only one way to find out.

"So, you with this meathead?" I pointed to Jax. I could tell by his body language that his patience was wearing thin and I had limited time before shit hit the fan. I expected Raul to make an appearance at any moment.

"No!" she shouted.

The crowd in the far corner increased their shouts as a man came through the rear curtain. He came alone, head down, shoulders set forward. He made his way to the ring, opening the cage door as he reached the top of the steps. He looked like a wet back, mean as hell with a Mohawk the color of ash. His ripped body was covered in ink. Maybe they were his trophies. His badges of honor.

Jax chuckled. It was a sound I didn't think the big ogre was capable of making. "She's with everyone." His lips formed a sneer, revealing a faint scar at the corner of his mouth. I didn't find his retort funny, but at least now I knew. I guess the ones Raul didn't sell he pimped out.

Another fighter came through the heavy curtain. He was as black as the night, torso oiled, rippling with muscle. He vaulted the steps, prancing into the ring like a dancer. He did two circuits, circling his arms like a windmill. The Mexican stood there; pensive, breathing, weighing up his quarry.

I focused my attention back to Jax before he could use the distraction to his advantage. "Well hell! Where do I sign up?" I wasn't joking. If I could just get Hope all to myself, maybe there was a chance to get us both out of this alive.

"You need to make an appointment with the big man," Jax replied. "Here's his card."

The thick, black rectangular card felt heavy and burned through my palm. *Finally, I had Raul*. Finally, I could end this. Hope and the other girls would be safe, and I could go on with my life. I just had to figure out a way to get to her without him knowing it was me. That part would be tricky. And I needed backup which meant Johnny needed to drop whatever bullshit drivel he was tending to and get his butt to Vegas.

"I'll give him a call. And I'll be seeing you soon, babe. That's a promise."

"Lucky for me you aren't known for keeping your promises." The venom in Hope's voice was evident. She blamed me.

It was like a knife to my soul, but she was right. The look of disgust and defiance on her face was enough to fuel the madness that burned inside. I needed her to stoke that fire;

the one that had been simmering so long but was probably better left smoldering. The anger that had rooted itself deep inside was not something I wanted to let loose from its cage, but maybe it needed to happen. Maybe, once and for all, it was time for everyone to know the *real* Blake. Hope needed to be scared and I knew just how to do it.

I moved to a vantage point as the fighters came to the center of the ring. The crowd was screaming for action. They rattled their beer bottles against the wire fencing that encircled the crude ring. Hope was suddenly lost in a sea of bodies, heading off to do her duties. I could still make out the giant knuckle head. He towered over the rest of the onlookers. I'd paid twenty dollars, so I may as well see some action.

The referee was in the center of the ring, giving the fighters the pre-fight rules. Yeah right. Like there were any. He was probably saying that anything goes except Uzi's. I scanned the crowd looking for Raul. Trying to catch a glimpse of him in the sea of carnage. No luck. He could be anywhere. Hell! He could be standing behind me with a 9mm aimed at my head. I shook the thought as the bell chimed. Both fighters advanced to the center, flicking out hands and taped up feet. Their gloves were sparring mits, barely offering any comfort for the body part it was about to smash into. If one of the dudes connected with those, it was goodnight Vienna.

This wasn't boxing. Madison Square Garden was a world away. This was hell. This was a trip to the hospital, or worse. The black fighter was all about show boating, whipping the crowd into a frenzy as he feigned and flicked out his jabs. The Mexican was methodical, dodging any attack as he pursued the other man across the ring, waiting for his chance. In a whirl of speed, the black fighter attacked with the speed of a cobra. The other guy fell back against the cage, bringing his arms up to protect his head as the blows peppered him. The referee was close by, bulging biceps that were ready to pull these guys apart if needed. The black guy sensed his chance as he switched to hooks, trying to club the other dude's arms away from his head. Ready for the kill. The Mexican seemed to be waning as the blows struck home, each one finding their target. He looked to the crowd, hoping to draw that bit of extra fight from their baying fury, before he finished the guy, but he'd underestimated his opponent. Classic trick. Mohawk was playing possum. As the younger fighter's hand dropped a few inches, the Mexican flicked his finger into his opponent's eye. He was off balance for a split second, waving his hand to his face. The veteran brawler took two steps forward and butted him square in the face. It was a blow that could have killed a guy. His black legs buckled as his head snapped backward, almost snapping his neck. That's when the Mexican went for the kill. He circled the younger fighter, wrapping his arms around his waist from behind. In one fluid motion he performed a belly to back suplex. This was not staged. Not choreographed. This was not Smackdown. The black fighter went over backwards, arms flailing as he headed for the mat. I could hear the sickening crunch as they landed.

The crowd sighed in unison. The Mexican climbed to his feet, looking at his twitching opponent. He spat in disgust on the other fighter as he lay prone on the floor. Something was wrong with him. His head was at a funny angle. The referee was signaling for someone from the crowd to help. I caught a glimpse of the downed fighter's eyes before a sea of bodies blocked my view. He was dead. His neck snapped like a twig. The Mexican was stood on the far side, swigging a bottle of water like he was shooting the breeze. Not like he'd just ended a life.

I exited the dive a few moments later as the noise levels died away. The crowd grew quieter as the news was spreading. I had to get Hope out of there. And I knew what needed to be done.

5

"Johnny, where you at, man?"

"Blake?"

I sighed. "Who else would it be, dipshit? Now answer my question. Where you at?"

He chuckled on the other end of the line. "Texas, man. What's up?"

I could hear female laughter in the background, along with the rustling of covers. I rolled my eyes, thinking how long it'd been for me. To say I'd hit a dry spell was an understatement.

"Johnny! Focus!" My tone was curt. I didn't have time, nor did I want to hear all about his romp in the sheets.

More rustling on the other end of the line. "Sorry, dude. I'm listening."

I filled him in on what had happened the night before and told him my plan. "I need you here, man. If Raul comes sniffing around he doesn't need to see me. He has no idea who the hell you are."

"Calm your panties, princess. When do you need me to be there?"

"Tonight. By six o'clock. Your plane ticket will be waiting at the counter." I'd already taken the liberty of making the arrangements. Him saying no wasn't an option.

He laughed heartily. "First class?"

"Don't be an ass dude. Be at the airport at two and don't be late!" I hit the end call button and tossed my phone on the couch in frustration. Lacing my hands behind my head, I paced more. Seems I was doing a lot of that these days, but it helped me think.

The doorbell rang at exactly six o'clock. I peeked through the peephole, squinting one eye for a better look. I was sure it was Johnny, but given the chance it could be Raul, I'd be a fool to open it without checking first.

"Alright, princess. I'm here to save the day." Johnny threw his duffle on the floor next to the entrance and waltzed right in as if he owned the place. I shut the door and slid the chain lock in place.

A good smack to the back of his head got his attention. "C'mon, pretty boy. Ain't got all damn day." I grabbed his bag from the floor and tossed it his direction. "Follow me."

He did as I said, no questions asked. Perhaps this would go smoother than I had anticipated. If we could stay on track this should be a piece of cake. I led him to the spare bedroom. "Get changed. Something nice. I just paid twenty grand for a date. If they show up and you look like, well this," I waved my hand up and down his direction, "things will look suspicious." He looked slightly offended, but I didn't care. Facts were facts. He looked like he'd been on a drinking binge for over a week and hadn't shaven in at least that long.

His eyes went wide with surprise. "Twenty grand? Are you shittin' me, dude? Who is this broad anyway?"

My hands curled into fists as I reigned in my anger. "She's not a broad, asshole. She's a woman. A woman who needs my help. All I need you to do is answer the damn door and get her inside. Think you can handle that?"

Johnny stepped back a few paces and held his hands up. "Sorry, man. I was just joking around."

I pinched the bridge of my nose, trying to curb the massive headache that was forming just behind my eyes. "It's fine. Just get dressed." I checked my watch. "She'll be here in fifteen."

I walked out of the room, carrying along a sinking feeling in my stomach. If this went south, I was a dead man. Hope's life would most likely be on the line, too. Raul didn't like to play games, at least not those he wasn't the creator of. One wrong move on my part, or Johnny's, we'd all be in for it.

I'd stewed over Hope's reaction to me all night and the better part the day. I couldn't figure her out, though to be fair, there was no telling what she'd been through in the last year since Raul had taken her. He was a horrible man; the vilest you'd ever have the displeasure of meeting, and I could only imagine the things she'd seen in that time. Not only that, but what she'd experienced personally. I hadn't been strong enough to stop Raul that day. To get her to safety like I promised, but I wouldn't fail her this time.

"This better, boss?"

Johnny was standing there in black dress pants and a white button up, with the sleeves casually rolled up, exposing his tattoos. I didn't check men out. Not my thing, but I'll admit it was a vast improvement from the sweats he'd shown up in. "You'll do."

He nodded cautiously. I went over the plan for the tenth time, satisfied that he had it down pat. Time would tell.

"Calm down, princess. I got this." Johnny stood and straightened his shirt. "Go hide out in the other room. She'll be here any minute."

I stood, reluctantly. "Don't screw this up." My tone was a warning. I wasn't going to let Hope slip through my fingers again and I wasn't about to let Raul get away. Not this time.

Johnny gave me a sarcastic salute as I walked away. I kept the door ajar ever so slightly, hoping to get a peek. I was so damn nervous, which was very uncharacteristic of me. I didn't do this shit. I didn't get bent over some chick. Not my style. I chalked it up to failure. That it was simply because I hadn't done my job and that pissed me off. I was a good agent. As good as they came, but I had blown it. I was cocky, too overconfident, and I got sloppy. This time I'd be more careful.

The doorbell chimed at exactly six. Johnny stood and walked with confidence to answer. The direction of the door swinging open obstructed my view momentarily, but I could hear her voice; that sweet voice that haunted my dreams almost every night. *Hope.*

"You have til midnight." The man's deep voice boomed, and I knew it to be Jax. The same beast from the fight last night.

"Sure thing." Johnny didn't appear to be phased in the least by the towering figure. I saw him reach his hand across the threshold to escort Hope inside. Just the thought of him touching any part of her sent anger shooting through me.

I saw her long, tan legs before anything else. Shit, she was built like no other woman I'd ever seen and believe me, I'd seen my share.

My eyes followed the trail, first catching sight of her barely covered thigh, all the way up her miniscule dress. It was green fabric, if you could call it that, and it barely covered her most intimate parts, somehow strategically held in place. My tongue hung out of my mouth like a dog thirsting for water.

Johnny shut the door and slid the chain into place before locking the deadbolt, just like we'd rehearsed. So far, so good. He led her over to the couch, his hand on the small of her back. I had to keep my cool. Five minutes. That was the agreement. Five minutes would give Jax time to leave, Johnny out the door, and me alone with Hope for the first time in a year. Five of the longest fucking minutes of my life.

I counted the seconds as my watch ticked in annoyance. "Hope, it's been lovely meeting you. Please, excuse me." He leaned down to kiss her hand, and she looked puzzled by his sudden departure. "She's all yours, princess."

Johnny waited until I reached the door, allowing me to shut and lock it once again behind him. "Told you I'd see you again, babe." I kept my back turned to her, trying to gain some sense of composure. Her current state of dress was making it almost impossible. *Deep breath. Deep breath.*

Hope was a statue on the couch, her eyes boring into mine when I finally got the nerve to face her. Immediately, something in the air changed between us. The detachment she had for me just hours ago was gone. I saw her falter, her body sagging against the arm of the sofa.

"It's okay, babe. I got you." I hauled ass to her side, reaching her in only four short strides. My long legs came in handy. "Hope?"

I waited for her to look at me and when she did, the dam burst. Tears spilled relentlessly out of her beautiful blue eyes, shattering my resolve into a million pieces. "It's you. It's really you!" Hope sobbed as she linked her arms around my neck.

I brushed the hair from her face, and the damp tears from her cheeks. "Yeah, babe. It's really me." Time was of the essence as we didn't have much, but I'd be a fool not to take the time to tell her how sorry I was. "Babe. God, I'm so sorry. Tell me you forgive me. It wasn't supposed to go down like that. He wasn't supposed to get to you."

Hope sobbed harder, wetting my t-shirt with her salty tears. I held her as she grabbed on for dear life. I knew then that anything I could've possibly imagined was a thousand times worse. "It's okay, Blake. It wasn't your fault."

I leaned back, gently prying her from my torso. The loss of our connection struck me hard, but I wanted to stare at her. I wanted to know she was really here and not just a figment of my imagination. "Are you okay?" It was quite possibly the dumbest question in the history of the world, but it's all I could think of in the moment.

She nodded her head yes and continued wiping her face. "Talk to me, babe."

"Oh, God, Blake. He's so awful. I can't…."

"Shhh, don't cry, babe. I'm here." I rocked her gently in my arms, feeling her heart beat alongside mine. Again, I was unsettled. This wasn't my typical reaction to a woman. I'd bed her and be done, not thinking twice about my actions. With Hope it was different. I wanted her to miss me. I wanted her to want me. And I damn sure wanted her to need me. Whatever the reason, I tried to let it go, realizing that trying to solve the puzzle tonight was of the least importance.

"Where's he keeping you, babe?" I sat up on the couch and turned so that our knees were touching. I needed the contact and I believe she did, too.

"The bunkers, where we were last night. That's what we call them. Raul holds us prisoner there."

I shook my head in disgust. "How many girls?"

Hope shrugged her shoulders and counted in her mind. "I don't know. Probably thirty, give or take a few. Some of them left out yesterday, but they didn't come back."

I knew what that meant. Sold for profit to the highest mother fucker that thought he had the right to own another human being. The men Raul dealt with were as evil as he was. "Where'd they go, babe?"

"I don't know. I heard Nicole, my friend, talking to one of the others, but I couldn't make out what they were saying."

"You didn't ask?" *Smooth, Blake. Real smooth.* This girl has gone through hell and you interrogate her like some piece of trash from the street.

Hope looked away as she spoke. "They don't exactly like me. I mean, we don't talk much."

"Why not, babe? Seems you all need to stick together."

"Because Raul favors me. I get more privileges. More food. More nights out. I don't know."

"You mean; Raul keeps you for his…. *personal use*?"

She gave a slight nod. I closed my eyes and took a deep breath, slowly letting it blow past my lips and then once more for good measure. "Yes." Her voice was barely a whisper, difficult to hear over the air unit that hummed in the background.

I stood and walked that same worn tract of carpet that still had my imprints from earlier. I didn't have the words. Actually, I did, but none that I wanted to say in front of Hope.

"What else?" I gritted through my clinched teeth.

"Well, you know about the fighting matches. That's how he makes money. That and pimping us out." She hung her head, embarrassed. I knew what she was thinking because I was thinking it, too.

"Who was it?"

Hope gave me a puzzled look, but it was fake. She knew exactly what I was referring to. "Who took that from you, babe? Gonna need an answer."

"Raul." She began to cry again, but I wasn't in a position to hold her. I was too mad. Too damn angry and I was afraid of hurting her.

"I'll end this, Hope. I swear, babe, I'll end this." I intended to keep that promise this time, or at least die trying.

She surprised me by walking around the couch towards me. She stood, rocking back and forth from foot to foot, unsure of her next move. I knew what she needed. Hell, I knew what *I* needed. I held my arms open wide and she came willingly, throwing herself at my chest. I closed my arms around her, breathing in the sweet scent of her hair. I squeezed my eyes tight, burning this moment into my mind. I'd never forget it.

A while later, after we'd composed ourselves, we ordered room service for dinner and talked through our plans. I knew I couldn't get her out tonight. It was impossible. The probability that Lurch was waiting in the wings was great and not worth chancing. We agreed that she would return tonight, but at the next bout I'd get her out. I'd get us both out and we'd run, never looking back.

The clock on the wall said eleven fifty-five. Five more minutes and Jax would be back to escort her to the compound. She'd be gone once again, but not for long if I could help it.

"Remember the plan, babe. I'll be there Friday night to get you. Back room, beside the stairs, just like we talked about. Eight o'clock sharp."

She nodded her head. "I don't want to go back." The pleading in her voice nearly broke me. I didn't want her to go back either, but I had to be the voice of reason. I had to be strong and not let on how scared I was.

"I know, babe. Just a few more days and we're home free. Okay?"

"What if we don't make it out?" Her fear was well-founded, but I'd keep that to myself. I'd already talked her down more than once and I didn't think either of us had the strength to go through that again. Not tonight.

"We will." I placed a kiss to her forehead, wanting to do so much more and yet, realizing that was as intimate as anything else I could do. Sometimes sex wasn't need. At thirty-seven that was just dawning on me and like I said, it was different with Hope. "You're a strong woman, Hope. One of the bravest I've ever met. You can do this. *We* can do this."

She seemed satisfied with my answer and even awarded me with a smile. "Okay," she agreed.

"Okay."

Just like that our plan was in place. I wasn't one hundred percent confident it'd work, but time would tell. Anything to get her away from that piece of shit Raul would be worth it in the end, even if I ended up dead.

Johnny was back in the nick of time. Jax would be arriving at any moment to take Hope back, and it was important I wasn't seen. "I'll see you Friday." I kissed Hope on the cheek and retreated back to my room once more, again leaving the door ajar.

Johnny blew out a breath. "Get things worked out, kiddo?"

“I think so.” Hope answered in a timid voice. She was shaking, and I immediately felt horrible for not introducing them. She must be wondering who he was and why he was there. Before I could react, the doorbell chimed.

“Thank you for a most lovely evening, Hope. I look forward to our meeting again.” Johnny kissed her hand in a gentleman-like fashion and once again my blood boiled.

“Let’s go.” I saw a meaty paw reach out and grab her by the arm. *Jax*! He pulled her away from the threshold and down the hall before Johnny had time to react. He started to go after them when I stepped from the room.

“I wouldn’t do that if I were you.” He didn’t have a clue the kind of people we were dealing with. They weren’t choir boys.

“Yeah? Why’s that? Didn’t you see him dragging her out of here?” He stood with his arms crossed across his chest, waiting.

“You don’t know who these guys are, dude. You have no fucking clue. Trust me, even with just the one, we’re outnumbered. She’ll be okay for tonight.”

“You sure about that? Cause you didn’t see the look on her face.”

“Ass in seat soldier.” I pointed to the dining chair where Hope and I had eaten earlier. Johnny looked at me with a smirk but complied. “These men…”

“These men are drug lords. I know. I’ve met Raul, remember?”

“Yeah, but things are a little different.”

"Because of the girl? She's a knockout by the way." He smirked again, trying to get under my skin. It was working, but I refused to give him the satisfaction.

"Yes. And the other thirty or so like her. Illegal fight rings. Whoring them out. Drugs. Money. Weapons. You name it, Raul's up to his eyeballs in it. These aren't people you screw with, Johnny. You make sure you have a damn good, fool proof plan in place, and you don't screw it up."

"I know who they are, princess. I grew up with half of them."

My mouth hung open. I was speechless, momentarily, but then my brain eventually caught up and the questions began to fly.

Johnny laughed heartily. "Settle down, man. I'll tell ya everything you wanna know, but you need to catch your breath and I need a beer." He excused himself from the table and headed for the mini-bar.

Looks like my night was just about to get even more interesting, if that was possible.

6

Johnny reared back on the couch and propped his feet on the glass table, again as if he owned the place. Hell, I didn't even own it, but it was my home away from home for now. At least until Friday. He could do whatever the hell he pleased so long as he gave me the info I wanted.

"Spill it." I sat across from him in a wing-backed chair, but I couldn't relax. My leg was bouncing all over the place, anxious to find out what the hell was going on. I knew he'd worked undercover, and had even worked a bit on Raul's case, but beyond that I knew nothing about him.

"I will, man, cool your jets. First tell me about this intriguing young lady."

"You know her from Tommy's, remember?"

He winked. "Yeah, I remember. What I mean is, what is she to you? Why the all-fired importance to save *her*? Why not one of the others?"

I rubbed the back of my neck, stalling. I'd never had to explain myself to anyone. Well, maybe the boss, but this guy was far from my boss. He was so far down the ladder he could jump without fear of breaking bones. The last thing I wanted to do was discuss Hope with him, much less that morning that she'd been taken so brutally.

"She's different. We kinda bonded. End of story."

He pointed towards the door where she'd made her exit just a little bit ago. "That didn't look like you guys 'kinda bonded'. That was more like someone struck a match and lit the two of you on fire. I was burning up myself just watching." Johnny chuckled, amused with himself.

"Shut the hell up, man. You don't know what you're talking about."

"Dude, I'm just saying…."

"Yeah, I know what you're saying. Forget it. Now tell me about these guys and how the hell did you get mixed up with them?" I was on the edge of my seat, waiting anxiously.

He grinned. "Dude, you won't even believe me if I tell you."

I lunged a pillow in his direction. "Start talking. I can't decide if I believe you or not if you don't tell me anything!"

He sat up, too, and placed his beer on the table. "Listen, this goes way back. All the way back to when Victor was alive. He and my father were…. Well, let's just say they were very good friends."

My head was spinning. I couldn't figure out who the hell he was talking about. I'd been running this job now for well over six years. I would've seen the guy at some point, right? "Go on."

"Not recently, but years ago when I was a kid." He twisted his mouth and tilted his head, figuring it up in his mind. "I'd say, oh, I don't know. Fifteen years ago, maybe a bit less."

"How did they know each other exactly?"

“Let’s just say I didn’t have the same upbringing as you. I made my father money, not the other way around.”

“Doing what exactly?” I thought about his job as an agent. Surely there was a background check on the guy somewhere. I made a mental note to contact George as soon as possible. I know I said I was giving the man space, but desperate times called for desperate measures. I needed to know Johnny wasn’t a rat. That I could trust him if it came down to it.

“Fighting.”

“What do you mean, fighting? On the street, in the gym? What?”

“I mean exactly what you witnessed last night. The underground kind. The highly dangerous and illegal type.” He shrugged his shoulders as if it was no big deal. “That’s how I got to know some of the guys. It’s actually the reason I was in Texas. You know, following up with old contacts and stuff. Thought it might be useful for the case.”

I was stunned. My mouth hung agape as I stared at him. “Who the hell *are you*?”

Johnny laughed again, rather loudly I might add. “Here princess, I got something for you.” He walked to the spare room where he’d stored his duffle bag earlier. “Here, George said you’d probably want some proof. It’s all in there. Psych evaluation, blood type, height, weight. All that good stuff. Oh, don’t look at the weight. I was retaining water that day.”

Well, wasn’t he just a comedian? I rolled my eyes and hastily looked through the stack of papers stuffed within the confines of the beige folder. Everything seemed to be in order as far as I could tell.

"Anything else?" he quizzed.

"Yeah. You know these guys. Any idea how the hell we take 'em out?"

He took a drink from the long neck of his beer bottle while he thought. "I'll have to do some poking around. Some of the guys I knew way back when have changed. They don't live the life anymore."

"Oh, Yeah, right. What about your dad?"

His reply was cold. "Dead. And before you offer your sympathies, don't. He was a miserable son of a bitch that made my life hell. My mom's, too. She was passed around like garbage to Victor and any other man he saw fit. He doesn't deserve an ounce of grieving."

I had no clue what to say to that. It was shocking, obviously, but what were the odds it'd go like that? "Where's your mom now?"

"She's in a nursing home. She never quite recovered from all they put her through and I travel too much to take care of her."

He was right. Saying sorry didn't fix anything. It sure as hell didn't help his poor mother and since Johnny didn't strike me as the type to accept pity, I let it go. "Sergio? Know him?"

"Yeah, I know of him. He wasn't around back then."

"Deuce? James? Otto? Any of those guys ring a bell? How 'bout this new guy, Jax?"

“Dude. Slow down, alright. Give me a damn minute to answer! Yea, I know them all. Otto and I used to tie into it all the time when we were kids. Dude was a punk then and he’s a punk now. He’ll be the least of our problems.”

“Our problems?”

“Yeah, *our* problems. I’m your new partner, Blakey-boy.”

I leapt from the chair. Did I just hear right? I hadn’t had a partner since Billy and I didn’t want one. It was just another person to get in the way. It’s not that I wasn’t grateful for what Johnny did tonight, but I could handle this on my own. “I don’t need a partner. I just need you to tell me the chances of me getting Hope outta here alive!”

“Sit down, Blake.” We faced off, a staring contests of sorts, to see who would back down first. I caved.

“Good. Now let’s go through this nice and slow so you’ll understand. Otto is easy to distract. He’s like a dog chasing a bone. No problem. Deuce isn’t the sharpest tool in the shed, if you know what I mean, but he’s a freaking bull. Trickery is the way to handle him. James is the same. Show him a pretty girl and he’s busy for days. The one we gotta watch out for is Jax. You didn’t see his face tonight when he drug her outta here. He’s a loose cannon.”

I shook my head, absorbing what he’d said.

“Raul, as you know, is also one to be reckoned with. I don’t have to tell you anything about the slime ball, as I’m sure you know much more than I do. I’ve only studied his file which as I understand is only a partial. That a lot of evidence went missing.”

"Yeah."

"Alright, so Friday night. Tell me about this plan."

I proceeded to fill Johnny in on my discussion with Hope. He agreed that it was solid, but he wanted to add a few elements into the mix.

"From here on out, we don't know each other. I'm a fighter. I can pull this off. Jax saw me tonight, not you. As far as any of them are concerned you're not even here. Let's keep it that way."

"I don't need you to swoop in and play hero. I'm perfectly capable of saving Hope on my own."

He guffawed. "Seriously? What are we? Eighteen? Dude, I'm not trying to steal your girl. But I'm telling ya, this is the way to play it. I get in and fight. I make Raul money. He'll trust me. We can get to Hope that way and the others, too."

I knew he was right, but it didn't make me feel any better. I was a selfish bastard like that. I didn't want her to depend on him, I wanted her to depend on me.

"Fine." I relented, knowing his idea was much better than mine. Raul spoke the language of money. It's what drove him to do all the shit he did. Johnny could be invaluable for that. "But Hope is expecting me Friday. If I don't show…."

"No worries. I'll explain everything to her. You still got that card?"

"Right here." I pulled Raul's card from my pocket and handed it to him.

“Get ready. You’ve got another date tomorrow night. Get your wallet out.” Johnny strode to the other side of the room and made the call.

7

Johnny and I hit the gym just before dawn. Laying low was key, at least where I was concerned. Johnny, on the other hand, needed the exposure. We knew this was the place to be, as it was usually bustling during the day with fighters looking for a match. Word needed to get around to Raul that Johnny was the best of the best in order to get our plan off the ground.

"Let's see what you got, cupcake." Johnny and I had our protective gear on and were in the ring, bouncing from foot to foot, sizing each other up. It'd been a while since I'd suited up and the excitement was almost too much. Adrenaline pumped through my veins like a raging wildfire.

"That all the smack talk you got, princess?" I could barely see Johnny's pearly whites through his mouth guard. "C'mon, let's see what you can do, big man."

The taunts ceased momentarily while we circled the cage. I advanced and lunged, landing my first upper cut to the left side of his jaw. It was more of a tap, but I was just testing the waters. I didn't need the training. I wasn't the one who'd be fighting for Hope's honor. I was more interested to see what Johnny-boy could do and he didn't disappoint.

"That's your one, princess." Without warning, he unleashed. A right hook and chop to my abdomen had me stumbling to keep my balance. He packed quite a punch and while this would normally piss me off, I couldn't have been more pleased.

Johnny continued his assault and I continued to be impressed. I purposely let him land a few and a few I didn't. He was quick on his feet, his body bounding around as if he weighed nothing more than a feather.

After a good thirty minutes of friendly sparring, we decided to call it quits. At least I did. "You know the plan. Guys should be showing up here any minute. Challenge a few and let's see how you fair against a real opponent."

"You're the boss." Johnny and I tapped hands before I exited the cage.

"I'll be right over there, watching. Give 'em hell, cupcake." I unstrapped the Velcro on my mits and tossed them to the side. I'd grab them later. Right now, I needed to remain as inconspicuous as possible. Fighters were starting to filter through the door and not to my surprise, Jax was leading the herd. He saw me and smiled. A wicked smile, full of malice. He'd seen me now, so it was pointless trying to hide. I ambled over to his posse as Johnny did some stretches in the ring to warm down.

"Hello again sweet cakes. What brings you here? Looking for a date?" He was trying to get a bite. He was huge. Probably a good four or five inches taller than my respectable six feet. He also outweighed me by a hundred pounds. He was indeed big, but dumb. If he wanted to spar with words, I was more than happy to oblige.

"Not really my ideal choice for a pick up joint. Too much testosterone and bad breath for my liking." Bingo! That hit the spot. His face looked like he'd just sucked on a lemon. Johnny heard the exchange and sauntered over, wiping perspiration from his brow with his forearm.

“Everything okay Blake?” he asked as he sized Jax up.

The dumb giant looked at Johnny like he’d just scraped him off of his boot.

“This your girlfriend, Blake?” he said, pointing toward Johnny. He smiled at the jibe, seeing an opportunity present itself.

“Nah. Blake’s not my type. Too skinny. I prefer someone with a bit more meat on the bones. Like you.” He pointed towards the ring. “Care to dance, sweet thing.”

Two minutes later I was standing with Johnny in the corner of the ring. Jax and his goons were in the other. They seemed excited. They looked like kids in line for the coaster. They were whooping and high-fiving. Did they know something we didn’t? Johnny looked relaxed. Hell, he almost looked horizontal. How could he be so laid back, looking at what was about to come his way?

“Okay, so what’s the game plan? You can’t trade with this guy. He’ll win.”

“Who said anything about trading?” Johnny smiled his most devilish smile. “We’re all the same size when we’re flat on our backs. That’s the plan. Take this asshole down, then go to work on him. I have a few tricks up my sleeve bro. Just keep a watch on his pals. If it gets ugly I may need you to step in.”

“Ugly.” I tried to push that thought from my mind as Jax headed over. He was stripped to the waist, opting for gym shorts. Black, the same color as the mitts he was strapping on. He was built like a train. Long and heavy. His arms almost fell to his knees. He suddenly looked very big. I looked at Johnny who was now all business, the jokes finished. Now it was time to dance.

"Okay Johnny, how do you wanna do this? Rounds. Or to the death?" Fuck. That sounded like this was some medieval duel.

"To the death." We all exited the ring, leaving the combatants to do a few last-minute stretches. One of Jax's goons rang the bell in the far corner. Okay. Showtime.

Jax came in fast. Real fast for a guy of his size. He cornered Johnny, peppering his body with an onslaught of testing blows. Johnny grunted in discomfort as he dealt with the shots. He seemed to be waiting. *Bang*. There it was. As Jax was pulling back for a straight left, Johnny fired his own right, catching the monster on the left temple. It was a shot that would have put me out. Jax merely shook his head as he swung a wickedly fast elbow at Johnny's throat. He ducked under it, coming up behind Jax, slamming a left, right combination into his kidneys. This time Jax felt the hard punches. He spun around, his back making contact with the turnbuckle. He paused, catching his breath.

"You can dance sweet thing." Johnny smiled. That was as close to a compliment he was going to get. Quick as a flash Jax was on him, grabbing Johnny in a bear hug, propelling him into the ropes. Two quick knees caught him in the chest as Jax pressed the advantage. This was bad. I could see the look on Johnny's face. It was the look of someone who'd been hit by a train. Jax propelled him across the ring with all his power. As Johnny bounced back off the ropes he was cut down by a wicked clothesline. He hit the mat in a crumpled heap. Jax smiled at me before stooping to pick my friend up by the hair. He scooped him into his arms before dropping him across his knee in a well-executed back breaker. Shit. It dawned on me. This guy wasn't just a fighter. He was a wrestler, too. *Double jeopardy*. Johnny was in trouble. He could be heading for the emergency room real soon. Jax could finish it now. He could turn Johnny over and deliver the killer blow. But he didn't. He wanted to enjoy this. He wanted to send a message to both of us. A 'you-don't-want-to-fuck-with-me' message. He lifted him to his feet. Johnny's legs were rubbery as he was backed into the corner. Jax slammed home two body shots that I'm sure cracked some ribs. Johnny winced as they reined in, pulling his arms down to ward off the attack. Jax lifted his opponent's arms, draping them over the ropes to open up his target. He caught Johnny across the chest with a thunderous back hand chop, sending his head backwards against the padding of the turnbuckle. Grabbing his arm, Jax propelled him across the ring, running with him, almost throwing him into the opposite corner. Johnny hit the corner chest first and seemed to crumble to the mat. He was done for. Jax was a killer. And it could end that way. Should I throw the towel in? I suddenly realized I had no towel. *Shit!* Jax pulled Johnny to the center of the ring, laying him out in a crucifix pose. He stood over him, breathing like an angry bull, almost snorting. "Big splash," one of his goons shouted from outside the ring. Jax nodded his head and headed for the corner, climbing up backwards he sat on the top turnbuckle, his feet on the second rope. I tried to warn Johnny, but the words caught in my throat. I was frozen. I'd seen what was about to happen on TV, but this was real, and it was ugly. Johnny was lay there, about to be hit by a three-hundred-pound train. I stood paralyzed as Jax launched himself off the ropes, stretching his frame out as he prepared to land on Johnny. Preparing to drive the last of the air from his lungs and crush him into the mat. A split second before impact, Johnny, the sneaky son of a bitch, brought his knees up, and they drove into Jax's stomach. The giant rolled off his knees onto the mat. He lay writhing in silent agony, his knees pulled up to his chest. Johnny straddled him, pushing the giant's arms flat on the mat. Two straight punches to Jax's face was enough to stun him temporarily. He climbed off him, picking his limp legs up. He held them straight as he looked down at his fallen opponent. What the hell was he going to do now? Break his legs? He stepped through the two legs with his own left leg. In one fluid motion, he crossed Jax's legs over his own, in a figure four shape. Before the giant knew what was happening, Johnny flipped him over onto his front, leaning all his weight back against him. It was a classic submission move. One I'd seen in wrestling matches over the years. Jax's face turned purple as an excruciating pain erupted all over his body. He was caught in a death grip. One that Johnny would never let go of. He leaned back some more, threatening to snap the bigger man in two. "Enough, enough! I submit. Fuck, get him off me!" One of his boys jumped through the ropes as Johnny let go of the hold, falling to the mat in an exhausted heap. I was over there in a split second, helping him out of the ring.

"You okay Johnny?" I asked, as he almost collapsed in my arms.

"Never better," he said through gritted teeth. I handed him a bottle of water which he chugged down in one go.

8

Johnny was licked pretty good, but I'll give the man credit, he didn't complain. He winced in pain, holding his rib cage as he stretched to pull his shirt on over his head. A few grunting noises came from his mouth, but he never uttered a word.

"You okay, man? You took quite a beating in the ring today." I grimaced, watching as he sat gingerly. He looked like he was holding his breath.

Once settled he cut his eyes up to look at me. A slow grin spread across his face. "Step one complete."

"What's that?" I chuckled. "Getting your ass kicked. Good plan, cupcake."

He lazily threw a pillow my direction, missing its mark. It was obvious that even that little bit of movement was painful. "No, smart ass. Step one was to let Jax think he had the upper hand. He doesn't see me as a threat if he thinks he can beat me."

I stood puzzled. "I was there, man. He tapped out. He surrendered to you. How is that letting him win?"

Johnny thought for a moment. "True. Perhaps I shouldn't have let my temper get the best of me. What can I say?" he shrugged. "But he was kickin' my ass before that. Pretty well, judging by the bruises I'll have tomorrow." He lifted his shirt, showing me his body. There were already the first signs of damage. He wouldn't be shooting hoops for a few days.

I looked away with a grimace. "Okay, so what now?"

"I imagine Jax has already run back to Raul, detailing the day. I don't think it'll be long before we hear something."

"You're forgetting one important detail," I reminded him. "Jax saw me. He knows I'm here. He won't let that go and neither will Raul. I may have just blown any chance at getting to Hope."

"Nah, man." Johnny waved it off, chalking it up in our favor. "Raul loves the thrill too much. He'll want you involved so he can taunt you with her."

He had a point. That's exactly how Raul would react. "I hope you're right. I'm gonna grab a quick shower. Hope will be here in thirty, if we're lucky."

"She'll show. And don't be surprised if Raul is with her."

The thought had crossed my mind, too. He'd want to see me for himself. Make sure I wasn't a threat. I'd need to let him know that I was no longer with the FBI and that I was here truly for the sport. Maybe even being Johnny's wing man and trainer could get me closer. Let Raul think I'd changed. The plan had merit.

I showered but didn't bother with shaving. A little stubble never hurt anyone, and I was too anxious to see Hope. Time, as always, seemed to drag slowly as I watched the seconds tick away on the clock. My palms were sweaty, and my breathing was erratic.

"Calm down, princess." Johnny had just returned from whatever he was doing in the other room and plopped himself gingerly on the sofa. "She'll be here soon. You need a drink to settle your nerves."

"I'm not nervous about seeing her. I'm nervous about Raul and what he might do to her because of me."

I walked to the mini bar and brought out two beers. One for me and one for Johnny, though downing them both crossed my mind. "Here." I twisted the cap and handed it to him.

"Look, I got your back. Raul isn't stupid enough to start something in a plush hotel with witnesses. He prefers seedy hotels bathed in darkness. Besides, you paid the twenty grand for your night with Hope. He'll deliver."

"Yeah, cause he's a stand-up guy." I chuckled at the thought. "I'm surprised the price didn't go up because it was me."

"Remember, they think I'm the one paying," Johnny reminded. "Sure, Jax saw you, but he doesn't have to know you're here. Like here, here. He could just think it's a coincidence. Hope is a babe; it's not like I wouldn't be interested in her. Why not leave it at that? Same as last night, I'll answer the door then the two of you can have your night." He shrugged, making perfect sense of it all in his mind.

I pinched the bridge of my nose and squeezed my eyes shut. "First, don't call Hope a babe. Keep your damn eyeballs to yourself." Johnny laughed, but I wasn't joking.

"Second, you may be onto something. Maybe I only need to make an appearance when necessary. Perhaps I find out, in front of Raul and the guys, that you've been spending time with Hope behind my back. That would definitely put a wedge between us and give Raul the excuse to believe you're on his side. Of course!" I was almost elated. This shit plan could really work.

"Of course, it'll work, princess. Now quit acting like a teenage girl and assume the position." He pointed to the room for me to go and hide. The doorbell chimed as soon as I'd shut the door.

"Hello, beautiful." Johnny's southern drawl echoed in the empty room. It was unfair he was getting to make the call; to be the one to call her that, but I understood. He was playing his character. At least I hoped that's all it was.

"Hello, Johnny," Hope drawled back. An icy draft descended my spine. She didn't sound like herself. At all. Something was definitely off. Her usually sweet voice was lustful and needy, and red flags started flying up everywhere. She was high as a kite, portraying the woman she was sold out to be. *Shit! Shit, shit, shit*! I was fuming mad but had to keep my rage under control for the moment. At least until Raul and Jax, or whoever the hell was out there was gone.

"Johnny, my boy!" Raul's voice boomed loudly, as I'm sure that was the point. If he thought I was here, he'd want me to know he was, too. "Heard all about you today. You and Blake. Where is he anyway? Thought he'd want to come say hello to a dear old friend."

Johnny laughed. "Is that what you are? Old friends?"

"You could say that."

"Well I don't know where the asshole is and quite frankly dude, I don't give a damn. In case you didn't notice, I've got a beautiful woman draped around me right now and I've paid for the night. I'd like to take full advantage of my purchase." Johnny's voice was even and cool, never giving away his deceit.

"Very well then. But I would like to speak with you in private sometime. About the fights. Jax said you gave him a run for his money today. Not something many people can do."

"Yeah, and?" Johnny's agitation was noticeable and full on.

"And no one else will fight him which means no one will bet against. I can't turn a profit like that. It may be illegal to hold bouts in the underground, but it doesn't mean people don't still like to join in once in a while. It's really quite profitable. Having someone that would face Jax could really bring in a lot of revenue. Put your name on the map, son."

"I'm not your son. Now go." Johnny held the door open wide for Raul to exit.

Upon passing, Raul handed Johnny his card. "Give me a call. We'll discuss at length. I think you will find my …. *terms* acceptable." He looked directly at Hope, a carnal expression plastered to his ugly face. He leaned into Johnny and whispered. "She's the best I ever had. Likes all sorts of things. Do with her whatever you will and enjoy. Compliments of me."

Johnny slammed the door in disgust and I bolted from my room just in time to grab Hope before she hit the floor. "Son of a bitch!" I wailed. "He's drugged her. Heavily. Get me some water."

Johnny did as I asked and helped me to support her weight while I forced the cool liquid down her throat. Her eyes rolled back in their sockets and a sinking feeling overwhelmed me. "You think she's like this every time?"

Johnny looked at me and then away; the hurt evident. "Yes. It's the same thing they would do to my mother. Keep her so drugged that she had no recollection of what happened to her the next day. Keeps them protected from lawsuits and assholes going to jail for rape."

Johnny's fingers flexed and squeezed, as did his jaw muscles. I knew this wasn't easy for him and it damn sure was killing me. "Blake? Baby, is that you?" Hope's words were slurred immeasurably, but thankfully she still had enough wits about her to know it was me.

"Yeah, babe. It's me. I'm right here. I'm gonna take care of you." I stroked her silky blonde hair from her face, noticing for the first time the discoloration under her eyes. She'd been this way before; many times, I'm assuming. I pushed the venom from my voice and continued to soothe her.

"You got this?" Johnny stood and braced his hands on his hips.

"Yeah, man. I'm good." I nodded once, letting him know it was okay. I knew this brought back painful memories for him and there was no point in him sticking around to relive it all over again.

"I'll be in my room if you need me." He walked away, head down in defeat. Once the door was shut, I refocused my attention back to Hope.

"C'mon, babe. Up you get." I lifted her in my arms with ease and cradled her against my chest. She began kissing and biting my neck, causing certain parts of me to react instantly.

"Hope, stop. C'mon, babe. Not tonight. Not like this."

"You want me, Blakey. I know you do. Ever since that first night…" Her voice was seductive and longing, and uncharacteristic for her normally reserved self. I had no doubt she could be a little hellcat in the sack. The shy ones always were, but there was no way in hell I was taking advantage of her. For one it wasn't my style. I liked my lovers to be participants, not spectators, and I sure as hell liked them responsive.

"Yes, babe, I did. But that was different. Now cut it out and let me take care of you."

Hope scoffed. "Take care of me? Since when do *men* take care of anything but themselves? Huh? Tell me that, Blakey."

Her hands continued exploring my body; my back, my neck and my chest. I needed to get her sat down and away from me. I kicked the suite door open and closed it again with my boot. By the time I reached the bed, Hope had all but ripped my shirt clean from my torso. "Here, babe. You need to sleep it off. C'mon." I pulled her body towards the headboard and situated the pillows for her to get comfortable.

She continued to paw at me. "Let go, babe." I pried her hands from around my neck. She was strong to be as far gone as she was.

"C'mon, Blakey," she purred. "Just one little kiss?" Hope rose up to her knees and before I could stop her, she had pulled her slinky dress up over her head and tossed it on the floor. My mouth went dry; a man wandering in the desert for days couldn't have had more of a thirst than I did in that moment. God, she was incredible. Her red lace bra and matching panties were enough to give me a heart attack. I stepped away once again, putting some much-needed space between us. "Babe, lie down. Get some sleep. I'll be in the other room if you need me."

I began walking away, but Hope was determined. She lunged at me, barely giving me enough time to catch her mid-air. "Please, Blake," she begged. "Make me forget. Please. Take it all away." Hope began to sob uncontrollably, transporting my mind to that first night and the way she'd reacted. It was obvious that time hadn't made her any more of the woman Raul wanted her to be, regardless of the clothes and makeup. She was broken.

My hands held her bottom as her thighs clamped around me tighter. She wasn't turning lose anytime soon. I sighed and led us back across the room and to the edge of the bed. I sat with her still clinging to me for dear life and rocked her back and forth. "It's okay, babe. Let it out." I drew soothing circles and imaginary lines on her back until she had calmed, and her breathing had evened out. When she was finally asleep, I moved us both further onto the bed and watched as she laid cradled in my arms. I knew nothing would ever compare to this night. This night where I willingly held a woman and fell in love with all the different parts of her; the physical and otherwise. Even the parts of her she thought were damaged beyond repair I saw as beautiful, and no one would ever convince me otherwise.

9

I woke a few hours later, bathed in the warmth of Hope. Her legs were thrown over mine and her arm was over my chest. I listened to the thumping of my heart, knowing it beat only for her. I would normally be freaking the hell out over such thoughts, but I knew when I was licked. There was no point in hiding what I'd denied for so long. I loved her.

She stirred ever so slightly, mewing and stretching herself into a more comfortable position. I watched with a curiousness, wanting more than anything to do this with her every day; to wake with her in my arms. She felt around, her eyes still closed. She squeezed them shut tighter, almost painfully and shrieked. "Shit! Not again, Hope!" She fought to free herself from my grip, but I held on even tighter.

"Let me go you ass!" Hope jerked herself away and landed on the floor with a thud. She looked down at herself, realizing she was barely dressed. Humiliation took over and she hung her head.

"Babe, it's me." I barely whispered, having to force the words past my lips.

Her head snapped up quickly, the thought finally dawning on her. Hope's eyes went wide, barely containing the tears threatening to escape. "I… I … I'm sorry, Blake."

"You thought I was someone else." It didn't take a rocket scientist to figure it out.

"Yes."

I scooted off the bed and sat next to her on the floor. "How often does this happen? How often does Raul drug you and send you out like this?"

She shrugged her shoulders. "I don't know. I lose track of time, sometimes days. I don't know how many men...." Her whole body shook, wracked with guilt and embarrassment. She didn't ask for this, however, and I'd be damned if I let her carry any shame for her circumstances.

"Look at me, babe." I gently pried her hands from her face. "Hope, we're gonna fix this. *I'm* gonna fix this. I promise. And you don't have to be ashamed of anything, babe. This. Is. Not. Your. Fault." I enunciated each word, hoping to better get my point across.

"Thank you." I knew my words had yet to sink in and I wasn't sure if they ever would, but I wasn't about to give up. I'd never give up on her.

"C'mon. Let's get you a shower and then something to eat. You'll feel better."

I helped her to her feet, suddenly remembering she was in nothing but her underwear. Football, puppies, and my grandmother quickly flooded my mind, breaking the spell Hope had cast on me. It wasn't the time.

"Did we....?"

I should have been mad at her question, but I wasn't. She was used to men taking advantage of her no matter the cost. "No, babe. We didn't. And we won't," I amended. "Not until this is over and you're truly mine."

She gave a slight smile and meandered to the on-suite bathroom. "What the hell is that!?"

She stopped mid-step, confused at my outburst. “What’s what?”

“That damn bruise covering more than half your back! How did I not see this last night?” The urge to kill Raul had suddenly reached epic proportions.

“Oh, that,” she waved off. “No big deal, Blake. I um, I fell…”

“Don’t lie to me babe. I can’t fucking help you if you keep secrets from me!”

She shrunk back, cowering at my outburst. *Shit!* “Hope, I’m not gonna hurt you. Hell babe, how could you even think that?”

Realizing what had happened, she stood tall and walked to where I stood. “I’m sorry, Blake. I don’t think that. Not really. It’s just a knee-jerk reaction. I can’t help it.”

I sighed in frustration. I knew she couldn’t, but it didn’t make it any less painful. “I know, babe. I know. Let me see.”

Hope turned slowly and when she revealed the magnitude of the bruising, I wanted to be sick. This wasn’t from a mere slap on the back. Not even a single punch. Her entire back was covered in one giant, blackish-blue contusion. Welts and gashes were visible through the discoloration, with small droplets of blood dried around each one. “Hope, how did you not feel this last night? How the hell did *I* not feel it? I rubbed your back for what seemed like hours.”

“Probably the drugs. I guess. I don’t know. Either that or I’m used to it.”

"What do you mean, *used to it*? How often does this happen?"

"Not very, but Jax was really mad yesterday when he came back from sparring. I guess he didn't get it all out in the ring. I was the next best thing."

"Jax? He's the asshole that did this?" I immediately felt responsible. Because of me and Johnny, she'd paid the price. A high price for the embarrassment Jax had suffered at the hands of Johnny. He was sending a message, knowing she'd be here tonight. Message received loud and clear. He'd be receiving his own very soon.

I grabbed some sweats from my suitcase that had yet to be unpacked. "Put these on." I tossed them to her, slightly chuckling as she gathered them in one hand to keep them from falling. "Wait here."

I left, searching the suite for Johnny. He was still in his room. "Hey, man. Gotta a sec?"

The door popped open within seconds. "Everything okay?" he asked, rubbing sleep from his eyes.

"No. It's not. Follow me."

Johnny did as I asked, hot on my heels. "Babe, Johnny and I are coming in. Turn around." It took a lot for me to allow this, but I forced myself to get over it. It was just a damn bra for goodness sakes and I'm sure Johnny had seen his share. At least her bottom was covered.

"What the hell is that?" Johnny walked over to Hope, almost brushing his chest against her back. I stepped in between, nudging him back a few paces.

"This is compliments of Jax. For this morning."

"Shit!" He paced the floor, huffing and puffing. His meaty hands curled into fists, tucked in close to his sides.

"Calm down, man. Hope doesn't need this. I just wanted you to see. This shit can't happen again. You make sure it doesn't. You finish him next time. No more games, Johnny. No more. We go in and pick them off one by one until Raul is begging for mercy like the punk coward he is. Are we clear?"

Johnny turned slowly. His head down and his inky black hair fallen over his forehead. He was a menacing figure in the shadows, the whites of his eyes barely visible as he cut them upwards. His chest heaved with every breath as the sound whooshed out of him. "Crystal. Consider it done."

He started for the door but stopped short. "I'm sorry, Hope. For what's it's worth, you weren't supposed to get hurt in this."

Hope peered at me through wet lashes before striding across the vast room. She laid her delicate hand on his broad shoulder, each in stark contrast of the other. "Johnny, it's okay. It's not your fault."

He sighed heavily. "Thank you for that, peaches."

Huh. A pet name? I let it roll around in my brain. I let it mingle and sit, and finally came to the conclusion I didn't like it. Not one damn bit. They weren't supposed to be close. They weren't supposed to care. They damn sure weren't supposed to have pet names for one another. "You're welcome. Now be careful. Raul is dangerous, but so is Jax. Maybe even worse."

I found that hard to believe, but I didn't dispute it. She knew them better than I did, after all. "I will." Johnny left the room without another word and then I heard the main door close with a sickening thud.

"You need to go after him!" Hope shrieked.

"He'll be fine. C'mon, let's get you cleaned up." She started to protest, but instead did as I asked. I hoped Johnny would be okay, but right now she was my only concern. I needed to get her wounds cleaned and bandaged before infection set in.

Two hours later Raul was there with yet another bodyguard to get Hope. I answered this time, not giving Johnny the satisfaction of ripping his head off. "Long time no see, asshole." I stood in the doorway blocking them, arms crossed over my bulging chest, feet shoulder width apart.

"Well, well, well," Raul tutted. "If it isn't Blake, the dirty rat that tried to do me in. Tell me, how is Heather? Such a lovely, beautiful girl. She was good, too. Oh, to have a taste of that again…"

I lunged forward, shoving him roughly into the man towering behind him. "You shut your fucking mouth. Don't you mention her name in front of me, we clear? It's time you listened to what I've gotta say. I suggest you take it to heart, Raul, else this is all gonna turn ten shades of ugly."

He swallowed down the lump in his throat, and for the first time ever, I saw fear in his eyes. I stepped back, allowing space for him to enter the suite. Johnny was stood in the corner, protectively shielding Hope behind him. He turned slightly. "If this goes south, get to the bedroom and lock the door. Got it?" She shook her head vehemently.

Raul stood at the edge of the couch, looking uncomfortable when his eyes landed on Johnny. He was well aware what he was capable of.

"Sit down." My voice was calm but threatening and he did as he was told. I wasn't foolish enough to believe he was caving. That wasn't his style. But he knew he was outmatched in this setting, leaving him little choice.

"Here's how this is gonna go," Johnny stepped in. "I'm gonna fight for you. I'm gonna make you shitloads of money. And you're gonna release Hope."

Raul sneered. "And why would I do that?"

I motioned for Hope to come closer. She was reluctant and scared, and my heart broke. "It's okay, babe. I got ya." I put my arm around her and turned her so that her back was facing him. Johnny flanked her other side, again in a protective stance. I lifted the t-shirt I'd given her, revealing the carnage Jax had done. "Because of this," I spat. "Because if this shit *ever* happens again, you're all dead."

Raul was having a hard time maintaining his composure. He wasn't upset in the least. In fact, he almost looked pleasured by the fact she had been beaten so badly. "You think this is funny, asshole?" Johnny stepped around us both, and towering over Raul, he picked him up by his shirt until his feet were dangling from the floor.

"This happens again," he warned. "You're mine. I will hunt you down like the animal you are. I will gut you and I will enjoy every minute of ending your miserable life. Do we understand each other?"

Raul's olive skin was turning shades of blue as he struggled against Johnny. He nodded profusely as he pawed at him to turn him lose. "Good."

Johnny finally let go, literally tossing the worm in a heap on the floor. And just when I thought he was done, he stood over him once again. "I'll be at your place tomorrow at ten sharp. Be prepared." He began to walk away, stopping just short of where I stood with my mouth gaping open. "By the way, Hope stays here."

The burly man that was stood with Raul started to advance. My eyes widened, and my voice stuck in my throat. Johnny didn't need my warning however; he knew the man was coming for him. Within arm's reach, Johnny turned and grabbed the well-built man by the throat. The man started to turn crimson, then purple as Johnny literally squeezed the life out of him. He dropped to his knees, a cawing sound escaping from his mouth. Johnny let go of the hold, kicking the guy square in the balls. He writhed around on the carpet in silent agony. Raul was on his haunches, watching the exchange take place. Powerless to do anything. He knew when to pick his battles.

"This isn't over," he warned. I'd never seen his eyes look as black as they did in that moment, and I realized we'd unlocked the beast. The demon hidden within. I'd always known he was evil but seeing him now I knew we'd yet to see the depths of that. Hell was coming, and Raul was leading the pack.

"You're right. It's not over. Not until I'm standing over you and pulling the trigger, finally putting that bullet in your brain. Take your crumpled henchman and go. We'll see you tomorrow at ten."

Raul wiped blood splatter from his nose. "Bring the girl."

He stood and left, his worthless friend trailing along behind. I bolted the door and secured the chain, then secured Hope in my arms. "You okay, babe?"

She was shaking uncontrollably. "I... I'm fine."

"You're not fine, babe. Let's get you in a warm bath."

I paused long enough to shake Johnny's hand, thanking him for what he'd done. "Don't thank me til this is over, princess. It's far from done." I nodded my head in understanding, knowing now wasn't the time to discuss.

"Get some sleep. We'll see ya in the morning."

10

The night came and went quickly, and before I knew it morning was here. Time to go and deal with Raul. I blew out a breath of resignation, a little louder than I meant to. Hope roused next to me, springing up quickly like a jack in the box. "Babe, it's okay. You're safe."

Her eyes were wide as saucers as she frantically wracked her brain, finally realizing where she was. "Sorry. Old habits."

"Don't apologize." I held her close, just long enough to calm her down. If I stayed any longer I wouldn't be going. It was hard enough leaving her as it was. "I've gotta get up and get ready to go, babe. I don't want Johnny doing this on his own. It's already a shit storm, don't need it turning any worse. Not now anyways."

Hope nodded her head as she sat quietly contemplating. "What if this doesn't work? What if something happens to you or Johnny? I'd never forgive myself."

I kneeled beside the bed, placing my hands on either side of her face and forcing her to look at me. "Nothing's gonna happen, babe. Not to us anyhow. I spent a lot of time with Raul. I know what makes him tick. I can handle him."

"And Johnny?"

"What about him?" He stood in the doorway, surprising us both. Hope pulled the covers around her tightly as she gaped at his astonishing presence.

"Hope is worried we'll get hurt." I grabbed the first shirt my fingers touched and pulled it over my head. I ran my fingers through my hair, trying to coax it into some sense of normalcy. It wasn't working.

Johnny let a slight chuckle escape. "Peaches, we'll be fine. I promise." He tipped his hat to her in an old-fashioned, gentleman way and she smiled. While I despised the pet names and innocent flirting, it made Hope happy. It made her smile and I'd take that over my happiness any day.

"If the two of you are quite through," I interjected. "We need to hit the road."

Johnny gave a wry smile, knowing exactly what I was thinking. "Okay, princess. Calm down. Ain't nobody proposing." He laughed heartily as Hope turned a thousand shades of red. "See ya later, peaches." Johnny left the room, his laugh echoing loudly behind him.

"Okay, babe. Lock and bolt the door behind us. Don't open it for anyone, understand?" She nodded. "Good. Be back as quickly as we can." I leaned over the side of the bed, giving her a peck on the cheek.

Johnny and I grabbed a taxi and headed to the outskirts of town. His leg bounced the entire way as I struggled to keep myself under control. We both knew we were walking into the lion's den, and after the way things had gone down last night there was a good chance we were in for an ambush.

"Keep your eyes and ears open. Raul's out for blood."

"Yeah, I know." Johnny stared out the window. The city of gold and bustling crowds soon made way to the vast expansion of darkness. Even in the light of day, everything just seemed black. The grey slabs of concrete came into view, a stark contrast to the life of the rich. The place looked deserted, though I knew better. Raul would have men watching from their secret posts, ready to take us out with a single bullet.

"Here? Are you sure?" the cab driver asked.

I nodded. "Yep, this is the place." I handed him money for the fare and reluctantly climbed out of the car.

The driver sped away, anxious to be far away from this place. Dust spun around us, reminding me of a standoff in an old western. If you listened close enough, the silence screamed danger; a warning to outsiders who didn't belong. "See anything?"

"No. But they're out here. Mark my words. Raul knows to be expecting us." I walked forward a few paces, stopping every now and then to listen. "Main building is this way." My feet scuffled over that same broken asphalt as I recalled being here just a few days ago.

Johnny trailed me, his shoulders and back stiff. Neither of us were stupid enough to believe we'd walk in, shake hands and make peace. Raul didn't operate that way. I felt he'd be more lenient with Johnny, however, since he was his meal ticket. We stopped just outside the door I'd entered through the last time I was here. "This is the place. Where the fights are. Think they're in here?"

"Don't know. Only one way to find out." Johnny stepped around me and made his way to the door. He didn't bother with knocking. Instead he pushed it open roughly, the slamming of metal against concrete giving way to a deafening clap. The place was a ghost town; the same as everything else around here. It was too quiet, and a feeling of dread settled in the pit of my stomach. "No one's here. Let's go."

He turned and walked away calmly, able to control the fear I knew we both felt. "Hope said the girls stay in that one," I pointed. "We'll check there."

As we moved closer we could hear the cries. The sounds of women being beaten; the torture they were enduring too great. Johnny took off, bolting towards the carnage. My feet quickly caught up and we wasted no time barging through the door. As soon as I took stock of our surroundings, I immediately felt sick. At least ten women were chained to the walls; cold shackles bound their wrists and feet. Much larger men stood in front; their hands, belts and whatever else they could find as their weapon of choice digging into the flesh of these poor girls, causing them to cry out.

"What the fuck?" Johnny voice was barely a whisper, but the disbelief was coming through loud and clear. Another group of women were off in the corner circled around a figure I couldn't quite make out, though I had a pretty good idea of who it was.

"Enough!" I shouted. Everyone stopped, simultaneously turning to see where the loud voice had come from. The men turned with a gleam in their eyes, ready for the fight of their lives. Johnny and I were severely outnumbered, and things weren't looking good. Just then I heard Raul.

"Well, you did decide to show." He walked from the blackness, checking the time on his Rolex. "Punctuality. I like it." An evil smirk flashed across his face as he gestured for the men to pause. "These are our friends, gentlemen. We'll do them no harm."

Part of me wanted to laugh, but the other part knew it was wise to keep my mouth shut for the time being. Right now, Raul thought he was in control and it needed to stay that way, at least until we had a better plan. It'd been stupid to waltz in here without one and Johnny and I both knew better. I guess love will make you lose your shit and do all kinds of things you didn't think possible.

"Let them go." Johnny stood his ground as he glared at the half naked women dangling from the cinder-block walls. Most had their heads down, ashamed and exhausted, but a few were staring at us as if we were their knight in shining armor. I knew then we were truly in over our heads. There was no way to get them all out. Not today anyhow.

"I'm afraid I can't do that. You see, they've been bad and as such they need to be punished." Jax met Raul in the center of the room, flanking his side as they stalked towards us.

"And what about Hope? What'd she do, Jax? Turn ya down? Realize what a piece of shit you are?" My voice sounded unrecognizable even to me. Rage coursed through my veins like never before.

He shrugged his shoulders. "Had to teach her a lesson, but she learned pretty quick. Don't reckon I'll be having any more trouble from her." He winked. The dumbass actually winked and then it was on.

Johnny had shoved his way through and had Jax by the throat, squeezing the life outta him. "Boys, boys," Raul yelled. "C'mon now. We're all on the same side, aren't we? I can't have my two best fighters at odds with one another. How would that look for business. Come, come!" He motioned for us to follow.

"Oh, and clean this up, Otto. Angela can take care of the púnta's from here."

We walked through the shadows of a long corridor before it finally opened up, revealing a set of large mahogany double doors. Again, a stark contrast from the musty hellhole we'd just come from, but I knew Raul. He had only the best money could buy. "Come in, gentlemen." He threw open the doors to his office, lavishly decked out in leather and even more mahogany. He set behind his intricately carved desk and folded his hands together. "Sit, please."

"I think we'll stand." Johnny and I stood at the entry way with our arms crossed across our chests. It was a good vantage point should we need to make a quick getaway.

"Suit yourself. Jax, I've asked Johnny to fight for me. You two will be sparring, for real this time. None of this gym nonsense. That doesn't bring the money in."

I could tell he was less than pleased. Johnny had already shown him up once, and that was in front of just a few onlookers. In a crowd of hundreds, he'd be humiliated. Jax started to protest, but Raul held his hand up, stopping him. "My mind is made up. Need I remind you who you work for?"

"No, boss." I'd never seen him so humbled, but it was obvious he was intimidated by Raul. It wasn't unusual as most were, but for a man of his size I was taken aback.

"Good. Glad we understand one another. Now, since I'm in a good mood, I'll let you sit this one out," he said, directing his attention to Jax. "Seems you've been humiliated enough for the time being." Jax glared at him.

His stance looked to be one of anger, ready to strike, though even he seemed to be too smart for that.

"Johnny, I've yet to see you in action for myself. Before we discuss terms, I think I should at least get a sampling of what I'm buying." Raul's lips turned up, giving off an air of vengeance. "Jax, bring James in."

He left the room, shouldering us as he passed. He had a chip on his shoulder, and Johnny and I had targets on our backs. A short time later, he returned, this James character in tow.

"Ah, James!" Raul stood and skirted around his desk, shaking hands with the man. "Glad you could join us. This here is Johnny, your opponent for today."

James stared us down before his eyes zeroed in on Johnny specifically. Spittle dripped from his mouth like a predator ready to devour his prey. He looked unstable at best. "Let's go to the ring, shall we?" As we descended back down the dreadful corridor, I noticed others fell in line behind us, anxious to see bloodshed.

"He's big," I said to Johnny. Not as big as Jax. But big and menacing all the same. He looked to be from the far north. An Inuit. He had fuzzy black hair that looked like as unruly as him. A wicked scar ran from his left ear to his chin, and his eyes were dark pits. Unreadable. He was probably an inch shorter than Johnny but made up for it everywhere else. His arms looked as thick as my thighs. Crude tattoos adorned his yellowed flesh in random fashion. Nothing about this guy screamed conformity. He was chaos from head to toe and Johnny was in trouble. Johnny grunted in a non-committal way. If he was scared, he hid it well. He'd stripped down to his shorts, his feet bare. He rummaged around in his kit bag, bringing out his mitts and gum shield. He looked at me and smiled.

"Don't wanna lose any pearly whites. I gotta image to maintain." I laughed, in spite of the melee that was about to take place. The other fighter was ready. He was stripped to a pair of faded red shorts, his feet also bare. They looked like they could break rock. Half the big toe on one foot was missing. He was just a nightmare, waiting to explode all over my friend. The referee climbed into the ring as I spotted Raul in the crowd. His eyes feverish. He was either high, or worse. The referee pulled both men together in the center of the ring to issue the usual halfhearted rules. No gloves were touched. Johnny walked back towards me, his face all business.

"Keep an eye out Blake. This may go south before it goes north." I nodded dumbly, not really knowing how to respond. The bell rang as Johnny put in his mouthpiece, turning to face his opponent. For a big man he was across the ring like lightning. He threw two quick punches that Johnny barely deflected with his gloves. He tied the Eskimo up, buying a few moments while the referee decided if he was going to intervene. Johnny was a tall, powerfully built man, but I could see that the Eskimo was stronger. He pushed Johnny into a corner easily. *Come on Ref, break em up*, I thought as the embrace continued. All of a sudden, Johnny cried out in pain. Not a hurt pain. An angry pain. Fucking, bitching pain. He pushed the James away, immediately holding his chest. "Fucking guy pinched me," he tried to say through his gum shield. I looked and could see straight away that the skin around his nipple was turning red. He stood there gloating at him, egging him to fight. The referee administered an empty warning that the guy ignored. He was purely focused on Johnny. His quarry. The ref waved them on, with the bulky man coming forward once more. Johnny feigned left before kicking the guy square in the balls. It was a lightning strike and I almost missed it myself. James's face contorted, somehow making him uglier, if that was even possible. Before he could act, Johnny had him pushed against the ropes, holding his huge arms by his side. Then it happened. Johnny butted him full in the face. I heard the impact above the crowds jeering as his head snapped back. I could see that it took some out of Johnny, too. *Bang*! He repeated it, as a spray of blood hung in the air like red vapor. Raul's man was sagging on the ropes, his face looking up at the stars. Johnny pulled the guys arms towards him, bringing his head on a level. For good measure he butted him once more, silencing the crowd somewhat. People looked on, mouths agape as he crumpled to the mat. He was out cold. Maybe worse. Johnny stood on rubbery legs as the referee quickly lifted his hand in the air before tending the fallen opponent. Johnny walked over to me as the crowd looked on expectantly. He was rubbing at his head with one hand as he fumbled awkwardly with his gum shield. "Got something stuck in my head," he said through gritted teeth. I took a closer look.

"Oh fuck," I said, part in horror, part in jest. "You've got one of the guy's teeth imbedded in your hair line. Brace yourself." I dug my nail into his skin, flipping the tooth out and across the ring in one fluid motion.

"Jesus man, go easy. Is it out?" He looked ready to crumple himself.

"It's out. Do you wanna give it to him as a memento?" I chuckled. Johnny laughed as he sagged in the corner, blood trickling down his face.

Through the silence of the crowd, a one-person clap could be heard loudly. It was Raul, looking well pleased. "Holy shit, son. James is one of my best and you took him out like it was nothing." The pleasure in which it gave him was sickening. What kind of man enjoyed the pain of another at the expense of money?

"Already told ya, I ain't your son."

Raul glared devilishly at him. "We'll see. Be here Friday night at five, ready to go." He walked away, barely giving James a second glance. "Do away with him."

11

"We've got work to do." Johnny was tending to the gash on his head while I mused over what to do. The training part would be easy. The guy was a beast for shit's sake. No, the tough part would be Hope. Getting her out, unscathed amid Raul's fury, and for that matter, an asshole that Johnny embarrassed in the ring. I imagined there would be quite a few of them in the coming days and weeks.

"Relax, princess. This ain't my first rodeo." The tone of Johnny's voice set me on edge.

"What do you mean?"

"Let's just say I didn't have the same upbringing as you. I wasn't born with a silver spoon in my mouth. Didn't go to college and get a degree. I've fought my whole life, Blake. It's no big deal."

Sure, he said it was no big deal, but his uncomfortable squirming told me otherwise. "Fill me in. Make me understand."

Johnny gave me a warning glare, but I diffused him quickly. "Look, if I'm gonna train ya, I need to know what I'm up against. This isn't a damn therapy session. Just spill it and let's move on."

He let out a disgruntled sigh. "Fine. My father made me fight. From a very young age. I didn't have a childhood. Spent nights and weekends at the gym with some mean sons of bitches. We'd exchange licks for a couple hours and I'd go home, all bandaged up."

"What about school? Didn't your teachers say anything?"

Johnny waved his hand dismissively. "Nah. I just sucked it up and went on about my day. When I went to school anyways. Didn't graduate. Dropped out when I was sixteen. Father's orders."

"What?" I chuckled. "Was he in the mafia or some shit?"

"You could say that." Johnny looked stoically out his window and I knew that was the end of our conversation. A million thoughts ran through my mind. *Who were these people? Is this how Johnny had gotten so good?* The man was practically unbeatable! Then one thought stood out above them all. Hope.

I smiled like a doofus. A big 100% grade-A doofus. I'd definitely been bitten by the love bug. Who'd have thought? A big, tough guy like me could be taken down by a petite blonde with beautiful eyes. *Hmph!*

My head sudden ratcheted forward with force. "What the hell?!"

"Just waking you up from your daydream, princess. We're here." Johnny laughed. "You've got some drool right there." He wiped at his own chin in mockery.

"Shut up, asshole!" I threw a few bills over the seat to the cab driver and we headed upstairs. Upstairs to my Hope.

I knocked on the door lightly, afraid of startling her. She hadn't been keen on the day's events as it was. Now I understood even better than before. I'd dealt with Raul for years, but I hadn't even begun to uncover the depths that pig would go. Today had been a real eye-opener. Just another reason to wrap Hope tightly in my arms and never, ever let go.

“Hope, open babe. It’s us.” Several long seconds passed before I heard the deadbolt and the clanking of the chain against the door. As soon as there was enough clearance, she lunged herself at me, wrapping her legs around my waist and her arms around my neck. Best feeling in the world. I buried my head in her hair, inhaling deeply the scent of honeysuckle and jasmine. I’d never grow tired of it.

“I’m so glad you’re back,” she breathed against my neck.

“I’m okay, babe. Told you. I’ll always come back. Always.” She squeezed once more before quickly releasing me.

“What the hell happened to you?” Hope’s voice was a cross between a high-pitch and a whisper.

“S’all good, peaches. Just a battle with a brut of a man today.” Johnny waved her off, same as he’d done to me earlier. “Nothing a hot shower and a beer won’t cure.”

Hope scurried to the bar and fetched him a cold one. “Who?”

“Who what?” I was cautious as I took in the exchange between them.

“Who did this? Holy shit, Johnny! You need stitches!”

Johnny looked at me and rolled his eyes. “Promise. I’m good. Night guys.” He gave a slight wave with his back already turned. His bedroom door shut with a click and Hope immediately turned to me with a scowl.

“How could you let this happen?” She was actually furious with *me*? Okay, time to set this shit straight. Didn’t matter how I felt about her. I wasn’t about to take any lip.

"What do you mean, *how could I let this happen?* This is Raul we're talking about. What'd you think we were gonna do? Have a fucking tea party?"

Hope looked shocked at my harsh words. "No. I just thought… well I didn't expect…"

"You didn't expect what? Shit, Hope! You of all people should know what we're up against. This is serious. It's dangerous. There's gonna be fights. People are gonna get hurt, babe. Maybe even die." There. I'd made my point.

Hope dropped her head and began to sob. And once again, I'd reverted back to the asshole I'd been when we met. "C'mon, babe. No tears. I'm sorry, alright?"

I moved closer, taking her in my arms. She didn't protest, just melted into me and cried harder. I lifted her effortlessly. "Wrap your legs around me, babe." I walked us to the master bedroom, once again closing the door with my foot.

I didn't bother undressing her or myself. I pulled the covers back with one hand, still supporting Hope's small frame in the other. "C'mon. In ya get." Setting her down easily, I waited for her to scoot over. I kicked off my boots and climbed in, pulling her close.

"It's gonna be okay, babe. You'll see. Johnny will be fine and we're gonna get you back. You're here now, aren't you?"

She nodded her head. "See. It's already working out in our favor." I gave her a toothy grin and then laid my head back on the pillow. I took a deep breath and blew it out slowly, hoping she wouldn't notice. I wasn't a pep talk kinda guy, especially when it came to Raul.

Truth be told, Raul was being overly generous letting her stay for a second night. I wasn't naïve enough to believe this was from the kindness of his heart. He had something up his sleeve, I was sure of it. I just didn't know how or when he would strike.

I would never tell her anything other than it would be okay. I couldn't. I couldn't break her heart. I couldn't watch her crumble. *Again*. And I damn sure couldn't let her lose hope. If she did, then surely, I would, too.

12

The week flew by. Johnny and I spent most of our time training at the gym while Hope stayed tucked away in the safety of our hotel. It wasn't ideal, and I hated leaving her alone, but I couldn't be two places at once. It was merely a tradeoff for the time being, but I didn't plan on this lasting much longer. Johnny would continue to win and make Raul his bank roll. I'd get Hope and we'd never look back. At least that's what I kept telling myself.

"Block with your left, undercut with your right, man!" I beat my fist on the side of the ring, frustrated that Johnny was getting his ass handed to him by some old chump with flabby arms. Johnny wasn't even trying!

"You wanna get in here, princess? Take a shot." Johnny stopped and glared at me, removing his mouth guard. "Well? Do ya?"

I paced the outer corner of the ring with my hands braced on my hips. Now was not the time to be losing my cool, but if he pulled this shit Friday night, we were in trouble. Hope was in trouble. "No. I want you to do your fucking job. Do I need to remind you what's at stake here?"

"No. You don't. And Hope ain't the only girl in this mess. You remember what we walked in on, right? It ain't always about you, cupcake. Understood?"

Johnny and I hadn't been this curt with one another. At least not seriously. We joked and threw insults back and forth all the time, but it had always been in good fun. This was different. I'd pissed him off. He'd pissed me off. Tempers were flaring, and I knew we were headed down a dangerous path, but whatever. So be it. I had a bit of adrenaline pumping through my veins. Just enough courage to be an idiot and climb in the ring with him.

"You're out, old man." I motioned for Johnny's sparring partner to vacate while I grabbed my gloves and mouth guard from my own bag.

I laced up and bent down, throwing one leg at a time over the ropes. "You wanna go, dumbass, let's go."

I bumped my gloves a few times and bounced from one foot to the other. I was ready for this. More than ready. I'd spent so much time training Johnny that I'd let myself fall behind. It wasn't unusual for me to spend a bit of time at the gym myself, punching away on the bag or an unworthy opponent. It'd be good to get all this angst out. And Johnny needed to beat the piss outta something to get his head back on straight. If he needed it to be me, then so be it. If it meant him winning Friday night's fight and me getting Hope, it was worth it.

"Let's see what ya got, princess. I ain't going easy on ya." Johnny smirked, his teeth gleaming behind his clear mouth piece.

"Never thought you would."

We danced around in a circle, each sizing the other up. I was a big guy. In fairly good shape. But Johnny? The man was a fucking brickhouse. Not an ounce of fat on him. He was all muscle and I knew his punches would pack some heat. I braced myself for the first blow.

With one quick jab, my head snapped left. A quick ringing in my ears left me a bit dazed. Momentarily. I recovered quickly and dealt a few one-two combos of my own. Johnny was braced against the ropes, head down and arms crossed across his chest for protection. I tapped him on the side of the head with my fist. "C'mon. That all you got?"

I retreated back a few steps, still bouncing from foot to foot to keep my heart rate up. That's when it happened. Johnny raised his head, his eyes glaring at me with a ferocity that would make most people shrink back in fear. "Not. Even. Close."

Within a split second he had me on the mat, trapping me in some sort of complicated leg maneuver. I wasn't about to tap out. No fucking way. I kept delivering punches to any part of his body I could reach. His ribs. His arms. His back. Didn't matter. Just something to wear him down and get him to back off.

"I'm not tapping out, asshole. Might as well figure out a new move." I grunted, wiggling myself lose from his hold. "Get it outta your system. You wanna punch something?"

"Yeah, I do. Mainly that smug smile off your pretty boy face." Johnny breathed heavily, spittle flying from his mouth.

I held my arms open, giving him a free shot. "Well here you go. Take it. I'll give you a free one. Do your best."

He stalked towards me until we were toe to toe. "No."

"No? Why not?"

"Because I'd kill you."

I laughed out loud. "I think *kill* is a bit strong, but alright. We'll go with that." I turned my back to leave the ring, knowing he was done. I was done. I still didn't think he'd gotten it all out, but what else could I do. I wasn't gonna ask the man to beat the shit outta me. Even I wasn't that stupid.

"Stop. I'm under control. Let's go." Johnny's voice sounded off, but I pushed the thought away. If he was willing, so was I. I just wanted to get this shit over and get back to Hope.

"Alright, boss. Let's do it. Ready?" I grinned and nodded my head, waiting. Johnny gave a quick nod back and then it was on.

Both of us were giving it all we had, each taking turns delivering blows. I could feel blood trickling from my temple. I could also taste the tang of it running from my nose. Johnny didn't look much better. The gash I'd given him across his cheek looked deep and painful. Welts were rising up on his forehead and chin. Hope would lose her shit when she saw us, but it was all for a good cause, so I kept on.

"Had enough?" I panted.

"Nope. You?"

I shook my head. "Then let's finish this."

We sparred for another thirty minutes at least. My body was spent and so was his. Probably not the smartest since he'd need at least a day of recovery and the fight was in three. We'd lost a day because of my brilliant idea and ego. We both lay on our backs on the mat, trying to regain our breathing while onlookers just shook their heads. Finally, once I felt like I could move, we left the ring, both with a newfound respect for the other. Or so I thought.

"We good?"

"Yeah, we're good, princess." Johnny was busying himself with removing his gloves, not once looking my way. I could tell something was still really bothering him.

"Look, I've told you before. I'm not trying to be your therapist. But I know something's going on. You need to talk to someone. Talk to me. Get it out. Yell. Scream. Cry. I don't give a fuck. But don't blow it in the ring Friday. Don't pull this shit. You got it?"

Johnny threw his gloves where they landed with a thud against the cement floor. "Yeah. I fucking got it. Anything else, *dad*?"

Ah, so that's what this was about. Now it was starting to make sense. "I'm not trying to be your dad. I'm trying to help you win so that Hope doesn't end up back in that rat-infested shit hole!"

"Yeah, and what about my mom? What about her? What about the other women we saw? You think their boyfriend's and families don't want them back, too?"

I rubbed my temples in frustration, then wiped my bloodied hands on my shorts. "I'm sure they do. And we'll work to get them all out. But Hope is my main concern and I won't fucking apologize for it!"

I grabbed my gear and slung it over my shoulder, bounding for the door. Fuck him! He could get his own taxi back to the hotel. He could do whatever the fuck he wanted as long as he showed up Friday night and won.

13

My temper hadn't ceased by the time I reached our hotel room. Instead of a soft knock, I pounded on the door like a crazed lunatic. "Open the door, Hope." There was no answer. Not even a hint of footsteps on the other side. I beat on the door again. "Fuck, Hope. Open the damn door!"

Guests were starting to peek their heads out of their rooms to see what the commotion was all about. I'm sure my appearance put them on alarm, too. I was sweaty and bloody, and still panting from my anger. I could only imagine what was running through their minds and I was only minutes away from security being called.

"It's fine, folks. Just left my key card." I waved my hand apologetically and turned back to the door. This time I decided to be a bit softer.

"Babe. Please open the door. I'm starting to draw a crowd out here. Please." Nothing. Not a peep. The hairs on my neck stood and my pulse beat rapidly. *Raul.*

I bolted down the hall, finding a gentleman still standing with his mouth open. He tried in vain to shut his door, but I stopped him. "Please. Sir, I'm not gonna hurt you. I'm just…. Have you seen a young woman come out of that room? Blonde, petite. Beautiful."

He seemed frightened, so I sweetened the deal. "Look. She's my girlfriend and she may be in danger. You talk to me. Tell me what I need to know. Put your stay on my tab. How's that sound?"

He pondered it for a bit. His meaty fingers rubbing over his bald head. "Deal."

I shook his hand and then grilled him like I'd done to suspects time and time again.

"Some men came to get her. I don't know who they were. She didn't put up a fight, so I figured she was okay." He shrugged while adjusting his trousers over his rotund belly.

"Can you describe them?"

"Well, of course I only saw them through the peep hole of my door…."

I sighed heavily. He was wasting my time. Precious time. Time Hope probably didn't have if I was right about Raul. "Look, I don't give a shit about your perverted fantasies or why the hell you're peeping out your door. I'm not here to bust you. I just need to know what the guys looked like. I need to find her. Please…"

"Tall. Muscular. Dark hair. Tattoos…."

"Scar over one eye?"

"Yeah, that's him!"

I rubbed my head, praying to all that was holy that I'd find her. Raul wasn't stupid enough to take her back to the compound. There's no way. He'd have her hidden in some place secret. His place, perhaps. And Johnny? Shit! I had no clue where he was and there was no way I could do this without him.

I thanked the less than stellar man and ran down the hall, past the bank of elevators. The stairs would be quicker. I ran down them, skipping two or three at a time and almost losing my footing in the process. I reminded myself to be careful; that I was of no use to Hope if I was hurt.

I ran outside, flailing my arms around trying to hail a taxi. A yellow car skidded to a halt and Johnny popped the door open. “Get in!” I yelled. “They’ve got her. They’ve fucking got her!”

I pushed him out of the way while the cab driver looked uneasy. “I don’t want any trouble guys.”

“Just drive the fucking car.” Johnny had clambered back in and the door wasn’t even closed when the driver pulled into traffic. I gave him the address of the gym; the only place I could think of. Maybe someone there would give Raul up. Tell me where he lived. It was doubtful, but I had no other choice.

14

Hope~

Cold metal shackles dig into my flesh. My ankles are bound, as well as my wrists, which are hanging over my head. With every movement, they dig further and further into my skin, leaving welts in their wake. Possibly even blood, though I can't be certain. The cold cinder block is unforgiving. It's wet and cold from the rain that has seeped in through the cracks. My naked flesh rakes against the harsh surface, causing me to wince in pain. The blackness is all encompassing, but I don't need my sight to know I'm in hell. This cold, musty dungeon is only the beginning of my punishment. The putrid stench of death invades my senses and I know, without a shadow of a doubt, that I'm not the first person that's been here. And I surely won't be the last.

Raul had sent Jax after me. For revenge. For Blake. For Johnny. For being put in his place. Raul didn't take well to being second-best. He sure as hell didn't like to be embarrassed and that's exactly what he was. Blake and Johnny had shown him up. They'd exposed his cowardliness, and I was about to pay the price.

I let my thoughts drift to Blake. It's all I can do. He's the only hope I have. Part of me wants him to come. I want to be rescued. The other part of me hopes he stays away. Even if it means my end, and it surely does, but I love him more. There's nothing I wouldn't do for him, and that includes dying. I finally give in, letting my head fall forward. Giving into the pain; the blackness. And the end.

15

I didn't even wait for the cab driver to put the car in park before I'd thrown open my door and stepped out. My shoes scuffed against the pavement, sending vibrations up my legs.

"Shit, Blake. Hold on a damn minute!"

Johnny was shouting behind me, but I was already at the door. "Tell him to wait," I hollered back. I knew this time of day it'd be hell to grab another cab. I didn't care that the meter was still running. Didn't make one damn bit of difference. There was no price I wouldn't pay to get her back.

I threw open the door, letting it slam against the stucco exterior. My eyes searched frantically, looking for anyone who might be connected to Raul. *Bingo!* I didn't know the guy's name, but I didn't need too. I'd seen him hanging around Jax. I marched over to where he stood with a sense of purpose. I didn't even pretend to make introductions, nor did I care. In one swift move, I grabbed him by the collar of his shirt and slammed him against the wall. "Where the fuck is he?"

A sneer and a furrowed brow told me all I needed to know. The asshole wasn't going to cooperate. *Fine.* I'd play this his way. I leaned back, pulling his body weight with mine then reversed the momentum, ramming his body and his head against the cement wall. The back of his head made a crunching noise as the two connected. "Do I need to ask again?"

This time, less of a sneer. He was in pain; of that I was sure. His buddies stepped back, obviously wanting to steer clear of the altercation. Funny. They could talk the talk, but not walk the walk. Not surprising. Most of the scum I'd dealt with over the course of the years were the same. All tough on the outside, scared shitless little boys on the inside. When the man made no effort to divulge the information I so desperately wanted, I tried a different tactic.

"Okay, asswipe. Don't say I didn't give you fair warning." I knocked him to the ground, using my body weight as leverage. He was fortunate that his head hit the mat this time and not the concrete. I straddled his chest, pinning his arms with my knees. I delivered blow after blow, losing myself and any coherent thoughts I should have had. I just kept pummeling away, not caring that his face looked like it had gone through a meat grinder.

"Where. Is. She?" I enunciated each word as my fist connected with his jaw. Blood was now pouring so fast that all I could see were the whites of his eyes, but even that didn't stop me.

"I don't know!" was his garbled response. He tried to maneuver himself from underneath me, but I was stronger. Add to the mix that the woman I love was in grave danger and it made me fucking unstoppable.

"You do know. Where's Raul taken her?"

"Enough!" Johnny came from behind, grabbing me around the biceps and pulling me up. "Enough, Blake!"

I shook loose from his grasp and turned suddenly. "No! Not enough. Not until I know where she is." I stalked off, knowing the guy laying in a crumpled heap on the floor was now less than useless. I didn't look back to see if Johnny was following or not. I didn't have the time and honestly, I didn't care.

I'd just made it back to the front when I heard a low hiss. "Psst!"

A petite woman was hunkered down, hiding herself behind the counter. She held out a slip of paper with one hand, using the other to place a finger over her lips. "You didn't get this from me," she whispered.

I nodded and took the paper from her frail hand. "Thank you." I nodded and left, climbing into the backseat of the stench-filled cab once again. Johnny was running to catch up.

"Thinking of ditching me again?"

I didn't answer. I stared at the folded paper in my hand, silently pleading for it to lead me to Hope.

"Look. I was an asshole earlier. Don't deny it. But you need my help and I'm here. Let's go get your girl."

I offered a half-hearted smile and handed him the paper. "The lady handed me this."

"What lady? I didn't see any lady in there. Believe me, I'd have noticed." He waggled his eyebrows up and down mischievously.

"You weren't supposed to. She doesn't want anyone to know she gave it to us."

"Oh."

Johnny tapped the driver on the shoulder and handed him the note. "Take us here."

I heard the crumpling of paper and the sound of laughter erupt from his throat. "This is an hour away. Gonna cost you a fortune."

I glared at him in the rearview mirror. "Do I look like I give a fuck? Screw the cost. Now drive. Fast!"

I rested my head against the black vinyl seat, not caring who or what may have been there. I needed to get myself under control. Raul would be expecting for me to come in, guns blazing. If I did, I'd surely be dead, as would Johnny. I wouldn't risk it. I wouldn't risk not being able to save her.

It seemed like I'd just closed my eyes when Johnny thumped me on the chest. "We're here."

I shot forward and looked around. Of course, this was Raul's place, although palace might have been more appropriate. He let his men stay in squalor while he was living it up, surrounded by all the lavishness money could buy.

We were on a secluded drive, the property clearly marked with security cameras and a guard, stationed just up the path. "This is as far as I go," the cabbie announced.

"Fine." I threw a few hundred dollars over the seat and climbed out, my anger raising to dangerous levels. I heard Johnny sigh and murmur. "Here we go."

I walked with purpose towards the small building that set just to the side of a rod-iron gate. A guard, decked out in full gear that included an earpiece, stepped outside and held his hand up, as if that was gonna stop me. I snickered as I advanced on him further.

"My beef isn't with you. Open the damn gate."

"Sir, you can't..."

"The hell I can't. Either move, or I'll move you myself. Your choice." I stood, crossing my arms over my chest. Johnny flanked my side, mimicking the same.

"I... I ... I need to call..."

"No," Johnny interjected. "What you need to do is close your trap. Don't say a word. Clicky-click your little button and open the gate. We'll handle it from there."

The guy was young. No more than twenty-five I'd guess. Short, but stocky. Fit, but not muscular. Unsure and scared shitless. I mentally high-fived myself at how easy this was. *So far*. He shuffled to the side and pushed a button and viola. Just like that the gate magically opened.

"Now that wasn't so hard, was it?" Johnny pinched his cheek as we proceeded past. "Take the rest of the day off. You've earned it."

I chuckled. Loudly. Okay, in hindsight a lot louder than I should have. "Would you shut the hell up?" Johnny slapped the back of my head. "How the hell did you make top agent again? Ever heard of a covert operation, 'cause now would be a good time to put it into practice."

"Sorry, dude. Just the look on that guy's face. I think he was pissing himself."

"Yeah, that was kinda fun." We snickered and cajoled before regaining our composure. Now wasn't the time.

Hope could be in real danger and us acting like pubescent idiots wasn't helping.

I motioned with my hand, signaling for him to stay back while I surveyed the area. The lush landscape was easy to navigate, with large trees enabling me to stay hidden. Soft lighting lined the shrubs, emitting enough of a glow to better see the main house. As far as I could tell, there was no movement. There were no men standing outside with guns like I had expected. In fact, it looked fairly normal. Totally out of character for Raul. Maybe we'd been set up. Maybe that dear lady wasn't as friendly as she pretended to be. Perhaps she'd led us here on purpose. I don't know why, but all of a sudden, I had a sinking feeling about this.

I began to retreat, walking backwards while keeping my eyes peeled on the extravagant mansion before me. About step four, my body collided with something hard. Something stout and unmovable. "Looking for someone, senór?"

Shit! Not going as planned. "My men have already found Johnny. He's inside waiting for you. Let's join them, shall we?"

Raul's condescending tone didn't surprise me. That much I had expected. What I hadn't planned on was his cool demeanor. He was too calm, if there was such a thing. I knew his question was simply rhetorical and that we would, in fact, be joining the men regardless of whether I objected or not. I sighed, knowing this would end badly. It always did when Raul was involved.

He waited for me to catch up, keeping his back turned. He knew I'd follow. I had no other choice. I also had to keep my cool. The egotistical side of me wanted to beat on my chest and demand he tell me where Hope is, but Raul didn't operate that way. With him it was always tit for tat. You have to give him something first and it's almost never an even playing field. Not even close.

We entered the house, greeted by Hilda, the maid. "Good evening." She held the door open wide, her dark eyes piercing me. Her smile was beautiful and sincere. I wondered if she knew what kind of a monster Raul was. The devil that she was working for.

"Thank you, Hilda. Would you please ask Jax to bring Mr. Roman's friend into my office? We'll meet in there."

"Yes, sir. Right away." Hilda curtsied. She actually fucking curtsied. This seemed to please Raul immensely.

I watched his face as she walked away. For an older woman she was stunning. Jet black hair pulled neatly into a low ponytail. Dark eyes and red lips. She was short and had a bit of weight to her hips, but no doubt she was still a looker. Judging by Raul's expression he knew firsthand for this to be true.

"She's lovely, isn't she?" He placed his hands in his trouser pockets and rocked nonchalantly back and forth on his heels.

"Yes. She certainly is. Does she know?"

"Know what?" Raul guffawed, seeming offended by my question.

"Know who you are. What you *do*. To women." I furrowed my brow and looked at him through hooded eyes.

Raul snickered. "Hilda has been with me for quite some time now, Blake. And I keep her…. comfortable, let's say.

There's no need to involve her in the business aspects of it."

I shook my head in disbelief. "Yes, I'm sure you do. Looks like you're doing quite well for yourself." I motioned around the vast room and the double staircase leading to the second floor.

"It'll do." Raul's typical reply. Nothing was ever good enough for Victor and he was coming up to be just like him.

The shuffling of feet grabbed my attention. I turned to find Jax leading Johnny into the room, blood trickling from his lip. "Now, now, Jax. Is that any way to treat our guests?"

Jax mumbled his frustration. "No, sir."

"You really must be more careful. Johnny here is one of my most valuable fighters. We wouldn't want him hurt before he has a chance to make me some money, now would we?"

Jax hung his head. "No, sir."

I stared in disbelief, taking in their exchange. Why in the hell would a big guy like Jax be cowering to a squirt such as Raul? Probably the same reason the girls did. They were all brainwashed. Told they were trash. Useless. Tell a person that enough and they'll believe it. It was obvious that Jax certainly did. While I wasn't his biggest fan, I didn't agree with Raul's methods.

"Come!" Raul began walking down a long corridor, eerily similar to the one at the compound. Dim lighting on dark paneling and expensive artwork were the only difference. We passed door after door, each one peaking my curiosity as to what might be hidden behind them. My imagination ran rampant, conjuring up everything from torture chambers to trophies of his conquests. I shivered, suddenly feeling uneasy, as I should be. After all, this was Raul we were talking about.

"Here we are, gentlemen. Jax, leave us." Raul's commanding voice had Jax turning on his heel and making a beeline for the door.

Raul skirted around a giant mahogany desk with a marbled top. Large windows sat along the back wall, again almost identical to the concrete dwelling where he held his captives. "I know; spectacular isn't it?"

He must've caught me looking around, but no mind. In reality it wasn't anything I hadn't seen before. I grew up in places such as this, just without all the frills and opulence Raul seemed to gravitate towards.

"More like déjà vu," Johnny mumbled.

"Glad you like it. Now, to what do I owe the pleasure?"

My blood boiled. He Raul knew exactly why we were here.

"I want her."

He reared back in his chair, laced his hands together and smirked. The smug bastard. "Who might that be? As you know, I have several to choose from. I didn't know you had a preference, but I'm sure I can accommodate your fantasy…."

"You know who, asshat. Hope. Where the fuck is she?"

"I'm sure I don't know what you mean, Blake. I haven't seen her. You mean you lost her? Did she run away?"

My patience was wearing thin. "You took her. I know you did. Now. Where. Is. She?"

Johnny stepped closer, leaning down over his desk. "He asked you a question. I think you should answer. Now."

Raul contemplated the question to himself, seemingly unthreatened by either of us. "Let me show you something I think might be of interest to you." He flipped the monitor of his computer around and clicked a few buttons on the keyboard. It was a video of some sort. Grainy at best, but it was definitely a live feed from somewhere.

"What the hell is that? I don't have time for your games, Raul. Tell me what you did with Hope, or I'll go to work on you. Slowly."

He clicked a few more times on the keyboard and the video became clearer. *Hope*. Chained up and naked. Her head hung limp; her beautiful hair cascading around her. I couldn't see her face, but I knew she'd been crying. I knew she was scared. And I knew she'd been waiting for me.

"You sick son of a bitch!" I leapt across his desk, taking his shirt and tie in my fist. "I'll kill you!"

Johnny swiped his meaty arm across the table, sending lamps, picture frames and an expensive box of cigars flying through the air. "I'll tear this fucking place down. Answer him!"

Instead of being afraid, Raul sat perfectly still. He didn't make a move. He didn't flinch. Didn't try to get away. Didn't fight back. He didn't do any of that. Instead he laughed. The asshole actually laughed. This was all a game to him, and we were nothing more than pawns he would use to manipulate and win.

"Now men, what would be the fun in my telling you? You've seen her for yourself. She's fine. Completely unharmed." His casual tone sent a whole new wave of anger through me.

"Does she look fine to you!? She's fucking naked. And crying. Exhausted. And no doubt frightened out of her damn mind. What did you do to her?" I demanded to know and then realized maybe I didn't want to. Maybe I should just kill him while I had the chance. The thought sounded good, but then I might never find her. His resources were endless.

"She doesn't look any worse than anyone else. She'll be fine." He waved his hand around dismissively. "Tell you what. Johnny my boy, you win Friday and I'll give you a clue. One clue for every week that you make me money. Do we have a deal?"

I pounded my fist on the desk. "No! We don't have a fucking deal!" I felt Johnny's hand on my arm, trying to calm me.

"You tell us where she is, or I don't fight at all." His voice was low and threatening.

"You don't fight; you never get her back. It's that simple."

I knew Raul. I knew what made him tick. The smell of money and cheap women. Drugs. Mayhem. Blood. And he was out for blood now. He'd waited years to find my Achilles heel and he'd just uncovered it.

"You don't harm one hair on her head. Not. One," I threatened. "If you do, they'll never find your body. No one will even think to look for your pathetic carcass by the time I'm through with you. Clear?"

He grinned wide. "Crystal. Now if you gentlemen don't mind, I have plans for the evening." He stood and stretched, removing his belt in the process. Just then the door opened, and Hilda entered, two stunning blondes following behind her.

Hilda ushered us out, shooing us with her arms in the process. "Out. Out. Give them some privacy." Before the door latched completely, a woman's loud cries could be heard, along with the cracking of Raul's belt.

16

"Jake will take you home." Hilda led us to the front door and as soon as it closed, I hit my knees. Distraught and defeated didn't even come close to what I was feeling. I had no doubt that Johnny would win. That he would fight even harder to win Hope's freedom, but what would happen to her in the meantime? Raul wasn't a stand-up guy. He wouldn't keep his word. I just knew it.

Johnny knelt down beside me. "Let's get outta here. She's gonna be fine." He pulled me up by my arm and led us down the stairs. At least I think he did. I don't remember too much, only that my heart was shattered in a million pieces.

"What if… what if she thinks I'm not looking for her? What if she thinks I'm not coming?" The words flew from my lips in a rush, but I didn't care. I didn't care that another man, hell *anyone* for that matter was seeing me break down. Nothing would be right until I had her in my arms.

Johnny stopped short, causing me to run into him. "Pull it together. That's not gonna happen. She knows you. She knows you love her. We'll fix this."

I thought about his words carefully. Did she know? Did she know I'd do anything for her? Be anything she needed me to be? I'd never told her how I felt. I'd shown her. I'd been loving and patient with her, but it wasn't the same. What if she mistook all of that for friendship? Or worse, what if she thought it was a big-brother complex? I'd wasted so much damn time and the thought of not getting the chance to tell her how I felt…

"I never told her, man."

Johnny sighed and rubbed his temple in frustration. "She knows, princess. Trust me. I've seen the way you look at her. There's no way in hell she doesn't know. And I feel for ya. I do. But we gotta get the hell outta here. Now."

We bounded along the path to a waiting car and to whom I assumed was Jake. He nodded and held the door open for us. "Where to?"

I don't even remember the ride back. My mind was in a fog. The bright lights of Vegas seemed subdued and far away. The hotel appeared drab. Not nearly at lustrous as before. Johnny stopped by the front desk to get a replacement key card. I don't know what story he gave them, and I didn't care. I just wanted a hot shower and to forget this damn night ever happened.

We rode the elevator in silence. At least I think we did. I don't remember that either. Johnny may have spoken. I don't know. Everything was muffled. People rushed by in a blur and yet my world had ceased to exist. It was weird, frightening, and uncertain.

He opened the door and I entered without a word. I took in the room; furniture overturned, and pillows torn. The coffee table upended on its side. There had obviously been a struggle, or at least Jax wanted me to believe there was.

"I'll get this cleaned up. Get a shower." Johnny's disgust was unmistakable, and I didn't argue. I didn't want to be here. In this room with thoughts of what Hope may have gone through.

I vaguely remember my feet shuffling along the carpet. The way it sounded against the soles of my boots. Rough.

Not soft like before. I pushed open the door of my bedroom, Hope's perfume immediately knocking me on my ass. I wouldn't lose it again, at least not in front of Johnny. I was stronger than that. I calmly closed the door and let her scent envelope me. That damn honeysuckle and jasmine had never smelled so sweet. I closed my eyes and leaned against the door; it was the only thing holding me up. I felt a hole deep in the pit of my stomach, like part of my soul was gone. An ache in my heart unlike anything I'd ever felt before. She'd been all I could think about for the past year and I finally had her. I had her right fucking here. Within my reach and now she was just… gone.

When I dared to open my eyes, I noticed the room seemed untouched. The bed was neatly made. All of our clothes tucked neatly away in our suitcases and in the closet. At least there'd not been a struggle in here. I couldn't take it if I thought he'd…. I can't even say it. I can't think it. I'm too mad. I'm fuming. And I'm broken.

I threw my t-shirt haphazardly on the floor; my jeans quickly following. I needed a hot shower and then bed. The bed I'd shared with Hope. Where I'd comforted and held her. The thought filled me with dread and yet I couldn't help but want it more than anything I'd ever wanted in my whole life.

The fluorescent light in the bathroom caused me to squint and blink until my eyes had adjusted. After a few brief seconds they were open wide, taking stock of the chaos. The mirror was shattered into tiny pieces. I hadn't even noticed the blood trickling from my hand as I raked it across the counter. The shower curtain was barely hanging on the curtain rod. Towels were strewn about as well as

Hope's panties. They'd fought in here. He'd taken her by surprise.

I stormed out, the rage inside me unstoppable. Now it was my turn. I threw the bedside lamp into the dresser mirror, busting it instantly. The loud noise shattering the relative silence, but I didn't care. I ripped the comforter and sheets from the bed, throwing them in a heap in the floor. A wing-backed chair that sat in the corner soon found itself smashed against the window pane. I threw suitcases, shoes, and pulled the door from its hinges. I went crazy, but I didn't. Fucking. Care.

"Hey! What the hell, man?! Calm down."

Johnny was on me within seconds, pinning my arms to keep me from doing any more damage. "Stop, Blake! Stop. It's okay." His breathing was heavy as he struggled against me.

A sob ripped from my throat, completely unexpected. I was a man. I didn't fucking cry. Ever. But I couldn't stop it. I couldn't stop the dam that burst forth from my eyes. "She. I can't. John I can't…. breathe."

"I know, man. I know." Johnny put his arm around me and waited. Waited for what I don't know. I guess for me to be okay, but that wasn't gonna happen. Not until Hope was here with me and safe. "We're gonna get her back. I swear. Your bike's here, right? The Harley?"

I didn't even bother looking up. I couldn't face him, so I simply nodded.

"Good. I'll be back. You gonna be alright?" I nodded again not sure if it was the truth.

He left for God only knows where. I laid on the floor. On the sheets that smelled of honeysuckle and jasmine and cried myself to sleep. My dreams were of Hope. They haunted me.

17

Johnny returned sometime later, kicking me awake with his foot. “Get up, princess. Let’s go.”

I rolled over, rubbing my eyes in the process. It felt like my pupils were on fire, my throat as dry as the desert. I’d cried myself to sleep, something I can’t ever remember doing. Not ever. I groaned in protest, but he wasn’t having it.

“Now, Blake. Up. We got shit to do.”

I peered at him through squinted eyelids. “What time is it?”

“Five in the morning. C’mon. I ain’t telling you again.” He opened the curtains, the morning light seeping in and highlighting the mess I’d made.

“What the hell are you so pissed about?” I sat up fully this time, wiping the sleep from my eyes. “And where the hell have you been.”

“You’ll see. Grab a shower….” He hesitated, remembering the horrific scene. “Better yet, use mine. Be ready in twenty.”

I struggled to my feet. “I don’t feel like going out, dude. Just go without me.”

Johnny stood in the doorway that was now void of a door. The same door I’d ripped from the hinges last night that now lay to the side, amongst a pile of clothing. “I said get ready. Twenty minutes. Meet me in the lobby.”

I cursed him, behind his back of course, as I gathered the first bit of clothing I put my hands on. A pair of cargo shorts and a black V-neck tee. I ran through the shower, barely giving the water time to warm. It didn't matter. I barely felt it hit my blistering skin. I was sore all over, more from the turmoil of the last twenty-four hours than the spectacle I'd made of myself last night. I was exhausted, worn out, and in no mood to mingle with people of the world who couldn't give a rat's ass about me or Hope.

I dried, threw on my clothes, and ran my fingers through my hair. My wallet and dark shades to hide my bloodshot eyes were next. I could always blame a hangover if anyone asked, but even then, I didn't feel like explaining myself.

The elevator seemed to descend at an extremely slow pace, or perhaps it was just me. Everything seemed to still be moving in slow motion, blurring around me like a fog. When I finally reached the bottom, Johnny was nowhere to be found. I searched the lobby and the adjoining bar. Nothing. It wasn't until I heard a loud rumble coming from outside that I looked up. There he was, sat atop a brand-new motorcycle. And not just any motorcycle. A Harley Davidson Low Rider, blacked out with a cut fender. I was drooling. It didn't compare to my Daisy, mind you, but it was pretty damn sweet.

I strode through the lobby, feeling a sense of myself slowly returning. By the time I reached the exit, I was smiling. I knew what this meant. Sure enough, my bike was parked just behind his, the low purr of a well-oiled machine vibrating the sidewalk. "Ready to get this shit sorted, princess?"

I walked around, lowering my sunglasses and admiring the low profile and sexy lines of the motorcycle. I was envious, no doubt. "You did this, why?"

He laughed heartily. "Because there was no way in hell I was riding bitch behind you on your pansy ass Shovel Head, that's why. Now. We doin' this or not?" He pushed his sunglass over his eyes and waited with a smirk. No way in hell I was turning this opportunity down.

Without a word I grinned and nodded. "Let's ride."

I straddled Daisy, my prized possession, reveling in the feel of her beneath me. I recalled the night Hope sat behind me, pushed up against me as the wind rushed past us. Rubbing my hand up and down her cold thigh as she trembled. A knot formed in my chest and an even bigger one in my throat. I looked up to find Johnny staring, waiting for my signal. With a simple nod he shot forward, me hot on his tail.

We rode the strip of Vegas, sitting in traffic as much as anything. People were out in full swing, especially for this time of the morning. I imagined many of them hadn't even been to bed yet. Typical for this city. It was at night that the multitudes came out to play; their debauchery knowing no bounds. Then they'd sleep all day, recovering from hangovers and the loss of hard earned money, only to turn around and do it all over again. Women clattering around on high heels, still clothed in sparkly dresses from the night before. Men looking just as out of place with fancy suits and loosened ties; their shirt collars unbuttoned. It was almost comical. Johnny shook his head as we watched stumbling drunks make their way across the street. I chucked, glad I wasn't the only one who found this amusing.

Once on the outskirts of town, where the pavement met dirt, I ran through the gears, topping out at ninety-five before finally slowing to let Johnny catch up. The sun on my face and the wind in my hair felt freeing. Therapeutic and calming. It helped ease my nerves and it even made me smile.

Riding side by side, we made our way through the deserted streets towards Raul's compound. We hadn't made any headway with him, but hopefully someone here would be of some use. I knew their language well. It was money. And already having made up my mind that there was no amount I wouldn't pay to get Hope back made this even easier.

We pulled into the lot, a swirl of dust flying up around us. I settled my feet from the pegs to the ground, steadying the bike. "What's the plan?"

Johnny shrugged. "Don't have one."

I rubbed my face, the last couple day's scruff feeling rough under my fingers. I worried what we'd be walking into this time. One of the most important rules of the job was to never go in without a plan. I knew this, yet it hadn't dawned on me until now. I'd been so damn excited about getting Hope back and being on the open road that all else fell by the wayside. "He knows we're coming."

Johnny's shoulders sagged with weary. "Yeah. I know. But what choice do we have? You want her back right?"

"Of course, I do. What the hell kinda question is that?"

“Then we’ll wing it. Do whatever we gotta do.”

I nodded, looking far off in the distance. I noticed people spilling out of the door, a few women dragging along behind them. “What the hell is that all about?”

“Hell if I know. Let’s go.” Johnny threw his bike in gear, spinning up gravel in the process. I followed suit, an uneasy feeling settling in my gut.

18

I thought Johnny would lay his bike over the way he swerved through the uneven patches of asphalt. He barely had the kickstand down before he was climbing off. "What the fuck's going on here?" His voice bellowed loudly, causing everyone to pause.

A rather stout man walked towards us, a mean scar running from his brow to the underside of his jaw. "And what business is it of yours?" He walked directly to Johnny, standing a good foot shorter, but never backing down.

Johnny laced his arms across his chest, puffing himself out a bit in a show of authority. "All of this is my fucking business. I work for Raul now. I'm supposed to making sure you assholes don't screw shit up. So, I'm gonna ask again. Where are you taking the girls?"

The man shrunk back, the mention of Raul obviously having some effect on him. "Look, man. I don't want no trouble. Not with you and certainly not with Mr. Suarez."

"Good. Then take the girls back inside and leave them be. Who's in charge here?"

The man looked back to the others and waited. For what I have no idea, but it looked almost like he was asking permission. Begging someone to lend a hand. No one was willing to step forward, so I used it to my advantage. "It's obviously not you, else you wouldn't be looking around for someone else to carry your balls." I stood from my bike and removed my glasses, tucking the stem into the neck of my shirt. I walked languidly towards where they stood, placing myself in a stance similar to Johnny. Looking the part was key, especially in situations like this. If they thought you were important, the battle was half won.

"We'll handle it from here. Do what he said. Get the girls inside and leave." The man scurried away, speaking in another language to the ones behind him. I watched with humor as their eyes widened in fear. Perhaps Johnny and I still had it after all. Hell, I knew we did. We weren't outta the game yet.

The women ran back inside, and I breathed a sigh of relief. I knew if they left, the chances of them coming back weren't good. It still puzzled me as to where they were taking them, but at this point that was probably the least of our worries. The men encircled us, and we were again outnumbered. Nine to our two. My back was to Johnny's as we shifted together, keeping our eyes on them. "We got this, princess. You good?"

I grinned devilishly. "Yeah, cupcake. S'all good." With that I lunged forward, clotheslining two men at once. They hit the ground with a thud, what air they had left was expelled from their lungs. I gloated briefly before another was on my back, ramming his fists into my side. Before he knew what hit him, I reared back, slamming my fist into his throat. He went down, writhing in agony. Johnny had his hands full, too, and so I stepped in. I sure as hell couldn't afford for him to get hurt. Not with Friday's fight coming up. The remaining thugs were easy enough to handle. We outweighed and outmatched them without worry. By the time the scuffle was over, we had barely even broken a sweat. The other guys were a tangle of limbs and scattered teeth on the ground.

"Let's see if we can get the girls to talk." I headed towards the compound, noticing the curtains moving back and forth behind the barred windows.

I didn't bother with knocking as I knew they were afraid. They'd been taught to cower; to submit to a man. The thought disgusted me, so I wouldn't use that tactic unless I absolutely had no other choice.

Johnny and I entered, and about twenty different pair of eyes stared widely at us. Some filled with fear, some with lust. Some with anger and hatred. It was a mixture of emotions and I wasn't sure who to look at first. Luckily, I didn't have to make the decision.

"What can I help you gentlemen with?" An older woman, mid-forties maybe, came strolling in the room. She was well dressed in business attire and looked extremely out of place for this hell hole. She was outfitted for Wall Street, or perhaps the part of a receptionist. Definitely not a madam, though I knew that's exactly who she was. I remembered her from the last time we were here. She carried herself well, but I knew very well what was underneath that fake exterior. The woman was a snake.

I clenched my fists at my sides as I gritted my teeth. Smarting off to her was not going to help. Flattery. Now that I knew something about. This should be a piece of cake. I flashed my dazzling smile, dimples and all, but just as I was about to wow her with my debonair self, she cut me off.

"Sir. I don't know who you are, nor do I care who you *think* you are. But this is my show. I'm in charge of the girls and you have no business charging in here pretending you run things."

She jutted out her hip, one hand braced firmly as she stared me down. "Now. I'm going to ask you nicely to leave. If you refuse, I can always call Kellan to escort you out. Not as nicely, of course."

"How much?" Johnny's voice shocked me. Surely, he wasn't serious.

"Depends on what you're asking for. And of course, which one." The lady motioned behind her like she was offering up an entrée.

"What's your name?"

"Angela." She suddenly seemed nervous, fidgeting with her hair and stuffy jacket.

"You know," Johnny said, circling her. "You look very familiar to me. Very familiar."

"I'm sure you're mistaken, sir. I've never seen you before in my life." Her voice quivered.

"About twenty years ago. I was just a boy. I'd sit at the warehouse, or at Ringo's, and watch you. You were with Victor back then."

She straightened herself immediately, regaining her air of importance, just as Raul would. Looking down her nose at both of us, her voice was laced with condescension. "I don't know who you think you're talking to, little boy, but I don't know you, nor do I care too. Now. If you'd like to talk money or whores," she said, turning to face the girls. "Then I'm happy to do business with you. If not, there's the door."

"Why don't you give your boss a call? Tell him his prized fighter is here. Maybe mention he needs to blow off a bit of steam with some of the girls and that you're refusing my request. We're all family here, right? But hey, don't take my word. Go ahead, call Raul." I handed her my cell, hoping she wouldn't call my bluff.

She hesitated briefly before backing down. "There's no need to involve him. I'm sorry, Mr.?"

"Mr. Roman. Blake Roman. And this is Johnny Trevino. Raul's newest and best fighter. We were told to take our pick. Boss's orders." This time my dimples seemed to have the effect I was accustomed to.

"Well then, Mr. Roman, please." She stepped to the side, holding out her hand as an invitation for us to pass. The girls assembled themselves along the wall, something that was both rehearsed and shocking to me. They'd done this more than once. It was unsettling.

Johnny and I perused the selection, each of us knowing our motives were different than the usual men that had walked this same line. I was careful, not wanting to pick the wrong one. I studied their body language. Their stance. Their pose, and especially their eyes. The eyes always give them away. The plan was to find someone willing to talk. One that was too shy, or one that was too damaged and cocky would blow this whole thing, and the odds of getting another shot at this were slim to none.

There were brunettes and blondes. Black headed and red headed, though red was a definite no go. Busty and barely there. Thin and a bit thicker. The way they were presented made me sick, and to think of my beautiful Hope standing here doing the same thing made me even sicker. I pushed that thought aside and set my sites on a brunette. She was gorgeous. Stunning. Even in her drugged state, there was something beneath her blank exterior that had me intrigued. Not in a romantic way, but in a Hope way. I held my hand out to her, hoping she would take it willingly. At first, she seemed unsure, but I chalked it up to the fact that she wasn't used to being asked. She was used to being forced, just like all the others.

"I'm not gonna hurt ya, darlin. It's alright." I got a hint of a smile as she laid her fragile hand in mine.

We stepped back and waited. Johnny was taking his sweet ass time and I was growing impatient. We had already been here longer than I anticipated. I cleared my throat, urging him to hurry up.

"Ah, this one should do nicely. Turn for me, sugar." He motioned with his finger in a twirling manner and the girl did as he commanded. "Yes. Nicely indeed."

"Very well, Mr. Roman and Mr. Trevino. Bailey and Cassidy will be pleased to escort you this evening." Angela pulled a clipboard and began jotting notes.

"Um, just the evening? That's not gonna do for what I've got in mind." Johnny waggled his brows and put a firm arm around Bailey's waist.

"Tomorrow then? Will that be satisfactory?"

He grinned. "That'll be great, Angela. Thanks."

She focused her attention back to the girls that looked weary and distraught. I felt bad not getting them all out, but we were on our bikes so not much else could be done. "All of you. Shower and bed."

I shook Angela's hand, immediately feeling a sense of cold travel up my arm. If Raul was the devil, she was his queen.

19

Hope~

I heard a metal key jiggling in a lock; the creaking of a large wooden door being opened before the dreaded sound of footsteps drew closer and closer. My body was exhausted. I don't know how long I'd been like this. Naked and chained. It could've been hours or even days. With absolutely no light, it was impossible to know. My limbs were shaky. My heart raced inside my chest, beating out of control, and the thought of even trying to lift my head had me feeling nauseous.

The footsteps got closer. The only other sounds were the drip-drop of water and my shallow whimpers. Coming to a stop just inches from where I was chained, the intruder didn't speak a word, but I could feel their breath on my skin. Their fingertips that lightly brushed the tops of my breasts before moving lower. I cried out, anguish and shame taking over. I'd give anything to go back seconds ago when I could feel nothing.

"Please, don't do this." My voice was barely a whisper and my plea was for nothing. I knew this, but I had to try. "Just let me go."

Again, the figure said nothing, just continued touching and fondling me in places he was unwelcome. It was only when I heard the sound of a zipper that I dare look up. *Jax*. Tears began falling from my eyes and with no way to wipe them away, it wasn't long before I couldn't see him at all. Perhaps that was for the best.

“Hold still. I’ll be quick.” He leaned in for a kiss, but I snapped my head to the side, refusing his advances. In response, he slapped me so hard that stars filled my vision.

“You will learn, bitch, and I’m just the man to teach you.” He grabbed my face roughly, turning just enough to invade my mouth with his tongue. I tried to bite down, but the grip he had on my jaw made it impossible. I squirmed but it did nothing except tire me out even more.

When he finally released my face, he stepped back a few paces to look at me. “We can do this the easy way, or the hard way, but I will have you. Make no mistake about that. So, what’s it gonna be?”

“Jax,” I pleaded again. “You don’t have to do this. You’re nothing like Raul! Please!”

He laughed. “Nothing like Raul? Who do you think sent me down here?” Jax stepped closer again until his nose was touching mine. “I will break you, Hope. I will break you in every way. And you will learn to enjoy it.”

I dropped my head and let go. I let go of everything. Every feeling I could possibly have in that moment dissipated into the blackness. To not care and to not feel; it’s the only way I’d survive.

The last thought I had was Jax pushing himself into me. The cold, hard concrete digging into my spine. And then there was nothing. Just weightlessness. And I’d be that way from now on. Nothing more.

20

Cassidy, the girl I'd been unfortunate enough to end up with, chattered the whole way to my bike. Not only that, but her perfume was literally choking the life out of me. Thank God I didn't have to climb into a car with her. Otherwise, it would've been windows down the entire ride. I'm not sure what it was; inside she seemed fine. Demure even. But this girl was acting ridiculous and my patience was already wearing thin.

"Look. Cut it out. This isn't a date and we aren't in love." Hurt flashed across her face, but she quickly replaced it with a smug smile.

"I know, darlin'. Don't go flattering yourself. Just sex. I know."

I didn't respond, just threw my leg over Daisy and started her up. I handed Cassidy a helmet and motioned for her to climb on. This seemed to please her immensely, all the while making me cringe. The thought of another woman's legs wrapped around me didn't sit well. Judging by the way she mounted the bike, I had no doubt she'd done this many, many times. She scooted forward and wrapped her arms around me, nuzzling her face in my neck. I gave her a warning glance, but it did little to deter her.

Johnny was losing his patience as well. His girl, Bailey I think is her name, seemed to be having trouble maneuvering herself over the seat in her short skirt. Not ideal for riding unless you have plans that involve a quickie on the side of the road. I chuckled, my mood slightly improving. I couldn't help but feel sorry for the poor thing.

She looked ridiculous to begin with and she was really struggling with her outfit. Finally, Johnny had enough. He dismounted, yanked her skirt up to her thighs, picked her up and sat her on the seat. Shaking his head, he put on her helmet, buckling the strap under her chin. He was mouthing something, but hell if I knew what it was over the roar of my engine. I knew he was frustrated, making it all the funnier.

He gave me the finger and rode past, Bailey clinging to him for dear life. "Hang on," I advised Cassidy. Didn't have to tell her twice. If she held on any tighter I wouldn't be able to breath.

The ride back seemed to take forever, and I didn't enjoy it near as much as I had earlier. I sure as hell didn't like it that it was Cassidy. She was nothing like Hope. Hope was toned, but soft. Thin, but with womanly curves. The swell of her breasts; the way her curls framed her face and shoulders. She was all woman with an innocence that made her all that much more appealing. Cassidy was pretty, too, in her own way, she was just…. not Hope.

When we finally arrived back at the hotel, the girl's seemed pleased. It was quite nice, especially if you lived in the conditions they had.

"This way, ladies." Johnny led the pack, easily opening the door to our suite. The first thing I noticed was that it had been cleaned. Completely. The furniture was back in its place and new pillows were on the couch. All the glass had been swept up and a new door hung in my bedroom doorway. I looked at Johnny with a puzzled look, but he simply shook his head. I knew now wasn't the time.

"Would you ladies like something to drink?" I offered. They rattled off some fruity-tutee drink that I'd never heard of. "How about beer or water?" They giggled in that obnoxious way immature girls sometimes do. I turned my back and rolled my eyes in response. How in the world I could've ever been interested in someone like that was beyond me. Shallow, and fake. This was going to be a long night.

"Here ya go. Water for each of you." I wasn't about to serve them alcohol. Who the hell knew what would happen? Neither of them seemed to be able to handle it and I wondered if they were dumbing themselves down purposefully, like it was all an act, or if they were really that naïve. My money was on both. They'd been programmed to act a certain way. To play ditzy so the powerful, money-grubbing men felt bigger than they actually were. Classic.

"So," Johnny began. "We lied. We didn't bring you here for sex, so you can both relax." I looked at them both, noticing a stark contrast in their reactions. Bailey looked disappointed and Cassidy looked down right pissed. Apparently, I *had* chosen the wrong one. She would be useless for the rest of the time. I would focus my attention on Bailey. She'd be our best bet.

"Then what the hell are we here for?" Cassidy set up on the end of the couch. "This is such a waste of time."

"I'm sorry, darlin. Did you have something better to do tonight? Perhaps get on your knees for someone?"

Her face contorted into a scowl. "You know nothing about me."

"Really?" I challenged. "I know you're a spoiled brat. I know you've been done wrong, and you now believe everyone should pay. That none of this has been fair to you, but that your attitude will eventually get you killed. You're gonna piss off the wrong man, kitten, and you outta be thanking your lucky stars it ain't me. Get off your high horse. We haven't done anything to you, nor do we plan to. Just answer a few questions and I'll take you back."

She looked away, staring out into the city. It was early afternoon and not much was happening in the way of bright lights and street entertainment. Nothing to catch her eye. She was stalling after being knocked down a few pegs. She was right on the edge; the edge of being too far gone to save, but I knew there was still a chance for her. Raul hadn't broken her completely. If he had, my words wouldn't have bothered her. "Fine."

"Fine what?"

She crossed her arms in defiance. "Fine. What do you wanna know?"

Bailey tapped her on the arm. "C'mon Cass. They're nice guys. Better than the creeps we normally deal with."

"Thanks, Bailey, is it?"

She nodded, her bright green eyes lighting up. Her gaze drifted to Johnny, who I just now noticed seemed to be drooling a bit. I cleared my throat to get him to focus.

"Okay. So, here's what we need. Raul. Your boss and my nemesis. We're taking him down, but we need some help. That's where you girls come in."

The silence was deafening as they each thought it over. Cassidy erupted into laughter. "You're going to take down Raul? Do you have any idea who you're dealing with?"

I rose to my feet and walked to the edge of the couch where she sat perched, feeling untouchable. Time to rectify that. I leaned over, trapping her with my arms.

"Do you have any idea who Raul is? Kitten, I'm an FBI agent. An agent who's been working Raul for years. There are things I know about that man that would make you crawl out of your skin. Don't pretend you have a hand up on me because we both know you don't. Now, sit there and shut up. Got it?"

She shrunk back, and her eyes went wide. *Good.* I'd scared her. She should be scared. She should be worried. And she damn sure better heed my warning. I was willing to put up with a little bit of attitude because I felt for her, but crossing Raul, or one of his high paying customers was a wrong move that she wouldn't live long enough to regret.

"Now, as I was saying, we *are* taking Raul down. And Jax. And anyone else that stands in our way." I looked specifically at Cassidy when saying the last part. "My biggest concern right now, however, is Hope. You ladies know her."

"Yeah, I know her." Bailey shifted uncomfortably. "She's very sweet. Quiet. Kinda keeps to herself."

"Do you know where Raul might have taken her?"

Another bit of laughter from Cassidy. "I'm sure the queen is currently dining with his royal highness at his elaborate estate, sipping champagne and eating caviar. Then she'll probably end up in his large bed with satin sheets, where he'll ravish and worship her body. Please. The girl's a bitch. Always flaunting herself about to get his attention."

"Quit being so jealous, Cass." Bailey seemed as frustrated with her as I did. I really needed to rethink my whole judging character malarkey. Apparently, I'd lost my touch.

"Hope never did anything to warrant Raul's advances. Or Jax's for that matter. She kept to herself, or at least she tried to. But Raul always paraded her around. Told the rest of us we should only wish to be like her. How perfect she was; how beautiful. Some of the other girls got a bit jealous and bitter about it."

I sat back and took a deep breath. I knew Raul had his sights on her since way back, but I thought he'd have grown bored of her by now. He wasn't exactly a one-woman-man.

"Go on," Johnny urged.

"Well, I just know some of the other girls had a problem with her. They'd mistreat her. When she stayed gone for a couple days the rumors started about her and Raul. How she'd betrayed us."

"Betrayed you how?"

Bailey fidgeted with her hands, picking away at her nail polish. She also chewed her bottom lip. She was nervous. "Don't be scared, Bailey. You can tell us anything. Believe me, nothing will surprise us when it comes to Raul."

"I think the girls thought she sold us out. Hope was always the one comforting us. Telling us to stay strong and be positive. That some guy would eventually come find her and that he'd save us all. She never mentioned his name, but a lot of us just thought she was making it up. That she was just trying to make us feel better." Bailey began to shake. Johnny scooted closer and laid his hand over top of hers.

"Take your time, babe. We got all night."

"I'm okay," she assured. "A lot of the other girls thought she left with Raul on purpose. That she was leaving us behind because she lost faith in this knight-in-shining-armor that was coming to rescue her."

I sat forward and rested my head in my hands. She'd been waiting for *me*. She'd held out hope... *for me* and I'd let her down. Again, and again. I breathed in a lungful of air, releasing it slowly. "I was looking for her. I tried so hard."

"You're him?"

"Yes."

Bailey rose from the couch and squatted in front of me. "She's in love with you, ya know? And she never gave up. Not ever. I don't think she left on purpose."

"She didn't. She'd been staying here with us."

Johnny cut in, seeming agitated that Bailey had tried to comfort me. I'd have to remember to ask him about it later. "I agreed to fight for Raul in order to guarantee her freedom, but sometime during the night, Jax broke in here and kidnapped her. Either of you have any idea where he'd take her?"

Bailey looked remorseful while Cassidy remained her stoic self. "I have no idea. I swear I don't. I've never been anywhere except the compound. If men come to pick us up, protocol is we're blindfolded until we get to where we're going. I've been here for over a year and this is the most of Vegas I've ever seen."

"What about you? You have anything you'd like to share, kitten?" If looks could kill, I'd be on the floor dead at that exact moment. "Fine. Suit yourself. Bailey, thank you so much for your help. We'll get her back and then we'll get you all out safely."

She began to cry, and Johnny was by her side in two strides, pulling her from the floor and into a hug. The man was all heart, even when he pretended to be a gigantic pain in the ass.

21

"C'mon. You girls can have our rooms. Johnny and I will sleep out here on the couches." Bailey was still joined at the hip with Johnny, content to stay tucked in his arms, but I didn't think it was a good idea for them to get attached. Not now anyways. Johnny didn't need the distraction. He needed to keep his focus and win these damn fights.

"I'm going out," Cassidy announced.

"No. Don't think you are."

She crossed her arms in defiance. Again. She was a hell cat; I'll give her that. The shy little girl at the compound was certainly an act, and one that she had perfected well. "You're not my father. Don't think you get to have an opinion."

"Not tryin' to be your daddy. I've got enough to deal with. But you running off in Vegas is a bad idea. For you and for me."

"I can take care of myself!"

I scoffed. "Sure, you can. You've done a bang-up job of it so far." I regretted the words the moment they slipped out of my big, fat mouth. She didn't ask for this. None of them did. I rubbed my forehead and apologized. "I'm sorry. I didn't mean…"

"I know exactly what you meant. I'm outta here." She stomped past me and out the door, letting it close with a slam.

Shit! “I gotta go after her. If Raul finds out one of his possessions is walking around town, we’re all screwed. You guys gonna be okay?”

“Fine. Go.” Johnny didn’t seem too upset by my impromptu departure and it didn’t take a rocket scientist to figure out why.

“Behave.” I glared at him, hoping he would get the message. This had disaster written all over it.

I left in a hurry, pretty much the same way Cassidy had. There was a line waiting for the elevator, so I decided the stairs were my best bet. I took them two at a time, racing for the bottom. I reached the lobby and finally the bar. She was nowhere to be found. The adjoining casino didn’t bring me any luck either. No surprise there. Maybe the concierge could offer some assistance.

“Excuse me. Did you see a young woman run out of here? Brown hair. Tight jeans?”

“Yes, sir. Just a few minutes ago.”

“Can you tell me which way she went?”

He held out his hand, waiting for an incentive. I pulled a twenty from the front pocket of my shorts and slammed it into his hand. “Now?”

“Yes. I believe she took a right.”

I rolled my eyes and took off in that direction. There was a sea of people mulling about, making it almost impossible. It was like searching for a needle in a haystack. The fact she was short didn’t help matters. I sped up, pushing past the slow walkers out sight-seeing. Finally, after several blocks, I saw her. Sitting on the edge of a fountain, her head in her hands. She was… crying. Not at all what I expected.

I sighed and casually strode over, tapping the toe of her shoe with mine. “Mind if I sit?”

Cassidy quickly wiped her eyes, her pride hoping I hadn’t noticed her tears. “It’s a free country.”

I grinned at her quick remark. “So, it is.” I took a seat next to her and crossed my legs at the ankles. I wasn’t good at apologizing, especially to someone who spoke so harshly against Hope, but I owed it to her.

“Look, Cassidy. I’m sorry. I didn’t mean what I said. I was a total jerk.”

“Yes.”

“And I didn’t mean to lash out at you. I’m just so damn frustrated. I need to find her.”

She giggled, but it wasn’t sincere. “Yeah. I’m sure you do. Can I ask you a question?”

“It’s a free country.” I shrugged, throwing her words right back.

“When is someone going to look for me, huh? When is someone going to give a damn about Cass?”

“I don’t know. I wish I could answer that for you. Do you have family?”

She fidgeted, uncomfortable. It was apparent she wasn’t as confident as she pretended to be. “No. None that ever gave a damn about me anyhow.”

“Boyfriend?”

"Lots. But again, no one that would ever waste their time wondering what happened."

I nudged her shoulder with mine, hoping she wouldn't take my words for more than they were. "You're a beautiful girl, Cassidy. I'm going to help you out of this. I promise."

"People promise shit all the time. Don't mean nothing." Another lone tear wiped away quickly. Another stare off into the distance. She was guarded, protecting what little of herself was left.

"Well, have I ever let you down?"

She rolled her eyes. "Do you not remember fifteen minutes ago when you accused me of asking for this?"

She was right. I'd treated her like trash. The same way she'd been treated every day for God only knows how long. Who was I to judge anything? I'd been in this business long enough to know that a person's circumstances weren't always black and white.

"You're absolutely right. I was outta line. And I've apologized. Forgive me?" Cue my smile and dimples. She ate it up, giving me a smile back.

"Yeah, whatever. Doofus. I forgive you."

I laughed out loud. "Good. Wanna head back to the hotel? Or I can take you back to the compound if you'd like?"

She thought briefly. "Is it okay if I stay? You know, to make sure your friend doesn't try anything with Bailey." The girl was full of pride, but I'd play along if it made her feel better.

"Yeah. You do have to be careful of Johnny. A real handful, that one. C'mon. We'll grab a bite to eat on the way back."

We walked in comfortable silence and I watched her from the corner of my eye. She seemed to be in a trance. Taking it all in. It was a lot for someone who wasn't used to the city, especially a city of this magnitude. I pried, hoping to gain her trust a bit more. "So, where ya from?"

"Oklahoma."

"Kinda far from home, huh?"

"You could say that. What about you?"

"I'm from California. Born and raised."

She smiled and brushed the hair from her face. "I've always wanted to go there. Be a movie star. Ooh, or a singer!"

"You sing, kitten?"

Her face turned fifteen different shades of red. "Not in a long time. I quit singing when…." Her voice trailed off and I knew I was pushing too hard. Changing the subject, I asked her what she'd like to eat.

"My treat. Anything you want."

"Mmm. A cheeseburger would be amazing!"

I laughed again. Something I found to be very natural around her. "A cheeseburger it is."

After a quick bite I suggested we head back to the room. We'd been gone for just a little over an hour, but that was more than enough time for Johnny to get himself in trouble and blow this whole damn thing.

I opened the door, motioning for Cassidy to enter first. There was silence, making me calm and anxious at the same time. That and the fact that Johnny and Bailey were nowhere to be seen. "Where are they?"

"I've got a pretty good idea." I darted across the room and stood just outside Johnny's bedroom, listening for sounds. Just as I was about to throw open the door, he cleared his throat.

"Looking for me, princess?"

I turned to see him standing behind me, a towel slung around his shoulders and wet hair. "Bailey's asleep. Took a shower in your bath. Hope you don't mind." He smirked, soliciting a giggle from Cassidy.

"Go on in, kitten. Get some sleep." I nodded with my head and stepped back, allowing her to pass.

"Thanks for everything, Blake. You're not such a bad guy for a doofus."

I grinned and nodded. "Anytime." She closed the door quietly behind her as to not wake up Bailey.

Johnny grinned wide and tilted his head like a damn lost puppy. "Wanna explain that?"

"Explain what?"

"That cozy little chat you two just had. Somethin' going on I should know about?"

"Nope. Just talked to her. Apologized and then took her for a bite to eat. No biggie." I shrugged and popped off the cap of my beer.

"Didn't look like nothin' to her. These girls' will attach themselves to anyone who treats them nice for longer than five minutes. Just be careful with her, okay?"

I stared in disbelief. How could he think I'd cheat on Hope, number one, and what kind of an asshole does he think I am? *Seriously?*

"I love Hope. Got no interest in Cass. Just being friendly, cupcake." I plopped on the couch, resting my feet on the marble table in front. I let my head fall back and closed my eyes. I could hear Johnny shuffling around, but I didn't bother with looking to see what was causing all the ruckus. Just as I was about to drift off, a pillow hit me upside my head.

"What the hell was that for?"

"We got shit to discuss, so listen up. Heather."

"What about Heather?"

"I know her."

I sat up, positioning myself more comfortably. "Yes, dumbass. Of course, you know her. You worked with her, remember? Tommy's Bar?"

He rubbed his temples, his annoyance obvious. "No. Before that. Way before that."

Hell, he certainly had my attention now. "Did you guys date, because Billy is not gonna like that."

"No! Just shut up and listen, will ya?" He paced as he gathered his thoughts. "This shit goes deeper than we thought, Blake, and it just might change the whole damn game. Look, I knew Heather when she was little. When we were just kids."

"How's that possible? I mean, they say it's a small world and all, but I can't imagine it being that small."

"Well apparently it is. My dad used to hang with Victor. Their history goes way back. Since I was born I guess. And he'd take me to meet up with him sometimes. At their house. I wasn't allowed to hear their conversations, of course, so I'd always be ushered outside, or into the movie room. There was this girl there. I didn't remember her name, just that she was really cute. And shy."

He smiled slightly, remembering her. Remembering Heather. "Her mother would be there with her sometimes. Sometimes I wouldn't see her at all, but I could hear her. With Victor. With my father."

"What do you mean *with?*"

He huffed. I knew this couldn't be easy for him and although I had a pretty good idea what he was talking about, I wanted the whole story. I needed to hear it.

"Having sex, Blake. What the hell do you think I'm talking about?"

"Go on." I sat back down, a sinking feeling that I needed to be off my feet for what was coming next. I wasn't wrong.

"That little girl was Heather, Blake. She was there. We played together. We stood outside the door, listening with our little ears as her mother was passed around the room. Man after pathetic man taking turns with her. And Heather would cry. She would cry so damn hard."

Johnny paused for a long time. He lowered his head, so I couldn't see his face, but I knew he was crying. Not something big, tough guys did, especially not in front of another guy.

"My mom was there, too. Being used. Being toyed with. I could hear my father, laughing at her screams. She was begging them to stop."

Fuck. What could I say to that? Not shit I could do to make it better. I thought of my own mother. Her cardigans and pearls; her well-coiffed hair. Johnny and I grew up on opposite sides of the track. I was from the upper class, well-to-do families with manicured lawns and servants. Johnny was from the complete opposite, but regardless, I felt for him. I knew how I'd have felt if that had been my mom, and rage boiled inside me. I know what I'd have done. I'd have killed them all. No questions asked, and that's when I knew. This vendetta wasn't just against Raul, or Jax. It wasn't just for me to get Hope back. This was for his mother. For Heather's mother. For what they'd been through and now what Bailey and Cassidy, and every other girl in there was going through. This shit had to end, and it had to end soon.

"Then let's end this. Once and for all. Victor's gone. Your dad's gone. Let's get rid of Raul and walk away. Done. Over."

"It's not that simple, princess."

"And why not?"

He turned his face towards mine and glared with fury. "Because of Angela. The woman we met at the compound."

"Yeah, what about her?" I was truly stumped. I had no idea where he was going with this.

"She's Heather's mother. She's the one that was there. She was always there."

"But… she's dead. Tom said…."

Johnny once again gave me a look that made me feel so small. "Tom had to have been there then, too. He's been in on this shit a lot longer than any of us thought, Blake. And I'm telling you. The woman ain't dead. That's her. I'm fucking positive! Did you see how she reacted today?"

I blew out a long, slow breath. I hadn't a fucking clue what to do. This had been a shit storm already. We knew what we were walking into, but with Angela involved, Johnny was right. This changed everything.

"We gotta call Billy. It's the right thing to do."

Johnny simply nodded and popped the top of another beer. This was gonna be a long fucking night.

22

"Hey, Blake. What's up, brother?" Billy's voice was loud and boisterous on the other end of the line, but he had no idea what I was about to drop on him.

"Not much. Not much." I filled him in on my time here, skipping over the boring parts and spending more time on Johnny and the fights. Raul. Hope. The girls. The compound. Everything I could think of, while skipping the whole topic of Angela altogether.

Johnny cleared his throat, clearly frustrated. "Put him on speaker."

I put the phone on the table between us. "You're on speaker, Billy. Johnny's here, too." They exchanged a few brief pleasantries and then Johnny nodded at me. "Go ahead. Tell him."

I had stalled long enough. "Billy, there's no easy way to say this, so I'm just gonna come out with it."

"Best way to do it." Billy was agitated. He knew as well as I did that these kinds of conversations never held good news.

"Heather. She doin' alright?"

"She's great, brother, but I feel you're beatin' around the bush here. You got somethin' to say, say it. Especially if it involves her. I need to know, man."

"You sittin' down?"

"Blake. I'm losing patience. I'll come beat it outta ya if I have to. Now. Spit. It. Out." I could hear his rugged breathing as the words shot from his mouth in annoyance.

"It's Angela. She's here."

"Angela who?"

"You know who. Heather's mother."

He laughed, but nothing about it was genuine. "You're shittin' me, right? This some kinda sick joke? 'Cause it ain't funny. Angela died when Heather was just six. There's no way…."

"Billy, stop." Johnny cut him off. "She's here. I've seen her with my own eyes. I knew her way back and apparently Heather, too." He pinched the bridge of his nose. "Look, Heather and I used to play together as kids. I didn't put it together until I saw Angela today, but it's definitely her and she definitely ain't dead. What I need from you is this. How do you wanna handle it?"

I chimed in my two cents, knowing Billy better than anyone. "Look man, however you wanna handle this, we got your back. It kinda changes things here; the plans we had for taking Raul down. It's not gonna be as easy, and I don't wanna do anything to hurt Heather."

Billy agreed. "She's been through enough, Blake. Shit, she's just now gettin' comfortable at the shelter, sharing her story and working with the kids. This will set her back. That is if it doesn't destroy her. When Tom died she finally laid all that to rest. I don't… I don't think she can handle this." I heard him say a string of muffled curse words before he came back on the line.

"Here's what's gonna happen. I'm on the next flight out. I wanna see Angela for myself. We go from there."

"And Heather?"

"I can't tell her. Not yet. Not til we tie up a few lose ends, brother."

"It's your call," Johnny interjected, "but there's not much time. Get here as soon as you can."

"See ya in a few hours, boys." The line disconnected.

I screamed out in frustration and threw myself backwards on the couch. My leg jumped up and down as I chewed my nails.

"Calm the hell down, princess. No need to go into hysterics here."

"Hope's life is on the line, Johnny. Do I need to remind you of that?"

"No, princess. You don't need to remind me of shit."

"I know Billy. He's gonna come in here, guns blazing, ready to kill the first person that stands in his way. It could blow all this shit. It could get Hope killed."

"Then we make damn sure that doesn't happen. He can't come waltzing in here like some deranged lunatic, Blake. He'll get us all killed."

"You ever been in love, Johnny?" I turned my head, slightly nodding towards the bedroom.

"Nope. And don't plan to be. I'm perfectly happy being a bachelor."

I laughed, remembering those same words I'd repeated to myself over and over again.

"Billy's in love with Heather, man. He's protective. He'd do anything for her. Same as I am with Hope. Same as any other man who's in love. You never think it'll happen, but just wait. When you see her, you'll know. Just one look can put you on your ass. The air gets knocked from your lungs when she enters the room. There's nothing you wouldn't do for her, including making irrational decisions."

"Well, thanks but no thanks."

"Sure I don't need to worry about you and Bailey? 'Cause there's a lot riding on these fights, cupcake. I need your focus at one hundred percent."

He stood quickly, knocking back the last of his beer and then crushing the can in his fist. "I got it. Don't need you tellin' me how to handle my business. Don't need you acting like my dad. We clear."

"As long as you do your job, man, yeah. We're crystal clear."

"Good. Now go to sleep. We gotta be prepared for the damn tornado that's Billy in a few hours."

23

Banging on the door woke us up. I knew it was Billy, so I jumped up quickly, dodging the mound of pillows strewn across the floor. I didn't want to alert the girls, who I hoped were still sleeping soundly in the other room.

Before the door was open all the way, Billy came barreling in, sniffing the air. "What the hell happened in here? A frat party?"

I gave him a half-hearted hug and pat on the back the way guys do. "Good to see you, too, man."

Johnny was sat on the couch, rubbing the sleep from his eyes. He gave a nod of recognition, but nothing else. "What time is it?"

"Just after four in the morning. I'm fucking bushed."

"Take my room," I pointed. "I'm gonna clean up out here and then grab a shower. We need to get moving on this."

"Agreed." Billy slung his duffle bag over his shoulder and walked away. Just before reaching the bedroom, he turned with a puzzled look on his face. "Why are you two out here if there's beds?"

"I can't sleep in there without Hope and Johnny's bed is occupied by two women."

"For fuck's sake! Can't you guys stick to just one?"

I doubled over with laughter. "Not mine, brother. Not Johnny's either." This got an eyebrow raise from Johnny.

"Then who?" Billy implored, a confused look creasing his brow.

"Two of Raul's girls. We brought them here last night to get info. Didn't do a lot of good. We gotta find out where he's got Hope. This ain't good, Billy. You know how he is. You know how he treats women. She's not gonna last long." The last sentence came out with a hushed whisper. It's the first time I'd said the words aloud. The first time I'd let myself show fear. The first time I'd admitted how unsure I was of our future.

Billy dropped his bag and came over to where I stood. He braced his arms on my shoulders. "She's gonna be fine. In the long run anyhow. Get the girls. We need to have a talk."

"What about being bushed?" Johnny finally stood, rubbing his hand over his stomach and stretching.

"Sleep can wait. I want to know about Angela."

"What'd you tell Heather anyways? When you left."

"Told her you needed my help with something."

I slapped him on the shoulder. "Shit, dude! Why you gotta make her mad at me?"

"Because you don't live with her and I do. I promised her I wouldn't get involved, but the fact her dead mother is alive kinda changes that promise."

We all nodded in agreement. "I'll get Cass and Bailey."

I tapped lightly, announcing my entrance. For all I knew they were naked, and while that thought would have aroused me in the past, it certainly did nothing for me now. "Girls, you awake?"

"Yeah," Bailey rolled over and stretched. I noticed she was wearing one of Johnny's t-shirts. What a gentleman he was. I rolled my eyes, wondering if he'd helped her into it.

"Can you ladies come out here please. There's someone I want you to meet."

Cass, in her usual snippy tone, sat up quickly. "Who the hell is here at this time of morning that we possibly need to meet? Forget it." She rolled on her side, facing away from me, and pulled the covers over her head.

"Not an option, kitten. Now get up!"

Her hand slid from underneath the covers and she gave me the finger. So that's how we were gonna play this? Fine by me. Bailey was already up, sliding a pair of Johnny's gym shorts on. She was covering her mouth, stifling the fit of giggles from bursting free. She knew what I was about to do.

I yanked the covers back and pounced on the bed, jumping up and down like a juvenile. I didn't care. Bailey seemed to be enjoying my childish outburst and believe it or not, so did Cass. I saw a hint of a smile just before I bounced her off the bed.

"Shit! You don't have to injure me, ya know?"

"Then get up, kitten. Not that difficult."

I heard someone clear their throat. A deep voice. An exasperated tone. "We through playing around?"

"Sure, Johnny. We'll be right out."

I climbed off the bed and straightened my clothing. "Put some clothes on." The playfulness had gone from my voice. Cassidy hadn't done anything wrong, but I was pissed at myself for getting carried away.

The truth? I was scared shitless. I was scared for Hope; for what she might be going through. For what she *was* going through. I'd tried to play it cool for everyone. I was a fucking FBI agent for shit's sake. I didn't let things get to me. Women didn't *get to me.* But Hope? She filled every fucking gap. Every hole. Every empty spot that had taken over; that had become part of my life and part of me. Those parts that over the years I'd become numb to. I'd distanced myself, just like Billy had. True, I'd not done it with excessive booze like he had, but I'd kept everyone at arm's length. I'd pretended I didn't care. Faked everything to stay on top of my game, and the little charade I'd just displayed for everyone proved that. Masking the inevitable. Masking the hurt and the pain. I was fucking tired of it. I was tired of me.

I composed myself and joined the others in the main room. Cassidy was right behind me, tugging at her clothes and sweeping a hand through her hair.

"Ladies," I began, "this is Billy. An old partner and good friend."

The three of them exchanged hello's and handshakes before I explained about Heather and Angela.

"What can you tell me about her?" Billy sat on the arm of the sofa, focused intently on the women. I'd not seen him this intense in years.

"Well," Bailey started. "she's our boss I guess you could say. I mean, technically Raul is, but she watches us."

"Supply you drugs?"

"Sometimes, but only a few of the girls take them willingly. If we refuse, we're injected, or they're put in our food."

"And where does she stay? Where can I find her?"

Cassidy threw her head back with laughter. "Seriously? Dude, there's no way you're gonna get to her. She's always got bodyguards. If they aren't around, then Raul is. There's no way to *get to her*," she said, making quotations with her fingers.

"We'll see about that." What neither Cassidy or Bailey knew, is that this wasn't new to us. We had dealt with this shit day in and day out.

"We can handle it," Johnny cut in. "No need to worry." He spoke to them both, but his eyes were fixed on Bailey's. He was making her a promise, specifically. One that I wasn't sure he could keep.

Bailey's lips turned up into a smile. That smile that I'd warned Johnny about earlier. The one that made men do stupid things and make spur of the moment decisions. *Shit.*

"Thanks for your help, girls. Mind if I talk to these knuckleheads alone?"

"Be my guest." Cassidy stood up and waited impatiently for Bailey to follow. She did a poor job of hiding the disgust on her face. It was obvious to everyone that Johnny and Bailey had something going on, though neither would admit it. The two reluctantly parted ways and finally it was just us guys, standing around trying to figure out what the hell to do.

"I don't like this. Not one damn bit." Billy chewed his lip while pacing the floor. "Heather's gonna lose it."

"Maybe we can do this covertly then. She never has to know." Johnny was mimicking Billy. Both walking back and forth, both thinking of how to play this.

"That's suicide. He can't keep this from her. No matter how it plays out, she'll be even more pissed that Billy didn't tell her."

Billy agreed. "I need to see her. Angela."

"We're taking the girls back in a bit. You wanna follow us?"

I groaned, dreading the ride back with Cass. I didn't think I could stand it. She was an alright girl, but she wasn't Hope. "I've got a rental, should seat all of us," Billy interjected.

Johnny fidgeted, and I knew what was coming next. It was written all over his sly face. "I think Bailey and I will take my bike. You guys can follow."

"Johnny, I swear if you…."

"Cool your jets, princess. It's just a ride."

"Yeah, you say that now. You gotta focus, dude."

He glared at me with nostrils flared. "I've already warned you once. I won't do it again."

I stood toe to toe with him, not willing to back down. He was slightly taller and a bit more muscular, but I knew I could hold my own.

"Then quit acting like such a damn love-struck fool when it comes to Bailey. When all this shit is said and done and you wanna get involved with her, fine. Be my damn guest. But not til this shit's over and Hope is safe. Got it?"

Billy got between us, giving us a shove backwards. "This ain't helping guys. Get it together. Both of you." His voice was stern. "Tell me about Hope. Where do you think Raul has her?"

"No fucking clue, man. I'm about to go out of my mind." I heaved myself back on the sofa and blew out a deep breath. My stomach was in knots.

"We'll find her. Maybe we can use Angela as a bargaining chip?"

"How so?" I was intrigued. Maybe Angela wouldn't be such a road block after all.

"Not sure yet. But it won't hurt to feel it out. Test the waters. I'm as anxious as a cat on a hot tin roof. Let's go."

Johnny got the girls and we made our way downstairs, each of us as solemn as the next. The girls, because they knew what they were going back to, and us because we had no damn clue.

24

Hope~

Jax's breath reeked of alcohol. I knew the scent well. My father had it oozing from his pores from daily over-indulgence. I begged and pleaded for Jax to stop, but my garbled words did nothing to deter him.

He grunted and groaned, and in the back of my mind I heard him mumble a string of incoherent words. I think at one point I even blacked out as a way of protecting myself. I didn't want to remember this. Not ever.

My body had been battered. Bruises from his rough hands would appear within days. My lip was split from his teeth and I could taste the tang of blood on my tongue. The cement walls had left gashes on my flesh with each thrust of his hips. I felt the burn with each scrape. I silently prayed for this to be over. Whether for him to stop, or for me to simply die, I didn't know which.

After what felt like hours, though was surely only minutes, his onslaught was over. My body was exhausted. I hadn't eaten, nor had I had anything to drink. My hair was damp with sweat. I shook, the cold chilling me to the bone. Silent tears flowed down my sunken cheeks as my head hung low. I wouldn't let him see me cry. I wouldn't show the fear that plagued me. It wouldn't do me any good anyhow.

Jax didn't say a word as he backed away from me. All I heard was the sound of his zipper and then…. clapping? Slow, methodical clapping.

"Well done, my boy." *Raul.* He'd been watching? "You're a man now, Jax. My right-hand man to be exact. You passed the test. Go and enjoy a night out on me."

From the corner of my eye I watched him nod at Raul, but not a single word came from his lips. Despite what had just happened, I knew this wasn't Jax. This was Raul. Completely and totally Raul's doing.

"Hello there, púta. You're looking a little.... what's the word? Pale? Ah, yes, pale. Perhaps you would like to come upstairs and have a hot shower and a warm meal?"

I knew this was a trap. It had to be. Raul wasn't a nice man. He didn't do things out of the goodness of his heart because he didn't have one. Yet, a hot shower and food sounded too good to pass up. It beat the rodents crawling over my feet. I'd been around Raul long enough to know what he expected me to say. Swallowing my pride would be hard, but if it got me out of this rat-infested hell, I couldn't say no.

"Yes, sir. I would like that very much. Please, Raul, will you take these shackles off." I sweetened my voice as much as possible, knowing he expected gratitude.

He smiled. A demonic, evil smile as he seemed extremely pleased with my words.

"There, my beautiful girl. Now that wasn't so hard, was it?"

He moved forward until the lapel of his expensive suit was touching my skin. "Any funny business and what Jax just did to you will look like a walk in the park. Understand?"

"Yes, sir. No funny business. I promise."

"Good." His tongue snaked out from his lips, licking my face. "Sex tastes good on you. Perhaps I'll have a sampling for myself later."

My stomach lurched. Raul had raped me many times since I'd been in his company, but this sounded like something entirely different. The tone of his voice was all wrong. My guard went up immediately, but I forced myself to remain calm. He ate up a person's weakness, especially a woman's, and I couldn't afford to show him my cards just yet.

He undid one cuff around my wrist and then moved to the next. I sagged with relief, trying to get the feeling back in my arms. They felt heavy and uncooperative. I slumped over his shoulders to hold myself up. "Eager, are we?" He turned his head to gaze at me with eyebrows raised.

"Sorry, sir. I suppose I'm a little more tired than I thought."

"Well," he explained. "You've been chained up here for two days. It's understandable. Raul's going to take care of you now. It'll be alright."

Two days? I knew it had been a while, but two days? Blake must be going out of his mind.

Once Raul had my ankles free, I took his hand for support. It repulsed me, the way our hands fit together. His dark skin to my pale. The fact that I needed him.

My legs failed me after a few short steps. Raul bent at the waist, swooping my up in his arms. I hissed when his jacket raked along my back, my wounds protesting in pain. "Love. I'm so sorry. We'll see to you at once."

He took the stairs two at a time. I could see a soft glow of light from the crack underneath the doorway. We stepped into a hallway, void of anyone's prying eyes. "This is the back of my house. We'll take the maid's quarters up so no one sees you, love. No worries. I'm going to take care of you."

Exhausted, I laid my head on his shoulder and let myself go. My head involuntarily nestled into his neck, getting as close as I could. *Comfort.* It's all I needed and at this point, even my captor's comfort would do. I was falling over the edge. Ready to spiral downward and I was grasping for straws to stay afloat. This, too, seemed to please Raul as he gripped me tighter, pulling me in closer.

"My beautiful girl. You'll see, Hope. All of this will work out."

I heard the creaking of hinges as we were yet traveling down another hallway.

"Mr…."

"Not now, Hilda. Please, bring some extra towels up to my room and some antibiotic cream." Raul's voice was curt and sharp.

I heard the woman huff as she scurried off to fetch the items.

"Here we are, my dear." Raul lowered me onto a massive bed, decorated in hues of cream and gold. "I'll be right back." I heard water running in what I assumed was the en-suite bathroom. Sweet smelling oils permeated through the air, calming me almost immediately.

Raul sauntered back into the room, tossing his blood-stained jacket over the arm of a chair. "Just running you a bath. Should be soothing to your aching body."

The last thing I wanted, other than him, was to show any appreciation whatsoever. I wouldn't be in this state if it weren't for him, but I knew my place. I also knew being ungrateful would get me thrown right back down into the pits of hell. He left me little choice. "Thank you, sir. I appreciate your kindness."

Again, and with a twinkle in his eye, Raul smiled. "You certainly are being a gem. I think you may have been one of the easiest to break."

I lowered my head in shame. Deep down I wasn't this girl. I wasn't shakable. Moldable. I damn sure wasn't compliant when it came to being raped, or being told what to do, but I had a part to play. It was survival 101 and I would do it to stay alive.

Hilda entered without knocking. I grasped for bed covers and anything else I could reach to cover my naked form. "Here you are Raul." She handed over the items, rubbing his hands gently.

"That'll be all, Hilda. You're dismissed."

She started to argue, but he cut her off immediately. "I said dismissed!" His tone was one of annoyance.

With a look of disdain for me, she left, slamming the door behind her. "I apologize. She can be a bit… territorial."

I nodded. *Did she not know who he was?* How he broke women? That I needed the medical supplies *because* of him.

"We'll get you treated after a nice bath. I've added some bath salts to help with your wounds. It'll help them heal quicker. Come." He held out his hand. I took it, without hesitation. I didn't want him carrying me again.

My jaw hit the floor when I saw the sheer elegance and size of the bathroom. Only kings and queens in storybooks had things like this. Gold, ornate carvings and painted cherub ceilings. Marble surrounded every square inch and a gold chandelier hung with thousands of tiny crystals, glowing from the candlelight.

"You like, my beautiful girl?"

"It's a lot to take in."

He chuckled, sincerely. I'd never heard that before. Not from him. "You'll get used to it."

"Get used to it?"

"Yes. This is where you'll stay. My room. With me. All of this," he gestured around, "will be yours."

That's when it clicked. The reason Raul was being so nice to me. Why he was taking care of me. This was about him *owning* me, and the thought terrified me more than anything Jax had done.

25

We pulled up at the compound just as the sun was setting. We'd told Angela we'd have the girls back in twenty-four hours and we were pushing it. Not that I felt we needed to answer to her but keeping her on our good side could only work in our favor.

"So, this is it?" Billy furrowed his brow, not liking the less- than-stellar accommodations.

"Home sweet home." Cassidy hadn't missed a beat, voicing her opinion quickly.

Sighing, I turned to face her. "Cass, I know this isn't ideal, but you've gotta give us some time. We're gonna get you outta this. You gotta trust us."

She scoffed and folded her arms. "I learned a long time ago not to trust anyone."

Billy threw the truck in park and turned in his seat, resting his arm over the steering wheel. He lowered his sunglasses, never a good sign, and began laying the law down the way he did.

"Darlin', I understand you got issues. I do. And believe it or not, I feel for ya. But no one, and I mean no one, is as important as my girl. And I'm gonna do whatever it takes to make sure she's safe. That she's taken care of. That means Angela isn't going to be a problem for you. Get what I'm sayin'?"

Cassidy nodded in silence, her eyes wide as saucers. "Now, don't blow it. We get inside, you keep your mouth shut. Play along no matter what. Understand?"

Again, she nodded. "Good. Let's go." Johnny had parked between us and the side of the grey building. He and Bailey were involved in some deep conversation, judging by the looks of it. I cleared my throat. "Ready, cupcake?"

"As I'll ever be." I watched as he squeezed her hand and then laced his fingers with hers. Not involved, my ass.

We waltzed in as if we owned the place. Kellan, also known as Angela's bodyguard, stood immediately and stalked towards us.

"You guys can't come barging in here."

"Like hell we can't." Billy stepped forward, his six-foot-five frame towering over the much smaller man. "I'm here to see Angela. She and I have business to tend to. Now," he wiggled his fingers, "run along and fetch her for me, will ya?"

Kellan looked unsure. I doubt anyone had the nerve to speak to him the way Billy had, and it caught him off guard. He stuttered as he tried in vain to come back with a witty retort. Before he had the chance, Angela came walking in, same clipboard in her hand.

"Well, hello again gentlemen. I see you finally decided to bring my girls back." She began making marks on her paper, as if she were keeping inventory.

"Yes ma'am. Told you we would. Had a great time, too, didn't we sweet thang." I slapped Cassidy on the ass, eliciting a yelp and a grin. I could tell underneath her fake façade, she wanted to deck me, and I couldn't blame her. I kinda wanted to punch myself. Still, it did the trick. Angela bought the act and that's what mattered. Johnny and Bailey were a different story. They were too busy making goo-goo eyes at one another. These girls weren't used for the purpose of falling in love. They were used for sex and bringing men in to bet on the fights. Period. Anything else was taboo and forbidden.

"Bailey. Here. Now." Angela's voice was stern and menacing. Demanding and degrading. Johnny's head dipped slightly, as his eyes cut her direction, telling her it was okay. He was within five feet of Angela, so one wrong move and I knew he'd be all over it.

"Yes, ma'am." Bailey's heels slid across the floor with a heavy scraping sound, almost as if she were being dragged. Her reluctance was hard to watch. As long as we were standing there I knew she was alright, it was after we left that I worried for her safety. These girls were as expendable and replaceable as the next.

"We need to have a chat." Billy stood firm, his arms crossed over his chest. Johnny and I flanked his side, ready for whatever goon might advance. Kellan was looking rather eager to pounce, judging by his posture and dead-set eyes.

Angela seemed taken aback, unsure of why he would need to speak to her. "If the girls were unsatisfactory…."

Billy cut her off mid-sentence. "No. My complaint isn't with the girls. This is of a more… personal matter." She straightened her glasses that had slid down the bridge of her nose, trying her best to maintain indifference. It was obvious she was rattled.

Her shaky hands smoothed out the wrinkles in her shirt, an involuntary tic of nervousness. "Fine. Right this way, Mister?"

"Willis. Billy Willis."

"I don't believe I know you, Mr. Willis. I'm not sure what we could possibly have to discuss." She slowly backed a few paces, wanting to put distance between herself and Billy's intimidating figure.

"You'll know me soon enough." He advanced on her, the wall behind her caging her in. Kellan made his move, aligning himself just in front of her to stop Billy's movements.

"That's close enough." Kellan's hand pushed against Billy's chest, but he didn't budge.

"Just need to talk with the lady. This doesn't concern you." Billy grabbed Kellan by the wrist and removed his hand from his shirt. "Touch me again and I'll be doing more than talking to you."

Johnny and I both advanced, our backs almost touching as we surveyed the possible threat around us. There were three other men besides Kellan, but none of them seemed too concerned with the showdown that was taking place. If anything, they seemed completely bored and disinterested. I relaxed my stance, but not my guard.

"You got five minutes," Kellan warned. He stepped aside, making room for Billy to move past. He grabbed Angela's bony arm and led her down the hallway to a more private area. Johnny and I followed for good measure, keeping our eyes peeled at all times. God only knew who was lurking around this creepy hellhole.

The musty smell combined with piss and cigar smoke was enough to coat the back of my throat. I briefly felt for Cassidy and Bailey, and the other girls' too, of course, who had to endure such lowly conditions. I also wondered what kind of hellish accommodations Hope was having to survive. It couldn't be as bad as all this, or at least I hoped not.

The burgundy-suede walls reminded me of something from the Godfather. Amber lamps hung from the walls, giving a soft, but eerie glow. Tackiest shit I'd ever seen in my life. I prepared myself for an ambush of mobsters, complete with tasseled loafers and pinstripe suits.

Billy pinned Angela in, his arms resting on the wall beside her head. I had my back turned, but I could feel the tension rising in the air. He waited a few moments, giving himself time to calm down. I knew this wasn't easy.

"Angela, do you have any idea who I am?"

She let out a whoosh of air. "Of course not! How could I? I've never seen you before." She seemed appalled at his simple enough question, but then suddenly her demeanor took a turn. "I'd remember you," she continued in a sultry voice.

"Don't touch me, woman. I'm not here to flirt and I damn sure ain't here 'cause I wanna be. You see, I was hundreds of miles away. Content. Happy with the woman I love. The most amazing, kind-hearted person I've ever known. We're engaged, planning our wedding. Moving on with life."

I turned just in time to see Angela stiffen. Her back was flat against the wall as she jutted out her chin. "Then why the hell are you here?"

"Because rumor has it that the woman I'm in love with…. you see, she was told her mother was dead. Years and years, she believed this lie, and it took her just as many to get over it. So, imagine my surprise when I get a phone call saying her mother really isn't dead. That she's here. Now what am I supposed to say to that? What am I supposed to tell my fiancée? Should I shatter her world into a million pieces, 'cause I gotta tell ya, lady, her damn world has been shattered one too many times. I won't put her through that again."

Angela's hands began to shake as tears filled her sunken, tired eyes. "What's her name?"

Billy sighed and took a step back, putting distance between himself and the mother that Heather had longed for. The mother that had betrayed and abandoned her. "Her name is Heather."

Angela gasped in shock. Her eyes widened in disbelief and her body sagged against the wall. I had no doubt she would have fainted had it not been holding her up. Billy continued, not letting her get another word in. "Now, here's how this is gonna go. Blake here," he pointed to me, "the woman he loves is Hope. Ring a bell?"

Angela nodded.

"Good. Raul has her somewhere and we want to know where. Give me the info I need and we're outta here. Forget you ever saw me. Forget this conversation ever happened."

"I – I can't do that. My daughter…"

"What about her?" he gritted through his teeth. "The daughter you lied to? The one who has spent every single day believing she wasn't good enough for you. For Tom? He's dead by the way, in case you were wondering."

Angela hung her head. I didn't know if it was shame or if all of this had just been too much. Probably a bit of both, but either way it was hard to fathom she had a heart. "Raul killed him, didn't he?"

"Yes. But that's the life you chose. You put yourself in this. Screwing around. Lying. Betraying your family. Don't expect pity from me. Shit, don't expect it from anyone."

"What about George?" she stammered.

Billy chuckled at her gall. "He's back home, with Heather. Mending their relationship that they should've had from day one. Did you know?"

"Know what?"

"That Tom tried to kill her. Poison her? Burn her alive? The hell she went through. Fuck, the hell *I* went through trying to get her back. That's the thing Angela; your screwed-up decisions don't just affect you. They affect everyone around you. Those that don't have a damn choice other than to be a casualty of your life. Do you even care?"

"Of course, I do." Angela's voice was a pained whisper. A woman who deep down was still a mother, though a shit one at that.

"Then prove it. Do something right for a change. Take us to wherever Raul has Hope." Billy's voice was gravelly as he struggled to hold back his emotions. I was on edge, my hands clenched into fists at my side. Briefly, I thought of Heather and the ordeal she had gone through. What Billy had gone through. How I felt powerless to help my friend as he mourned the woman he loved. Now the tables were turned, our roles reversed.

"He'll kill me." Angela's voice wobbled with fear. She knew Raul to be a monster, just as we all did.

Johnny spoke up, his furious tone unmistakable. He'd seen what Heather had been through as well, and their relationship had been a close one. True he knew next to nothing about Hope, but it didn't make her situation any less dire.

"That's a chance you gotta take, lady. You got Heather into this. Now you've dragged Hope into your shit storm and you're gonna fix it. Now."

Angela straightened immediately. Even surrounded by three burly men, I was surprised at her lack of trepidation. And just as quickly as the tears came, they stopped, a belligerent look taking their place. "I can't help you. I'm sorry."

Billy chortled and swiped his hand across his face in disbelief. "No. No, you're not sorry, but you will be." He pulled a knife from his back pocket and held it to her side. "I never wanted it to come to this, but you've left me no choice." Grabbing her by the arm, he placed her in front of himself, nodding for us to fall in line. As we reached the main area, all chatter and commotion settled to nothing as people eyed us carefully. Kellan made a motion to stand, but Angela shook her head slightly, telling him to stay put.

We walked out the front door, past the graveled lot and sparse bushes to Billy's truck. "Things are gonna go a little differently now, Angela. I was gonna go easy on ya, but don't worry. I always have a plan B in place." He opened the door and pushed her inside, placing his hand over her head for protection. "Arms behind you."

Angela followed directions without making a peep, but her eyes narrowed into thin slits, giving him a go-to-hell look. He secured her wrists with a zip tie, pulling it snug. No point in taking any chances. “Sit quietly.” He slammed the door, cursing in the process.

“Fuck!” He kicked rocks and tugged at his hair in frustration. “I’ve just kidnapped Heather’s mother. You think that shit’s gonna go over well? Forget the damn fact she’s *alive*. Dammit! Blake, what the hell are we gonna do?”

I strode over and braced my hands on the tailgate, shuffling a few rocks of my own.

“First thing you’re gonna do is calm the fuck down. You know how this shit works, Billy. You can’t let Angela see your emotions. You can’t let on that we don’t have a fucking clue what we’re doing. You damn sure can’t let her know that your feelings for Heather have anything to do with this. She’ll use that against you.” I sighed and stood up, my eyes squinting in the afternoon sun. “We have to play this cool. Johnny’s got a fight coming up Friday. Two more days. Raul will be there. His money is on the line.”

“Think he’ll show with Hope?”

My eyes darted away, unable to look at him. At anyone. “I don’t know. Maybe.” I shrugged my shoulders, feigning disinterest, though we all knew it was a lie. I was dying inside; going crazy not knowing where she was, or if she was alright.

“We’ll get her back, brother. I promise you, we’ll get her back.” Billy rested his hand on my shoulder and squeezed.

Johnny's bike came to a roar next to us, Bailey straddled behind him. He lowered his shades and smirked, riding off into the sunset as if nothing was wrong. Just as I was about to make a fuss, Billy reminded me of something. "You know, he's no different from us. Remember how you were with Hope in the beginning, and I thought it was a bad idea to get involved with her?"

I laughed heartily. "Yeah, I do. And look how that's fucking turned out."

"Point taken, brother." Billy sighed, bracing his hands on his hips. There wasn't anything else to say.

"Let's get outta here and figure out our next move. Raul or Jax might be showing up at any minute."

I rounded the truck, pausing by the passenger side door. Kellan was standing just outside the building, arms crossed, and feet spread apart, grinning maliciously. I knew we were on borrowed time; time that was slipping away.

26

Hope~

Raul left me alone, allowing me a few moments of privacy. I was shocked, and thoroughly relieved. I stepped into the tub of scalding water, sinking in slowly as my open wounds made contact. A long, slow hiss came from my lips, pushing the pain from my lungs. I sat still, letting my body acclimate to the blistering feel of the oils on my back. Within minutes, it felt soothing to my battered body. Resting my head on the bath pillow, I closed my eyes and dreamed of a far-off place; the only place I'd ever felt safe in my whole entire life. *Blake's arms.*

I felt his presence before I ever opened my eyes. The bubbles had dissipated in the murky water that was now tinted red with my blood. Covering myself was futile, not that Raul hadn't already seen me naked. "You're taking an awful long time, my beautiful girl. Let's get you tended to, shall we?"

I knew from his tone that it wasn't a request. He wasn't asking if I was through bathing, he was telling me I was done. "Yes, sir." My voice was soft as embarrassment took over. A flush rose up my body, though not in a needful way. This was demeaning and unnecessary. I was perfectly capable of getting out of the tub myself, though I knew it was unwise to thwart his services.

Bracing my hands over the side, I rose gently from the now tepid water and waited. Raul strode over with a white fluffy towel in hand. "Here, my dear. Let me dry you off." I winced as he gently blotted my skin. It was less painful than before, and no doubt the bath salts had helped, but nonetheless it wasn't pleasant.

He was careful, taking his time and being methodical about where he placed his hands. It struck something in me; how sweet he was being. Something I'd never seen from him before. He was always rough. Taking what he wanted, when he wanted. No questions asked.

When he seemed satisfied I was dry enough, he stepped back, his eyes perusing me. I watched myself in the mirror behind him, taking notice of my flushed cheeks and the bruises on my otherwise pale skin. Jax had been rough, not caring the damage that he'd done to me. Even Raul seemed a bit uncomfortable as he took me in, full view. Breaking the silence, his voice croaked.

"Let me get some cream on those cuts, then we'll have a nice dinner. Hilda has prepared steak and potatoes. We'll dine on the patio. It's a beautiful night."

I held back the laughter that threatened to burst from my throat. Did I just hear him correctly? Dine on the patio? Beautiful night? The man was delusional. We weren't a couple in love. We weren't anything but captive and captor. He repulsed me; he made my skin crawl. There was nothing normal about this whole situation and I knew now that I needed to be on my guard more than ever.

"That sounds nice." Sweetly smiling, I placed my hand in his as he led me over to the vanity. There laying on top were the items he'd requested from Hilda earlier.

"Turn," he ordered. Exposed in the mirror, I watched his reflection as he moved to stand behind me. He inhaled sharply as his eyes roamed over my backside. "I'm sorry,

Hope. I'm afraid these look worse than I thought." He opened the antibiotic cream and with extreme care, began applying it to the gashes. I squeezed my eyes shut, preparing myself.

He blew gently across the one, spending a great deal of time making sure I wasn't in any more pain than necessary. When the burning subsided, I opened my eyes to find him watching me; our dark brown eyes boring into one another.

"You feel it, don't you?" he asked, stepping closer so our bodies were touching. He lightly ran his fingertips down my arms. "You feel how much I want you."

Brushing my hair to the side, he leaned down and placed a chaste kiss to my shoulder. Needing the comfort of another human being was normal. I recognized this, but I was afraid my body would betray me. I didn't want this. I didn't want Raul, but I closed my eyes anyway, relishing in the tenderness of his touch.

"Mmm. You smell so sweet, my beautiful girl." His hands moved from my waist upwards, until he was cupping the full weight of my breasts. "Perhaps later, my dear. I know you're in no shape at the moment, and I want you cohesive for what I have planned."

My gaze fell to my hands that were tightly gripping the edge of the sink. "Yes, thank you. And I am famished."

He grinned widely, making his harsh features look human for once. His dark eyes twinkled with mischief, childlike almost. In that brief few seconds, I tried to imagine what he'd be like if he hadn't had Victor for his father. I thought of the charming man Raul could have been; how the ladies would've thrown themselves at him. How his whole life could've been different, and I actually felt sorry for him.

I followed Raul to the bedroom. There, laid across the gold, satiny duvet was a crimson-colored robe. It looked soft and inviting. "I thought this would be easier to manage." Raul cleared his throat and rested his hands in his pants pockets. Again, he seemed unsure of himself, like a pubescent teen asking a girl for a date. Was I in the twilight zone? Who the hell was this guy? Not the cocky, confident, overbearing monster I'd come to know, that was for sure.

I traced my hand over the fabric, letting the silky belt fall from my fingertips. "It's lovely. Thank you, Raul."

"My pleasure." He stepped forward and held it up. I placed my arms through, sighing with delight as it molded to my body. It felt luxurious, like something from a world-class spa, encompassing me in warmth. "You look stunning."

I blushed again, uncomfortable with his compliments. "Come. Let us eat, drink, and be merry."

Raul led us out the back patio. He'd had someone light candles that surrounded the perimeter. The moon shone off the water from the pool, its gentle tide twinkling like a million stars. "Fancy a dip?"

"No, thank you, but it does look beautiful."

He smiled with satisfaction. He thought he was getting to me. Thought he had me pegged as broken. What he failed to realize is that my spirit was broken a long time ago. Years before he came into the picture. I wasn't that easy to figure out, and this was as much a game to me as it was to him.

Raul waited for me at the table, holding my chair like any respectable gentleman would. I nodded, thanking him with a silent recognition I knew he craved. "There you are, Hope. You look just lovely. I could get used to sharing a meal with you every night."

"Every night?" I spit, my gulp of wine getting stuck in my windpipe as I tried to process his words.

"Yes. Every night. I've told you, Hope. All of this," he waved his hand through the air, "is yours. And me? I'm the biggest prize of all."

And there it was. His arrogance right back in place, along with his smug smile. "Well, you do have a lot to offer a girl." I played along with the charade, batting my lashes as I peered over the rim of my wine glass. A few more smiles, a flip of my hair, a finger to the tip of my lips and I'd have him eating out of the palm of my hand.

Hilda came from the house with a scowl on her face. She was attractive I suppose, once you overlooked her snarky attitude. She set Raul's plate down gently, seducing him as she reached over to refill his wine with her breasts pressed into his face. If she expected me to be jealous, she was sorely mistaken. I'd gladly trade places with her.

When it came time to deliver my food, she dropped the plate haphazardly, letting it fall to the table with a rattle. "Thank you, Gilda." I winked and turned my chin smugly, not letting her get the best of me. Raul's laughter floated across the table, making her even angrier.

"It's Hilda," she scolded. "With an H."

"Oh, my apologies. Must be this delicious wine that has my brain all fuzzy." I took another sip and held my glass out to her. "Another refill, please. This really is good. Too bad you can't sit and enjoy it with us." My flippant tone knew no bounds, but this lady was barking up the wrong tree. She was naïve if she thought she could run me off. Little did she know I'd dealt with worse people than her, namely the one who sat across from me now, running his foot up and down my leg.

"That'll be all, Hilda. Leave us." She turned to stomp away in a huff. "Oh, and leave the wine." She did as he bid, leaving us without interruption for the rest of the evening.

Dinner passed quickly with little conversation and I was grateful. What would I say to him anyhow? Thank him for the delicious meal? For tending to my wounds? He was the cause of all of this and I couldn't forget not just the past few days, but the last year with him. He was a horrible, ruthless man. I'd do well to remember that and not allow myself to get caught up in the lavishness of his world. Besides all of that, there was Blake. My love. My protector. My savior. I couldn't forget him. Not ever. Not for all the money in the world.

"Sir, we have a problem." A large man busting out of his too small suit came barreling out on the terrace. Raul threw his napkin on the table in annoyance and excused himself from the table. I waved my hand dismissively, anxious for a few moments to myself.

They stepped out of earshot, just inside the door for privacy. I meandered over to the pool's edge, dipping my toes in the warm water. It was a balmy night, as summer had appeared early. I wouldn't complain. I was a Cali girl who loved the sun and warmth. At least if I was being held against my will, it wasn't in Alaska.

"I have to go." My back was turned, but I knew it was Raul and I knew he was angry. I felt his breath on my neck and heard the gruffness in his words.

"What's wrong?" I feigned interest, once again reeling him in. I laid my hand gently on his chest, moving my fingers back and forth in a soothing motion. He seemed taken aback by my loving gesture, but he didn't ignore. He cupped his hand over mine and squeezed lightly. My touch seemed to ease his anger somewhat, his voice more mellow when he spoke.

"I'm sorry, my beautiful girl. I didn't mean to be harsh. Forgive me?"

This really threw me for a loop. Raul didn't ask for forgiveness and sorry wasn't in his vocabulary. "It's okay, Raul. If you need to go…"

His hand stroked my cheek lovingly, again as if we were a couple. My stomach lurched as my meal threatened to come back up. I shivered at his touch, but not in a good way. I knew all too well what those hands were capable of. Just as he'd done moments before, I placed my hand over his, only to get him to stop.

"I do have to go. But I'll be back. *Soon.* Why don't you wait upstairs for me?" I knew what he was insinuating. I knew what he expected, but I didn't have it in me. I could play this game as well as the next girl, but sex wasn't going to happen. Not willingly anyhow.

"Sure, but I'll probably be asleep. I'm beat." The words were out before I realized what I'd said. I covered my mouth with my hand, surprised how quickly I'd forgotten. Raul smiled in recognition. He was pleased. And damn was he good. He'd done exactly what I'd said wasn't going to happen. He'd made me forget.

His arm snaked around my waist and pulled me in closer. He buried his nose in the crook of my neck and inhaled deeply. "You smell delicious, edible even, my love. Sleep. They'll be other days." His lips grazed my collar bone; his tongue darting out to run along the ridge. I tightened my thighs, afraid of what was happening. Raul was a good-looking man and my body was once again betraying what I knew to be right. It was both satisfying and infuriating. I closed my eyes, a twinge of fluttering in my stomach causing a soft sigh to escape my lips. I felt his mouth turn up as he smiled against my skin. Even that felt nice and send a jolt of pleasure to my core. I needed him to go, and I needed it five minutes ago.

Luckily, nosey Hilda showed herself, reminding Raul that he had people waiting for him. "Right. Thank you, Hilda." He brushed his hand along the small of my back before striding away gracefully. He briefly stopped beside her, his orders no more than a quip. "Leave her be. I mean it."

I scurried quickly to his side for protection. Not physically, as I didn't think she'd lay a finger on me, but I didn't have the energy for a verbal confrontation either. "Walk me inside?"

"Anything for you." Raul placed my hand into the bend of his elbow and escorted me through the French doors. "Up you go." I ascended the stairs lazily, for the first-time, dreading being alone.

27

Angela thrashed around the back seat. We'd not laid a finger on her and didn't intend to, but the way she was carrying on was sure to draw attention. Billy slammed on the brakes, stopping her ridiculous display. She slid forward on the leather, her heading colliding with the back seat.

"Cut it out, woman. You're not making this any easier for yourself."

Angela used her legs to push herself up and spit in his direction. "You asshole. You won't get away with this!"

Billy guffawed, wiping her spittle from his sleeve. "Really? We'll just see about that."

We continued on until finally he ventured off a dirt path, far from the hubbub of the city. "Where are we going?" I quizzed.

"Someplace a little more private than the hotel. Too many prying eyes there." Billy waggled his eyebrows.

I grinned, knowing my old partner well. "You had this planned, didn't you?"

He nodded. "I may have been out of the game for quite some time, but I haven't forgotten how this works. Just thought it was smart to have a backup plan."

I agreed. The man had tenacity, that was for sure. He didn't give up. "She's our bargaining chip, but we can't show our cards just yet. I wanna see what Raul has up his sleeve first. You can never be too careful when it comes to that snake."

"Bingo." The rest of the ride was spent in silence; me looking out the window, wondering if Hope was okay and Billy, I'm sure, was daydreaming of Heather. We were both lucky. We didn't deserve the women we had, but I'll be damned if I'd want it any other way. Then I briefly thought of Johnny. Of what Billy had said. Was there ever a right time to get involved? Probably not. And who was I to say he didn't deserve exactly what we had? Who knows, Bailey might be good for him.

A tiny, run-down cabin appeared off in the distance. Dirt swirled around the truck, gravel pinging off the exhaust. "Well, whatcha think?" Billy threw the truck in park, waiting for me to answer.

"Looks perfect. Looks a bit run down though."

He glanced over the seat at Angela, who was breathing like a rabid dog. "I'm not staying in that hell hole!" she exclaimed.

"Again, we'll just see about that." Billy climbed out of the truck and opened the back door. She slid to the other side, kicking her scrawny legs in the process. With ease he was able to subdue her futile attempts as he drug her across the seat. "It won't do well for you to play games, Angela. You're not the first vile piece of shit I've dealt with. Listen and things might go a little smoother for you."

He had her out and, on her feet, but she continued attacking him, finally landing a good kick to his shin. I knew he'd never hit a woman, but if anyone deserved it, it was Angela. I ran around to assist. I took one of her arms and Billy took the other. Together we lifted her with ease as she continued flailing her limbs about.

I'll admit the place wasn't ideal and needed a lot of work. The porch looked a bit unstable with loose boards and nails protruding through the flooring. A broken window cast a cylindrical beam of sunlight to the inside, which was covered top to bottom in cobwebs and dust. It did have all the modern amenities of comfort, including running water and an inside bathroom. That should make the ungrateful woman happy.

"Home sweet home," Billy announced, kicking the door open. I coughed as the dirt invaded first my mouth and then my lungs. It smelled of must and animal piss.

Angela wrinkled her nose in disgust. "Oh, come on, woman. It's no worse in here than the company you keep."

"I'm not staying here." Angela stomped her foot like an errant child. It was rather amusing considering she was a woman of at least forty, dressed in a business suit.

"You are, and you will. Don't worry," Billy smirked, "by the time you're through cleaning, it will be as good as new." He pointed to a small kitchenette with bags sat atop the counter. He led her over and unloaded them. Pine Sol, Pledge, Windex and Lysol were just a few of the items he'd purchased. "I even splurged and bought your highness a pair of rubber gloves so as not to ruin your nails." He smirked again as he tossed the heavy yellow mitts in her direction.

She huffed, infuriated. "How dare you think you can manhandle me and then demand that I clean this dump. You... you…."

Billy tutted. “Angela, Angela, Angela. Let me explain this to you one more time.” He bent down so they were eye level. “I don’t give a shit about you. I don’t care about your fancy suit, or your perfectly coiffed hair. I certainly don’t give a rat’s ass what you think of me, or even Blake for that matter. You see, you spent years not caring about your own daughter. About Tom and George. I suppose one could look at this whole situation and realize that it all started with you.”

Angela glared at him icily. It was in that moment I realized just how evil and narcissistic she was. Maybe even more so than Raul. “That little bitch never did anything but cause me grief. Why should I give a damn what happened to her? What about me?”

I stepped in before things could get out of hand. Again, I’d never seen Billy hit a woman, nor did I think he would, but when a man is as desperate as he is, one would be foolish to push the limits.

“Angela, what Billy is trying to say is that regardless of how you feel, you will clean this place up. You will follow orders and you will do it without any lip. Neither of us care how you feel about this, so you’re wasting your time and ours. You had your shot to lead us to Hope and you refused. This is our plan B. Deal with it.”

Billy pulled his knife from its sheath and walked until he was standing behind her. With one swift, downward motion, he’d freed her wrists of the zip ties. “One attempt to be foolish is one attempt too many. I will kill you and I will feel nothing as I stand over you and watch the blood drain from your body. Do I make myself clear?”

I watched her carefully. Angela's whole body shook with fear. For the first time, I saw uncertainty in her eyes. She knew, beyond the shadow of a doubt, that Billy wasn't bluffing.

"Whatever you say. *Boss.*" Her voice was dripping with sarcasm and distain for her future son-in-law.

He stood up straight and puffed out his chest. "That's more like it. Now," he grinned, "get to work. This could take a few hours."

Billy and I stepped out front, leaving Angela to the task at hand. He pulled a pack of cigarettes from his pocket, lighting the end and inhaling a long drag. "Thought you quit?"

"I did. But if this shit doesn't justify starting back up, I don't know what does."

"True, brother." The wooden post held me up. I was beyond exhausted and knew that wouldn't change anytime soon. I crossed my feet at the ankles and leaned back, the warm summer sun beaming on my face. "Aren't you worried she'll run off?"

He took another drag of his cigarette and blew it out slowly. A sly look came upon his place, filling in the rough lines around his eyes. "I've taken precautions. She's not getting out unless she comes through this door."

"I'm impressed, man. As always, I bow to the master." I held my arms up and bent over in an exaggerated manner.

"Alright, smartass, knock it off." Billy flicked the burning embers from his cigarette and squashed it with the toe of his boot. "So, here's what I'm thinking. Raul will show

Friday night to the fight with Hope in tow. We'll take Angela and strategically place ourselves where we're sure to be seen. He needs Angela. She's worth more to him than Hope. You've seen it. She runs that damn place and those girls. Without her, there's no business. No business, no money. He'll trade one for the other and you and Hope ride off into the sunset." He beamed as he stood there, waiting for my reaction. To be honest, I didn't have one. Not the one he was expecting anyhow.

"Billy, he's not gonna let her go that easily. He wanted Heather and he didn't succeed." I ran my hand over the back of my head. A nervous tick I had. "Angela may be invaluable to him, but so is Hope. Think about it. It puts the two of us in our place once and for all. This is all just a game to him. He can find girls anywhere and his drug connections are all over. He's got nothing to lose and everything to gain."

He pondered over my words. His face turned up in a scowl as he tried several times to reassure me. Each time he stopped, realization dawning that maybe, just maybe I was right. "Blake, I…"

"I know, man. I know. Look, we can try. We've got nothing to lose either. Chances are, he already knows anyhow. Either way we need to be prepared. You good here?"

"I'm good. Go on. You need to get some rest. You're looking a bit peaked." We shook hands and I began to leave. It hadn't dawned on me that my bike was at the hotel and I had no way of getting back. Calling a taxi wasn't a smart move.

Just as I turned around, Billy's keys landed at my feet. "Be back here at eight sharp to pick us up. We're heading to the gym for some training. Bring Johnny."

I nodded and gave a half-hearted salute. "Will do, brother. See ya in the morning."

28

I arrived back at the hotel to find Johnny and Bailey crashed on the couch, tangled around one another. I started to slam the door, wakening them rudely with my displeasure, but it wouldn't do anything but start a fight. A fight I wasn't in the mood for.

I closed the door quietly and crept to my room. Hope's perfume wasn't as noticeable as I breathed in deep, trying to bring it back to memory. I stared at the well-made bed with its obscene number of pillows; the floor, no longer littered with her clothes. A pang coursed through me. A realization that her absence was more than I could bear.

I grabbed my jacket from the chair and headed back out, leaving as silently as I came in. The bar was crowded, overrun with couples and singles alike, all lost in their own world. I picked a spot in the back, away from everyone. I didn't want to see lovers displaying their affections towards one another, especially when I wasn't sure I'd ever have that again. I was jealous. Envious of every man in here. I scoffed to myself at the ridiculousness. Since when had I ever been jealous of anyone?

I slid in the booth, raking my hand through my messy mop of sandy blonde curls. Everything on the menu looked enticing, though I wasn't all that hungry. I couldn't remember the last time I'd eaten. I suppose with the situation I'd forgotten all about it. My stomach growled on cue, just as the waitress approached to take my order.

"Sounds like you're in dire need of my services." She laughed, her bright blue eyes twinkling with mischief. "What can I get for you?"

I quickly skimmed the menu again, hoping something would jump out at me. Aha! "I'll have the double bacon cheeseburger, side of rings, and the largest beer ya got."

She winked, but not in a flirtatious way. This girl seemed too young, too innocent, and I liked that about her immediately. She was sincere and, in my opinion, too good to be working a dive like this. Don't get me wrong, the bar was first rate, as was the hotel. But I imagined she had to endure a lot from the men that traveled in and out of those revolving doors.

"Be right back." I watched her go, again, noting how she didn't sway her hips, or flaunt her backside. I think it's the first time I've ever seen that. A woman *not* trying to get with me. Not batting her lashes or licking her lips. I sat in stunned silence. The only other girl to ever do that was Hope.

Shit, I missed her like crazy. Her smile. Her infectious laugh. Her clumsiness even. I think sometimes she did it on purpose; dropped something, or fell over, just to have a reason to touch me, but she never needed one. I lowered my eyes, my gaze following the faint pattern on the table. What I wouldn't give for Hope to be sitting across from me now. To have her outstretched hand in mine, my thumb absently drawing imaginary figures on her skin.

"Fancy meeting you here." His voice was low and gripping. "I took my chances. Maybe I need to place a few bets tonight seeing as this is the first place I checked. Maybe luck is on my side after all."

Raul sat down, placing his arms on the table and lacing his fingers together. He leaned forward, attempting to keep the conversation as private as possible. "Where is she?"

"Where's who?" I was growing increasingly worried as I thought of Hope.

"Angela." Raul's dark olive skin was turning a blustery shade of red as he spoke. If he was any more high-strung, smoke would be coming from his ears. I took delight in his discomfort.

"I've no clue what you're referring to. I've been here all day." I sat back against the booth, relaxing into a comfortable, carefree pose. I had one up on him and Billy had been right, he seemed eager to get her back. Maybe more so than keeping Hope. Angela just might be my bargaining chip after all.

"There will be all kinds of hell to pay if you don't release her at once!" His body was stretched over the table and drawing attention as his voice grew louder. I remained calm, refusing to take the bait. I needed to be smart about this.

I copied his movements, leaning over the table and pushing him back into the seat. "Well, I might be able to help, Raul, but of course I'll need something in return. You see, my services aren't free either. Everything has a price."

"And what might that be?"

I was surprised the little shit even had to ask, but I'd oblige. "Hope. I want her. Give her back and you can have Angela, and this shit is done. The end. You won't see me again, and I'll stop hunting down the nasty dog you really are."

He seemed to ponder this over and over. He was taking too long for my liking, which with Raul was never a good sign. It usually meant he was coming up with an ulterior plan, and one that benefited him greatly. "No."

My pulse raced as sweat began to bead on my brow. My eyes narrowed in disbelief. How could…. "No? What do you mean, *no?* Angela is way more of an asset to you than Hope is!"

"Perhaps," he smirked in amusement. "But Angela is washed up. Old. Used. You know the likes. Hope, on the other hand, wow. Just wow, Blake. I've never seen a more beautiful creature in my life. Her soft lips, the curve of her back as it dips down to her ass. Oh, and her full breasts." Raul closed his eyes and hummed to himself in pleasure.

"You sick bastard! If you touch her… and Angela isn't washed up." The words escaped my lips before I thought them through. The thought of her turned my stomach sour, threatening to expunge the bile, but since I'd started it, I needed to see it through. "I don't know why you'd think that, Raul. She's an attractive and vivacious woman for her age. You remember how hot Heather was, don't you? Add some experience to that and you've got Angela. Not to mention she's somewhere right now, doing my laundry and cleaning up. What's that you called it before?" I snapped my fingers and pretended to search for the word, already on the tip of my tongue. "Oh yeah, earning her keep. Hope isn't much for housework so looks like I'm getting the better end of the deal. Two for one special, if you will."

Raul was seething. Spittle flew from his taut lips and his breath was ragged. I'd never seen him so unglued before. "I'll do whatever I want to Hope. She belongs to me." He leaned forward again, our pissing match getting a bit too heavy for our surroundings. We were once again drawing attention.

"You do, and they will never find you. They can pull the best of the best, all the blood hounds they have, but not one shred of your vile body will remain. Not even bone." I gritted my teeth, keeping my words just above a whisper. "Don't fucking touch her! Not ever."

"Interesting," Raul replied, a huge grin giving way to the laugh lines around his demonic, dark eyes. "When I left her earlier, she told me she didn't want to be alone. That was, of course, after her bubble bath and our delicious meal together. She should be waiting for my return, which I expect she's rather anxious for. I must be going. Don't want my beautiful girl waiting too long."

Raul moved to stand just as the waitress was bringing my food. He eyed her speculatively, as did I, though I'm sure our reasons were very different. One was a predator and one a precautionary.

"Here's your burger and rings." She sat the plate down gently, hyper aware of Raul's eyes boring into her.

He stood and moved closer, brushing his hand along her arm. She shivered, though to her credit, it was barely noticeable. "Is there anything else I can get for you?" She ignored him and his creepy advances, keeping her eyes concentrated on mine.

Before I could respond, to tell her to run as far and as fast as she could, Raul bent down to whisper in her ear. "Such beautiful, creamy skin you have, púta. You really should be more careful the company you keep. All sorts of predators lurking around out there."

Raul walked away calmly, as if he'd not just willingly threatened an unsuspecting girl. I was fuming, my body trembling with rage. I noticed Jax and an unfamiliar man fall in line behind him as he exited the door. It wouldn't be smart to go after him. Not yet anyhow.

I took the waitresses by her wrist and led her to sit. It was obvious she was in shock. "Ma'am? Can you hear me?"

She nodded in response but stared ahead blankly.

"If you see him again, you go, understand? Don't let him near you. He's a bad man and for what it's worth, you seem like a sweet girl. Be careful of men like that."

Again, she nodded. "Do I need to call someone for you? Are you gonna be alright?"

"No. I- I think I'll be alright. He's intense, huh?" she chuckled uncomfortably.

"He is," I agreed. "Even more than you know. Just promise to be careful. I'd hate for something to happen to you."

The girl bounced back like a champ. "Pssh," she dismissed. "I've got three older asshole brothers. Trust me, I can hold my own."

I challenged her. "Really? Cause you looked scared shitless three minutes ago."

"I've seen him before. Underground fights, right? That's what caught me off-guard. He's always there and it's like he's burning a hole right through me. I don't know, I always thought he was kinda interested in me, but I guess not." She shrugged her shoulders and sat back with defeat.

"Trust me, he's not the kind of guy you want to get mixed up with. It's better this way." I took a swig of my beer and pushed my plate across the table. I'd lost my appetite.

"What's your name, darlin'?"

"Tammy." She eyed the plate speculatively.

"Nice to meet ya. I'm Blake." I nodded towards the uneaten plate of food. "You're welcome to have that. Kinda lost my appetite."

"My boss will kill me for eating on the job." She glanced at her watch. "What the hell. I'm off in five anyway. Mr. grumpy britches will just have to get over it." I watched as she pulled the plate closer, devouring the savory-looking meal within minutes.

When she caught me staring, her cheeks reddened with embarrassment. "Oh my God! I must look like the biggest pig to you!"

I laughed. "Not at all. I'm glad you enjoyed it." I stood and reached in my pocket to pay the tab. Tossing a few bills on the table, more than enough to cover dinner and a sizeable tip for her, I decided to head back to the room and get some shut eye.

"It was nice meeting you, Tammy. And please, remember what I said. Stay as far away from Raul as you can."

When her eyes met mine, all playfulness was over. She could sense my worry. "You're serious, aren't you?"

"As a heart attack."

"What has he done exactly? Can you at least tell me that?"

I sighed. *Women.* Always had to have a damn reason. Couldn't just accept shit and move on. "Can't share that with ya, Tammy. I wish I could. But he's dangerous. A predator. And young, beautiful girls like yourself are his poison. So please, heed my warning."

"You think I'm beautiful?" she smiled, twirling her hair around her finger. Cue the flirting.

"Out of all I just said, *that's* what you picked up on? Jesus." I braced myself on the edge of the table, glaring down to her hopeful face. "Yes, you're beautiful. Very much so. But Raul isn't worthy of that. Of you. Hell, of anyone. Stay away from him, darlin'. That's all I got to say. I'll see ya around, kiddo."

I threw the kiddo part in to make a point. No matter how beautiful she was, she was just a kid compared to me, and Hope had my heart. She always would.

29

Raul had been gone for quite some time. I used his absence to gather myself. I'd acted off pure emotion earlier, taking his arm and letting him lead. The truth is, he terrified me. The abuse he could inflict was no doubt great, but it was the emotional part that bothered me the most.

I felt foolish. A young, stupid girl with a crush. It happens to the best of us I suppose, but he wasn't a white knight in shining armor. He was my kidnapper. My deviant captor with no regard for anyone, or anything except himself. Deep down I knew who he was, but that hadn't stopped me from wanting to be close. Blake had my heart. Every single piece had his name written all over it, but Raul's arms just happened to be what I had. Nothing more, nothing less.

I shut his bedroom door behind me, resting my head against its white-washed frame. My breathing became shallow as I felt the true weight of my predicament closing in around me, squeezing at my chest. How was it possible to develop feelings for a monster like Raul? How did any sane, rational person let their conscience flit away? I huffed in frustration and kicked the door, howling in pain when my toes made contact. I was still extremely sore from the past few days, though thoughts of him had made me momentarily forget.

I turned and looked around the room. Its opulence unmatched, even by the queen's standards. The gigantic bed sprawled across the expansive room, taking up more than half. It had to have been custom made, as I'd never seen anything of its size before. The intricately carved headboard towered over my five-foot-four frame, its rustic, golden panels gleaming in the overhead light. To the left sat an antique wardrobe with pedestal feet. It reminded me of something from Beauty and the Beast, with its charm and whimsy. It still screamed of wealth and money, mind you, but it didn't feel as stuffy as the accommodating pieces. It was my favorite part of the whole room. A large stone fireplace took up the wall to the right. A pair of ivory reading chairs and a bear rug sat facing the elaborate structure, enticing to anyone looking for a spot to relax. The whole room was breathtaking, but if I'm honest, I missed the simplicity of Blake's place. Not the hotel, but the place where we'd first stayed the night he rescued me from the party. It seemed like ages ago.

My weary body flopped down, exhausted beyond comprehension. I wasn't even sure how my eyelids had managed to stay open. As tired as I was, however, I couldn't relax. The bath and the full tummy hadn't helped me either way. I was on autopilot, just going through the motions. My nagging feelings for Raul weren't helping either. I couldn't seem to get myself under control when it came to him, and I sure didn't like that Blake could potentially become a distant memory if I continued down this path.

The clock chimed half past midnight. It was time for Cinderella to turn back into the abused step-sister, the girl I felt myself to be. I wasn't pretty, or beautiful. I wasn't delicate, or soft. Years of neglect had hardened me. It had made me bitter towards everyone I'd ever met. Everyone except Blake.

Somehow, he'd been able to break down my walls; to move past the barriers I'd carefully put in place. Without my knowing, Blake and done the unimaginable. He had loved me. He saw something in me that he believed to be good and worthwhile, and his love had brought me from my dark place, even if for a brief time. I cherished the memories I had of him. The few fleeting nights we'd spent together. We'd not made love, but what we shared had been even more intimate. I couldn't have felt any closer unless I crawled inside his body and pressed my ear to the rhythm of his beating heart.

I wondered if we'd ever have that again. Those stolen, innocent moments that made us who we were. I didn't feel complete without him. Without knowing he was in the next room or curled up behind me in bed. My world had spun out of control for years and when I least expected it, there he was, setting things straight again. I needed him more than I cared to admit. I had never been dependent on anyone, learning from a very young age that people always let you down. But not Blake. He was as solid as they came.

Silent tears ran down my face, soaking into the thin material of my robe. I let them flow freely, allowing myself the release I so desperately needed. I had tried to remain strong and so far, I'd done a bang-up job. But here, alone in Raul's palace, I had no one to hear my cries. No one to judge my weakness. No one to tell me it would be alright.

Footsteps just outside the door startled me. I jumped up, quickly wiping away the remainder of my emotions. Voices carried through the massive vaulted ceilings. Whoever was speaking didn't sound like they were very happy. I recognized one as being Raul's, the other I'd not heard before. Angry tones and sharp responses had me cowering like an impish child being scolded. Not wanting to be on the receiving end of Raul's wrath, I quickly ducked under the covers and pretended to be asleep.

30

"Get a move on, Angela. Dinner ain't gonna make itself!"

She padded around the small, dingy kitchen as if she hadn't a clue what to do. Apparently, Heather had learned her cooking skills from her mother, meaning they were non-existent. "For shit's sake, woman, it's just spaghetti. Boil water and drop in the noodles."

She glared at me with all the hatred she could muster. "I'm not making anything for you, you cowardly pig!" Angela slammed the steel pot on the stove in defiance. "I don't know who you think you are…." She began advancing towards me with her scrawny finger poking at my chest.

Without thinking, I grabbed her wrist and twisted, pinning her arm against her back. "Let's get one thing clear, Angela. You don't have a fucking choice. You will do what I say, when I say. I can't be any clearer than that. And if you don't like it, tough. It ain't up to you. Do you understand?"

A whimper escaped her lips as I tugged harder on her arm. She pushed up on her tip-toes, trying to relieve the pressure. "Fine! Just let me go. You're hurting me!"

"Like you hurt your daughter?" I spat. I let go, lightly shoving her forward. "Difference is you don't give a shit. You never did. The only reason I haven't put a bullet through your miserable brain is because she wouldn't want me to. Because Heather is nothing like you. Nothing at all. Thank fuck for that!"

I turned my back but stayed on alert. I'd already made sure to remove any knives from the cabin, but a frying pan could do just as much damage. I heard movement behind me and then finally running water.

"Glad you see things my way." I grunted and moved to the couch, plonking my boots noisily on top of the milk crate, and positioning myself so I could keep an eye on her. She couldn't be trusted. Not one bit.

The tiny cabin was sparse, per my request. This wasn't a damn vacation and I wasn't about to give Angela the luxuries of everyday life. I'd slept under the stars on gravel, in the pouring rain. This was nothing to me. Hell, if anything it was a step up, but Angela wasn't used to slumming it. And no way in hell was I about to let her little ass get comfortable.

Dark, paneled walls made the space seem drab. The green shag carpeting looked and felt gross, caked in years of dirt, but it was nothing a good scrubbing couldn't fix. The linoleum in the kitchen was curling around the edges, the underside coated with mold, but again I was sure her majesty would have it looking good as new before our little stay here was over. Yep, she had plenty to do, and I had the perfect vantage point from right here on the couch in which to supervise.

"You done in there yet?" I knew she wasn't; I was only goading her. Seemed like a good way to pass the time.

She huffed and puffed, blowing her hair away from her face. Pots and pans clanked around in the sink as she tossed them about carelessly. "Does it look like I'm done, Sherlock? It'll be ready when it's ready." She mumbled under her breath, but it wasn't hard to decipher her words.

She unleashed, calling me every name in the book and then some.

"Is there a problem in there? You know, a temper tantrum for a woman of your age is very unbecoming."

She glared at me, her eyes wild with condemnation and fury. If she could've burned me on the spot, I'd be a pile of ashes right now. Undeterred by her outburst, I shrugged my shoulders and picked the frayed fabric of my jeans.

"You'll get what's coming to you, ya know?" Angela leaned against the counter, her arms folded over her bought and paid for chest. "Raul won't stand for this. He'll make you wish you were never born."

"Really? Want to place a wager on that." I removed my cell from my shirt pocket and waggled it in the air. "'Cause Blake just called me. Seems he and Raul had a meeting. Blake wanted to exchange you in return for Hope's release, but seems ol' Raul said you aren't worth the trade in. Guess he wanted a newer model."

The look on her face was priceless. Who knew a face could contort and twist in so many ways? It was quite impressive really. "You're lying! You're lying to me!" Angela was frantic, pulling at her disheveled hair and pacing the small space.

"I'm not. Seems no one wants you."

That did it. Apparently, those were the magic words to make her flip her shit. I'd seen her mad. Hell, I'd seen her down right rude and crude, but what happened next was pure, unadulterated evil. Without warning, she lunged at me, hurling all one hundred pounds of herself at my torso. Her fingers clawed at my flesh as she tried her hardest to pluck my eye from its socket. I felt the rip as my skin tore open, and blood as it trickled down my cheek. Her scrawny legs were flailing about, landing jagged kicks to my legs and groin. Lucky for me, I was leaned forward, blocking her before she could inflict any real damage to my manhood. I laughed at her before effortlessly stopping her pathetic assault.

I pushed her to the ground and stood over her. She shielded herself with her arms, only making me laugh harder. "Angela, if I wanted to hit you, believe me I would've already done it. Matter of fact, one blow is all it would take to be rid of you for good. But I'm not Raul, and like I said before, Heather wouldn't want me to hurt you." I slowed my breathing as I wiped the blood from my face onto my shirt tail. "Consider yourself warned, however. One more outburst like that and no one's feelings will be a consideration."

I walked away, knowing I needed time to reign in my temper. I needed to cool off and remember why we were doing this. This was for Hope. To get her back to Blake where she belonged. I leaned against the porch railing, missing my angel more than ever. I'd lied to her again. The biggest lie I'd ever told in my life, and it nearly broke me. After all we'd been through; I swore to her I'd never break her trust again. All I could hope was that she would understand my reasons for coming here. That it was for her. To keep her safe. To keep our world intact. And to help Blake. If it hadn't been for him, Heather and I probably wouldn't be where we are today. I owed him my loyalty. My respect. And my life.

31

Raul quietly entered the room, his anger from just moments ago having subsided. Even though I was facing away from him, I kept my eyes closed and concentrated on breathing lightly. I was too on edge and couldn't bear a conversation with him tonight. The thoughts of him pressed against me wasn't an idea I wanted to entertain.

I felt him standing on the other side of the bed, his eyes boring into me. I felt the heat as it rushed through my body and pooled between my legs. *Dammit!* I needed to get a grip. This was wrong on so many levels. A low growl escaped his lips and it was almost my undoing. *Almost.* My brain was pleading to turn and look at him, but I shut it off, refusing to give in. My heart wanted Blake. My body was a different story, though I couldn't figure out why.

The rustling of his clothes hitting the floor pounded in my ears, perking them to attention. The silky covers pulled back and seconds later I felt his hardness press into my backside. "I'm back, my beautiful girl." His hand swept my hair away from my neck as his lips gently grazed my shoulder. I bit my tongue to keep from moaning. His hands glided sensuously over my hip and down my thigh, pulling the thin material aside as he made his way back up. I was naked underneath, which he knew. A few more inches and all would be bared.

I had to stop this from going any further. "Raul, I'm exhausted. I'm sorry. Can we just sleep for tonight?"

Surprisingly, his hand stopped moving and he rolled onto his back, staring at the ceiling. "Of course. We'll wait until you're ready."

At his response I had no choice but to turn and face him. It's not at all what I'd expected. Raul didn't take no for an answer. Ever. His hand was laid across his bare chest; his impressive, muscular, tanned chest. My breath caught as I realized for the first time just how handsome he was. I'd seen him in expensive business suits. I'd seen him casual. I'd even seen him all sweaty in gym clothes after a long run. But there was something different about the way he looked now. He seemed content. Relaxed. A far cry from the strung-out drug lord and sex-crazed lunatic he was. Maybe he was changing. Maybe he needed me.

I shook my head, desperately trying to rid myself of the idea he could be a good man. It wasn't possible. He was holding me against my will for goodness sakes! Who in their right mind does that?

His thick voice disrupted my reverie. "Was Hilda a problem for you tonight?"

I sat up, pulling my robe tighter across my chest, tying the sash more securely. "No. I didn't see her after you left."

"Good. I'd hate to have to fire her after all these years. She's a great cook." I waited for the punch line, but his lack of humor told me he was dead serious.

"You'd fire her? For me?"

"Of course, I would." He seemed offended that I would think otherwise. "I'm changing for the better Hope. For you. I want to be good enough for you."

"Oh." Maybe I should have thanked him. Told him that he was good enough, but 'oh' was all I could manage. I felt stuck in the twilight zone. Or maybe this was a real-life version of Alice in Wonderland. Had I fallen down the rabbit hole? Everything was backwards. Right was wrong, up was down and left was right. My mind spun out of control, so much so that I became dizzy. I grabbed my head and fell back against the pillow, attempting to focus. Things seemed to blur instantly. I could feel movement and hear shuffling, but I couldn't see anything.

Suddenly Raul was over me, pressing his weight and me into the mattress. "It's okay, beautiful girl. Just let go." His lips sealed over mine, his tongue invading my mouth.

I floated through the clouds, my mind and body disconnected. I'd never felt anything like this before. I was acutely aware of his hands roaming my curves, his tongue lapping greedily at my breasts, his body as it moved over mine, but I couldn't say anything. I let go, drifting off into sweet surrender. The next morning, I would remember nothing.

32

Bailey and Johnny were in the main room, enjoying room service in fluffy white robes. They looked cozy. They also looked happy, and so I decided to let this one go. I knew when to pick my battles. This was one fight I wouldn't win. He was too far gone.

"Hey, cupcake. I'll be ready to hit the gym in twenty minutes." Johnny wiped his mouth, tossing the cloth napkin onto the coffee table. He bent down and kissed Bailey on the forehead before making his way over to me.

"Look, I know you said…"

I put my hand on his shoulder and shook my head. "Forget what I said. If you're happy, then I'm happy for you. I'm gonna grab a shower and then we can head out."

"But…"

"Hang on tight, Johnny. If you have feelings for this girl at all, hold onto her with all you have. Don't fuck it up."

With his hands braced on his hips, Johnny's shoulders shook with silent laughter. "I won't, princess." He turned to look at her. I watched as their eyes locked. I knew that feeling well. There was no coming back from this, whether I objected or not. It was the same connection Hope and I had, and it was a once in a lifetime shot.

I patted his shoulder and tossed a wave to Bailey over my shoulder, excusing myself from the room. It was intense and suddenly I felt intrusive. I needed to get away from it all. It was suffocating me. I showered and tossed on a ratty muscle tee with loose shorts. I needed this workout today;

to let the aggression I felt go. I was looking forward to pounding the bag, maybe even pummeling Johnny, wiping that dumb look from his pretty boy face.

"I'm ready," I announced.

Johnny and Bailey jumped up quickly, hoping I'd missed their display of affection. I hadn't. They were on the sofa, tangled limbs in every direction. I didn't begrudge them, but damn if I wasn't jealous.

"Let's ride." Johnny took Bailey by the hand, and I followed them out the door.

The parking garage beneath the hotel looked empty compared to normal. Buzzing sounds from the overhead fluorescents seemed to be roaring at an unusually obnoxious decibel. I covered my ears for all the good it did. A high-pitched, squealing noise had us all jumping. My eyes darted every direction, looking for even the slightest of movement. Something felt off; terribly off as alarm bells started ringing in my head.

Johnny grabbed Bailey by the waist and moved her behind him. She clutched his t-shirt in her fist as she buried her head between his shoulder blades. "It's okay, baby. I've got you." He protectively kept his arm around her, his adrenaline-filled veins protruding through the skin beneath.

He looked at me with narrowed eyes. Silently, we communicated the way all agents are trained to do. Thankfully it was something that never left you and we were able to keep our wits in situations like this. Our bikes were visible across the littered concrete of the parking structure. If we could make it over to them, we were home free. Normally I wasn't one for backing down, but Bailey's presence made that one a no brainer. No way were we going to drag her into this. There would be enough casualties by the time this was all over.

To our left, two figures emerged from the shadows. Kellan and another beast of a man. Both with scowls on their faces, and both punching a fist into their hands. I roared with laughter, as it reminded of some lame eighties movie with bad sound effects. Kellan was a puss. No danger of him doing us any harm, but the other guy? He might have been a different story. He looked too big to be fast, but so was Johnny and he'd surprised me more than once. Guess the saying's true; you can't judge a book by its cover.

"Well, well, well," Kellan boasted. "Looky who we have here." We stood our ground, letting them come to us. "I hear you have something we're looking for."

"Yeah? What's that?" I reached around my back, feeling the butt of my gun tucked in my gym shorts. I was a quick draw and didn't worry of being bested by these two buffoons.

"Angela."

Johnny howled while Bailey grabbed him a bit tighter. "You should know. You were there when we took her. Shit, man, how much dope you been smokin'?"

The bigger man turned on Kellan at once. "You failed to mention this, rookie. Why the hell didn't you tell Raul?"

Interesting. I watched in fascination, the slightest of hope that they would turn on the other. I could feel it brewing.

Kellan stuttered his words. "I- I-."

"Save it." He grabbed Kellan by the neck. "Good day, gentlemen. Sorry to have bothered you." His voice was a low baritone. I could feel the rumbling of its deepness in my chest as he spoke. He dragged Kellan away, stepping into those same shadows they'd come from. The next sound we heard were those of popping bones and screams. When he emerged again, he calmly placed his shades over his dark face and walked away. Kellan wasn't with him.

Bailey was in hysterics. "Get her outta here." Johnny pulled her into his side and walked briskly away. He covered her head with kisses and then his spare helmet as they mounted the bike and drove away. I, on the other hand, couldn't bear not knowing what happened. Seeing no one in sight, I strode to the place the men had disappeared. One glimpse had my stomach churning. There, on the pavement, was Kellan. His head cocked at a weird angle. His eyes were still open and staring straight ahead into nothing. He was dead. I sighed, feeling somewhat sorry for the kid. He was *just a kid.* Too young and stupid to know what he'd signed up for. I shook my head and mounted my own bike, peeling rubber to get the hell outta there as fast as possible.

The gym was packed as usual. A lot of the guys I recognized from the last underground fight. They were beasts in the ring, but most were pretty cool once you got to know them. It was never personal, but business was business. And the kind of money that flashed around those illegal fights was enough for most of these men to kill their own families. It was a fight of the fittest; men struggling to put food on the table for their kids. I got it. I didn't agree with it, but I got it.

Johnny and I both had earned a bit of respect after they had seen what we were capable of. Especially where Raul was concerned. People never stood up to him, and we never backed down. That was in and of itself enough to earn us badass legendary status. It was kinda nice to walk in and have everyone stare, though I imagined Bailey had something to do with that as well.

Girls didn't come in here. Not normally. The few that did were paid by the hour to stand by and look pretty. All for show, but not Bailey. She stuck out like a sore thumb, in a good way of course. The girl had class. And manners. Both went a long way in my book.

"Hey, man. What's up?" Bruce, one of the trainers always greeted us with a smile. True we'd only walked through those doors a couple times, but that was enough to get people talking.

"Good. Good. And you?"

"Ah, can't complain. Who is this pretty thing?" He eyed Bailey cautiously, knowing Johnny would take him down in a heartbeat.

"This is my girl, Bailey. Bailey, this is Bruce." The two shook hands.

"Nice to meet you." Her voice was timid and squeaky.

"Likewise." He grinned mischievously.

"Watch it, Bruce, or you'll be picking your teeth up off the floor." He was serious as a heart attack.

Bruce backed away, holding his arms up in surrender. "Not even thinking it, man. Not even thinking it."

"See that you don't." Johnny placed a chaste kiss on the top of her head and released her. "Watch her for me, will ya? Make sure these assholes keep their hands to themselves."

"You got it, boss." Bruce put his hand on the small of her back and led her over to a row of chairs sat against the wall. He was an older man and one I believed to be harmless, but Johnny could lose his shit in zero-point-two seconds. It would pay for the old man to behave.

Johnny geared up, and I tightened the Velcro on his gloves. "Block and jab. Bob left and right. Keep moving, don't let yourself be a target like last time."

He smiled wide. "Don't worry. I've got someone to impress now." I looked over my shoulder to see Bailey making googly eyes at him. Jesus, would they ever get over the honeymoon phase? It was sickening.

"Yeah, yeah, cupcake. Just concentrate on the guy throwing punches at your face, how 'bouts. They'll be time for hanky-panky later."

He shoved in his mouth guard and shot me two birds between his padded red gloves.

33

I woke with a pounding head. It hurt to open my eyes and every movement sent shockwaves through my extremities. A groan escaped my mouth as I attempted to switch positions, rolling to my side. I buried my head in the pillow and prayed for death. I'd never hurt so bad in my life.

"Good morning, my beautiful girl." Raul strutted over with a tray of tea in his hands. "How we feeling?"

"Like hell," I murmured. I shielded my eyes from the sunlight beaming through the windows. "Please make it stop." I pleaded with him to end my misery and he chuckled at my discomfort.

"There, there," he patronized. "Raul will make it all better." The bed shifted with his weight, as he moved to draw the curtains closed. I sighed with temporary relief. "Take these, love. They'll have you feeling better in no time."

Raul handed me two blue pills and a bottle of water. My throat felt as thick as cotton balls. I guzzled the cool liquid, along with the medicine he had placed in my palm. "Thank you."

He scooted closer, caressing my cheek with his hand. "My pleasure, beautiful girl. I'm here to take care of you. Anything you need." Raul placed a chaste kiss on my lips and waited for me to reciprocate.

A million thoughts flooded my psyche. Vivid memories flashed through my mind as I recalled the evening before. Raul carrying me up the staircase, gently tending to my wounds; dinner and him excusing himself moments later. It was all right there at the forefront of my brain, taunting me. I remember him coming back later in the evening; touching me, possibly more, but it was just out of reach. My body refused to cooperate, denying me any conclusion as to what might have happened.

"Are you okay, my dear?" Raul's thick accent oozed sexuality. His hands continued their ministrations, exploring my thighs before moving to my breasts. He pawed at them roughly, causing me to gasp. His hands felt all wrong and yet so right. I couldn't explain it.

"Just let go, Hope. Close your eyes and let me take care of you, baby. I know what you need." He moved closer still and licked his way up my neck, finally stopping at my jaw. "I know what you want."

Just like the previous night, I wanted to object. I wanted to tell him no; to stop what he was doing. The words were on the tip of my tongue, but when I moved my lips there was no sound. I felt paralyzed, unable to voice my objection. Even my arms and legs felt heavy. I remember him pulling me by the ankles, scooting me down the bed until I was lying flat. Then he was over top of me again, taking everything, I didn't want to give.

My eyes rolled back in my head as blackness stole my vision. I didn't try to fight it, for I knew it was as useless as a water-logged boat. I drifted off to Raul's head moving between my legs and the low rumble of his laughter.

I awoke what seemed like days later, though I knew it'd only been a few hours. I sat up to stretch, crying in pain when I did. My whole body hurt. My arms, my legs, my head. Even between my legs. It felt like I'd been ripped in two. It was then that I realized my robe was missing as well. I was as naked as the day I came into the world. Covering myself with my arms, I winced with the overwhelming effort it took to sweep my legs over the side of the bed. I gave myself a pep talk. *You can do this. Yes, it's gonna hurt like hell, but you're strong, Hope. Dammit, pull yourself together!*

Raul was nowhere to be seen and the hallway seemed empty of any activity. Now was my chance. In one quick and most ungraceful motion, I was on my feet and sprinting to the en-suite bathroom. One look in the mirror had be scurrying backwards in disbelief. I didn't even look like myself. The bags under my sunken eyes were tinged a deep shade of purple, my lips the same. And though I'd always been pale, my normally creamy complexion seemed to have turned a transparent shade of silver. Bruises appeared on my arms and torso, and bite marks covered my breasts. I gasped in horror at the unrecognizable girl staring back at me.

Suddenly it all came rushing back. Memories of last night and this morning flooded every square inch of my mind. Running to the toilet, I wretched and dry-heaved what little was in my stomach. I grasped the sides for support as my body continued jerking in protest. The pills. The food. The drinks. He'd drugged me. Raul had actually drugged me. Tears ran down my face as I relived for the first time exactly what he'd done. We'd not made love. He'd not been tender and kind. He certainly wasn't a changed man, worried about my well-being. He was as evil and sadistic as everyone believed him to be. The man had no soul.

Rage grew, and my blood boiled. Finally, it all made sense. The inappropriate thoughts and warm, fuzzy feelings; it was all the drugs. The drugs Raul was feeding me to keep me complacent and incoherent. I wasn't losing my mind after all. Part of me wanted to be elated at this newfound revelation, the other part seethed with anger, wanting to burn his playhouse down.

I hoisted myself from the floor and dried my tears. Right then and there I thought of Blake. Of his strength and determination. How much he'd endured and what he'd gone through since my disappearance. I knew he felt guilt and that it weighed heavily on his shoulders. I also knew that he felt responsible for me. That he felt remorse for letting Raul get to me in the first place. He'd revealed as much during our late-night talks. Without success, he'd tried for years to take him down; all of it wasted thanks to his crooked boss.

I sighed, once again staring at my reflection. I'd made a decision, and one that I'd have to live with, no matter the consequences. I'd have to be careful to pull it off, but it just might work. It could totally work, and Blake would be none the wiser. He'd no longer have to carry the burden that wasn't his to bear in the first place, and I could finally prove myself worthy of a man like him.

I turned the shower as hot as it would go. I would scrub every inch of my skin, removing Raul from all the places he'd touched and the damage he'd done. After today I would no longer think of him. I wouldn't allow him the power he dangled over me. No. I hold the cards now, and I have one hell of a poker face.

34

Johnny was in the ring with Chase. He was a worthy opponent, giving Johnny a run for his money. This is exactly the kind of sparring partner I want him to have. Without a doubt, Raul will bring the most ruthless of fighters, not lightweights. It was pertinent that he practiced with the likes of the men he'd be up against.

I pounded my fists on the mat, coaching him what to do. "Roundhouse! Drop him! Drop him!" My body ducked and swayed as I imitated the moves. "Watch the left, princess."

They continued delivering blows, though nothing hard enough to knock the other out. This was only to keep his mind sharp and his body tuned, not to beat him into oblivion. He needed to save that for the ring tomorrow night. "Good job, guys." I clapped my approval.

Johnny stepped from the ring covered in sweat. Apparently, it didn't bother Bailey, as she came barreling into him, wrapping her arms around his neck. His toothy smile was genuine as he locked his arms around her waist and swung her around. "Ah, isn't that just precious." Raul mocked them loudly, drawing the attention of others around us. You could've heard a pin drop.

Johnny sat her down gently and blocked her with his body. "What are you doing here, asshole? Shouldn't you be hiding under the rock you slivered out from?"

Raul threw his head back with laughter. "Oh, Johnny. So clever. Good thing I'm not paying you to think. I just dropped by to see how my star fighter was, but I must say, I am surprised to see Barbara here." He peered around Johnny's shoulder just to get a rise out of him.

"It's Bailey, and don't look at her."

Raul pompously raised his chin as he tugged at the sleeves of his shirt, pulling them down further over his wrists. "I own her. She's my property. I think that justifies a look, don't you?"

Like a flash of lightening, Johnny was in Raul's face within a millisecond. "You don't own shit. She's a fucking person, not a piece of property."

"The signed paper releasing her into my custody says otherwise," he responded, arrogantly.

He turned to glance at her, wondering if it could be true. She lowered her head in shame. I moved to stand next to her, throwing my arm over her shoulder. "It's okay. No worries," I whispered.

"How much?" Johnny's face reddened as he stood here in front of a crowd, putting a price on the woman he loved. It was degrading and mortifying for her, and it pissed him off royally.

Raul snuck another glance. "She's used goods so… let's say… ten thousand should do it."

From behind Johnny, I could hear his teeth scraping together as he clenched his jaw. "Done. I'll get you your money and you burn whatever piece of paper you claim to have. Then you leave her the fuck alone. Clear?"

Raul smirked. "Crystal. Pleasure doing business with you." He turned to leave but stopped short. "Oh, by the way, the girl comes with me. I'm afraid I can't release her to you until I have payment in full."

Johnny stalked forward, pinning Raul against the ropes. His brow creased, and his eyes narrowed into thin slits. "She stays with me. End of discussion. You can take that piece of paper, my money, whatever you want, and shove it up your ass." He pushed off, giving Raul just enough room to escape. Which he did. Quickly.

Once he was gone, Johnny took Bailey by the hand. "We're out. See ya." She followed behind, trying to keep up with his long stride.

"Son of a bitch!" I yelled, loudly.

"Calm down, Blake. It's all gonna be alright. I wish someone would put that smug son of a bitch in his place." Bruce wasn't one for mincing words, and I had a feeling the rest of the guys shared the same sentiments.

"Thanks, Bruce. See you guys tomorrow night." I waved over my shoulder as I exited the gym.

I threw my leg over Daisy, not even bothering with my helmet. I needed to feel the wind in my hair, the sun on my face. I just needed to ride. To get the hell away from this place for a while. I stood her up, kicking the stand with my foot. She roared to life immediately and I smiled as she rumbled beneath me. All I needed was Hope behind me; her thighs and arms clinging to me for dear life. One day. One fucking day.

35

Johnny~

I sat perched on the window sill, watching her sleep. The moonlight bathed her skin in a soft glow. I was convinced she was an angel, sent to save me from myself.

Bailey hadn't said a word the entire ride back. She barely looked at me in the elevator. I'd embarrassed her. I'd *bought* her, for shit's sake, just like Raul had. She had every reason to be angry with me for acting so foolish. I'd let my temper get the best of me, and she got hurt in the process.

As I continued to watch her, I thought back over my life; all the years I'd wasted trying to outrun my demons. My father had been a brutal son of a bitch, and my mother and I had suffered greatly because of the life he chose. I didn't want that for Bailey. As much as I felt for her, I wondered if I was good enough. I was a fighter. It's all I knew, and from the moment I stepped in the ring, I became a different man. A man that didn't deserve her.

Most of my life had been a game. One that I wouldn't have chosen for myself and one that was riddled with pain. No one ever showed me that there was another way. That it was possible to have it all, but Bailey changed that, and I finally understood what Blake meant. Her smile alone made me feel as if I could conquer the world; that I could once and for all silence those demons that plagued my every waking thought. Her laugh made my heart ache with joy. Just knowing she was happy could sustain me in the darkest of times. I knew I should let her go. That I wasn't enough for her, but God help me, I couldn't. She calmed my soul and quieted my thoughts. No, I could never let her go. All I could do was love her to the best of my ability. Maybe then the dark clouds would blow away.

I gently climbed in the bed next to her, pulling her close. I kissed her temple and stroked her cheek. She sighed softly in contentment, and for the first time in years, I drifted off into a peaceful sleep.

36

As I was not about to put that damn robe back on, I went in search for clothes. I padded to the wardrobe, crossing my fingers that I could find something. Raul had lost his damn mind if he thought I was gonna parade around here naked or stay chained to his bed.

Opening the door of the closet, my eyes were met with rows and rows of women's clothing. All with the tags still attached and all in my size. I seethed with anger when it hit me. Raul had planned this. He'd orchestrated my kidnapping; it wasn't a spur of the moment decision. I ripped a pair of jeans from the hanger and pulled them on. They fit like a second skin, which I'm sure was his intention. My hands grazed a rack of blouses, finally settling on a soft knit tee. It felt nice against my delicate skin.

I bolted from the room and stomped down the hallway. I was livid as the events of the past several days took hold in my mind. Raul had another thing coming if he thought he was going to get away with this. With my mind preoccupied, plotting his slow, painful death, I hadn't been paying attention to where I was walking. My body crashed into something, causing me to stagger backwards. The first thing I noticed were a pair of black boots and jeans.

"Hope," Jax's whispered. Unable to look me in the eyes, he hung his head in shame.

Well tough shit. I wasn't going to give him the easy way out. He owed me an apology and a hell of a lot more. "Jax. Coming to pay me a visit again? Didn't you take enough from me already?" I poised my hands on my hips in an attempt to look menacing, but he towered over me, squashing the plan. He was a good foot taller.

He cleared his throat, still keeping his eyes to the floor. "Um, no. I was just going to my room down the hall. I'm sorry to have run into you." Jax moved to step around me, but I blocked his path.

"Your room is down the hall? You live here?"

"Yeah. All us guys do. It's easier for Raul when he needs us to do ……" A string of curse words flew from his mouth when he realized what he'd said. It only angered me further.

I stepped forward, crossing my arms over my chest. "Like rape girls? Is that what you meant?" My finger poked him in the chest with each word. I showed no fear, nor would I. These two men had already taken everything from me. I had nothing left to lose.

"Hope, I'm sorry. God, I'm so sorry." His ice blue eyes cut to mine and it was only then I was able to see the remorse hidden within. They were red-rimmed with unshed tears, threatening to spill over at any moment. He looked at strung out as I felt.

I laid my hand on his forearm and asked, "Is he drugging you, too?"

Jax shrugged and moved back, putting distance between us. For whatever reason, he either didn't trust me, or he didn't trust himself. "He drugs us all. Brainwashes us. It's all about control with him. I didn't want what happened between us, Hope. I didn't want to……"

I believed him. I did. I knew what a devious monster Raul was. I knew how he manipulated people to get what he wanted, no matter the expense. While I couldn't forgive Jax entirely, I had to believe there was some good in there somewhere.

"Where's he now? Where's Raul?"

Jax's head snapped up as he shook it vehemently. "He's not here, but don't go looking for him. Stay clear of him, Hope. He'll break you. He'll break you into a million pieces and then walk away laughing at the carnage he leaves behind."

I moved closer once again, looking him square in the eyes. "You can't break what's already broken, Jax. But there's a difference in being broken and giving up. I'm not a quitter, and I don't think you are either. We can take him down. Me and you. Together we can do this."

Jax's eyes grew wide as he pondered my words. It was there in that hallway that a pact was made, and forgiveness was given. Raul would pay for all he'd done, and he'd pay dearly.

37

Tonight, was the big night. Do, or die. Shit, or get off the pot, as my grandfather would say. I'd been a nervous wreck all afternoon, causing Johnny and Bailey to retreat to his room. He said he didn't need the added stress of watching me wear a hole in the carpet.

Bailey had been attached to his hip ever since the gym incident with Raul. Not that I blamed her. And she seemed more quiet than usual, but I attributed it to Johnny fighting tonight. She and I were both worried, but for very different reasons. I knew he could hold his own. The man was a beast, after all, but he also happened to be the man she was in love with. That would be enough to put anyone on edge. For me, I was riddled with fear. Fear at seeing Hope in a drugged-out state. Fear of seeing her covered in bruises and lacerations, suffered at the hands of Raul. Fear that he'd already gotten to her; that she wouldn't love me anymore.

I gently tapped on the door. Johnny answered almost immediately, pushing me back into the main room. He held his finger up to his lips, shushing me until we'd moved out of ear shot.

"How is she?" I nodded towards the bedroom.

"She's okay. Nervous and fidgety, but otherwise she's fine."

"Good. Good." I stuffed my hands in my short pockets, resisting the urge to look at my watch for the fifteenth time in the last twenty minutes.

Johnny looked as cool as a cumber, as usual. In that moment, I wished I had his confidence, his optimism, but I knew Raul all too well. Deep down, all the way to the pit of my stomach, I knew that bastard would pull something tonight. I wouldn't tell Johnny, however. He needed to keep his head clear, no matter what.

"I need a favor," he spoke, solemnly.

"Name it, brother. Anything." I'm sure I sounded overly eager, but he was fighting for Hope, after all. I'd have given the man a kidney if needed.

He grinned and patted my shoulder. "I knew you'd say that. I need you to keep an eye on Bailey. Keep her with you. Hold her hand. Don't let her outta your sight. Got it?" His demeanor had turned from playful to serious in a matter of seconds.

"Of course, Johnny. I'll keep her with me. No worries, no one will touch her."

"I'm holding you to that. If I know she's with you, I'll be fine. If I'm searching for her, or worried about some douchebag with his hands on her, then I won't be able to concentrate on whatever asshole Raul decides to throw at me tonight."

I nodded in agreement. He wasn't wrong about Raul. He would find the meanest, nastiest son of a bitch he could. He'd been put in his place at the gym. Again. Revenge was in order and no one served it better than him.

"I won't let her outta my sight. You can count on me. I promise."

The sound of a door shutting cut our conversation short. "I told you I can stay here." Bailey seemed agitated that we'd been talking about her.

"Nonsense," Johnny countered. "I'd be just as worried if you were here by yourself. At least this way I'll know where you are. And Blake is going to stay with you. Don't leave his side all night, okay?" He stroked her face with a tenderness that surprised me. I'd never seen this side of him before. To be honest, I didn't think he was capable. I guess love really could change a person.

"He can't watch me and have your back," she argued. "Who's going to be watching out for you?"

I stepped in, trying to relieve the tension with a bit of lightheartedness. "Who, this guy? Psh, Johnny doesn't need my help or anyone else's. Did you see this guy in the ring?"

Her green eyes bore into mine, waiting for a glimmer of reassurance. "Bailey, the man's a machine. I'll be with you the whole time, Johnny will pulverize whatever jackass is dumb enough to get in the ring with him, and we'll come home and celebrate. You'll see. It'll be fine."

"Okay." Her voice suggested it was anything but okay, but I knew she wanted to please Johnny.

"Well, I'd better get a move on. I told Billy I'd pick him up. I'll see you guys there?"

Johnny gave me a fist bump. "With bells on, princess."

I smiled and gave Bailey a peck on the cheek.

"Hey, lips off my girl!" I'd already made it to the door, a safe distance from his right hook, and flipped him the bird. I heard his boots pounding the floor behind me in hot pursuit, but he was too late. I laughed all the way to the elevators.

38

Raul exited the bathroom, affixing his cuff links and straightening his tie. He looked dapper, for a cunning son of a bitch. He always dressed like this to attend the fights. I think it made him feel superior to the others. In fact, I know it did. His money gave him power and he wanted everyone there to know it.

"Can you help me with this?" He had tugged on that damn tie so much I would have to start from scratch. I imagine that was his plan all along; to get me closer.

"Sure thing," There was a sweetness to my voice that made even me want to gag. I sauntered over, sashaying my hips like a model on the catwalk. His eyes turned to black pools of liquid as he watched me closely, desire burning deep. I also noticed a bulge in the front of his trousers, though I refused to pay it any mind.

His hands found my hips instantly, pulling me close. I felt every part of him from the torso down, only this time it didn't have the same effect on me as he wanted it to. It took great restraint to resist the urge to knee him in the balls. I leveraged my hands on his shoulders and pushed back slightly, putting some distance between us. "Raul, we need to leave in a few minutes. We don't have time for this."

"They can't start without me. They'll wait." He leaned in for a kiss. I pursed my lips, hoping he'd take the hint. He didn't. He kept on, running his tongue along the seam of my lips until I opened and granted him the access he felt entitled to. Despising this whole thing, I obliged, keeping to the plan. It wasn't easy, but I had committed to this. I wasn't a quitter and I wasn't backing down.

His hands explored my backside, rubbing back and forth over the swell of my ass and the dip in my back. Mine stayed firmly planted on his shoulders, digging my nails into the thick fabric of his suite jacket.

"Mmm, that was nice." His lopsided grin stirred me, anger bubbling to the surface. I wanted to slap him, but again I refrained.

"Yes. Now we need to be leaving and you've cost us precious minutes." I worked with his tie, making the perfect knot. Thoughts of choking him with it briefly touched in my mind. I could end this right now.

"What are you wearing?"

I nodded to the edge of the bed. "Just a pair of jeans and a tee. It's not like we're going somewhere fancy."

He contemplated my words, tilting his head. His devious expression told me he had other ideas. "A beautiful woman such as yourself shouldn't be in something as common as jeans, my love." Raul strode to the wardrobe with purpose. I knew whatever he chose would be as ridiculous as his getup.

"Here, try this. It will look beautiful with that creamy skin." He pulled an emerald green dress from behind him. No doubt it was gorgeous, but for the opera or some art exhibition, not for a fight.

"Raul, it's a bit much, don't you think? I mean, it's beautiful, sure. And any woman would be lucky to wear such a dress, but I think I'll just stick to my jeans."

He barreled across the room, grasping my upper arm tightly as he pulled me up on my toes. “You’ll be with me. You really need to learn to dress the part. You will not embarrass me like this, understand?” His teeth ground out the words as his face reddened with fury. His grip on my arm tightened to painful proportions.

“You’re hurting me!” I cried. “Raul, please let go.”

He released me, shoving me in the process. I fell to the floor, gripping my aching arm. His fingerprints could be seen on my flesh, small purple blotches already forming under the skin. My head lowered as I cried silent tears.

I could hear his heavy breathing and his shoes scuffling across the carpet. He disappeared into the bath, returning within a few short minutes. “Here. Take these.” In one hand was a glass of water, the other, two small, blue pills. I recognized them as the same ones he’d given me before.

My shaking hands took the glass, a bit of water splashing over the rim. “Thank you.” I took the pills from his palm. His eyes roamed over me, sending tingles up and down my spine. I couldn’t refuse and anger him further. I tipped my head back and popped the pills, chugging a large gulp of water to wash them down.

“There. Now you’ll feel better. You know, if you just do as your told, things like this wouldn’t happen.” He rose to his feet and sat the glass on the nightstand. Checking his watch, he huffed. “Meet me downstairs. Fifteen minutes. Green dress,” he ordered. He paused before opening the door, keeping his back to me. “Oh, wear your hair up.”

The door slammed behind him. I scrambled to my feet, trying to pull myself together. I ran to the bathroom and removed the pills from under my tongue. I'd save them for later.

I tidied up my face, wiping the tears and my ruined mascara. I applied another thick coat and lined my pale blue eyes with a charcoal liner. My lipstick was bright, making me look more like a clown than a classy woman. It didn't fit with the dress, but Raul had picked this, too. I raked my hands through my soft curls, pulling them into a knot at the top of my head. I twisted and secured my hair with bobby pins, letting a few tendrils fall around my face. I hardly recognized the woman staring back, something I found to be happening a lot lately. I looked sleazy. Like a street walker. Exactly how Raul liked all his women.

I found the green dress draped across the back of the chair. I sighed, resigning myself that this whole damn night was a sham. A mockery, and I would be the butt of the joke. People at these fights knew me as the ring girl, which was bad enough. I'd paraded around in front of these animals like a dangling piece of meat, and now I was going to go in, dressed like money on Raul's arm. Rumors would fly within minutes of our arrival about how I'd secured such a position. I rolled my eyes with dread.

The slinky green fabric slid over my curves with ease. It felt silky smooth and hugged every part of me just right. I turned from side to side, feeling a tad giddy inside at my appearance. I would never tell Raul, but this dress was amazing. It dipped low, barely covering the peaks of my breast. The back was the same, showing the dimples of my lower back, just above my tailbone. It flared slightly at the hips, stopping just above my knees. I twirled and spun, admiring every angle. A soft knock on the door brought me from my thoughts.

"Are you dressed?" Jax's booming voice said from the other side of the door.

"Yes, come in."

His jaw dropped when he saw me standing there, like a deer in headlights. "Wow," he murmured.

"I know. I look ridiculous." I bowed my head with embarrassment.

"No. You look beautiful. Um, you… wow." He rubbed the back of his head and looked away.

I giggled. "Thank you, Jax. Shall we?"

"Yes, we'd better. Raul sent me up here to look for you. Did he…?"

I opened the matching clutch. "Yes. But I didn't take them." I opened a tiny square of toilet paper, the hidden pills inside.

"Good girl."

I gave a rueful smile. I wasn't sure I could do this. My nerves were all over the place.

"It's gonna be alright. We just stick to the plan, okay?"

I shook the bad thoughts and what ifs from my mind and laced my arm through his. "Okay. I'm okay. I can do this."

Descending the staircase, only one thing ran through my mind. *Blake*. Tonight, my pink stained lips would lie to him. They'd break his heart and I'd stand there and watch as if it were nothing; as if *he* were nothing. By the end of the night, he'd hate me forever.

39

We entered through the back as instructed by Raul. He'd called Johnny on the way over, also adding that he'd better not lose. He had important people attending tonight. People that had paid a lot of money to see a good fight, and he'd better not disappoint.

Bailey's heels clinked on the floor. From the opposite end of the corridor, shouts of excitement could be heard, along with a few raucous catcalls. Johnny stopped short, grabbing my arm.

"I'm supposed to wait in here until they call my name. Keep Bailey with you. Remember our deal." He turned to her and caressed her face gently. "I'm gonna be alright, baby doll. You'll see."

Bailey whimpered, holding back the tears. "Promise you'll come out of this in one piece. I need you." Her last words were spoken with a whisper, barely audible over the noise level just down the hall.

"I promise. Now stay with Blake."

He handed her off to me and I clinched my arm tightly around her waist. I felt her tremble beside me with worry. "Don't worry, man. I won't let you down."

"Ditto." We shook hands before Bailey and I made our exit, leaving Johnny there in the hallway alone.

"Stay close. Don't let go of my hand, no matter what." Bailey nodded, her eyes wide with fear.

I opened the door, pushing through the crowd. I positioned us close enough to the ring, so we could see the action, but also near an exit in case we needed to make an abrupt departure. People pushed against us as she struggled to keep her footing. "Watch it, asshole!" I shouted over the crowd. "You okay?" My attention turned to Bailey. I could see she was visibly shaken.

"I'm okay. Just ready to get this over with."

"I know. Me, too," I agreed. This whole place gave me the creeps, though I'd been in worse dumps. I still couldn't shake the feeling that something was going to go wrong, but no way in hell would I let on.

Commotion from the way we'd just entered caught my attention. The people gathered seemed to part at once, making an aisle. Surely Johnny wasn't coming out already. They'd not even announced his name. The tip top of a head of blonde hair caught my eye. My throat went dry as my eye's stung with unshed tears. I was the one trembling now, and Bailey stared at me expectantly.

Raul was leading her, dragging her along as she staggered on her heels. My God, she was beautiful, even if overly dressed for the occasion. She kept her head down, gripping onto the back of his jacket for support. She looked like some drunk girl leaving prom. As they approached, I noticed her arm, a bruise forming on her perfect skin, and I saw red. I stepped forward to block their path, but Bailey grabbed my arm, bringing me to a halt. She shook her head discreetly, reminding me that now was not the time. I turned, averting my eyes to look anywhere but at Hope.

They passed us by and continued to the other side of the ring. Purely strategic, I'm sure. He wanted me to watch. He wanted me to know she was there… *with him*. I gritted my teeth as my grip tightened on Bailey's hand. She poked my shoulder and pointed to our joined fingers.

"Mind loosening the hold a bit? Can't feel my fingers." I apologized profusely, rubbing life back into her delicate hand.

"Long time no see!" A jolt to my shoulders sent me forward, crashing into an unfortunate bystander.

I turned to see Billy standing behind me, Angela in tow. "Billy, you remember Bailey?"

"Of course, how could I forget such a lovely young lady?"

"Hi, Billy." Bailey ducked her head and tucked a strand of hair behind her ear. I could see her cheeks reddening.

"Seriously? Lovely? This tramp?" Angela's vulgar mouth hadn't changed, I see. Perhaps Billy should invest in a roll of duct tape when he goes to buy more cable ties.

"Yes, lovely. Now watch your mouth, woman. Keep it shut." Billy's gruff voice caused her to stiffen. I didn't hear another peep from her.

My eyes searched once again for Hope. I needed to see her for myself. To know she was okay. I nodded to Billy as he followed my field of vision. His eyes locked with Raul and it was game on. "Watch her." Billy shoved Angela my way and took off like a bat outta hell.

I couldn't read their lips to make out the conversation. I could only imagine it was more of a pissing contest than anything. I was so preoccupied, watching the exchange, that Angela almost got away. *Almost.* I grabbed her by the elbow just before she was about to make her escape. “Ah, ah, ah! I don’t think so. You’re staying right here with me.” Between Bailey, Angela, and trying to keep my eyes on what was happening across the room, I had my damn hands full.

Hope was hidden in the shadows, but I could see her enough to know that something wasn’t right. She kept stumbling around, grabbing onto Raul’s arm for support. She swayed back and forth, her head lulling from side to side as she tried to remain upright. She was definitely drugged. Just as I was about to release the girls and head over, Jax came forward, pulling Billy aside. The conversation looked heated and intense, but it didn’t look like they were arguing.

They kept their heads low, Raul nor Hope giving them any thought. Raul was speaking to a man, a rather large man, and the referee judging by his attire. The man kept nodding his head and shortly after, Raul slipped something into his hand that mysteriously disappeared into his pocket. A fucking payoff? Seriously? Raul was betting against his own fighter? What the hell was going on here?

I turned abruptly to Bailey, barking out my orders. “Stay here. Keep an eye on this one.”

Before I could make it five feet, Billy had me by the collar. “Where the hell are you going? You gotta job to do, right?”

“What the hell was that all about? You switchin’ sides on me, bro? You and Jax in cahoots or something?”

Billy narrowed his eyes as he leaned in closer. “How could you ask me that? After all we’ve been through, you really think I'd turn my back on you? Unbelievable," he sighed.

"Then what was all that coziness over there? And what the hell is going on with Hope? Did you even check on her? She's outta her damn mind!"

"Calm the fuck down, Blake. I can explain." He pinched the bridge of his nose, exasperated. "Hope is strung out, but she's gonna be fine. Jax was telling me to have Johnny throw the fight."

I went fifty shades of ballistic, swinging my arms around like a mad man, not caring if I landed a target in the process. "Why the hell would he want him to do that, huh? So, I never get Hope back? Look at her, Billy! Look at her! She's twenty damn feet away, she needs me, and I can't be there for her! How do you think that makes me feel?"

"I know. I know, but you have to calm down. Look, I don't know all the particulars, okay, but he seemed pretty desperate for Johnny to lose."

"I've got a bad feeling about this, man. A bad feeling."

"I know," Billy agreed. "Something's not sitting right with me either."

"I promised Johnny I'd watch Bailey tonight. And I will. But if shit starts going south, you take her and get outta here, got it? I'll jump in if need be. I can't let him take a beating for me, even if it is for Hope. This shit ain't right!" I was about to break down from frustration, something that would get my ass beat in a place like this.

I stared at Hope across the ever increasingly crowded room. Our eyes locked and for the briefest of moments, I saw her in there, hidden deep behind those baby blues that were almost unrecognizable. She quickly looked away, breaking the spell. I wished I'd have done the same. I couldn't unsee what happened next, and believe me, I'd have given anything to wipe it from my mind. She grabbed Raul by the chin, turning his lips towards hers. My world turned on its axis in slow motion as she kissed him, and my heart shattered into a million pieces, all over that floor. The room spun as my ears struggled against the muffled sounds of laughter. A pounding in my head thumped in time to my dying heart.

"Hey! Blake? You okay? Answer me! Can you hear me?" Billy was slapping my face, pulling me from my trance.

"I…I…"

"Blake, words. I need words. What the hell happened?"

"Hope. Raul. They kissed. I… I..."

Billy mumbled under his breath. "Christ. Okay, well I'm sorry, bro, but right now we gotta focus. Johnny's about to come out. We need clear heads for this. Can you do that?"

"Yeah. Screw her. She's made her damn choice." I waved it off as if it were no big deal. Deep down I was hurting so badly that all I wanted was to die. To let that concrete floor swallow me whole and be put out of my damn misery.

I took Bailey's hand in mine, intending to keep my promise. "Stay close, remember? Anything happens, or if shit gets crazy, grab ahold of Billy and do what he says. He'll get you outta here."

Bailey panicked. "What's gonna go wrong? You said he'd be fine!"

"It is gonna be fine, sweetheart. I'm just sayin' in case. That's all." I was lying to her. I could tell by the atmosphere in the room. It grew eerily cold despite the fact we were packed in here like sardines. Rusty lanterns hung from exposed wires, swinging back and forth overhead. Cloth sheets were spread in the corners, covering old furniture. One wrong move and this place would go up in flames.

Bailey tucked her head under my arm and latched around my waist. I felt a few tears soak through my shirt. Shit, she probably should've stayed at the hotel. I had no clue what was coming, but I had a feeling I was about to break my promise to Johnny. Something bad was coming.

40

Fog machines went off at the entrance of the corridor just before the announcer made the introductions. Smoke seemed to fill every crevice as people fanned it away from their face. Billy still had ahold of Angela, Bailey was to my left. Screams and screeching pierced my ears as the whole room broke out in commotion. People were pushing and shoving, banging on the edge of the ring, demanding a good fight. Strobe lights bounced from the walls, a dizzying array of pomp and circumstance for such a lowly crowd. This was Raul's style, however. Flashy and overdone.

A man climbed into the ring with a bullhorn. "Ladies and Gentlemeennn!" I laughed at the sentiment. There were no gentlemen here, only thugs looking to make a quick buck, and the only two females present who could actually call themselves *ladies* were Hope and Bailey.

The ring announcer, who looked more like a Vegas magician than an announcer, put the microphone to his mouth as a man burst through the curtain. "Making his way to the ring, from Riga in Latvia, weighing in at two hundred and sixty-four pounds, dressed in black shorts with black trim. Undefeated in all contests. Ladies and gentlemen, I give you the Baltic Juggernaut, Viktors Borisovs."

I caught sight of him as he strode past. My stomach turned to ice as we locked eyes for a split second. His face was flat, featureless. His piggy eyes seemed almost black. His hair was dark, cut short. He was all business. The stare was broken as he moved past me, climbing into the ring.

The guy was a fucking beast. I pegged him at just under six feet. His legs and arms were massive. His chest a hairy barrel. He looked like a nuclear bomb would bounce off him. I felt for Johnny in that moment. He may not need to throw the fight. This guy was a killer.

"And now, making his way to the ring from Las Vegas, Nevada, weighing in at two-hundred thirty pounds, dressed in blue shorts with white trim. Also undefeated in all contests. I give you The Tank, Johnny Trevino."

Johnny came through the curtain, winking at me on his way to the ring. He climbed through the ropes as the crowd cheered for blood. It was downright ugly in this joint. It was enough to give Mike Tyson the jitters. I needed to focus. I walked a few paces to Bailey and Angela, putting them either side of me as I watched the two men in the ring sizing each other up. The referee, a short black man with salt and pepper hair, called the two fighters to the center of the ring. I couldn't hear the words over the baying crowd, but Johnny looked focused. The Latvian just looked like a machine, ready to destroy my friend. They walked over to their corners as the announcer informed the crowd it was to be last man standing. No rounds. *Shit!* This would be brutal.

The bell sounded as Johnny turned, gloves up, ready for a dust up. The Latvian was cagey. He was probably nearing forty. To be unbeaten at that age took some doing. It also took ring smarts. He was not about to go all out. He wanted to dismantle Johnny, piece by piece. They traded a few initial blows, feeling each other out. Johnny connected with a straight right. It was a blow that would have taken most men down, but Viktors never flinched. If anything, it seemed to affect Johnny more. I saw the look in his eyes. It was not fear. It was respect. If he came through this, it would be the sternest test of his life. Johnny swung a right haymaker, hoping to cause some damage. The Latvian was a split second too fast, ducking underneath the swing. It left Johnny exposed and Viktors knew it. Quick as a flash, he hit my friend's side with a high knee, propelling him into the ropes. As he headed back across the ring, clearly winded, the Latvian shoulder charged him, sending him flying backwards, onto the mat and out of the ring. Johnny landed on his knees on the padded flooring outside the ropes, sucking in lungsful of air. The crowd went wild and I looked over to see Raul smiling. He was enjoying the thrill of the battle. Hope was looking at the ring, her eyes out of focus. She was totally out for lunch. What had that bastard given her?

My mind snapped back to the action as Johnny climbed to his feet. He rolled back into the ring, getting to his feet as a barrage of blows rained down on him. He deflected most of them, taking a stinging blow to the left arm. It hung by his side as he fired out a short right that caught the Latvian on the chin. It rocked him, ever so slightly. Johnny noticed it but couldn't take advantage. He had a dead left arm, which would be useless for a while. Viktors knew this as he covered up. No blows from Johnny's right would get through as the beast circled him.

"Come on Johnny," I yelled. "Stick to the plan."

"Shut up asshole," a voice said to my left. On any other day I'd have been over there, kicking ass. Today, I had to concentrate on my friend in the ring and the two females either side of me. Johnny was shaking his left arm, trying to get some mobility back into it. Viktors looked poised; a coiled cobra, ready to strike, and strike he did. He barreled into Johnny, pushing him into the corner turnbuckle. The referee tried to pry them apart. He managed to do so, breaking the fight only momentarily. Johnny looked over at Bailey, his focus lost for a split second. It was the opening the Latvian was waiting for. He butted him in the side of the face, snapping his neck back over the turnbuckle. The crowd collectively winced as the noise rang out. Even the most seasoned thug cringed at the sound. Johnny's arms hung over the ropes, his head hanging forward as the Latvian brought his knee up into his sternum. Once. Twice. Three times. He was out on his feet. I'd never seen Johnny get manhandled like this. Viktors grabbed his elbow, pulling him across to the other corner. He staggered blindly towards the other side of the ring, the Latvian propelling him with everything he had. He hit the corner chest first, his head snapping forward. Johnny collapsed to the floor as the Latvian rained blows down on his head and shoulders in a chopping motion. I couldn't take this. The referee was just standing there, letting it happen. Before I knew it, I was in the ring, stamping my heel between the Latvian's shoulder blades. He looked up, his face contorted in a rictus of pain.

"Get the fuck off him, asshole," I yelled. "He's done!"

The referee tried to shove me out of the ring. "Get out! You'll get him disqualified!"

"Disqualified? Look! He's almost fucking dead!" Before the referee could answer, he was flying out of the ring, courtesy of a kick to the side of the face. I tried to see where he landed, but I had other things to worry about.

The Latvian. He was all over me, firing shots at my head and body. "Fucking bastard. Attack me from behind like girl. I'll show you. I'm going to fuck you up, pretty boy."

He threw another punch that grazed the top of my head, shooting stars through my vision. I kicked out, my boot raking his bare shin, drawing blood. He grunted in pain as I fired a one-two combination, connecting with both. Johnny had rolled out of the ring. I could see him trying to get to his feet. I looked to the crowd, seeing Billy stood with Angela and Bailey. I motioned with my head and Billy knew what that meant. *Get out of here.* I just managed to see Raul's sour expression before Viktors was on me again. He tried to envelope me in a bear hug, hoping to either squeeze the life out of me, or maybe to perform some brutal wrestling move. He was quick, but I was quicker. A split second before we came together, I planted my left leg behind me, bringing my head forward and down in a lightning strike. My forehead connected with the bridge of his nose, shattering the bone. The Latvian howled in pain as I grabbed his shoulders. I butted him again, causing me to stagger back a few steps. I saw Viktors in front of me, clutching his nose. The contest was over a long time ago. Now it was about survival. *Our survival.* I kicked him square in the balls, watching with satisfaction as he melted to the mat. I stood over him, driving the heel of my boot into his head over and over until his face resembled a car crash. I may have killed him, but I didn't care. I needed to get Johnny and get the hell outta here.

41

The place was mayhem. People were shoving and pushing, some even standing over Johnny, taunting him. I blocked it all out, including the giant who still laid unconscious in the ring. Getting to Johnny and getting outta here was my main focus. It wouldn't be long before Raul got to him.

I did my fair share of pushing and shoving, as well. "Get the hell outta the way!" I screamed. People stared, eyes wide, as they took in my bloodied state. For all I knew I may have been hurt, too, but I was running on pure adrenaline and thankfully didn't feel a thing. Not yet anyhow.

As I rounded the corner of the ring, I saw Johnny's bare feet and crumpled body still lying on the cold floor. Just as I suspected, Raul was barreling over to him. No way in hell was I gonna let that asshole do him more harm. I quickened my pace, running smack dab into Hope. Her eyes were sorrowful, pained even, as she looked at me. I momentarily let myself get lost. It was the closest I'd been to her in days, and for a brief moment, she was all mine.

Raul's angry tone broke through the ruckus, bringing me back to the here and now. "Get him out of here. Sorry piece of shit!" His tasseled loafer drew back, ready to kick Johnny in the ribs as he lay motionless.

"Better rethink that, asshole. I'll ram that shoe so far up your ass you'll be tasting leather for months." My stance was poised, ready to strike. My feet were shoulder width apart for balance, in case he decided to try something stupid.

We stared one another down. The patrons circling us took notice as a hushed whisper descended amongst the chatter. "Raul, let's just go, okay?" Hope pleaded with him, pulling on his arm. He didn't budge. We were now toe to toe.

He jerked his arm free from her hold, sending her flying backwards. She landed hard as the unforgiving concrete broke her fall. I had two choices; rush to her aide, forgetting all about Raul, or letting her go, to live with the decision she'd obviously made. Before I had a chance to decide, Jax was there in a flash, helping her to her feet.

Johnny was finally starting to come to. His groans beckoned me to look. He was struggling to his knees, bracing himself with his one good arm. His left still hung limp and useless. Raul backed up a few paces, allowing him barely enough room. I kept my eye on him, blindly helping Johnny to stand. Over Raul's shoulder I watched as Hope's sad eyes turned to worry. For the first time tonight, she seemed stone-cold sober. She kept mouthing *I'm sorry. I'm so sorry*. I nodded discretely. Now was not the time.

"C'mon, buddy. Let's get outta here." I took Johnny's arm and put it around my neck, practically carrying him out the door. The crowd parted easily to make way. His toes scraped along the floor as his legs drug behind him. Other than a few gasps, no one said a word.

Finally, we made it to the hallway we'd entered through. Stale cigar smoke filtered through the small space, along with the stench of blood. Probably Johnny's. There was so much of it, I wasn't even sure where it was coming from. "Just a little bit further, Johnny. C'mon. Help me out, big guy."

Upon exiting the building, I remembered his bike. *Shit!* There was no way he could ride. He couldn't even stand upright. I thought quickly, remembering Billy's truck. Maybe he was still here. My eyes searched the grassy area, trying to locate him. A slight incline proved to be challenging as I maneuvered us forward. Johnny was struggling, but it wasn't until I heard a gurgling sound that I became increasingly worried. He needed medical attention, and he needed it now.

A loud rumble broke through the chilly night air. Billy's truck came barreling around the row of cars, flinging grass and dirt along with it. It jolted to a halt right in front of us. He jumped from the vehicle, running around to offer assistance.

"Bailey?" I questioned.

"She's in the truck. And she's pretty fucking tore up. Probably shouldn't see him like this, but I don't know what choice we have. He can't ride."

I nodded. "Yeah. Just help me get him in. We gotta get him somewhere quick!"

Billy took Johnny's other side, careful of his dangling arm. On three, we both grabbed a leg, carrying him the rest of the way. Even his feet were bloodied from dragging the concrete, which I'd not thought about.

Bailey was screaming hysterically by the time we got him in the truck. She was in the back, sitting against the door. Johnny's head fell over in her lap and then rolled to the side. I tried to keep a brave face for her, but even I knew his state was grim. "You promised!" she wailed. "You both promised!"

"Bailey, I know. And sweetheart, I'm real sorry, but he needs you right now. We gotta be strong for him, okay?"

Billy threw it in drive and took off through the field while I tried in vain to calm her. "He's a tough son of a bitch. He's gonna be fine."

Unfazed by my words, Bailey cried even harder. Her whole body shook as she struggled to get her breath. I leaned over the seat and took her hand, placing it on Johnny's chest. "Feel that? It's his heartbeat. Concentrate on that. He's gonna pull through, but he's gonna need you."

Her gaze stayed glued to her hand where it met his battered flesh. Blood coated her pale pink sweater, her palms and her jeans, but she didn't seem bothered in the least. Her eyes never left him as we bounced through the rocky terrain towards the highway. I cut my eyes to Billy and spoke discreetly. "When we hit the pavement, floor it."

I rested my head against the seat, for the first time feeling the effects of my own beating. Cuts covered my hands, my knuckles sustaining the worst of the damage. I moaned in agony as I remembered what had happened. It was bad, just like I knew it'd be. It was a blood bath, and it was carnage. My friend was hurt badly, thanks to me, and I'd not been able to stop it. Not in time, anyhow. And the worst of all? Hope's face. Her haunted eyes. Her pink lips that kept saying she was sorry. *Sorry for what?* I couldn't help but think there was more to it, but it was only wishful thinking. I saw how she was with Raul. The way she looked at him. The way she kissed him. I squeezed my eyes shut, running my fingers back and forth across my lids, as if it would magically erase the vivid images.

Soft sobs filtered through the cab from the back seat. Only then did it dawn on me that there was one voice I'd yet to hear. I moved abruptly, almost banging my head on the windshield. "Angela?"

Billy grinded his teeth as his jaw flexed. "She got away."

"Shit."

"Yes, quite. Not happy about it, but I'll figure something else out."

I stared out the window, lost in my own mind. Lost in Hope. Heather. Everyone in this God forsaken truck as we sped down then highway towards the lights of town.

"Y'all act like somebody died. Mind cheering up a bit?" Johnny's voice was faint and croaky, but he was alive and that's all that mattered. I chuckled loudly, breaking the solemn atmosphere.

"Leave it to you to be an ass when you're in the shape you're in." I looked back just in time to catch a glimpse of a smile. Cocky bastard.

Bailey's sniffles didn't go unnoticed either, as Johnny took extra measures to reassure her. I tried to tune them out, feeling intrusive during their private moment. "Baby, don't cry. I'm okay. Shh."

And there it was. The man I knew him to be under all that rough exterior. A man who cared for his woman. Who'd move heaven and earth to make sure she was alright, putting her needs first. Yep, he was all grown up and in love. After tonight, I couldn't think of anyone who deserved it more.

42

Hope~

Well, I got what I wanted. Blake bought my façade, and I bought my penitence. A life without him.

On the outside, I kept my face stoic. Raul couldn't see me break. I'd bury the guilt and betrayal so deep, no one would ever know the true depths of my heartache. I watched Blake's face; how it fell flat with defeat when I kissed Raul. How his insides wrenched at seeing his friend and partner beaten to a pulp. I could never make up for what I'd done, for how foolish I'd been, but for now Blake was safe. Far away from the train wreck that was my life.

The ride back to Raul's place was tense. Jax sat across from me in the expansive limo, drumming his fingers on the seat. He was wound tight, as was I. Raul and a few of his men were in a heated argument, one that I tried my hardest to block out because I knew the subject of their conversation. *Blake.* How to get rid of him once and for all. He wasn't supposed to jump in and save Johnny. He wasn't supposed to beat the star from Latvia that Raul had secretly brought in to do his dirty work. My only saving grace in that moment was that Blake was heartbroken. I'd done what I set out to do. After tonight he wouldn't want me, and I was sure it would stay that away. It had to.

Jax's eyes locked with mine. His dark stare pierced right through me, and I knew what he was asking for; the pills I'd hidden in my purse. The same pills Raul had tried to drug me with earlier. I nodded, discretely removing the handkerchief from my bag. I stretched across the aisle and handed it to him as he faked a sneeze. Raul, nor the other men even flinched. I leaned back and inhaled a deep breath, relieved. Raul had no idea what was about to happen.

Johnny looked at the fully stocked bar, glowing in the ambient lighting of the car. His large meaty hands grasped the crystal tumbler, pouring a hearty amount of brandy. Raul's poison. Then turning to shield the dark amber, he ground the pills between his strong fingers, turning them to powder. Both went in without so much as a splash. His finger swirled the liquid, mixing it until it was dissolved.

"Here, boss. Drink this. It'll take the edge off." Jax handed the glass to Raul, waiting with bated breath for him to take the first swig. I watched as his body visibly relaxed, satisfied that any traces of the drug had gone undetected.

Over the next several minutes, the chatter inside the car grew increasingly quiet. The other two men had been dropped at the front gate, while Raul, Jax and myself winded through the trees, up to the front lawn. Hilda came rushing out the door as soon as she saw us approach. I rolled my eyes. Just what I needed.

Jax exited the vehicle first, holding his hand out to assist me. Raul was slumped over in the seat, and of course required the most assistance of all.

"What happened to him? What did you do?" Hilda addressed me with an accusatory tone.

"Save it, Hilda. Hope didn't do anything. Raul just doesn't know when to quit drinking." Jax easily hoisted him up over his shoulder and strode inside, as if he were carrying nothing more than a gallon of milk.

I scurried away, trying to catch up to his retreating form. No way did I want to be alone with miss fifty questions.

I followed Jax up the stairs, stopping to open the bedroom door. "Put him down on the bed." I ran to the bathroom, quickly changing into a pair of sweats and a tee. I washed the theatrical makeup from my face, pleased to see by bright skin reflecting back. The dark circles were finally starting to disappear, and other than my red rimmed eyes, I was beginning to look like myself.

Fumbling outside the door grabbed my attention. I jerked it open, startling Jax who was struggling to remove Raul's shoes. "Here, let me help." I took one while he took the other. Expensive Italian shoes hit the floor with a thud.

"Let's go. He's out for the night."

I found myself once again following his lead, shutting the door quietly behind me. "Follow me," he instructed.

We passed door after door until finally he stopped short. He jiggled the handle, leaning against it when it refused to budge. Finally, it gave way, revealing the unexpected. "It's not much," he said, flipping the light, "but it'll do for the night. It's like all of our rooms."

It certainly wasn't what I expected, but it would be more than fine for me. I was astonished that Raul hadn't bothered decorating every square inch of his mansion, but perhaps he wanted to save all those luxuries for himself. *Selfish bastard.* The pale walls were void of any paintings. No shelves, or anything. A rickety cot sat along one wall with barely enough dresser space for a toddler. There were no doors, meaning no closet and no bathroom. It was bare minimum; nothing more and nothing less.

"This is great. Thanks, Jax."

"Well, if it weren't for me you wouldn't be in this mess." he huffed out a breath, resting his hands on his hips. "Hope?"

"Yes?"

His hand immediately went to his forehead as he tried to rub the tension away. "My life. It's been hard. Real hard. And this life is all I've known. But I'm not a bad guy. Not really. What I've done to you…."

"What you've done is help me." I laid my hand across his arm, comforting him. "I know you were drugged when you did those things to me." Tears rolled down my cheeks as I recalled that horrific night.

"It was the drugs. The things Raul makes us do in order to survive. I have these blackouts, sometimes losing days at a time. But with you," he winced, staring me straight in the eyes, "I remember. I remember it all. The look in your eyes as I violated you in the worst possible way. Your voice, begging me to stop. It haunts me every day."

Jax trembled as he bared his soul. I knew it was hard for him. These were big, strong men. They didn't have feelings. Macho egos and bulging muscles weren't supposed to care about anything but steroids and winning, right? Yeah, I used to think so too, but Jax was different. I didn't think he was spouting words to make me feel better. He was truly remorseful.

"Jax, it will take a long time for me to forget what you did," I responded, truthfully. "But I do forgive you."

His shoulders dropped, as did his head right before he burst into tears. I must say it was quite a humbling sight. I put my arms around him, as much as they would reach around his bulky frame and squeezed him tight.

"Thank you. I don't deserve it," he cried.

"Everyone deserves forgiveness, Jax. Even you." I let him cry it out, wiping away a few tears of my own.

Jax released me. "So, the plan's still a go, right? Me and you?"

I smiled bright. "Yes. All is still a go. If you want?" I corrected. "You know; you could just run. Get out of here and away from this life. You can make something of yourself, Jax. It doesn't have to be this way."

"This is all I've ever known, Hope." He smiled, ruefully. "Maybe one day."

"Okay then. Well, step one is complete. Raul's drugged and hopefully out like a light. Blake is far away from the danger and safe. That was my two main objectives for now. Tomorrow is a new day. We'll see what happens."

"Yeah, tomorrow," he agreed. "Night, Hope."

"Night, Jax."

I watched him pad down the hallway, counting the number of doors he passed in case I needed him. Four down on the left. I repeated it over and over to myself, so I didn't forget. I seriously doubted any of these other ogres would be so quick to help in my time of need.

I laid back on the cot, lacing my fingers behind my head. The stark white ceiling became my backdrop, a blank canvas for all the memories I wanted with Blake. I dreamed of his arms, wrapped tightly around me. Holding me when I was sad, or just for no reason at all. I smiled, remembering the way he would hum through his nose, content. Nothing had ever felt as good as being bathed in the security of him. If I closed my eyes, I could feel him. His breath against my skin. His fingertips lightly grazing the flesh between my thighs.

My eyes sprung open, knowing my fantasies would always be just that. Endless dreams that would never be. I'd hurt him. Maybe almost as much as the Latvian had hurt Johnny. Broken bones heal, hearts not so much. The ache inside me was almost unbearable, the need to be with him great. To tell him every day how much I loved him; how he was everything to me.

I rolled onto my side and into the fetal position as I let the tears take over. The room felt chilly and cold, just like everything else in this place. I drifted off, hearing Blake's voice in my mind. His soothing, husky voice, telling me it was all gonna be alright. I didn't know if it would or not, but I trusted him with everything I had. I trusted that he loved me; that maybe one day, whether it be in the near future, or in some parallel universe, that he'd forgive me. That he could love me and I him. I held onto that for dear life, knowing it was the only thing that would get me through.

43

Billy and I bust through the doors of the ER, holding Johnny up between us. Bailey was running along behind us, sobbing her eyes out.

"What happened?" A nurse came flying around the corner, catching her scrubs on the desk. She called out to a few nurses behind her as they scrambled to get to Johnny. "Bring a cart!"

We helped him up, laying him as gently as we good. Bailey squeezed her way through the bodies, nudging her way to his side. Through swollen eyelids, he fumbled around blindly, searching for her hand. "It's gonna be okay, baby doll. Stay with Blake. I'll see you soon."

He groaned with pain as she bent to kiss his busted lip. "See you soon," she repeated.

With great urgency, they whisked him away, down the bright hallway and through a set of double doors, marked *authorized personnel only.* We were instructed to wait in a small room off to the side. "We'll come and find you as soon as he's been evaluated." The nurse hurried along, leaving us with our bleak thoughts.

"Want some coffee?" Billy offered. I shook my head and found a few empty chairs over in the corner. Bailey plopped down, emotionally exhausted from the night's events. I followed suit. I worried for my friend; the one who was in here because of me. Because I was trying to get back a girl who wanted nothing to do with me. I'd lost her, and Johnny was the one paying the price.

Billy's boots scuffed the tile floor as he paced, sipping his hot cup of joe. The smell of coffee beans mixed with sterile alcohol was never a good combination, as tonight had proved to be true. He took a few more sips before tossing the cardboard cup into the trash. "Stuff's nasty."

"I could've told you that." I mumbled under my breath, finding myself annoyed with every breath and sound someone made. I was irritable that my friend was possibly fighting for his life, and we were all out here enjoying shitty coffee.

"Gotta problem with me?" he asked, cutting his eyes up to look at me through his lashes.

"Nope." The sarcasm was thick, hanging in the air like billowing storm clouds. Shit was brewing, but now was not the time.

"Guys, please don't do this. Not here. Johnny wouldn't want you out here fighting." It was the first time I'd heard Bailey sound anything but timid. She was assertive, taking charge, and acting like the only adult between the three of us.

I stood abruptly and walked out, leaving them to talk behind my back, or whatever they were doing. Probably blaming me. Saying how this was all my fault. And truthfully, that was the root of all this shit. It *was* my fault. Because I fell in love with a girl. This is why I didn't do this shit. I'd never let my guard down precisely for this reason. I'd never let anyone in before Hope. Lesson learned.

"Johnny Trevino's family?" A doctor came from the forbidden corridor, pulling a bloody cap from his head.

“Yes, we’re his friends. What can you tell us?” I rushed my words, anxious for any news that would alleviate some of this pain.

The doctor flipped through his chart, scribbling notes. “I’m sorry, but family only.” His curt voice stung the already gaping wounds.

As I was about to unleash on the guy, Billy stepped in, flashing his FBI badge. “Doc. He’s our partner. There is no family. We were working a case, so this needs to be discreet. We can’t blow cover, and we can’t have people poking around asking questions. We’re the closest thing to family he has, so spill it. Or do I need to call my superiors?”

The greying man shrank back, intimidated by Billy’s authoritative tone. “Perhaps we should speak some place more private then. Follow me, please.”

Bailey slid her hand in mine as we waited for the worst. “So, what can you tell us? How bad is it?”

“I’ll be blunt. Your friend has suffered some pretty significant injuries. He’s still in radiology, but from what I can tell, he’s got a broken clavicle, several broken ribs, and a bit of swelling on the brain. Now,” he adjusted his glasses, pushing them up the bridge of his nose, “the bones will heal with time. My concern at the moment is the swelling on his brain.”

“So? You’re a doctor. Fix it!” I demanded.

“It’s not that simple,” he explained. “We will watch him closely for the next few hours. If the swelling doesn’t subside, we’ll need to take him into surgery.”

"And do what exactly?" Bailey stepped forward, crossing her arms over her chest.

"We'll have to open his skull to relieve some of the pressure. It can be risky, but it's even more dangerous to do nothing. At this point I'd say there's a good probability that he'll have to have the surgery. I would need to see remarkable progress in the next few hours for this not to be an option."

Bailey's head dropped in her hands. Billy stepped forward and wrapped a comforting arm around her shoulder, pulling her in close. "Can we see him?"

"As soon as he's out of imaging and in a more private area, we'll have someone bring you to him. Just for a few minutes though. He'll be sedated so he can't respond, but just talk to him. Let him know you're there."

"Will do, doc. Thank you." Billy extended his arm in gratitude and the two men shook hands.

I stood at the door, debating what to do. Part of me wanted to crumble to the floor as I thought about Johnny; the arrogant, pig-headed asshole that always gave me grief. The man who'd stood by me even though we barely knew one another. He'd never asked a single question. Just jumped right in to do what needed to be done. Now he was laid up, hurt, possibly even worse.

"Do you need to be looked at, son?" The doctor pointed to my bloodied hands.

"Nah. I'm good, but uh, I'm gonna get going. Call me if there's any news." I waved half-heartedly, looking anywhere but at my friends who thought I was a sack of shit for bailing.

"You're just gonna go? Leave him like this? That's not the Blake I know. The Blake I know isn't a coward!"

Billy spoke to my back. I couldn't face him, not after everything we'd been through. "A coward?" I questioned. "Who do you think sat with you for weeks when you got shot, Billy. Who picked up the slack? Oh, and who was it that helped you get your girl back after she'd left you? After Raul took her, too. You think I'm a coward, then fine! I can't do anything to change your mind. But don't pretend to know what I feel. You're my best friend in the world, Billy. Johnny's a close second. If you think any of this is easy, then fuck you!" I slammed the door behind me, earning me a look of disdain from the nurse across the hall.

The bitter wind bit into me as I exited the stark white structure of death. I'd always hated hospitals, but even more so because it seemed everyone I cared about kept ending up in one. My thin tee did little to deter the chill that ran through me, but I wasn't convinced the weather was the sole cause.

Hope's words played on repeat in my mind. *I'm sorry. I'm so sorry.* What was she sorry for? It just didn't make sense. She was sorry she kissed Raul? Sorry for Johnny? I hadn't a clue. The only thing I knew for certain was that she was gone. Lost to me.

I continued walking with my head down, clueless as to where I was headed. It was only a few blocks to the hotel. Perhaps I should head there and start packing the few belongings I'd brought with me. Maybe it was time to move on. To forget everything. My job. My friends. Hope. Maybe I'd travel back to Montana, or even California, and settle down. Lay low for a while. No one really needed me.

Billy had Heather, and now Johnny had Bailey. No one wanted to be a third wheel, including me. I wouldn't force my friendship on anyone, and I damn sure didn't want pity.

Shoving my hands in my pockets, I had made up my mind. It was time to leave Vegas and flee to the solitude of an old rustic cabin. Breathe the fresh air. Be one with nature. A slow smile crept across my lips, proud of myself for coming to this conclusion so quickly. Yep, a change of scenery would do me some good.

My phone buzzed in my pocket. I looked at the screen to see Billy's mug staring back, AC/DC blaring as the ringtone. They were his favorite band. I declined the call, shoving the phone back in my shorts. Outta sight, outta mind, or so they say. When it went off for a fourth time, I decided to turn the whole damn thing off. He could leave a voice mail and I'd get it later.

The sound of screeching tires warranted my attention. A black car with dark tinted windows jerked to a stop alongside the curb. I stop, perplexed. And I was just pissed off enough to do something stupid. Which I did. Not knowing who was on the other side of the glass, I began ranting like a lunatic. "What the hell do you want?" My fist beat on the window with anger.

Ever so slowly the window lowered. Jax leaned across the console, looking as menacing as ever. "Get in."

"Fuck off!" I continued my stride down the sidewalk, ignoring him. Within seconds, I heard those same damn tires and that loud ass engine that would give anyone a headache.

"Hope needs you." His car rolled forward at a snail's pace as he continued alongside me.

After about twenty feet, his words sunk in. *Hope needs you.* Then Hope's words; *I'm sorry. I'm so sorry.* I grabbed at my hair in frustration. Needed me for what? So she could bury the knife further in my back? Had she not done enough damage.

"Funny thing," he continued. "Sometimes we're so busy licking our own wounds that we can't see others around us are hurting, too."

"What the hell is that supposed to mean? And since when did you become all psychological and shit? Been reading books?"

"Insult me all you want," he replied, unfazed, "but I'm trying to help you. I wouldn't be here otherwise. Now get in the damn car."

"How do I know this isn't a trap?"

He shrugged his shoulders. "You don't."

I stood and contemplated my choices. Montana, or Hope. California, or Hope. Feeling deflated, I grabbed the door handle and climbed in. This might be a fool move, but I would always wonder what he meant. I'd regret not getting in this car; not hearing him out. Maybe he could shed some light on Hope's cryptic message.

"So, talk."

Jax shifted the car into gear and took off, leading us away from town. "I can't tell you everything, but I'll give you as much as I can."

"Fair enough. So, what's this about Hope needing me? She didn't seem too busted up about seeing me tonight." I pouted like a child who hadn't gotten his way and was now going off to sulk in the corner.

Jax sighed loudly. "You know, for an agent you really are dumb."

"Who said anything about me being an agent?"

"It's written all over you," he answered. "The way you walk. You have an air of cockiness about you. A holier than thou attitude, if you will."

"Right. What else?"

"The glasses. Those damn ridiculous glasses. I keep waiting for Don Johnson to jump from the shadows as your wing man." He laughed heartily, the car bouncing with his hefty weight.

"You done?" I was sharp and quick with my words. To the point. So far this had been a big, fat waste of my time.

"Not even close. Look, I'm trying to make amends here. We need to work together."

"Work together for what?" I quizzed. The lights of Vegas flashed by in a blur as we sped along the highway at dizzying speeds.

"I promised I'd keep things quiet, but I think you need to know. And I'm sorry about what happened to your friend. Johnny didn't deserve what happened to him tonight. He may not be my favorite, and neither are you by the way, but it was a real shit move on Raul's part."

"Agreed. So, what's this about us teaming up? You honestly expect me to believe you want to help take Raul down?"

Through the darkness of the car, I could see Jax's pearly whites gleaming. His devious smile seemed to back up my theory. "Damn straight I do. That asshole deserves everything that's coming to him."

Well of all the things he could've said, I certainly wasn't expecting that. "But you work for the guy."

"No," he corrected. "I did work for him." He fidgeted uncomfortably in the leather seat next to me. "A lot of shit has happened the past couple of weeks. Things I'd rather not discuss. Let's just say I've had an eye-opening experience. It's made me rethink some decisions I've made."

"Okay. I still don't understand what your epiphany has to do with me being in this damn car." My frustration was growing. He was being very vague, and I was a big believer in just spitting it out. "Get to the point already."

"A couple nights ago, Raul drugged Hope. His usual M.O. Shit went down. Bad shit. Shit you don't wanna know about."

He was right. I didn't. I clenched my jaw, flexing the muscles underneath. My vision blurred as thoughts of putting a bullet through his skull seemed more appealing with each passing second. I nodded for Jax to continue.

"Hope figured it out and tonight he got those same pills he'd been giving to her. Asshole is down for the count." Jax pulled the car to the side of the road, cutting the engine. Draping an arm over the steering wheel, he turned in his seat, as much as his towering figure would allow. "She and I came up with a plan. A plan to take Raul down, or at the least to get her out. What you saw tonight was all an act. The kiss. Hope laughing. Her hanging on his every word. She wasn't trying to hurt you, man, she was trying to protect you."

Stars filled my vision. She was trying to protect *me*? So that's what she meant when she apologized. She wanted to keep me away. Of course! It made perfect fucking sense!

"I was gonna let it go. Stick to our deal and see this through. Keep you outta the loop like she wanted. But I passed by her room tonight and she was crying. Hope doesn't deserve that. She doesn't deserve any of what's happened to her."

"So, you're a nice guy now?" My words were laced with uncertainty as I questioned his motives.

"An epiphany, as I believe you called it earlier." The large giant next to me was really a big softy. Who would've ever guessed? "Look, Raul's estate is just up the road. I can't drive you through the gate. It'll draw attention. But we can get in around the perimeter. You get in, get Hope, and then get the hell out."

He tossed me the keys to his charger. "Don't look back, just go. Away from here. I'll hold Raul off as long as I can."

"Why are you doing this?" I sat staring in astonishment.

"Because she forgave me," he answered, quietly.

Did I want to know? Did I really? If I had to guess, I'm sure I could've figured it out. "Forgave you for what exactly?"

"It doesn't matter now. And she's gonna be mad as hell about me bringing you here, but if the shoe was on the other foot, I'd want someone to tell me."

"I appreciate that." And I did. With all the sincerity I could muster, I thanked him.

"Stay low. There's a covered patio to the right of the fence line. Lights are always on, so stay clear. I cut the cameras for the garden. Go left until you come to the walk next to the pool. There's a terrace. Meet you there in ten."

"Where are you going?"

"To let you in. Unless you wanna climb the side of the brick."

"Not particularly," I deadpanned. "So, what? You're just gonna waltz through the front gate on foot? Won't that look a little suspicious?"

"Nah," he waved off, "I stagger in here drunk all the time. I'll tell them I had a friend drop me off. It's all good."

I had no choice but to believe him. If he said Hope needed me, then no way in hell was I gonna turn my back on her. I extended my hand; a good faith gesture and a thank you to him for coming to find me. "You didn't have to do this, ya know?"

"Yeah, I did." He climbed awkwardly from the car, almost getting stuck in the doorframe. He was one hulk of a man.

I took off on foot, making as little noise as possible. I followed Jax's directions to the t, taking extra precautions at the patio, just like he'd said. The terrain was easy to navigate. Plush sod. *The extravagant bastard.* The terrace was just ahead, within thirty feet, or so. I was almost home free when voices deterred my advances. I knelt, shielding myself behind a row of shrubs. The two men dressed in fatigues talked for a few minutes before departing to their respective posts. I gave them several seconds before moving from my cover. I needed to make certain they were out of range.

Once I felt comfortable, I darted across the dew-soaked grass. Johnny was already there, waiting for me. "This way," he motioned.

We crept up what appeared to be a back staircase. It was bare, and obviously meant to be used by the staff. Johnny turned halfway up, pressing his finger over his lips. He stuck his head around the corner, checking for any signs of life. Out of habit, I checked behind us, making sure any uninvited guests weren't creeping up to deliver a cheap shot to the back of our heads. He waved me on, walking quickly ahead. I took stock of our surroundings, making mental notes of how I'd get Hope and myself out of here. There seemed to be doors every few feet, brass numbers on each one. It seemed more like a hotel than a home.

Number three. That's the door Johnny stopped in front of. "She's in there. Enter quietly, and don't startle her. These other rooms are occupied by men just as bad as Raul. Just because he's out of commission doesn't mean one of these other assholes won't jump at the first sign of trouble. They'd eat it up. Take her out the same way we came in."

"Wouldn't it be safer to hole up here for the night? What time to the guards do shift change?"

He checked his watch. "Midnight. You've got a couple hours. Alright, two hours. That's your max."

"Understood." I thanked him again and opened the door, shutting it quietly behind me. I turned the lock, avoiding any interruptions.

The room was pitch-black, only a sliver of moonlight shining through the shadows. My eyes adjusted quickly as I searched for her. Lying across the room, curled into a ball, was Hope. I moved closer, gingerly stepping across the wooden floor. It was then that I noticed her tear-streaked face. She'd been crying. Possibly for me. I knelt down beside her, whispering her name. "Hope, I'm here. Wake up for me." Her lips beckoned me. I needed to kiss her; to taste her. I sealed my mouth over hers, flicking my tongue out over her petal soft lips. She tasted like heaven against my sin. Light against dark. Hope against fear. She was everything I remembered and more.

44

She moaned into my mouth, instantly recognizing my scent. I can't even begin to describe the feelings that ran through me. Jax had been telling the truth; it had all been an act.

"You're here. You're really here." Hope's delicate hands grabbed my face, touching and tracing the outline of my jaw, the creases of my eyes; my nose and chin.

"Yes, babe. I'm really here." I smiled with relief. The weight of the world broke from my shoulders, floating away. Peace filled me, head to toe, and I knew without a shadow of a doubt this is where I belonged. With her. Always with her.

"Blake, *why* are you here?"

Well, that quickly deflated my bubble. "I'm here for you, Hope. Why else?"

She sat up, throwing her legs over the side of the makeshift bed. I sat back and waited. "*How* did you know I was here?"

"Jax."

She stood abruptly, shaking her head back and forth. "He promised!"

"Babe, calm down. He thought he was doing the right thing. He *did* do the right thing." I tried to wrap my arms around her, to settle her down, but she fought against me.

Pulling at her hair, her face reddened as she looked like she was about to burst. She was angry. Angrier than I'd ever thought her capable of. "You have to go. You can't be here, Blake! It wasn't supposed to go like this. Please, just go!" A half-whisper, half-scream erupted from her.

"I'm not leaving," I said, with finality. "I'm here, Hope. For you. Because damn it, I'm in love with you. Because I've lost you twice now, and I'm not willing to tempt fate. Because I fucking need you!" I wasn't giving her the option of backing down. This shit had been building for a while now. Better to clear the air and get it over with. Now she knows. She knows how I feel and the ball's in her court.

Her beautiful blue eyes penetrated me. "You love me?"

Simply and easily I replied, "Yes."

"Blake, I…"

"Just say it Hope. For fuck's sake, for once in your life, just say what you want!"

She hesitated. She was warring within herself about what to say. Deep down I knew she loved me. It was written all over her face, her body language, but I knew what her response would be. It would be to push me away. Because she really thought that's what would be best. But she was wrong, and I was tired of letting her run. Not this time.

"What. Do. You. Want?" I moved closer, inching her backwards until she was against the wall. Her chest heaved with desire; her breath catching in her throat as she watched my lips. My need for her was evident as I pressed my body into hers. I was not backing down.

"What I want doesn't matter," she said, breathlessly. "It's what *needs* to happen. What I need you to do to be safe. That's what all this has been about. Don't you get it?"

Her eyes drifted to the floor. I knew this was hard for her. Right and wrong. Black and white. That's how she viewed the world, and there was no in between. I put my finger under her chin and lifted it slightly until our eyes met again. "What you want does matter, babe. It matters very much. And I need to hear you say it. You can deny it all you want, but you and I both know the truth here. We've been dancing around it all this time. We've wasted precious moments, Hope. Moments we could've had."

I moved my hands up the wall, pinning her in as bent lower to whisper in her ear. "Now. Tell me, Hope. What. Do. You. Want?" My tongue darted out, flicking that spot just below her ear, down her neck and to the hollow of her collar bone. I felt her tremble beneath me as I waited for the words I'd longed to hear.

Hope's hand pushed against my chest, coaxing me back. "Blake, I…" she sighed, exasperated. "I can't do this."

I turned away, composing myself. *Damn, she was so stubborn!* So trapped inside her own head that she couldn't for one fucking second let her guard down enough to let someone in. "I'm sorry," she cried from behind me.

I guffawed. "Really? Because it's always up and down with you, Hope. One minute you want me and the next you push me away. You're giving me damn whiplash!" I was beyond frustrated, but I needed to push her. Years of training had taught me a great deal, including how to get people to talk. This wasn't my preferred method when trying to get my girl to confess her love for me, but if this was the only way, then so be it. "I can't take this, Hope. Either you want me, or you don't. Plain and simple. The choice is yours. But if I walk out that door, I'm done."

"What do you mean *you're done*?"

She was panicking. Good. "Just what I said, babe. I'm tired of doing this same song and dance with you. Maybe you aren't the woman I thought you were."

I turned again, praying to all that was holy that she'd call my bluff. I'd almost made it to the door when I heard a painful cry escape her lungs.

"I want you! I want you, Blake. But I'm trying to protect you! Can't you see that?"

I spun on my heels, once again backing her against that spot on the wall. She was close to cracking; to revealing all her secrets that I so desperately wanted to know. That I *needed* to know.

"Why can't you just say it? Tell me how you feel, Hope."

Her chest heaved with her every breath, the pale moonlight illuminating her flawless skin. My eyes fell to the delicate curve of her breast, peeking out through the thin material of her shirt. Her tongue licked her luscious, full lips, begging to be kissed. I felt her pulse quicken as her heart beat wildly; I watched her pupils dilate, a classic sign of desire. I pressed into her more, the full length of our bodies touching.

"I want you," she whispered, as I lifted one arm above her head, holding it against the wall.

"And?" I prodded.

"I need you." Her eyes closed in satisfaction. I almost had her.

"What else, babe?" I held both her wrists secure in my hand, above her head. My other hand traced her face, her neck, and down to her waist, finally stopping to rest on her hip.

"I love you, Blake."

That was it. The three words probably spoken more than any other in the English language. Words that people threw around too easily with no thought for the ramifications. But I didn't feel like these were just words between us. I knew they weren't. They were the building block to everything we'd ever been or would be in the future. They were my lifeline; the reason I wanted to try. The reason I *would* try every fucking day to be the man she deserved.

Keeping my body in line with hers, I leaned only my head back to look at her. Her hooded eyes were filled with lust, mirroring every emotion coursing through me. It was sensory overload and suddenly I couldn't get enough. In a frenzied hurry, I released her hands as I grabbed the hem of her shirt, pulling it over her head.

"Blake," she moaned, letting her head roll to the side. My lips found that sweet spot that I knew drove her crazy. Her arms wrapped around my neck, pulling me in closer and closer.

I kissed her like the starving man I was. I wanted to leave my mark, trace every line and curve of her body. Only then would she know, could she *possibly* begin to understand the love I had for her.

"I want you Blake. I need to feel you." That was all the encouragement I needed as I kissed her. Hard and urgent, our teeth clashing. She bit my lip, drawing blood. The salty tang tasted good. She was not the scared girl of a minute ago. She was a woman. A real woman, with one thing on her mind. *Me*.

She pushed me backwards, my legs touching the side of the bed. I sat down heavy, Hope pushing me flat as she climbed on top of me. We kissed again, her hair tickling my nose as it draped over my face, before pushing her off to the side. She landed in a tangle of long hair and longer limbs. I climbed over her, swooping down to kiss her neck. She was breathing heavily, her skin flushed. We looked into each other's eyes, but no words were needed. I kissed her neck again, her hand wrapping around my nape.

"Your skin tastes incredible." My shorts threatened to burst open when my hand met her bare breast.

"Oh, Blake," she moaned, her head pushing back into the pillow. In one swift movement I had her shorts flying across the room. She looked into my eyes, suddenly conscious of her nakedness. I smiled as I leaned in, taking a hard nipple in my mouth. I licked and sucked at it, as Hope writhed underneath me. My other hand was cupping the other breast, kneading the nipple between my fingers. Hope's hand was still around my neck as I started moving south. She let go, moaning some more as my lips made a trail down her perfect stomach. I noticed faint blond hairs around her belly button that made me smile as I kissed her. She was just perfect. She was mine, and I hers. And it was time to become one. She looked down, willing me to do something. Her breathing was now ragged. I smiled as my lips found the silky skin on the inside of her thighs. My arms wrapped around her legs as my mouth slowly worked its way north. I could smell her arousal and it took my breath away. It was her own musky scent. My arms broke out in goosebumps as I inhaled her.

"I love you Hope," I said, as I gently kissed her most intimate of places.

Her body writhed like she'd been given an electric shock. She was neatly trimmed, as I guess was the way these days. She looked so right, so perfect, and I didn't want to leave this room. *Ever*.

She began panting as my tongue flicked over the folds of her flesh, sending shockwaves throughout her body. I was ravenous for her as I pushed my tongue deep inside, drawing louder moans from the woman I loved more than anything. She was so wet. So slippery, and warm. I was doing that. It made it feel all the more right. I began to kiss her, holding my mouth tight to her body, my tongue rolling back and forth inside her. Her legs were quivering as I picked up the pace. Hope's whole body was tensing up, and then it happened. I tipped her over the edge. "Oh, Blake!" she yelled, quickly biting her lip to stifle her outburst. I tightened my arms, riding her like a bucking bronco. Damn she was strong. It took all my strength to keep my mouth on her, keeping her orgasm going with my lips and tongue. I felt drunk. Intoxicated with her. I would never tire of this. I gradually loosened my grip on her legs, my mouth coming away from her flesh, giving her respite. Her whole body was covered in a light sheen of sweat, as I licked her body, my mouth making its way to hers.

45

Banging on the door startled me from a deep, peaceful sleep. I peered down at Hope, who lay sleeping quietly beside me, her blonde hair covering her beautiful face.

"Hope! I know you're in there! Open the damn door!" Raul's voice was laced with anger as he continued his fisted onslaught against the door. Keys jangled as he fumbled for the right one.

I jumped quickly, searching for my clothes scattered around the floor. Hope was jolted awake in the commotion, the blood draining from her face once she realized what was happening. Panic set in. I dropped to my knees in front of her, brushing the hair from her face. "It's okay, babe. This changes nothing. You hear me? Nothing!"

I could see the guilt written all over her. It was eating her alive, wondering what she'd done. The price she'd pay for drugging Raul, or for my being here. It was killing her; quickly deluding and erasing everything that had happened the night before. I was fast becoming a regret and that was something I refused to let happen.

I took Hope's face in my hands once again, squeezing just enough to get her attention. I didn't speak a word of assurance, knowing sometimes actions mean more than anything I could say. Glaring into her eyes, I conveyed what I wanted her to know. That I loved her. That last night was everything it should've been and more. That we were getting out of this alive. More importantly, that we were getting out of it together. She shook her head slightly, acknowledging our unspoken words. I kissed her gently, backing away and resting my forehead against hers.

"Follow my lead, babe. I'm gonna get you outta here."

Without further prodding, Hope took my hand, squeezing it in hers, and that was all the confirmation I needed. She was back. I grinned a wide, toothy smile of my own, already making plans for our future together.

Gingerly stepping across the floor, I braced my ear against the wooden slab and listened for any footsteps outside. It seems Jax had stayed true to his word, leading Raul away and allowing our escape. He'd told me to go out the way we came, through the back stairwell and through the French doors to the back patio. Seemed simple enough, but because of my lapse in judgement, we now had people looking for us. Dangerous people and walking outta here scot-free didn't seem as feasible now. I wouldn't share that with Hope, especially in her already fragile state, but I myself was feeling a faint bit of nervousness. Raul was a brutal beast of a man, his goons being no better.

With one last kiss to her temple, I told Hope to stay close. "Don't let go of my hand. If I run, you run. If I stop, you stop. We go together. Got it?"

"Got it."

"Good girl. Let's move." The door creaked in protest as I opened it, echoing loudly in the otherwise silent hallway. I hesitated for the briefest of seconds before making a run for it. Hope stumbled behind me, quickly gaining her footing once again as we picked up the pace. I could see the stairwell closing in. A few hundred more feet and we'd be home free. A smile broke out across my face, thoughts of our future together once again invading my psyche. Her walking down the aisle with flowers in her hair. Her belly growing with our child… all the things I'd never wanted and yet at this moment they were so close I could almost taste them.

Then out of nowhere it happened. Every dream; every plan and moment of perfection was replaced with sheer terror. A jolt to my body. My feet tangling up, causing my abrupt fall. A shrill scream mixed with pain and fear. An empty feeling in my hand as Hope's grasp was ripped from mine. A momentary blur of panic and disbelief.

"Move and she's dead." Angela's tone struck me viciously, as if she'd smacked me across the face. There was no remorse. No feeling. Not one ounce of guilt as her hand held the gun steady against Hope's temple.

"Let her go. Take me," I pleaded. Every ounce of training and my years as an agent no longer mattered. I threw it all out the window. I didn't care as long as Hope was alright.

"I don't want you, but this pretty thing here," she motioned towards Hope, "is my ticket to fixing things with Raul. I bring her back; he has no choice but to accept me again." Her devious smiled told me she was screwed just enough in the head to believe that.

"You really think Raul cares about you?" I scoffed. "That he gives a shit what happens to you? Tell me, Angela, did he come looking for you, even once?"

She threw her head back, shaking out her stringy hair. By the time her eyes met mine, they were hollow pools of black. "He. Loves. Me."

"Maybe he does. So, let Hope go and take me. I'm the one he's had a beef with all these years. I'm the one that tried taking him down. Hope is innocent in this." The desperation in my voice made me sound more like a teenage pubescent than a man, but it didn't matter. Nothing I said was going to penetrate Angela's hard exterior or change her soulless mind.

An evil grin spread across her face, highlighting years of self-inflicted abuse. Age lines were made more prominent from the alcohol and cigarettes she consumed daily. Her rotting yellow teeth baring a hint of black around her gum lines. She was despicable, both physically and emotionally, and a few screws loose in the head was just the tip of the iceberg.

"She's leaving with me. End of story. You've got five seconds to get moving before I start firing rounds. One, two…"

I reached for Hope, Angela pulling them back at the same time. "This is not a game!" she screeched. "Go. Now!"

Hope shook her head, silently pleading for me to follow Angela's orders. How could she expect that of me? How could she think I'd ever rescue her from Raul just to turn around and leave her in the hands of another monster?

"Hope. No," I vehemently argued. Tears slid from my eyes as defeat washed over me. I'd left Jax's gun in the room, tucked under the pillow in case I'd needed it overnight. I'd been careless to forget it this morning. Another reason why I never got involved. You lose your shit. You forget important stuff and errors are made. Costly mistakes, just like this. And there wasn't a damn thing I could do about it.

They backed away in unison, Angela's grasp tightening around Hope's throat. Garbled sounds came from her as she struggled to keep upright and move alongside her. Hope mouthed *'I love you'* as they disappeared around the corner and out of sight.

I continued staring in the direction they'd gone, waiting for her to reappear; for all of this to be nothing more than a bad dream. Crumpled in a heap, I let the tears continue to fall as I plotted my next move. This wasn't over. Not by a long shot.

46

"C'mon! Get up! We gotta move!"

Someone was shouting at me, but their face was nothing more than a haze through my clouded mind. *Hope*. She was gone. Tugging on my arm finally brought me out of my reverie.

"Blake!" the stern voice shouted. "Let's go!" Jax pulled me up, hooking my arm around his shoulders for support. I barely felt the tips of my toes bouncing on the stairs as he ran, my feet offering no assistance. The aggregate patio and smell of fresh cut flowers whizzed by in a blur as he ran across the lawn, getting us out of harm's way. Just on the other side of the shrubbery, he let go, my body hitting the ground with a jolting thud.

Jax paced as he spoke in a gravelly voice to someone on the other end of the phone. "Yes. Now. I don't know. Probably. I have an idea."

None of it made sense, but then again it didn't seem anything ever would. What the hell had happened? It had all been so fast that I didn't react. I couldn't. One-minute Hope was mine and I could finally see light at the end of the tunnel. The next it was all ripped away, leaving a searing burn in the middle of my chest. I stared at the dew-soaked ground, the wetness seeping into my jeans. It was cold and yet I felt nothing. Nothing but an emptiness I couldn't describe.

Jax hit the screen of his phone, shoving it back into his pocket. "Let's go, lover boy. Our ride will be here in a minute." Pulling me up again, Jax wasted no time in hoisting me over his back, taking off with ease, my two-hundred-pound body not affecting him in the least. He didn't even get winded as he hurried us through a pillar of trees and overgrown bushes, my body bouncing about haphazardly. Tree branches and loose twigs assaulted us both as he ran without thought. I hung on for dear life, letting him do what needed to be done. I certainly wasn't in the right frame of mind to be making any decisions.

My head was still clouded; overrun with thoughts of Hope and the danger she was in. Raul was a brutal man, capable of any number of things, but I knew he wanted her. In an extremely weird and uncomfortable way, that thought was consoling. It brought a teeny bit of relief, albeit skewed. Angela, on the other hand, was simply using her as a pawn. She was disposable, and I knew Angela wouldn't think twice about killing her at the first sign of trouble.

What felt like hours in my mind was only mere minutes. Two tops. Jax stopped, planting me back on my feet. I swayed to and fro as he looked on, his head tilting to the side, puzzled. "You gonna make it?"

"I feel sick," I grumbled, as I grabbed my stomach and emptied its contents.

He patted my back and looked around, listening carefully for signs that anyone had followed us. "Better?"

Jax was a man of few words and right now I appreciated that. "Yeah."

"Good. Let's keep moving. We've got another five miles or so before we make it to the back road. Billy is picking us up."

“Billy?” How the hell had he gotten in touch with Billy? And what the fuck was I gonna say to him? I’d left him and Johnny high and dry, alone in the hospital. I guess not much had changed after all.

“Yeah. Billy. Look,” he huffed, exasperated, “I’ll explain everything later. Right now, we don’t have time for this shit. Raul’s guys are gonna be on to us soon and trust me, Raul looks like one of Santa’s elves compared to these guys.”

That was all I needed to know. “Let’s pound pavement then.” I took off, steadying myself to a slow jog in an attempt to conserve energy. Five miles was no joke and truth be told, I’d let myself go over the course of the last several months.

Jax caught up in no time and together we weaved through the dense foliage. The further we went, the narrower the path became, causing us to run single file. My breathing began to accelerate as shin splints grappled their way through my legs. I began running slower and slower until I could barely see the back of his head. I could only imagine the smirk on his stupid face now.

Once I felt rested, I began running again, surpassing my earlier jog. *We’re the hell had he gone?* Jax was nowhere in sight. An uneasy feeling settled over me, wondering if this had been a set up after all. Were he and Angela in this together? My mind was put to ease when I saw Billy’s obnoxious truck ahead, both of the bastards leaned against it with a smile.

“Bought time you showed up, princess. Thought I was going to have to come and rescue you.” Billy grinned his usual asshole smile, casually reared back without a care in the world. If I didn't know him so well I might have even believed his cool and collected demeanor, but he wasn't fooling me. Not one bit. I knew everything about this man, including that if he appeared calm, he was anything but. Inside, he was losing his shit.

"Yeah, yeah, yeah," I mumbled. "Let's get outta here."

Jax and Billy occupied the front of the cab while I licked my wounds in the back. I could tell by their unspoken nods and shifting eyes they were silently communicating my inability to keep Hope safe. In hindsight I should've listened to Jax. Last night shouldn't have happened. I should've gotten Hope outta there instead of giving in to what I wanted. Part of me wasn't sorry. I'd never regret being with her, I couldn't. But I wasn't thinking, and it had cost her. It had cost us both.

Billy took the roads at an alarming rate, turning the vehicle whichever way Jax pointed him. Each second led me further and further away from where I wanted to be, but I had no doubt these guys had already worked out a plan. Apparently, they'd done a lot of talking, unbeknownst to me.

"Where we going?"

"You'll see," Billy replied. "Just hang on. We'll be there in a few minutes."

I closed my eyes, letting the memory of last night wash over me. The feel of Hope's skin against mine. The taste of her still lingering on my tongue. Suddenly, my sweet memories were tainted and replaced with fury. *Angela.* That nasty hag had my girl. The look on her face as she held that gun to Hope's head was burned into my brain. She was demented and down-right scary. Worst of all, she showed no fear. No remorse. No heart. My head shot forward, my eyes opening wide as I tried in vain to dispel the image from my mind. I couldn't think like that. Not yet. It wasn't too late. It couldn't be.

47

"Why are we here?" Slamming the truck door behind me, I followed the guys inside.

"Because we need to check on Johnny. And there's someone else here we need to see."

I thought about questioning him further, but there was no use. Billy's answers were short and to the point, meaning it was on a need-to-know basis. Guess I'd be finding out soon enough.

The smells and sounds coming from the sterile hospital filled me with dread. I hated these places. Billy of all people could appreciate that better than anyone. Lord knows I'd spent enough time in one while waiting for him to get better. A woman weeping in the waiting room, a doctor knelt down in front of her, was precisely one of the reasons I hated hospitals. Not a lot of good news came from conversations like that one. Of course, I'd thought a lot about Johnny. I wasn't completely heartless. The guy had done a lot for me; taken the brunt of Raul to help me win my girl back. I owed him my life. I knew that. But it still didn't mean that I wanted to be here.

Billy paused in front of his door. "Ready for this?"

"As I'll ever be." My shoulders slumped.

"Bailey isn't very happy with you, ya know?" Jax chimed in, grinning like a fool.

"And how exactly would you know that?"

He shrugged. "Intuition, princess. Now, in ya go!"

Johnny's unrecognizable face was the first thing I saw upon entering the room. The sheets were pulled to his waist, his broken ribs bearing white gauze and tape. His left wrist was in a cast, strategically placed on a stack of pillows to keep it elevated. His bruised brow and cheeks rose with his smile. "Bout time your ugly ass mug came to check on me."

I grinned back, feeling awkward. Bailey regarded me cautiously before standing and throwing her body into mine. Her fragile arms wrapped around my neck, burrowing her head in close. "Thank you for coming back. He's been worried about you."

I squeezed her gently and patted her back, thankful she hadn't hurled the uneaten tray of cafeteria food at me. "Thank you for not killing me," I joked.

Bailey wiped a few tears and then moved to the side, telling me to take the chair next to his bed. "We'll be outside. You two catch up for a bit," she insisted. "Billy, take me to get food. I'm starving."

Jax laughed as Billy gave her a hearty "Yes, ma'am!" The three of them departed the room, leaving an uncomfortable silence behind.

The plastic chair felt as uninviting as it looked, but I forced myself to sit, coming face to face with Johnny. I never knew what to say in circumstances like this. Did I joke around like usual? Should I act more serious given the situation? I had no clue as to what to do, so I started with the basics and hoped he'd take it from there.

"How ya feeling, cupcake?"

He winced as he repositioned himself. “Been better,” he grunted. “but not bad. You?”

I shrugged. “Been better.”

“I heard about Hope. Sorry things didn’t go according to plan at the fight.”

My head perked up. *He was sorry?* For what? I shook my head. “No. *I’m* sorry. For all this. For getting you in this mess in the first place. I should’ve gone after Raul myself.”

I stood angrily, needing some space, but Johnny grabbed my wrist before I could escape the awkwardness. “No. Don’t you dare apologize to me! I got involved on my own because I wanted to. Because I know what Raul does to those women. What he’s done to Bailey. So, don’t you dare fucking apologize to me.”

I wiped my hand over my face, at a loss. “I don’t deserve what you’ve done, and you certainly don’t deserve to be laid up and in pain.”

“I look that bad?” he laughed. “I thought I looked pretty badass laying here like this.”

“You look like you got the shit beat outta ya,” I razzed.

Johnny laughed at the same time he grabbed at his ribs. Obviously, it was too soon. “Shit. Sorry,” I moved to help, but he waved me away.

“Don’t need a nurse, dude. That’s Bailey’s job.” He waggled his eyebrows up and down.

“So, this thing with you guys,” I gestured, “it’s serious?”

Johnny exhaled loudly. “It’s still early, but yeah, I think it could be.”

A wide grin plastered my face. “That’s good, man. That’s real good. I’m happy for ya, brother. And I mean that.” I reached to shake his hand, which he took gratefully.

“Ya know,” he countered, “If I hadn’t gotten involved in your screwed-up life, I wouldn’t have met her. So maybe there’s a reason for all this. Maybe it was supposed to happen this way.”

I was uncomfortable with where this was headed. The air in the room was thick, just like I remembered in times past. I couldn’t handle it. I leaned forward, bracing myself on my knees. Sure, I seemed like a baby, but no one knew what I’d been through with Billy when he’d been shot, and we didn’t think he would make it. People didn’t have a fucking clue what that did to me, seeing my partner and friend laid up like that, knowing I hadn’t been able to do anything to stop it.

“Johnny, I…”

“I know. Billy told me.”

“Of course, he did.” I rose from the chair again, pacing the floor.

“I’m gonna get outta here, princess, so no tears for me. Besides, I think Bailey secretly likes taking care of me.” He winked, another joke hanging in the air, but I wasn’t up for taking the bait.

“Johnny, she’s gone.”

“Gone where?”

“I have no fucking clue. Angela’s got her.”

“Shit.”

"Quite." I squatted down, ready to hit the floor. I was so fucking tired, and I just wanted all this to go away. Just one damn day without drama and turmoil, and uncertainty.

"Well, guess I'd better quit milking this shit then, huh?"

"What?" I questioned.

He smiled again, an impish smile if I'd ever seen one. Then he did something I didn't expect. The bastard sat straight up in bed, no cries of pain whatsoever. Not even a whimper. When I moved to question him, he threw his hands in the air, knowing he'd been caught. "Just waitin' on you to come around and gravel a bit. We're good now."

"You son of a bitch," I laughed, moving to give him a hug.

"Ouch!" he wailed. "Just 'cause I'm better doesn't mean it doesn't still hurt. Easy, killer."

"Yeah, I outta kick your ass for carrying on, making me think you were a goner."

He looked at me with a puzzled look on his face. "A goner? Me? Nah," he waved off. "I'm too damn stubborn. Besides, who else would keep your sorry ass in line."

"True," I agreed.

"Well, let's get me outta here and then we'll go get your girl."

It surprised me just how simple he thought this was gonna be. Perhaps he didn't understand just how bat shit crazy Angela was. Before I could explain, the door opened.

"Ready to go?" Bailey winked as she passed by me and dropped a fresh set of clothes on the bed next to Johnny.

I turned, eyeing Jax and Billy. It was apparent they'd all been involved in this. "So, you knew?"

Billy opened his arms and shrugged. "Who do you think is giving them a ride?"

Bailey busied herself with packing Johnny's things, what few he had, while the guys and I helped steady him long enough to get dressed. The nurse had come in at some point during all the commotion and handed Bailey the care instructions for when we got him home. "I understand. Follow up Monday."

Once that bit of business was over we were free to go. "I'll grab a wheelchair."

"The hell you will," Johnny objected. "I'm walking outta here."

Bailey obviously didn't like the idea, but she had a point to prove so she let it go. "Alright, tough guy. Lead the way. Don't need you falling over me when you pass out."

He kissed her on the cheek and then hobbled on his way. I was surprised when Jax walked beside him, ready to catch him if need be. I watched carefully, still wary whether or not he had the best of intentions in mind. Billy seemed to trust him though, and I knew he was normally a good judge of character. For now, I'd let it go.

When we pulled up at the hotel, it hit me how long it had felt since I'd been here. Days felt like months. A hot shower and a soft bed is just what I needed to clear my head and get a fresh start in the morning.

Solemnly, we all made our way upstairs, Johnny looking worse for wear. There were a few times I wasn't sure he'd make it inside, but his stubbornness knew no bounds. Plus, he was trying to look macho in front of Bailey. It was a guy thing.

Before we were fully inside, my eyes caught a brunette who was wrapped around Billy, kissing the living daylights out of him. Just as I was ready to pry them apart, which would've only been possible with a crowbar, I realized who it was.

"Heather? When did you get here?"

"Good to see you, too, Blake." Heather gave me a warm hug and then pointed to the couch. "Sit. We all need to have a talk."

48

Stunned, I sat on the couch, staring at everyone still standing around me. Billy and Heather with their arms around one another; Jax, legs apart and hands folded behind his back, and Johnny leaning over the back of the chair, Bailey with her arm linked in the crook of his elbow. It was surreal to say the least.

You could've heard a pin drop. They all appeared to have something to say, something to add to the story, but none of them wanted to start. To say it felt unsettling was an understatement. Had something already happened to Hope?

"Really don't like being left outta whatever the hell is going on with you guys, so someone get to spilling the secret you all seem to be in on."

"Fine. I'll start." Heather sat next to me and took my hand in hers. "You okay, Blake?"

I nodded my head slowly, stilling myself for whatever was coming next. I was sure it had to be about Hope. That Billy had called in Heather for reinforcement.

"I know about Angela. Billy called a few nights ago, telling me I needed to get here. That you needed me."

"So, you hopped on a plane for that?"

"Absolutely." She never even hesitated. Not until the next part. "He told me everything. About Hope and Raul. How he kidnapped her. The horrible things he's done to the others." Heather reached over and squeezed Bailey's hand. Apparently, she really did know everything.

"And about Angela?" Uncertainty hung in the air and I briefly wondered if I'd said the wrong thing.

"My mother, you mean?"

"Yes, your mother."

Heather lowered her head, covertly wiping a tear from her cheek. "She's a horrible, loathsome person. I asked Billy to tell me everything. Not to sugar coat anything, or water it down. I've lived my whole life believing she was dead. And after Tom told me everything, I was happy that she was. I'm very sorry for her part in this; for what she's done to you and Hope. And to you, too, Jax."

He titled his head, barely acknowledging her words, but I knew he'd heard them. I imagine he felt embarrassed considering he initially had a part in this whole thing. Heather left me and approached him. I had forgotten they had a history together.

"Jax. I turned out okay, didn't I?"

"Yeah. You sure did, Birdy."

Birdy? A pet name? I wondered how Billy felt about that. I was given my answer when he made haste towards her, securing a protective arm around her waist.

"She turned out wonderfully. Didn't you, angel?"

Heather blushed as she leaned into Billy, her delicate hand still on Jax's shoulder. "I should've stopped all this years ago. If I had…"

Heather cut him off. "If you had, they would've still found a way to disrupt everyone's lives. We're going to figure this out, Jax. For all of us. And we're going to get

Hope back to you, Blake. I refuse to believe that it's just over. Look at you guys. Your heads hanging down in defeat. That's not the men I know so stop it. Now. No more pity parties and no more blame. From here on out, we're all in this together."

"Agreed," Johnny chimed in. Somewhere during Heather's heartfelt plea, he'd moved to the chair. Bailey looked relieved, as he was as white as a ghost.

"You're not in any shape to get involved in this right now, princess."

Johnny cut his eyes towards me. "That's a helluva thing for you to say. I'm already up to my eyeballs in this, so deal with it. Two days' tops and I'll be good as new." Bailey didn't look convinced, and neither was I, but a little positive thinking couldn't hurt.

"Okay. So, what now?"

Heather chewed her nail as she walked the length of the room, back and forth. "Jax, where would Angela take Hope? I mean, surely she wouldn't take her back to the compound, knowing we'd check there. Is there any place you can think of?"

"It's possible she's holding her at Raul's. I mean, her whole objective to getting Hope was for leverage with him. She wants him. She's *always* wanted him. Angela would want to be close to him, wherever he is. And he wouldn't leave his house at this point to go on a witch hunt. He'd send the guys out to do it."

"What guys?" Billy asked.

"The other fighters. That's where they stay. The girl's get stuck in the pits of hell with Angela as the ring leader, and the guys get gourmet meals and luxury. The damn dirty pigs. Makes no sense."

Everyone agreed in unison before a somber lull once again filled the room. "I know where they might be, if they aren't there." Bailey's timid voice cut through the silence.

Heather being the comforting one of the group placed an arm around her bare shoulder. "Bailey, we made need you in this. And I hate to ask given what you've been through. But do you think you can help us?"

Bailey shrugged insecurely. "I'll do what I can, but…."

"You're stronger than you know, Bailey. I see women like you every day at the shelter. Beaten down and abused. And just like them, that's only part of your story. You are so much more than what's happened to you, darlin. You believe that in here," she tapped her heart, "and everything will be just fine. I promise."

"Okay," Bailey agreed.

"And these strong, strapping men will never let anything happen to you. Especially this one." Heather nudged Johnny on his good side and gave him a wink. They, too, had history together. He grinned wide and gave her a squeeze.

"Good. So that parts settled. Now, where else might we find this mommy dearest?"

We brainstormed for a bit longer until Johnny looked like he would pass out from either sheer exhaustion or pain. Maybe both. "C'mon, I'll help you get the old man in bed."

Bailey and I each took an arm, bracing Johnny's large frame between ours. He started to argue, telling us he was perfectly capable of getting in the bedroom by himself, but one curt look from Bailey had him shutting his mouth. "Okay, babe. You can help." He threw his head back and laughed, choking on his own spit.

"See what happens when you try to be a smartass?" Bailey jested.

After much struggling, we managed to get him in the bed. Bailey had decided to lay with him, in case he needed anything during the night. I smiled, catching on quickly. She would've stayed with him regardless, but I'd done enough razzing for the day. "Okay, Bailey. Sleep well."

I shut the door behind me, giving them some peace and quiet, and joined the others on the couch who were still hatching out a plan. Jax had grabbed a pen and piece of paper and was jotting down directions, drawing mock scale places of where we should start.

"I don't want you anywhere near Angela. She's not sane, angel. She may be your mother, but the woman is a monster. You being her daughter is of no consequence to her. I won't let you put yourself in harm's way." Billy spoke sternly to Heather, but with a gentleness as well. He certainly had a way with her.

"Billy, I can more than take care of myself. You can't tell me I can't see my own mother! I have questions I need answered. After all these years, don't I at least deserve that?"

Billy huffed and rubbed the sleep from his eyes. "Angel, you deserve a world that gives you nothing but happiness.

That world doesn't include your mother. She isn't the cookie-baking, apron-wearing mother you remember. Trust me when I tell you this."

"Heather, I'm not trying to pick sides here, but Billy's right." Jax dropped his pen on the table and laced his fingers together. "When we were kids, there were a lot of things I witnessed. Things no child should ever have to see. And after you quit coming to the mansion, things got a lot worse. Your mother… Heather she became the worst of the worst. Things you don't even wanna know about."

"Well, let's see," she interjected, "I know about the drugs. How she helps Raul sell the women to the highest bidder. That she keeps them so high and strung out they barely know their own name. What else could there possibly be?"

Jax walked to the mini bar and grabbed a cold brew. Flicking the cap into the trash, he took a big swig of the golden liquid and proceeded with the many reasons Heather should stay clear of her mother. "Heather, your mom is… well, let's just say she can be even nastier than Raul. You remember when he kidnapped you? What he did to you?"

Billy lunged from the couch and grabbed Jax by his collar, pinning him against the wall. "Don't ever fucking talk about that. Do you know what that did to her? Any clue at all how she had to fight to get past that?"

"I know enough," Jax said coolly, removing Billy's hands from his shirt.

I stepped in, separating the two before it got physical. A pissing contest wasn't what any of us needed at the moment. "Alright guys, cool it. We're all on the same side here."

The two parted ways, but not before throwing daggers in one another's direction. Heather placed her hand over Billy's knee and squeezed. "I'm okay, Billy. I'm not made of glass, so quit treating me like I am. Jax, please continue."

Billy looked pissed and displeased, but this was bound to happen sooner or later. Best to get it all out now so when it came time for us to move, animosity and egos were outta the way. We had one shot at best to rescue Hope and I was not about to let these two assholes jeopardize it.

"She's not crazy, Heather. Angela knows exactly what she's doing. How in the world you turned out as well as you did is beyond me." Jax took another long pull from his beer, laughing to himself. "Remember when we'd run through the gardens at Victor's and pretend we were the king and queen of the land? Or when we'd sneak in the kitchen and steal milk and cookies before dinner? God, even then everything seemed normal, ya know? I mean, sure we knew shit was going on, but we could block it out. We were able to pretend, for a brief few hours, that shit wasn't real."

"I remember," Heather whispered.

"Then know that when I tell you this, it's to protect you. I always tried to keep you safe, Heather, and I failed. I fucking failed. But I will not let Angela or Raul get to you this time. You go see your mother and get your answers if you need to. But all that bad shit you think you're over will come back tenfold. She's evil. She's callous. She's manipulative. The woman has no soul. And Billy's right, she won't think twice about killing you if she feels you're a threat."

Heather sat quietly, letting Jax's words wash over her. I began to get nervous when she stayed silent longer than anticipated. She wasn't normally at a loss for words, but he seemed to have rendered her speechless.

"Angel, you okay?" Billy asked, concerned. He rubbed her arm gently and pulled her closer, her head landing limply on his shoulder. Jax moved closer as well.

"Heather, say something," he urged.

"I know she's evil. You can't do the things she's done and be anything less. But she's my *mother*, whether I like it or not. And I didn't have a choice in that, but I have a choice in this. I should see her. I must confront her. For myself. For Hope and Bailey," she argued directly to me. "Even for you Jax. I can see this eats away at you every day. You're not the same little boy I knew. You're hurting. You're guarded and rough. You're also incredibly sweet and kind, but you've got to let the past go. It's controlling you and sometimes confronting the problem helps that."

"I'm not looking to be fixed!" Jax argued, loudly. He sprang from the chair and downed another beer. "Don't go looking to save me, honey. You wanna talk to your mom, fine. I'll take you myself. But don't put me in the middle of your love-conquers-the-world fest. Don't want it and sure as hell don't need it."

Jax threw his empty beer bottle in the trash and walked out the door, slamming it behind him.

Heather broke down in tears, Billy right there to pick up the pieces as usual. "I'm gonna go after him," I murmured.

Billy nodded and continued cooing in Heather's ear, trying to calm her.

"Jax, wait!" I called down the hall. He stopped at the elevator, punching the button repeatedly when the doors didn't open soon enough.

"Not in the mood for company, princess."

"Good. Neither am I. But I am in the mood for a drink. Buy ya a beer?"

"Yeah. Sounds good, man. Thanks."

We made our way to the hotel bar, deducing it was best to stick close by. I ordered our beers as we sat on our stools, drinking in complete and total silence. It was the perfect end to a shit day.

49

"You shouldn't be sitting here, sharing a beer with me like we're friends." Jax's low baritone voice carried through the empty bar, easily disrupting the TV announcer and the hockey game.

"True," I agreed, "it is an unlikely combo. But, you helped me out. Hell, you tried to help Hope. I owe you more than a drink or two for that."

Jax scoffed. "Not if you knew…."

"Knew what?" My easy-go-lucky tone was quickly dissipating. I had a feeling whatever he was about to say wasn't something I was going to like.

"Forget it." He threw his head back, downing every drop before slamming the bottle back on the bar. "Gonna need something a bit stronger. Barkeep," he motioned. "Shot glass and a bottle of whiskey."

The bartender gave me a questioning look and I nodded. He sat the clear shot glass in front of Jax and began pouring the golden liquid before moving to place the bottle back behind the bar. Jax grabbed his arm with one hand, the bottle with the other.

"I tell ya what," Jax squinted his eyes to read the man's nametag. "Mike. Just leave this with me so you can go on your merry little way. Don't need you pouring my drinks for me."

"It's fine. I'll watch him." The man looked unsure but shrugged his shoulders and busied himself with cleaning glasses.

"Wanna tell me what your problem is?"

"Nope," he replied, emphatically.

"Okay. How 'bout this? We sit here drinking our problems away in silence until you're ready. That sound good?"

"Fine by me. But neither of us are gonna be walking outta here on our own two legs, cause I ain't talking." Jax grabbed the bottle and poured a shot, gulping it down with ease. He poured a second and a third, repeating the process.

"Maybe you should slow down."

"Maybe you should mind your own business." Shot number four and five went down the same as the others, except after five, his lips pulled back over his imperfectly white teeth as he struggled to keep it down. If he wanted to drink until he was sick, who was I to stop him?

"So, tell me about your time with Hope. She's pretty closed off, huh?" I elbowed him mockingly, trying to get him to loosen up.

Jax huffed, seeming content with our no talking agreement. I, on the other hand, had a feeling he had a lot to say and I wanted to hear it. The old saying keep your friends close and your enemies closer was true. Maybe he was liquored up just enough that he'd start telling me what I wanted to know.

"She's a kid. Too stupid to know what's happening most of the time. But she was smart in trying to keep to herself. The other girls didn't like her too much." He snickered and downed another. This time he began swaying on the stool.

"Easy, killer," I joked. "So, why did they dislike her?"

"Raul's pet."

"Oh," I replied. "What did they do to her?"

"Just acted like bitches. Angela egged it on and encouraged it. Raul put a stop to it. Now she's got you and life is fucking great."

"You got a thing for her, cupcake?"

Jax guffawed. "Um, no. Women are too damn complicated."

"They are, but when you find *the one*, she's worth it."

"Yeah, well, you and Billy can have that life if ya want. Hell, even Johnny looks like he's been snared. So, good for all of ya, but I'll not be joining that club."

"Suit yourself." I was still nursing my beer, being careful to keep my wits about me. "But if you want my opinion…"

"I don't," Jax interjected, dryly.

"Well, all the same I'm giving it to you, so shut up. You'd make any girl feel lucky to be with you. I mean, you've got the looks. I've seen the way girls fall over themselves to get to you at the gym."

"I can *get* a girl. I can certainly get a girl to sleep with me. And that's all I'm interested in. Believe me when I say that's all they want, too. I'm not boyfriend material."

"If you say so." I kept pushing and pushing, knowing he was going to blow any minute. I wasn't wrong.

"What the fuck you want from me, man? Damn! I like women, okay? I fuck them. Sometimes because they ask for it, sometimes even when they don't. Alright? That what you wanna hear? Ask Hope if you don't believe me."

I jumped from my barstool, sending it backwards and crashing to the floor. Jax did the same as we squared off, toe to toe. I knew it. I fucking knew he'd done something to her.

"What. Did. You. Do?" I gritted. My hands clenched into fists, my breathing accelerated, heart thumping erratically, I stared down the drunken beast in front of me. "Start. Talking."

He grinned, mocking me. "You wanna know what I did to your precious little Hope? I gave her exactly what she wanted. I did everything to her I could think of and more, and she fucking loved it. She's not as innocent as you think she is. Another reason I don't trust women. They're all the same."

Jax's legs wobbled as he swayed from side to side. It was helpful given what I was about to do, but I was so damn angry I didn't need it. I reared back, punching him square in the jaw with everything I had. His head snapped back, and he stumbled, grabbing the ledge of the bar for support. The few patrons inside gasped in horror as they watched the scene unfold. Women were screaming for us to stop, the men egging it on, hoping for a blood bath. This was Vegas after all, and a free show is what they wanted. Couldn't disappoint them, now could I?

My heavy boots thudded against the carpet as I stomped his direction. I threaded my hand around his jacket and bunched it in my fist, landing blow after blow to his face. "Don't you ever fucking talk about her like that again! I'll kill you!"

Jax just laughed. The harder I hit, the more blood that oozed, he continued cackling as if he didn't feel a thing. It only pissed me off even more. The next thing I knew, someone was behind me pulling on my arms, yelling for me to stop. I didn't. I shrugged them off and kept going, out for revenge.

"Blake, stop!" Billy kept screaming, but it wasn't until Heather stepped in front of my fist that reality came back. I was a crazed madman and almost hit her.

"You're lucky you stopped. If you would've hit her, you'd have dealt with me. Now what the hell happened?"

"He… he." I braced my hands on my knees, gasping to regain control of my ragged breathing. "Hope. He…" I couldn't even bring myself to say it.

"Calm the hell down, man. It's all gonna be fine. Let's talk this out. Let him explain. Maybe it's not what you think."

"It's exactly what I fucking think, Billy. You don't know. You weren't here. You didn't hear what he said."

He crossed his meaty arms over his chest and waited. Looking over my shoulder, he watched as Heather tended to Jax, wiping the blood from his face with a napkin. "For what it's worth, I don't trust the son of a bitch either. But he's helped us this far. And whether I like it or not, he seems to have a soft spot for her," he nodded. "He might be our ticket to getting in. So, for now," he spoke sternly, "keep your mouth shut and your hands to yourself. When this is over, do whatever the hell you want. Heather needs answers, she's gonna get them. Don't blow this for either one of them."

Of course, he was right. He was always right. Didn't mean I didn't want to put a bullet right between his eyes. "Fine. I'll leave him be. Just keep him outta my sight."

I walked off, leaving the three of them there. I didn't care what happened to him. All I cared about was Hope. What he'd done to her. Hell, what Angela was doing to her right now. I wasn't waiting around for plans and schemes. Enough of this shit. I was going after my girl, and anyone who stood in my way would be nothing more than collateral damage.

I pulled my keys from my pocket, knowing I shouldn't get on my bike. I felt certain I could make it though; the driving force being Hope. I had to get to her. Tonight. Now. No matter what it cost me.

50

The cool night air felt unseasonably cold against my skin. A chill in the air lead the way to what I was sure was going to be just as chilling. Raul's place was huge; more than huge, and the number of rooms I'd have to check were numerous. I remembered Jax saying something about a basement. Perhaps that's where I should look first.

Even thinking his name caused anger to pulse through my veins. I pushed the throttle a little more, barreling me down the highway to the outskirts of town. Opposite the direction of the compound, towards the lavish homes that sat just on the other side of the dust bowl dessert. I gunned it, my speedometer pushing closer to eighty and then ninety. I knew Billy would be on my trail soon enough, and I didn't want him involved. I didn't want any of them involved.

I cut the headlight of my motorcycle just before I rounded the last curve to the drive. I also cut the engine, silencing Daisy's natural and unmistakable rumble. It was hard to miss. I may have been stupid for coming here alone, but I wasn't foolish enough to add to the already dangerous territory on which I was treading. I pushed the bike the last fifty feet or so, hiding it behind a row of bushes just to the left of the lawn. I would sneak in the same way I'd done before, feeling certain if there was a doorway to a deep, dark dungeon, it would be in that area.

The same men I'd seen previously were at their usual post, walking the lit patio and surrounding pergola. I waited in the shadows, careful to not make a peep. My gun hidden in the back of my shorts pushing against my spine reminded me just how serious this was. It also brought to mind that it was no match for three men with assault rifles. I had limited rounds, only one spare clip in my pocket. I would have to be sparing, only firing when absolutely necessary. Ideally, not using it at all would be best, but I was almost positive that wasn't a realistic probability.

The men chatted for a while, discussing everything from the weather to the latest bimbo in Raul's bed. I wanted to gag at some of the things they were saying, but considering the source of their information, I wasn't the least bit surprised. My ears perked up when I heard one of them mention Hope.

"Did you see that one earlier? Hot damn, I'd like a shot at that."

"Yeah, good luck. And don't let Raul hear you say that. That's his girl."

"Really? Cause she doesn't seem all that interested in him, and Angela made it pretty clear that *she's* Raul's girl. Either way, dude has more women than anyone I know. His bedroom might as well have a revolving door."

They laughed like all of this was just a fucking game and not people's lives at stake. I hadn't exactly expected that Raul surrounded himself with outstanding men, but even so it was hard to hear some of the things they were saying.

"The blonde? That the one you're referring to?" another man asked.

"The one and only. Did you see the rack on that girl?"

"Hard to miss. Hard to miss," he agreed.

"Like I said, just don't let Raul hear you talking about her. He may have other women coming and going, but Hope's the one he wants. He's pretty taken with her."

"I hear Jax is, too. Probably why he's gone missing."

"Missing? More like running. Raul said he's a dead man if he shows up. Won't be long til the guys are looking for him."

For the briefest of seconds, I felt sorry for Jax. I knew Raul's brainwashing tactics better than anyone and saying no to the guy just wasn't an option if you valued your life. I imagine it was the same with these losers. They didn't have much of a choice, not if they wanted to live. No matter though, some things were unforgiveable. What Jax had done to Hope was just one of many.

It seemed like hours passed before they finally departed. It was now or never. I ran, humped over, my knees almost skimming the grass. I made my way to the patio doors, peering inside. It seemed void of staff, so I turned the knob, listening for the click as it opened without pause. I waited for alarms to sound, but fortunate for me, nothing happened. I closed it gently behind me, moving quickly around the marble island and pantry. Four doors stood out to me, any one of them possibly being the one I needed. Quietly but quickly, I opened each one, peering inside. First was a pantry, second a storage room, the third a washroom. The last door had to be it. My palms were sweating and my heart racing. I reached around to my back, pulling my gun from the waistband of my shorts. I turned the knob quietly, an immediate smell of machine oil and dirt filling my nostrils, almost taking me to my knees. What the hell was going on down there? A set of iron steps led the way down, my boots making scuffing noises as I hit each one. I called for Hope, though my voice was no more than a loud whisper. I couldn't afford to give away my position. It was dark with only small hanging oil lamps lighting the way. It reminded me of Dracula's castle, an eerie feeling taking over. "Hope! Are you down here?"

I had reached the bottom, my boots sloshing in the wetness of the mucky ground. The dampness bore a musty scent, not helping with the rumbling happening in my already sensitive stomach. "Hope?" I called again. Still nothing. I grabbed a lantern from the wall, turning the knob to brighten the glow. I moved it about, holding my arm up overhead to get a good look. Shackles hung from the wall, chains with clamps laid on the floor. This was definitely the type of place Angela would've brought her. One small window caught my eye, bars obscuring any possibility of entrance, or exit. It was ground level, and barely wide enough for a small animal to fit through. But it was enough of a makeshift peephole that I could peer outside. I took my arm, knocking away the dirt and grime. I could hear voices, but they sounded faint enough that I wasn't worried about being seen. It wasn't until Raul's voice carried through the thick glass that I became alert.

"What have you done?" he shouted. "If you've harmed one hair on her head, so help me…"

"Why do you want *her*?" Angela whined. "I can give you what you want, baby. Haven't I always taken good care of you?"

I almost vomited in my mouth, thinking about it. She made a move to put her arms around his neck, but Raul caught her wrist, shoving her away roughly.

"No. I want nothing to do with you personally. You knew the deal from day one. I kept you alive when my father wanted you dead. I didn't do it for me. I did it because you were valuable to my business at the time. But let's not blur the lines here. Our time together has come to an end, Angela. Now you tell me where the fuck you have her, or else…."

"You'll what?" she countered. "You'll do nothing. And I tell ya something else. Until you learn to treat me with the respect I deserve, you'll *never* see your precious Hope again. She's a whore like the rest of them."

Raul's hand made contact with Angela's cheek, smacking her hard enough that she stumbled backwards. Shock crossed her hardened features as she moved to hit him back. Again, he grabbed her wrist, digging into her skin with his lanky fingers. "Don't cross me, Angela. It won't end well for you. You have twenty-four hours to bring Hope to me, or there will be a bounty on your head."

Raul stepped back two paces and straightened his suit jacket, completely composing himself as if nothing had happened. He walked away in true Raul fashion; head held high with an air of arrogance. I lowered the flame on the lantern, hoping Angela wouldn't see the faint glow through the miniscule opening. She stood, stock-still and stunned. She never even glanced in my direction. I continued watching her, hoping to observe which direction she went. Just as I was ready to throw in the towel, she moved slowly backwards, disappearing to the left side of the property, into the woods. Bailey's words came to mind as I remembered her talking about a small rickety shack just off the grounds. That had to be it.

I made my way up the iron stairs, shaking the muck from my shoes. The house seemed quiet as usual, so I carefully opened the door, peering outside. I heard voices, faint as they were, and I knew time was limited. I made a run for it, praying to all that was holy I'd make it out and be able to catch up to Angela in time. She was in heels, so surely, she wouldn't get too far.

I cleared the lawn with ease and kept running until I was several feet into the thick trees. I stopped and listened, hoping to hear any signs of limbs breaking or leaves rustling. Seconds passed without a peep, but then a loud crunching noise came from just ahead. Could've been nothing more than an animal, but I'll be damned if I didn't check it out. I moved lithely through the dense greens, and the fog that was beginning to settle across the leafy foliage. Branches tore through my shirt and scratched at my face, but I continued, not letting anything deter me.

Having gone several hundred feet, I once again stopped, shielding myself behind a tree. Listening. Watching. The darkness had settled, leaving an almost blanketed feel across the wooded area. The only light I had was from my cell phone, but I refused to use it and give myself away. I continued walking the same direction at a brisk pace, putting my arms out in front of me to feel my way through the black night. The trek felt long and hopeless as nothing stood out to me. No shack. No light. No Angela. "Dammit!" I turned in circles, feeling lost. I'd traveled further than I realized, Raul's mansion no longer visible. I had two options. Three really. Give up and spend the night here, which didn't seem likely. I was tired of giving up and settling for complacency. My second option was to continue, hoping I'd come across something, and my last option was to head back, putting myself smackdab in the middle of Raul's place, potentially getting myself killed. It was kinda a no-brainer. I kept going, determined to find this place Bailey had talked about. Hope had to be there. She just had to be.

51

I trudged up ahead, careful to keep my footing over the rocky terrain. Everything felt as if it were closing in; the surrounding mountains feeling as if they were sucking me further into a hole. Rocks and broken chunks of earth made it almost impossible to navigate. I needed to be careful. Injuring myself wouldn't be good, especially for Hope. How in the hell Angela had passed through here in heels was beyond me. Perhaps there was a trail, or some other paved way I wasn't familiar with. No matter now, as I was this far into it.

Small hills and valleys dipped and curved, turning me this way and that. It wouldn't be hard for a person to get lost, especially in the dark. I was careful to stay as straight as I could, making the return easier. Lose, stray pebbles shifted beneath my boots, causing me to slip. I steadied my hands, catching myself just before I wiped out. "Shit!" I cursed low. I dusted myself off, needing a light to lead the way. Against my better judgement, I pulled my cell phone from my pocket. No signal, of course, but the flash light app would be enough. I turned it on, keeping it pressed mainly against my thigh. Its glow was rather bright in the blackness of night. I shielded it just enough, turning it ever so slightly to the ground. It wasn't great, but it was enough. There were other things to worry about, too. Things like scorpions and snakes. Rocks were the least of my worries.

I don't know how far I had been. At this point, walking was the only option. There was no way to run. The further I went, the worse it got. Rocks turned into boulders, small shrubbery into giant pines. The temp also seemed to be dropping. My thin tee did little to shield me from the dampness of the misty fog. Coyotes howled in the distance, adding to the overwhelming creepiness, but I'd come too far to turn back now.

A few climbs up, faint lights greeted me. Nestled behind a row of large pines sat a rickety shack, just like Bailey had said. It couldn't have been as big as a small bathroom, a one-room cabin. And secluded enough that Raul may not even be aware of where it sat. He gave Angela 24 hours to return Hope. The question was; who was I more likely to win against? Angela was cunning and callous, but she was cocky, making her more prone to making a mistake. Raul was calculating, but careful. I'd hedge my bet with Angela.

I tip-toed closer, my chest tightening with every step. Twigs crunched beneath my weight, pebbles turning to dust. I peered around, and seeing no one in sight, I made a bee line for the small framed window. Crouching down, I peered through the dingy glass, sneaking a look inside. Angela appeared through a doorway, rubbing a towel over her wet hair, but Hope was nowhere to be found. I moved and situated, gaining optimal clarity of every single nook and cranny in the place. She wasn't here. My shoulders dropped in defeat as my body shook with anger. I should bust in there and take Angela down, but I needed her alive. I needed her to lead me to Hope, so I'd wait it out.

My legs gave way from sheer exhaustion, my body both physically and mentally exhausted. This game of cat and mouse was beyond comprehension; that people could be so cruel as to do this, especially to someone like Hope. She didn't deserve this, and I didn't deserve her.

The night lingered, bringing the cool air down to an uncomfortable chill. My teeth chattered as I wrapped my arms around myself for warmth. What I wouldn't give for a shot of whiskey right now. Jax came to mind; the bar we were sitting in just hours ago. What he said. What I did. It kept replaying in my mind, over and over. Jax had never said the words outright, but he didn't need to. He'd raped Hope, of that much I was sure. So why was he helping us now? Why was Hope so eager to work with him? To set Raul up. None of it made sense to me. And why the fuck was I sitting her like a broken-hearted fool? This wasn't the end. Not by a long shot.

I sprung to my feet, once again peering through the window. Angela was stretched out on the couch, one arm thrown over her eyes, without a care in the world. Well, she was about to have one.

I walked cautiously across the wooden floor of the porch. Just as I figured, the door was locked. Even Angela wasn't stupid enough to leave it open, especially with Raul's threats. Lucky for me I was good at picking locks. Occupational hazard or happy accident, depending on how you looked at it. Quietly, I jimmied the lock while slightly turning the knob, waiting for the click. Didn't take long as this wasn't my first breaking and entering.

Through the curtains I could see Angela was still lying on the couch. She hadn't moved a muscle. I pulled my gun once again, keeping it trained on her sleeping form. Shuffling gingerly, I moved closer, putting it flush with her forehead, right between her eyes. How easy it would've been to pull the trigger, but lucky for her, it wasn't her time. Not yet at least. Her eyes widened immediately, staring at me in what could only be described as horror.

Guns had that effect on people, especially spineless assholes like Angela.

"Where is she?"

"Who?" Her voice trembled, and I smelt the faint stench of urine. She must've peed herself.

"You know who. And I'm not playing games with you. It's over. This," I waved my hand around, "hold you think you have over Raul. The girls. Feeling indispensable. It's all over."

"Raul has Hope. Haven't you heard? He's gonna make an honest woman outta her." Angela laughed drunkenly, hiccupping and wiping spittle on her arm.

"Don't fucking lie to me." I dug the gun harder into her head. "I heard you. I heard him. I know you have her. However, unlike Raul, I'm not giving you twenty-four hours. You won't last that long. Now. Where. Is. She?"

Angela sat up, still eyeing me cautiously. "Fine. I'll take you to her. But you have to do something for me."

"Lady, and I use that term loosely, you seem to be forgetting that I'm the one holding the gun. I'm holding the cards. And I damn sure ain't doing you any favors. Now," I motioned, "get dressed and take me to Hope. Last time I'm gonna be nice about it."

"Fine." Angela stomped into the other room, me hot on her heels. "Wanna watch?" she asked, seductively.

"Hell no!" I winced. "But I am keeping an eye on you because I don't trust you. Seriously, get moving. Wasting precious time here."

She huffed and puffed but did as I asked without hesitation. “Where’s your car?”

“Not here,” she snarled. “How the hell do you think I’d get a car in this hellhole?”

Right. Forgotten that part. “How the hell did you get here so quick anyhow? I was right behind you.”

“Trail cuts off to the side. What? You went through the fucking dessert and rocks to get here? Desperate much?”

“You have no idea,” I quipped. “And you have no idea what a desperate man in love with a gun will do, but I fucking promise you, you are about to find out. My patience is running thin, Angela. I’m not here for pleasantries. I damn sure ain’t here to make friends.”

“And they say you’re one of the nice ones.”

“Not even close,” I deadpanned. “You have no clue what I’m capable of. Trust me when I tell you, you don’t want to find out.” Anger bubbled to the surface. I could physically feel my skin getting hotter and hotter. Wasting any amount of time with Angela was time I didn’t have.

“Again. Fine. Let’s go.” She grabbed a flannel shirt from the couch and wrapped it around her waist. I followed her outside, keeping her close.

“Try anything and it’s lights out for you. Understood?’

“Understood,” she laughed. “You know, you think you’re the big bad wolf, but you really aren’t. I can see why Hope is so into you. Talks about you all the time. Even in her sleep.”

"I know what you're trying to do, and it won't work. Keep walking." This time I had the gun at her back, pressing against her spine. She didn't argue with me. And I *did* know what she was trying to do. Diversion. Classic line of defense for anyone, but I couldn't give into it. I couldn't think about it. One wrong move and this gun would be pointed at me. Only difference is, Angela wouldn't think twice about pulling the trigger. I wouldn't either except I needed her at the moment. She was nothing more than a means to an end. She'd serve her purpose then I'd throw her to Raul. Let him take care of her. It was of no consequence to me.

52

Angela led the way to her car, tree brush smacking me in the face as she easily ducked out of the way. It was apparent she knew this hellhole like the back of her hand. "Over there," she pointed.

She tossed me the keys, but I threw them right back. "Oh no, you're driving. Last thing I need is for you grabbing at the wheel and running us off the road."

"How do you know I won't just do that anyways?"

I laughed loudly. "Because you aren't that selfless. You want Raul and you can't have him if you're dead. Besides," I added, "you aren't through making everyone's life a living hell, including your daughter, Heather."

"Leave her outta this," Angela hissed.

She shot me a sideways glance, her eyes as bottomless as a black pit. None of this had gone according to her plan. She was no different than Raul. She liked to play games, but only if it was by her rules. I'd thrown her off track; off guard, and she didn't know how to deal other than buck up.

"Like you did all those times you decided to play whore in front of your daughter? What about selling her out? Ya, that should earn you fucking mother of the year," I scoffed.

"You know nothing about me," she quipped with a scowl.

"I know enough. More than I'd like. You're trash, Angela. Pure and simple. And when I'm through with you, I'm throwing you to the wolves, just like you did to your daughter. Only this time the wolf is Raul, and he's far more dangerous than anything you'll meet in these woods."

Angela turned from a crimson shade of red to pale white, as if she'd seen a ghost. Perhaps for the first time since all this shit started, she finally figured out her odds and they weren't good. She was scared, as she should be.

I opened my door, waiting for her to get in the driver's side. "Try running and I'm not above shooting you in the back. Plenty of places out here to hide a body."

Once we were seated inside, I buckled up. I wasn't a stickler for safety, as evident by my constant need for all things adrenaline, but I had no doubt she'd make this a ride from hell if she could. I kept my gun dug into her side; a polite reminder that I held the power. One wrong move, I wouldn't hesitate.

Silence hung thick within the confines of the car, the engine sounding a dreadful lull as she took corner after corner at an alarming rate. I kept my mouth shut, praying to all that was holy we'd make it in one piece. Perhaps this wasn't the best idea after all.

Almost an hour into the drive, the sun went down completely over the horizon, giving way to the blackness of night. Although a blur, the area started looking more and more familiar. She was taking us to the compound.

"I told you not to mess with me," I gritted. "Why are we here. Even you aren't stupid enough to bring Hope here."

"There's places here that Raul has no clue about."

I gave her an incredulous look. "You expect me to believe that? Raul knows everything about his investments, and this dump is no different."

"You think I'm dumb? How do you think I got to where I am?"

"By spreading your legs," I deadpanned, and she laughed. "Just calling it like I see it."

"Raul isn't the only one who has secrets to keep. I have a few of my own. Where Hope is being held is just one of many." A slimy smirk spread across her ashen complexion, causing my stomach to turn.

Angela drove to the back of the lot, cutting the lights just before reaching the gates. She shut her door lightly and I did the same. "If you're setting me up, sure I might die, but not before I put a bullet in your brain," I whispered, hastily.

She rolled her eyes. "I got it, big man. Calm down."

Angela pulled a key from her pocket and told me to follow her. Just off the path, obscured behind heavy brush, was a metal door. The rusty lock echoed in the dead of night, the tines protesting with each turn of the key. I looked around, my eyes searching the dark for any sign of movement.

The door gave way, with the faint glow of lanterns leading the way down a narrow hallway to a set of stairs. They were steep and narrow, and not nearly wide enough for my large boots. I had to step sideways to keep from tripping. The further we went, the more the stench of death greeted us. I knew without a doubt that others had entered here but hadn't been fortunate enough to make it out. The thought that Hope had been held here all this time made my blood boil.

"Move faster," I ordered, my voice thick as I tried in vain to hold my breath.

Angela glared at me over her shoulder. "Almost there. Patience, lover boy."

"My patience is running thin…"

Angela stopped short, almost causing me to run into the back of her. "Here we are," she chimed, almost in a sing-song voice. How any human being could derive such pleasure in harming others was beyond me, but there was no doubt in my mind that Angela thrived on it.

She opened what I assumed was the last barrier between myself and Hope, but I was wrong. A large, circular room came into view, eight separate doors lining the perimeter. The cinder block was stained with blood and from the smell of it, urine. No windows, as we were obviously underground. I began to cough, the stench becoming too much. Angela just laughed.

"So much for being a tough guy." Her head fell backwards as her shoulders shook with laughter.

The cocking of my gun brought her back to reality. "I'm not playing with you anymore. Where. Is. Hope?"

"I'd like to know the same thing," a heavily accented voice boomed from behind us.

Angela once again turned white as a ghost, the words sticking in her throat.

53

"You've been lying to me quite a bit, it seems." Raul laced his hands behind his back, walking a slow circle around her. "And here I thought you could be trusted. You know, I tried to warn my father about you. Tried to tell him you were nothing but a dirty whore, but for some reason he kept you around."

As soon as he stopped, he violently and quickly grabbed a handful of her hair, jerking her head back to look at him. "I want to be sure my face is the last thing you see," he mocked. "You should have known after all these years not to cross me, púta." Raul drew his hand back, ready to deliver a blow, when my hand caught his wrist in mid-air.

"When she gives Hope to me, you can do whatever you want with her. Until then, she remains unharmed."

"You seem to forget, Blake, that you're on my turf." Raul waved his hand in the air, never taking his eyes from mine. Within seconds, two larger men flanked him, ready to strike on cue.

"You want Hope alive just as much as I do," I reasoned. "If Angela's gone, that ain't gonna happen for either of us. Thought you were smarter than that." Taunting him was a gamble, but it was a rule of the job. Never let them see you sweat. Never let them think they had the upper hand.

I gestured my arms, indicating the surrounding doors. We had no clue which one Hope was in, if any, nor did we know if any of this was a setup. This *was* Angela we were talking about.

"Deal," he gritted. "But after this is over, once I have her, you're dead." His eyes bore into mine, never wavering on his threat. I knew he wouldn't hesitate. We went back too far, had been through too much for him to let me walk outta here alive. And, since it was three against one, I knew I didn't stand a chance. The important thing was getting Hope out and to safety. If I could manage that, I didn't care what happened to me.

Raul still had Angela in his grasp. "Open the door, Angela. Now! And the right one, or this is gonna be over sooner rather than later."

The rumble of motorcycles closed in. Raul motioned with his head for beefcake one and beefcake two to go and investigate. I knew it was Jax and Billy, perhaps even Johnny, though I knew he was in no shape to be riding. They took the stairs two at a time, pulling their weapons from their holsters.

Now was my chance. Raul was distracted, and Angela was panicked, trying to figure a way outta this. I quickly drew my gun away from Angela and aimed it right at the temple of Raul. I had to give the bastard credit, he never flinched.

"Pull the trigger, Blake. I dare you. This place will be swarming in a matter of seconds."

"I don't think so. We're too far underground."

A brief look of terror crossed his face but was quickly replaced with stoicism. Shouting and the sound of thudded footsteps caught all our attention, coming from the stairwell. I didn't know who was coming, but whoever it was, there was a whole lot of them. I didn't know if I should turn and look or keep my focus on Raul, but eventually the latter won out.

I heard gunfire and smelled the distinct odor of lead. The two henchmen from earlier tumbled down the stairs, where they both landed haphazardly, blood pooling around their dead bodies. From the corner of my eye, I saw two larger men and a woman enter the sparse space, guns drawn and aimed at my two adversaries.

"You, in here," Billy ordered Raul. He had a personal beef with him, one I would gladly let him handle. He wanted revenge; revenge for what he'd done to Heather. He wanted to defend her honor, and as much as I loathed the piece of shit, there's no way I was taking that away from my friend.

As if Billy hadn't said a word, Raul released Angela, giving her a less than gentle shove away from him. "Heather," he mused with a devious smile. "You're looking well, my love."

"Don't speak to her," Billy said, gritting his teeth, spittle flying from his lips. He grabbed Raul, pinning his arms behind him, painfully. He winced as Billy pulled so hard that Raul had to come up on his toes to lessen the grip. Heather approached him cautiously. She glanced at Billy, making sure he had him secure. This had been a long time coming, no doubt, and as hard as it was, I knew she needed to do this. Billy did too.

As she got closer, I noticed Jax had stepped in line with her, keeping a protective arm on her back. He wasn't letting her do this alone and as much as I hated the man, I had to admire him, too.

"You can do this, Heather. I'm right here," Jax whispered. "He ain't gonna touch ya."

I saw Heather falter for only a split second before she put her mask back in place, and approach him fearlessly. Once she was almost toe-to-toe with him, she spit in his face.

Raul laughed. "That all you got, *doll*?"

"You don't deserve anything else. You sure as hell don't deserve any more of my time." Heather began to turn but stopped short. "Actually, I do have something to say. I have spent the last year of my life, looking over my shoulder. I've been afraid of the dark and being by myself. I question every noise and every shadow spooks me. But ya know what? Never again. After today, I won't give you a second thought. You will never again haunt my sleep or occupy my thoughts. You are nothing, Raul. You are *nothing.*"

Heather walked away, and as promised, she never looked back. She knew Billy had him, but she also knew Raul was a chapter of her life that was now closed. She could finally move on. She thought of Lauren and how proud she'd be, and Heather couldn't wait to get home and tell her. But first, one more thing to deal with.

Angela stood in the corner, her eyes wide as saucers. True to fashion, she bolted from the corner and began to cry. Victim was the name of her game, after all, but luckily Heather was too damn smart to fall for it.

"My baby!" Angela wailed. "Oh, Heather! Thank God you're alive, baby. You don't know the awful things that man has done to me."

She headed straight for Heather, but Jax was quicker. He stood between them and crossed his arms. "You'd really keep me from her? She needs me!" Angela begged. "I'm her mother!"

Jax scoffed. "You don't get to say a damn word. You're gonna go in there," he motioned to a door, "and you're gonna sit the fuck down and let *her* talk. Then, when she's done, you deal with me."

Angela straightened, her perfect façade carefully back in place. "Um, guys, there's still the matter of Hope," I reminded. "Angela goes nowhere til I get my girl."

"Of for fucks sake," she huffed, throwing a key at me. "She's through that door and down the hall. Follow the stench of pee. Should be easy enough."

"You mess with me…"

Jax eyed me. "Go get her. I got this." He nodded, and something passed between us. Some unspoken bro-code. For the first time since this whole shit storm started, I trusted the guy. I nodded back and sprinted in the direction Angela had sent me.

54

Their shouts faded as a I ran further down the narrow corridor. Angela wasn't wrong about the putrid smells, but I doubt it was coming solely from Hope. There was no way. This stench had been here for years; years of torture and even death. No telling what the FBI would dig up on the compound once all of this was over. The thought made me think of George, and that I needed to get in touch with him, but that could wait a bit longer. I was already ignoring orders and any protocol the agency had went out the window weeks ago. I could wait and get my ass chewed later. Right now, I needed to get to my girl.

I called out to her. "Hope!" Faint cries came from just feet away, and I knew I was getting closer. "I'm here, baby. Hold on!"

Pounding came from the other side of the door, causing relief to flood my whole body. I'd found her. She was okay. *We* were gonna be okay.

I fumbled with the key, clumsy in my haste to get to her. I wasted no time once I heard the tell-tale click of the lock, and threw open the door, taking in the frail shadow that stood just a few feet away.

"Hope, it's me baby. It's Blake." I moved towards her, cautiously. There was no telling what she'd been through and I didn't want to scare her any more than she'd already been.

She stood, stock still. Observing me. Squinting her eyes and shielding them from the light. She'd been in darkness for days now, and she needed the time to adjust. She was gaunt; shaking and covered in dried blood. Blood that I presumed to be hers, judging by the gash on her head. Unsure, she studied me for in inordinate amount of time. Her head tilted as she took me in, trying to remember a time when not everyone was a threat to her.

"It's okay, Hope. I'm not gonna hurt you. It's Blake, baby. I'm here to help you. To save you." I took a few steps towards her, cautiously. I held out my arms and waited. It was killing me to stand there. It went against every bone in body. Every cell, begging me to wrap her in my arms and never let her go, but this had to be on her terms. She'd had so much stolen from her already and I wasn't going to take any more; nothing that she wasn't willing to give freely.

After what felt like hours, Hope launched herself at me, clinging tightly and sobbing. It broke my heart and mended it all at once. "I've got you, baby. I've got you."

"I can't believe you came for me!" she cried.

"Why would you think I wouldn't come for you?" I was stunned, almost rendered speechless. Did she not know how I felt about her?

"I'm nothing," she cried harder, burying her face in my neck.

I sat her back on her feet and held her away from me, so I could look her in the eyes. "Hope. Listen to me and listen good. You need to hear what I have to say. Can you do that for me?"

She nodded and waited.

"You're everything to me. I don't know what you've been told, or how much you've been brainwashed, but baby, none of that shit's true. And I wanna know everything, when you feel like you can talk about it. I wanna help you get past all this, baby, but until then just remember one thing...."

"What's that?" Her voice had lowered to a whisper, mulling my words over in her mind.

I braced her face in my hands and moved closer so that our bodies were touching. Placing a soft kiss on her forehead, I said, "Remember that I love you. Always and forever, Hope."

"You... you... love me?" her words sounded unsure. I had told her this before, but in her state, it didn't surprise me that it escaped her mind.

"Yes, Hope. I do. I think I have since the first time I laid eyes on you."

She stepped away from me again and chewed her lip, thinking of a response. Maybe even a way to let me down easy. "But how can you love this?" she questioned, motioning to herself. "How can you love someone so broken?"

"Listen to me," I pleaded, taking her hands in mine. "You feel broken, baby, but you aren't. I will help you glue every piece back together if that's what you feel you need, but I love you the way you are. Just like this."

Disbelief was written all over her face, but I think another part of her wanted to believe it more than anything, and luckily for me, that's the part that won out.

"Let's get you outta here," I suggested. I walked us to the door and felt her pull back on my hand, stopping us both.

"We can't go out there," she whispered. "Angela…Raul, they'll kill us."

"Baby, Billy and Jax are taking care of them now. I promise you, it's safe. Ain't no way I'd walk you outta here if it wasn't."

She nodded and took my hand once again. I walked slow, giving her a few extra seconds to come to terms with it all. The fact that she was free; that she no longer had to worry about the assholes that were determined to ruin her life.

55

The sounds of scuffling and screaming reverberated in the sparse area. Blake turned and looked at Hope, securing her hands tightly in his.

"Babe, you ready for this?"

Hope thought for a moment, chewing on her dry, chapped lips. "I don't know if I can face them, Blake. I don't think I'm strong enough…"

He stood in front of her, blocking out the commotion just on the other side of the door. He worried his towering figure might cause her to feel frightened, but it did just the opposite. Hope felt shielded and secure. Something she only felt in Blake's presence.

"Hope, I will not let them harm you. Not ever again. Dammit, I have failed you so many times, and I don't deserve your trust, but babe, I'm tellin' ya, they ain't gonna harm one hair on your precious head. I'll do anything, Hope. Anything you need," he reiterated, "if you'll just believe me."

Blake waited, holding his breath, anxious she might falter. Truth be told, she had no reason to trust him. He'd let her down too much. When he was ready to hang his head in shame, he felt her cold hands press against his chest.

"Blake, now I need you to listen to me and listen good."

He smiled, loving the sound of her voice. It was strong; confident. Hope was still in there. They hadn't broken her.

He hadn't broken her. And he was so damn proud that he couldn't help but smile even broader.

"I'm not afraid of you. And I do trust you, Blake. You've never, ever let me down. Those people," she pointed behind him, "they're the monsters. Not you. Never you. I just don't know if I can look them in the eye. I don't know if I'm strong enough to escape what they've done."

Hope's head dropped to her chest. "You don't know…" her voice broke off into a whisper.

Blake didn't offer words. He knew nothing was adequate. That nothing he could say would help right now. He'd been around Lauren and Heather enough to know that it had to be in her own time, in her own way. He wouldn't push her, but he'd make damn sure he was there each and every time she needed to fall apart.

Blake held her close, her body shaking with the relentless sobs that fell from her lips. He rocked her gently, stroking her back and her matted, blood-soaked hair. It didn't deter him in the least. Underneath the filth, he knew she was beautiful. Every inch of her. Every freckle and blemish, every curve. Hell, she was beautiful even now.

Lost in thought, Blake felt her jump when the first gunshot sounded. He pulled her tighter to his chest, his hand covering her ear. The blast was deafening, the second almost his undoing. His ears were ringing, but he continued to rock her, hoping all she could hear was the beating of his heart and the low hum that rumbled in his chest. Blake didn't know how long they'd been like this, and he didn't care. He'd hold her like this for hours if that's what she needed.

The squeaking of the metal door broke Blake from his reverie. He was on guard, but that guard immediately dissipated when he heard Johnny's voice from behind him. With his voice barely audible, he told Blake to shield Hope and get her out quickly. He didn't have to ask why.

"Babe, I'm going to pick you up and get you outta here, okay? I need you to hold onto me, and keep your eyes closed. Please, just let me get you outta here."

A few more sobs escaped as Hope nodded her head. Blake lifted her small frame with ease, bracing one arm behind her back, the other behind her knees. She felt so fragile and it took all he had not to break down himself. Johnny walked out with them, flanking one side of Blake as Jax stepped in line on the other. Blake knew they were shielding her too, and for that he'd forever be grateful.

His brawny legs carried them across the blood-soaked floor and up the stairs, quickly. Once outside, Hope clung to him even more, a silent plea for him not to let go. Message received, loud and clear.

"I've got you, babe," he cooed in her ear, "and I'm not letting you go. Ever again, you hear me?"

As before, Hope nodded against his chest, but there were no words. He sat on the tailgate of Billy's truck, the sound of sirens closing in the distance. The only effort he made to move was to grab a blanket from one of Billy's duffle bags, using it to shield her from the cold night air.

It wasn't long before Jax and Johnny came trudging from the doorway, Jax lending support to a still injured Johnny. Blake nodded at him, a silent thank you, and what he hoped would be the beginning of burying the hatchet. He hated what Jax had done to Hope, but he could forgive in time.

Next came Billy, Heather walking alongside him with a blank look on her face. We all gathered around, everyone silent as the nights events ran through our minds. No words were needed at that moment. I didn't even feel like asking questions. There would be time for that later. Right now, I just wanted to marvel at the girl in my arms and the family that surrounded us.

56

I was in a trance, the finality of what happened settling in. Raul was finally dead. Gone. A pool of red blood surrounded his body. I had seen it for myself, otherwise I wouldn't have believed it. It was over; his reign of terror. His years of abusing women and breaking the law had come to an end, and seemingly my career. I was done.

"Blake," Billy spoke, breaking my thoughts. "We need to see to Hope. Let them look at her."

He motioned to the medics that were waiting beside the truck. I hadn't even noticed them. I gave a small nod, and moved back, separating her body from mine. Her wide, doe eyes looked at me in fear as she began to shake. Heather and Bailey were there, rubbing her back and comforting her.

"We'll stay with her," Heather said, softly. "Think you and the boys have some stuff to attend to."

I moved Hope from my lap. "I'll be right over there if you need me. Let these people help you, make sure you're alright, then we'll go home." I placed a chaste kiss on her forehead and stepped aside, her eyes never leaving mine. Bailey immediately stepped in and took her hand, and essentially my place.

"We're going to just check you out ma'am," I heard one of the paramedics say as I backed away. I kept my body turned so that she could still see me, and I her.

Jax, Johnny, Billy and myself stood just out of ear shot. "What happened?"

Blake blew out a breath. “They’re dead.”

I rolled my eyes. “I know that. I saw.”

“I shot her.” Jax’s face held no remorse, his features stoic. “Heather may never forgive me but can’t say Angela didn’t have it coming.”

In a million years, I never thought I’d see what happened next. Billy put his arm around Jax’s shoulder and squeezed. “I owe you, man. You saved Heather. I turned my back for two fucking seconds, and I almost lost her again. Anything you need, ever,” he stressed, “just say the word.”

Jax nodded but kept his head down. It was in that moment I realized he was just as much a victim as Hope was, or anyone else for that matter. Where I’d only been knee deep in this for a few years, he’d dealt with this his whole life. I reached out, an olive branch if you will, and shook his hand.

“Same goes for me, brother.”

Jax accepted my peace offering, but I knew it would still take time for the dust to settle. Things had been said and done; bad things that didn’t just heal overnight. We all had our own shit to work through, but that one small gesture had me feeling more confident than ever that we’d all be okay.

“Angela had her,” Billy’s low baritone growled. “By the throat. I took my eyes off her for only a second….” He shook his head and huffed out a disgruntled breath. “I was focused on Raul. Hell bent on getting revenge for what he’d done to Heather.”

"You were handling business," Johnny spoke up. "You can't blame yourself. It had to be done."

I seconded his words. "Look how many people you saved in return," I reminded him.

"You did, son." George appeared seemingly from out of nowhere and clasped Billy's broad shoulders. He had a way of doing that.

"Well you're a sight for sore eyes, old man." I grinned wide, more than happy to see my boss and Billy's father-in-law. "How'd you know?"

"Good to see you, too," George answered. "Billy called me earlier, told me shit was about to hit the fan and I should get here quick. I headed this way, especially when I realized Heather's sudden departure involved Raul."

"Yeah, about that," I mumbled. "I'm sorry I didn't keep in touch. That I didn't let you know what was happening. After all the shit with Tom and everything that went down, I didn't really know who to trust at the agency, and well," I stalled, "I just kinda needed to do this on my own."

"I get it, Blake, I do. But you forget in this business, you're never alone." George looked around to the group of men standing beside us. I nodded my agreement.

Heather came running over when she noticed George. "Dad!" she screamed, jumping in his arms. "What're you doing here?"

"Still my case, darlin'. Got business to handle." He patted her back then excused himself to talk to the chief.

Jax walked to the edge of the tree line, keeping his back towards us. I felt bad for the guy, I really did. He'd proven himself to be one of us, yet I knew because of the situation, he felt like an outsider. Before I could move, Billy whispered to Heather.

"I think you should go talk to him. He's got guilt he shouldn't have, and I think whatever needs to be said, needs to come from you."

Heather leaned forward and placed a soft kiss on Billy's lips for reassurance. Not that he needed it; there was no doubt these two belonged together, but it was a nice gesture. "I'll be right back."

Billy, not wanting to intrude on their conversation, turned his attention towards Johnny. I briefly heard him ask how he was feeling, before tuning them out completely. For me, a blonde-headed woman stole the show, once again and as she always would. Perched on the tailgate, Hope looked even smaller than usual, her body slumped forward with the weight of what had happened. As promised, Bailey was right beside her, holding her hand and answering as many questions as she could.

I made my way over and wrapped my arm around her protectively. She fell into me, nestling her head in the crook of my neck. I felt her sigh in contentment, as I did the same.

"Okay, ma'am," the attending medic spoke, "all done here. You've got some abrasions, of course, but they should heal in no time. The gash on your head, you'll need to watch closely. Any drainage, head to the emergency room and they'll be able to stitch it for you, but the bandage should do the trick. Minimal scarring," he added.

"Thank you," I offered, extending my hand to his. "I'll take good care of her." He shook my hand in return but shot me a glaring look. No clue what the dude's problem was, nor did I care.

"Ready to go home?" I asked. Hope looked at me again with that same blank expression, a million questions building behind her eyes.

Bailey squeezed her one more time and gave me a concerning look before bounding over to Johnny. I watched their exchange. He held his arm out and she tucked herself underneath, as if it's where she belonged. I reckon she did.

"Where's home?" Hope whispered.

"Home is wherever you want it to be, but for tonight, my hotel room. Tomorrow we'll figure all of this out. We have the rest of our lives, babe." I cautiously leaned forward, searching her eyes for any sign of fear. When she didn't resist, I placed my lips softly against hers.

"Just get me out of here," she murmured.

"Gladly," I said, picking her up and setting her down. I wrapped around her, shielding her from the cold and the stares. I walked us to where the rest of the group stood, waiting for Heather and Jax to finish their heart-to-heart. I knew the time it was taking was killing Billy, but I was proud of him. In a way, Heather probably needed it more than Jax did.

As we approached, Billy turned, catching sight of George. He was making his way over, men in suits following. I straightened, standing tall.

"Boys, this is Chief Morris."

"Hello," he greeted all of us at once.

"And these gentlemen," George continued, "are Steven and Ben. We all shook hands and exchanged pleasantries.

I waited for George to explain, but Steven jumped in before he had the chance. "Impressive work, guys. We've been after Raul for quite some time."

"We've been working it for years, but that didn't seem to work in our favor," I quipped. "Didn't go by the book this time."

"Never can with ones like him," Ben chimed in, jutting his head towards Raul's lifeless body. They were rolling him by on the stretcher, a surreal moment if there ever was one. "They don't play by the rules and there are no textbook cases."

"Yeah," Steven added. "You guys are free to go. We'll wrap this up and turn everything over. Hope to work with you guys in the future."

"Not me." I'd been thinking about it for a while, and no time like the present to let everyone know my plans. "I'm done, out. I've given a lot to this job. My loyalty, my respect, hell, even my life. Now I've got something more." I pulled Hope closer, smiling down at her.

"Don't blame you one bit," George lulled. "We'll get the paperwork done, son. Don't worry."

"Thanks, I appreciate it."

Jax and Heather started back in our direction. I didn't miss the way his arm was slung over her shoulder, and neither had Billy, but I had to give it to him. He stood his ground, hiding his displeasure rather well. As soon as they were close enough, Heather did what came naturally and took her place next to him.

"I um…." Jax started, but Billy interrupted him.

"Not sure what your plans are Jax, but I sure could use some help back home. Free room and board, and Heather here is one helluva cook. Job's yours if you want it."

I grinned. Big ol softy.

"You sure, man? I mean, I don't wanna intrude."

Billy hugged Heather a little tighter. "I'm sure, brother. Be glad to have ya."

The corner of Jax's mouth turned up in a smile, one that he rarely wore. Heather beamed, and Billy grinned.

"You, too, Johnny, when you're fully healed, of course," Billy added.

"And Bailey, Lauren and I could use some help at the shelter, if you're interested. We've got all sorts of upcoming events and new groups we're trying to incorporate. More hands are always welcome."

"I would love that," Bailey stated, "but I don't really have any experience with that sort of thing. I'm not really qualified to…"

"Don't need to be, darlin'," Billy added. "Just gotta have a listening ear, sometimes that's all people need." He was speaking to Bailey, but I knew his words were meant for me, as well. I barely nodded, but he caught it and that was good enough. It meant don't push. Let Hope come to me and open up when she was ready. I had a feeling the shelter could be good for her, as well, but it was too soon to mention it.

57

Hope didn't say a word on the drive back to the hotel. We took Billy's truck; he and Heather rode my bike. Normally I didn't let anyone else drive Daisy, but I figured at this point, Billy and I were one in the same, so it seemed only reasonable.

Hope didn't even sit next to me. She sat huddled up to the passenger door, gazing out the window as the lights flashed by. I didn't know which upset her more; the fact two people were dead, or that I hadn't gotten to her sooner. That she'd gone through so much more than even I could understand. Idle chit chat seemed meaningless at this point, so I didn't even try. Maybe I should have, but I didn't. Years of dealing with victims, and yet nothing prepared me for this. This was different.

The silence between us as we walked to the room was as deafening as it was in the cab of the truck. She didn't hold my hand, didn't place her arm in mine. In fact, she walked a few paces behind me, no matter how much I slowed my gait. I opened the door for her and stood back, allowing her to enter first. It seemed like forever since she'd entered those doors, but in reality, it had only been a little over a week. This time was in stark contrast to the last, however. There was no jubilation, no excitement. It felt awkward, but I wasn't sure why.

I cleared my throat to get her attention. The only thing she found interesting was the pattern of the carpet.

"You wanna take a hot shower?" I offered.

Hope nodded, but not a word was spoken.

“Okay, c’mon babe. I’ll help you.”

She didn’t move a muscle. When I looked back questioning whether she heard me, I noticed the tears streaming down her face.

“What’s wrong?” I implored, immediately, moving to take her in my arms. She shrank back as if I had scolded her, causing me to pause. I dropped my arms to my side and slid away, giving her space. Did she think I was going to hurt her?

“I can do it myself,” she said, her timid voice barely audible.

“Okay.” That’s all I had; all I could say. I didn’t understand why she was pushing me away, but I had to respect it.

Hope padded to the bedroom door, shutting it closed behind her. The weight of it felt heavy, felt final and foreboding of what was to come. I plopped myself on the couch and rubbed the wetness from my eyes. It had been a long day, but I had a sinking suspicion the night would drag out even more. What did this mean for us? What the hell was happening? I thought Hope would be happy, for fucks sake. This was finally over! Raul was dead, as was Angela. It meant no more looking over our shoulders, no more violence. We were free.

The sound of a door opening brought me back to the present, only it wasn’t the door I was hoping for. Billy, Heather, Jax, Johnny and Bailey filed in, all looking as worn out as the next. Billy held out his arms and looked around.

“Where’s Hope?”

I stood and rubbed the back of my neck, a quirk I had when I didn't feel like explaining myself; especially when trying to explain something even I didn't understand.

"She's taking a shower. Didn't want me in there," I mumbled, praying he'd drop it. I wasn't in the mood. We should all be celebrating instead of moping.

Heather was the first to approach me, while everyone else stood back and offered apologetic looks.

"Let me talk to her. I think maybe I can help." Heather disappeared behind the same bedroom door, shutting it quietly.

"Heather went through this exact same thing, Blake. Don't take it personal. You just gotta give her some time." Billy squeezed my shoulder, comforting me.

Jax cleared his throat and all heads turned towards him. "She loves you, Blake. I know you know that, just remember it when it feels like she doesn't. You were all she talked about; all she wanted."

"Thanks, Jax. I will." I said the words with little conviction. I knew she loved me, but I also knew sometimes that wasn't enough.

"Bailey and I are gonna try to get some shut eye, if that's alright? Just been a long day and my girl needs some rest."

Bailey jabbed him in the ribs. "Speak for yourself, old man. I'm not the one who just got released from the hospital."

"Old man, huh? I'll show you old man," he teased back.

Bailey was giggling as she tried in vain to escape his hold, for all the good it did her. The more she resisted, the more he tickled.

"Get a room, guys," Billy joked. The whole scene caused my stomach to turn. That should be me and Hope.

The tension looming in the ear caused Johnny to pause. "Sorry, princess," he offered, speaking to me. Bailey gave me a rueful smile before pulling him by the hand.

I waved them both off. *Why shouldn't they be happy?* They deserved it more than anyone, and I wouldn't begrudge them.

"It's cool, guys. Go have fun." The words sounded flat as soon as they came out, but I just didn't have it in me for anything more.

"Beer?" Jax offered.

"Thinking something a little stronger is in order."

I heard ice hitting the glass seconds later. Jax walked over, the hardball glasses filled with liquid gold. He set them on the table, one for each of us. "Bring the bottle," I admonished. One wasn't going to do the trick.

We sat in silence, Billy and Jax nursing their whiskey while I downed mine. Numbness. Numbness was the way to go.

"Think you might wanna slow down there," Heather quipped. I raised my brows at her tone.

"Why the hell would I wanna do that?"

Billy stood, ready to defend her as always. "Think you need to drop the attitude, princess. She's trying to help."

"Don't need help."

Jax sighed. "This really necessary tonight, guys? We gonna have another match or what? Just beat the shit outta each other and get it over with. Christ!"

Heather stepped between the two of them. "No more fighting tonight. Or a while, for that matter," she admonished.

Jax grabbed the bottle of Jack and strode to the balcony. "Just need some fresh air," he explained. No one acknowledged him, which was probably for the best.

"I think you need to talk to her," Heather offered.

"Tried," I snapped back. "She's afraid of me. She's fucking afraid of me, dammit!" I threw my empty glass, the remainder of ice and shards scattering across the floor.

"Wonder why that is, asshole?"

Heather crossed her arms and glared at me. "She's afraid of everything right now, Blake. *Everything.* Most of all, she's scared that you won't want her anymore. Fix that, and the rest will fall into place."

"What?" I asked, incredulously. "Why would I not want her anymore?"

Billy interjected. "Same reason Heather felt that way. The abuse. The brainwashing. The *rape*. Thought you were smarter than this, Blake. We've worked with hundreds of victims, Hope is no different." He squeezed the bridge of his nose, exasperated. "Put your feelings aside, and how you *think* things should go, and just fucking be there for her."

I stared at them both. They were right. I had this picture in my mind that we would just whirl in here and make love, picking up where we left off, not giving a second thought to what she'd been through in the days that Angela had her. *Selfish bastard!*

"You're right. You're both right. Sorry, guys, I just…"

"Just go to her, princess. Give me some alone time with my girl here," Billy motioned to Heather. I clasped him on the back and went in search of Hope.

58

3 months later….

Hope was doing good, and I was proud of her. She'd come a long way. I attributed the positive changes to the other girls and the amount of time that she'd spent at the shelter, but mostly it was just her. Hope was stronger than she'd ever given herself credit for.

We'd all settled in to a comfortable way of life. Jax lived just down the road, on the back acres of Billy's farm. He and Hope got together time to time for pow-wows and heart to heart talks, but it didn't bother me. Only they knew from first-hand experience what it was like to live under Raul's thumb, and it was beneficial for both to have that time. Whatever she needed, I'd gladly provide, and it was a small price to pay to have her come back to me a little more each day.

Even Johnny and Bailey had settled into a routine. Bailey was working on her cosmetology degree and Johnny was a trainer in town at the local gym. While he was through with fighting, he helped train and mentor kids, which was right up his alley. Life had taught him lessons that you could only get from personal experience, and he vowed to help those boys defend themselves the right way, unlike his father.

As I sat on the swing, the sun setting just over the tops of the trees, I sipped my beer and watched the scene before me. Lauren, Hope and the other girls were all doting over Sam and her new baby brother, Gunner. Jax and Johnny were tossing the football, and Luke and Billy were discussing business as usual. Burgers on the grill ignited my senses and caused my stomach to growl. George stood with the spatula in his hand and 'World's Best Grandpa' on his apron. Heather was due around Christmas, and for George it couldn't get here soon enough.

"Wanna give me a hand?"

"Sure, boss. Whatcha need?" I'd officially been retired from the FBI for 2 months, once the paperwork had been filed and the dust settled, and I'd never had a moments regret over my decision.

"Grab that cheese, will ya? These will be ready soon."

George finished the task at hand and then called everyone over to eat. It smelled delicious. Sam was first in line. That little girl was growing like a weed, and the spitting image of Luke. He beamed with pride as he watched her, and in that moment, I knew what I wanted. A family.

I couldn't push Hope on it though. She'd just gotten comfortable with me touching her again. She tolerated it, at least. I followed Heather's advice and learned not to take it personal. Instead, I allowed her the space she needed, and waited for her to come to me. It was best not to push, though inside I was dying to be with her.

We all stood around, Billy offering grace. I'd never been much for religion, especially after all I'd seen over the years as an agent, but I couldn't help but feel none of this was possible without some intervention from the man upstairs.

When I opened my eyes, Hope was standing next to me, Gunner in her arms. His light hair favored his mothers, but he still had Luke's features. Lauren vowed to keep trying until finally one of their children looked like her. I chuckled with the thought, knowing they'd end up with a house full of rug rats before that happened.

"Isn't he the sweetest?" Hope mused. She rocked him gently and brushed his cheeks with the back of her hand.

"He is," I agreed. I'd never been around babies much. To be honest, it freaked me out. They were so tiny and fragile. I'd held Sam when she was little, but she wasn't so new as Gunner.

"You look like a natural holding him," I added. Immediately I regretted my words, unsure how she would take it. My remorse was short lived when I saw her beautiful smile.

Hope's eyes never left him as she spoke. "I think we should have at least three. What do you think?"

What did I think? I think hell yeah! The air was briefly knocked from my lungs, not at the thought of having children with her, but to know that she'd considered it; considered letting me touch her.

I turned her towards me and placed my hands on her hips. "Babe, when you're ready, I'd be honored."

"Good," she said. "Because I'm thinking we might wanna get on that."

"You do?" I asked, incredulously.

"I do. See, I was thinking; you're not getting any younger, and neither am I. And if we're gonna have at least three, we should be thinking about it. And ya know, sometimes it takes a while for people to get pregnant, and I don't even know if I…."

She was rambling. Something she did when she was nervous. I placed a gentle kiss on her lips to shut her up, so I could speak. “We get this barbeque over babe, you’re mine for the night. Got it?”

I was a man on a mission, hurrying everyone up and shuffling plates into the trash. “Hey!” Jax called around a mouthful of food, “I wasn’t done with that.”

“Oh, sorry, it’s just that it’s getting late.” I tried to sound remorseful, but I just couldn’t. They all needed to leave, hours ago.

“Whatever reason could you possibly have to want everyone gone?” Billy teased, tapping his finger on his chin. The sarcasm was thick.

“No reason. Just think Hope needs to rest.” I shrugged my shoulders and threw a glance her direction, hoping she’d back me up. My girl didn’t disappoint.

She feigned a yawn and stretched. “Yeah, sorry everyone, but I am kinda tired.”

“Uh huh,” Heather chimed in. “Tired my ass.” She gave me a wink, and it wasn’t long before the others were teasing us. Hope didn’t seem to mind, though I did notice the blush that crept across her face.

Enough was enough. Taking matters into my own hands, I circled the table and held my hand out for Hope. She placed her tiny hand in mine and I helped steady her. “You guys clean this when you’re done and lock up.”

I offered no other explanation as I hoisted Hope up in my arms and made a mad dash to the back of the house. Pretty sure they didn’t need me to spell it out for them anyways.

Catcalls and cheers assaulted my ears, and Hope just laughed, burying her head in my chest.

I opened the door, kicking it closed with my boot. Setting her down gently, I made sure to keep my arms around her, so she didn't run. When Hope peered up at me through impossibly long lashes and bit her lip, I knew there was no possibility of that happening.

"You sure about this? Because once we cross that line, babe, I ain't stopping." My tone was stern, my voice gruff, but she knew I'd never go farther than what she was comfortable with. I wasn't the type, but I also wasn't backing down. Pushing her a little might be a good thing.

"Blake, I don't want you to stop. Ever."

Next thing I knew, Hope lunged at me, pressing her soft, beautiful lips to mine. I lifted her with ease, and she wrapped her legs around me. I carried her through the house, to our room. Normally I'd have thrown her down on the couch and saved precious time, but with a yard full of company, I didn't think that was a good idea. Plus, it had been a long time since Hope and I had been together. She deserved more than a romp on the couch.

Still holding her in my arms, I pulled the covers back and laid her down. Reluctantly she let go and leaned back, her beautiful blues never leaving mine. I stood back and stared in awe. The moonlight cast shadows in all the right places, highlighting her like the angel I knew her to be.

"God, you're amazing," I mused.

I had to remind myself several times that this was a marathon, not a sprint. I wanted this to last and pacing myself was key. We needed it, and most of all, Hope deserved it. She deserved to be loved and worshipped the right way.

I kicked off my boots and slowly removed my shirt and jeans. She watched me closely, every move seeming to turn her on more and more. I watched as she squeezed her thighs together, her teeth still assaulting her lip as she stifled a groan.

By the time I'd undressed myself, she was practically naked. All that remained were the few scraps of lace she wore. I leaned over top of her, softly planting my lips on her neck, making my way down to the swell of her breasts. I started to ask if she was okay, but one look told me all I needed to know.

"I love you, Hope. I've always loved you and I will till the day they lay me in the ground."

No other words were spoken. They didn't need to be. We continued that night and every night after, wrapped around one another in bliss. I'd been wrong all those years, thinking nothing was better than kicking ass and putting bad guys away, and I couldn't have been more wrong. The perfect life was sitting on the porch, Hope in my arms as we watched our children play. It was paying bills and fixing leaky faucets. It was holding her when she cried and walking away when I was so pissed off that I couldn't speak without hurting her. It was making up and laughing. It was having friends that would do anything for you, and you doing the same in return. It was changing diapers, kissing boo-boos, and sitting through school plays. Life wasn't defined by how much you had, but the ones you affected while you were here. I vowed to love her every day for the rest of my life and that's exactly what I'd do. Loving her was as easy as breathing.

The end.

Chance of a Lifetime…. Coming Winter 2018

Prologue

Sierra looked out over the field, the tall grass and wildflowers swaying gently in the wind. Summer had come and gone, and fall was starting to settle in. Cool, crisp nights had been a Godsend, as the summer had been unbearably hot. It'd been hard enough to get comfortable lately, and the sweltering heat hadn't made it any easier.

Resting her elbows against the porch steps, Sierra leaned back and rubbed her growing belly. Life had sure thrown her for a loop, and this little miracle was no exception. She thought back to what had brought her here; the life she used to live. A different town; different friends and family. It seemed like ages ago. The journey had been long and the road a bit bumpy, but she knew she wouldn't trade it for anything. It had brought her to him.

Chance.

Made in the USA
Columbia, SC
12 November 2024